W9-BQY-317

WITHDRAWN
Plainfield-Guilford Township
Public Library
1120 Stafford Road
Plainfield IN 46168

BELLE MORTE

BELLE MORTE

BELLE MORTE BOOK ONE

BELLA HIGGIN

wattpad books

wattpad books W

An imprint of Wattpad WEBTOON Book Group

Content Warning: mentions of blood, mentions of violence,
unwanted sexual touching, language

Copyright© 2022 Bella Higgin. All rights reserved.

Published in Canada by Wattpad Books, a division of Wattpad Corp.

36 Wellington Street E., Toronto, ON M5E 1C7

www.wattpad.com

No portion of this publication may be reproduced or transmitted,
in any form or by any means, without the express written permission
of the copyright holders.

First Wattpad Books edition: April 2022
ISBN 978-1-98936-589-2 (Hardcover original)
ISBN 978-1-98936-590-8 (eBook edition)

Names, characters, places, and incidents featured in this publication are
either the product of the author's imagination or are used fictitiously. Any
resemblance to actual persons (living or dead), events, institutions, or
locales, without satiric intent, is coincidental.

Wattpad, Wattpad Books, Wattpad WEBTOON Book Group, and associated logos are trademarks and/or registered trademarks of Wattpad Corp.
and/or WEBTOON Entertainment Inc.

Library and Archives Canada Cataloguing in Publication
information is available upon request.

Printed and bound in Canada
1 3 5 7 9 10 8 6 4 2

Cover design by Ysabel Enverga
Cover images: © Valerii_k via shutterstock; © PitakAreekul via iStock;
© Thomas Dumortier via Unsplash

To every dreamer looking up at the stars.
Dreams can come true.

CHAPTER ONE

Renie

My first glimpse of Belle Morte came as the limousine crested the hill of a sloping road. The vampire mansion was at the far end of the city of Winchester, where historic timber-framed buildings gave way to the green sprawl of the South Downs National Park.

The gated wall ringing the mansion was mostly blocked from view by a crowd of paparazzi. They clamored for a glimpse of the creatures that had become the world's most dazzling celebrities—alongside any people associated with them. As of two weeks ago, I had become one of those people, when my application to become a blood donor had been accepted.

The limo bumped over a pothole, jolting my stomach. I put down my glass of champagne. I was already a hard knot of nerves; the alcohol wouldn't help.

"I can't wait!" exclaimed a girl on my left. "Phillip and Gideon and Etienne—oh, and *Edmond.*" She rattled off the names of Belle Morte vampires like they were old friends.

She wasn't alone in her adoration. Vampires were now the epitome of fame—mysterious, beautiful immortals who had stepped out of the shadows ten years ago and proved they really existed. Now the world couldn't get enough of them. A-list celebs had been shoved down to C-list, and anyone lower had almost dropped off the map. Tabloids, gossip columns, photo shoots, and talk shows—they all belonged to vampires now.

Most people liked it.

I didn't.

"Míriam's my favorite," said the boy opposite me. "I can't wait for her to get her fangs into me."

Another boy shook his head. "Yeah, Míriam's hot, but if anyone's taking a bite out of me, I want it to be the ice queen herself: Ysanne Moreau." A dreamy look crossed his face.

The girl next to me scoffed. "You don't get to choose who bites you."

"Yeah, but a guy can dream."

I sank back in my seat, mentally shaking my head. Belle Morte was one of five Vampire Houses in the UK and the Republic of Ireland, and everyone in this limo was heading into that house as a blood donor. In our modern world, vampires didn't hunt their prey from the shadows anymore, but instead paid people like us to let them drink our blood.

It seemed like a good deal—apply to be a donor, get accepted, move to a Vampire House and live in luxury for months, let the vampires drink from you, and eventually leave with a very full bank account. People like me, coming from a poor family and struggling to find a permanent job, really needed that money.

But I couldn't forget the tales of blood and bodies, death and evil that I'd seen so often in movies and books, before vampires were reimagined as romantic heroes rather than villains. There had to be some truth to those legends.

As we approached the mansion, the flash of cameras grew more frenzied, and I had to clench my hands to keep them still. Maybe this was a mistake. Donors remained in a House until the vampires got bored of them—that could be weeks, months, even years—so once I went inside Belle Morte, I had no idea when I'd come out. That wouldn't have been a problem if I was in it for the money or the glamour, like everyone else who signed up.

But I wasn't.

Five months ago, my sister had walked into this house. She never walked back out, and all communication from her ended abruptly several weeks ago. I'd applied to be a donor solely to find out why.

The girl on my right fluffed up her pixie cut. "Got to look my best for the cameras," she said when she saw me looking.

As the wrought-iron gates barring the way into Belle Morte swung open and the limo crawled forward, the flash of cameras and the loud voices became overwhelming. I turned my head so a curtain of auburn hair hid my face. Unlike the other donors, I didn't care if my picture landed on the front of a magazine.

Three vampires strode out of the mansion grounds, flanked on both sides by human security in black uniforms. Vampires were strong enough to hold overeager press at bay without help, but they had cultivated an image of elegant, mysterious immortals. Tossing media vultures around like cheap toys would have a negative effect on their public persona, so human security did their dirty work for them.

The limo stopped close to the gates and someone opened the door to let us out. When it was my turn to exit, I found myself looking up at a man in his forties, a smile crinkling the skin at the corners of his eyes, moonlight glinting on the shaved dome of his head.

"Dexter Flynn, head of security," he said, helping me out of the car.

I ducked my head again as the press crowded around, shouting questions and barking my name.

"Renie Mayfield . . ."

". . . how do you feel about . . ."

". . . hope to achieve . . ."

". . . vampires . . ."

A vampire moved to my side, glaring at the press as they swarmed too close. "Easy now. Give the lady some space," he warned.

Like all vampires, he was classically handsome, his dark-red hair a striking contrast to his blue eyes, and when he smiled it was close lipped; I couldn't see his fangs.

Etienne Banville. Before completing my donor application, I'd done as much research as possible so I would know what I was heading into. Inevitably, I'd fallen down the rabbit hole of fan art and fan fiction, polls about favorite vampires and donors, endless forums speculating on which vampires were sleeping with each other. It all seemed so ridiculous, but at least I knew everyone's name.

Etienne's expression wilted as he looked at me. I had no idea why.

I wanted to get through the press gauntlet as quickly as possible, not stopping to answer any questions, but one man surged too close, almost hitting me in the face with his microphone. I reeled back, stumbling into the most beautiful vampire I'd ever seen.

Strands of raven-black hair fluttered around the pale planes of his face, the cheekbones sharp enough to cut glass, and his eyes were as dark and hard as onyx. Edmond Dantès.

"That's enough," he said, pushing the man back.

The man backed off, but the cameras continued to click and flash. So much for me wanting to keep out of the limelight. By tomorrow pictures of me and Edmond would be headlining every gossip magazine and vampire site in the country—maybe even in the world. Vampire mania wasn't restricted to the UK; there were Houses around the globe, and serious vampire fans—or Vladdicts, as they liked to call themselves—were always desperate for more gossip.

Edmond signaled to Dexter, who strode over.

"Get a handle on this situation. These people shouldn't be able to touch the donors," Edmond growled.

"Yes, sir," Dexter said.

Edmond looked down at me. "Are you all right?" he asked, his voice softer now, a faded French accent curling around the words.

Suddenly, I was breathless, a shiver rolling through me. Edmond lifted one dark eyebrow.

"I'm fine," I mumbled, feeling like an idiot. All those times I'd sneered at people who treated vampires like gods, and the first time I spoke to one I'd gone to pieces. *Good job, Renie.*

With a brisk nod, Edmond swept away. The girl who'd sat on my left in the limo gave me an envious, vaguely murderous look, but the short-haired girl winked. At least she was enjoying herself, pouting and blowing kisses like she was sashaying down the red carpet, knowing photos of her would appear everywhere. Vladdicts and other vampire fans always wanted to know about us—both the newest donors going into the mansion and the castoffs released from their contracts and tossed back into their old lives, where they went on to nab spots on talk shows, release books, and star in reality-TV shows.

"Okay, enough now," Dexter barked, using his forearm to push back another overenthusiastic photographer. "Let's get the donors inside."

The gates clanged shut behind us. No one was allowed inside without permission from Ysanne Moreau, the Lady of the House. Of course, she wasn't *actually* a lady—that was just the title used by female rulers of Vampire Houses across much of Europe and North America.

I gazed up at the mansion. Lit by huge spotlights positioned on the grounds, it was designed to look old—a towering, Gothic structure of gray stone, with oriel windows perching on ornamented corbels, their glass panes covered from the inside by UV-blocking shades. Above the brass-studded door, a stone bas-relief spelled out the House's name—Belle Morte. *Beautiful dead.* How appropriate.

How had June felt when she came here? My sister was a bona fide Vladdict, caught up in the vampire obsession of the last decade, so this would've been the greatest thing in the world to her.

There *must* be a valid reason she'd cut off contact. Mum thought I was overreacting, pointing out that no donor had ever been injured by a vampire, and if anything *had* gone wrong, then Belle Morte wouldn't have accepted June's sister as a donor, but I couldn't shake off the fear. And since donors weren't allowed visitors, my only way in was to become one.

As we walked up the stone-flagged path to the huge front door that Dexter was pushing open, my chest knotted.

No turning back now. I was here, and nothing would stop me from finding out what had happened to my sister.

Dexter led us into a spacious vestibule with parquet flooring and mahogany-paneled walls, lit by a crystal-drop chandelier. Marble plinths topped with flower-filled bowls bracketed the door, and burgundy drapes long enough to pool on the floor hung on each side of the windows. Various arched entryways led off the room, and a wide staircase with a scrolled banister sat at the far end.

Several people in Vladdict forums online speculated that secret passageways lurked somewhere in the mansion's depths, but they were probably the same people who believed vampires were angels or aliens.

Vampires gathered on the staircase, keenly eyeing us. Edmond stood at the head, alongside Isabeau Aguillon, a tall, willowy woman, whose chestnut curls fell almost to her waist. She surveyed us with the measured calm that seemed to come so easily to vampires. There was no sign of the vampire I'd expected—Ysanne herself. Belle Morte was her House, every vampire here answered to her; essentially, for as long as we were here, we belonged to her.

Aside from the security team there was no sign of any human staff, but it *was* nearly midnight. Maybe they'd gone home.

"On behalf of the Lady of the House, I formally welcome you to Belle Morte," Isabeau said. "The first floor is almost totally accessible to donors, comprising the ballroom, dining hall, library, the bar, feeding rooms, art rooms, the music room, meditation room, and the theater. The kitchens and supply rooms are out of bounds for donors.

"The second floor consists of four wings. The north wing is where we sleep. No donor is permitted there. The east wing is mostly additional supply rooms. You may visit these if you wish, though I cannot imagine you will find much excitement in doing so. The south wing is where donors sleep.

"The west wing is off limits to everyone." Isabeau's voice took on a warning note; without moving a muscle she'd become . . . different. The unnatural stillness of her body, the calm hardness of her face, the fathomless look in her eyes screamed *not human*. "The rules of Belle Morte are taken very seriously, and none more so than the west wing." Her eyes landed on each of us in turn, burning like lasers. "Any transgression of this rule will result in immediate termination of your contract."

I rolled my eyes. What was up there—a red rose in a glass dome?

Isabeau waited for that to sink in before continuing. "The other rules of the House were laid out in your contract, and there are copies in all bedrooms, but I shall run over the basics once more. Donors are expected to keep themselves in good shape. All meals are provided and donors must eat precisely what they are given. Good nutrition is essential to the healthiness of the blood. Smoking and drugs of any kind are strictly forbidden. Drinking is allowed, but don't get carried away. All items of clothing are provided, as well as any necessary cosmetics, which are found in your rooms. If you require anything else, you may fill out a request form. There are no computers in Belle Morte, and mobile telephones or other methods of internet access are not permitted."

The last words sounded awkward in her mouth, as if modern technology was something that she still struggled with.

"You may write to loved ones as often as you wish. All letters will be inspected before they are sent."

The boy next to me looked baffled at this, as if he'd forgotten pen and paper even existed.

"Until your contract ends, donors cannot refuse any vampire who wishes to drink from them," Isabeau continued. "But romantic relationships between humans and vampires are strictly forbidden."

My gaze shifted from Isabeau to Edmond, standing silently at her side, all ebony hair and moonlight skin. Okay, I could see *why* people were fascinated by these beautiful creatures, but I still didn't trust them. What happened if the world got bored and donors stopped signing up? Would vampires start stalking the streets and dragging prey into the shadows like the vampires of legend?

Isabeau's eyes briefly landed on me and something slid across her face; it was too brief to identify, but it made me uncomfortable.

The short-haired girl from the limo poked my shoulder. I was average height but she had a good few inches on me; I had to tilt my head to look up at her. "Hey, roomie!" she said.

"Huh?"

"Weren't you listening? We're roommates."

"Oh. Great." I didn't really care; I was here to find June, not to make friends.

"I'm Roux." She offered her hand. She looked about eighteen, same as me—apparently young blood tasted better—and her angular features and mile-long legs made her look like a runway model.

"Renie," I said, shaking her hand. Her fingers were long and slim, with polished nails.

Roux grinned, and I noticed a tiny ruby piercing in her nose, gleaming like a drop of blood. Was that a turn-on for vampires? I guess she'd find out.

New donors and existing donors never met on the same night, supposedly to give the newbies a chance to adjust, so I wouldn't see June until the morning, but as a blond vampire named Gideon led us to our assigned bedrooms, I studied every door we passed, wondering which one was June's.

Gideon didn't talk much, but I guess we were just food to these creatures. There was no need for them to socialize.

"I was kind of hoping we'd get to start feeding the vampires tonight," whispered the boy walking alongside us. Maybe a year or two older than me, he had the same model-like good looks as Roux, all coiffed hair and perfect skin and angled features. "My name is Jason, by the way."

Then I registered what he'd said—*feeding*. The word slithered through me, and I fought the urge to shiver. When I'd submitted my application, I'd known I'd be offering up my veins for vampires to suck on, but I couldn't imagine it actually happening.

Jason eyed Gideon's broad shoulders, lean hips, and long legs. "I'm keeping my fingers and toes crossed that this gorgeous piece picks me."

Gideon abruptly stopped. Jason was so busy admiring him that he almost walked into the vampire's back. Luckily, Gideon didn't seem to notice.

"Roux and Irene, this is your room," he said.

I cringed at my full name. I'd been Renie ever since I was born and June, then a toddler, hadn't been able to pronounce Irene.

"Awesome, thanks," Roux said. "See you tomorrow, Jason."

Jason hurried after Gideon as Roux pushed open our door, and I followed her inside.

"Wow," she breathed.

I silently echoed the sentiment.

The bedroom was generously sized, the walls papered in flocked velvet of palest gold, the cream carpet so thick it was like walking on a cloud. Darker gold curtains hugged the windows, even though they were fitted with shades that we couldn't open. At least we could go outside during the day.

The two beds were almost opposite each other, both featuring ornately carved mahogany headboards and draped with satin covers. A huge wardrobe dominated one wall, a long dressing table the other. Alongside one bed, a bronze Venus de Milo statue posed on a nightstand, and next to the other, an open door offered a glimpse into a cream-tiled bathroom. Another crystal-drop chandelier hung from the ceiling. The whole room smelled faintly of roses.

It was a far cry from the tiny bedroom that June and I had shared all our lives.

Roux squealed and pounced on the bed next to the bathroom, knocking the pillows to the floor. "This place is *amazing*."

I couldn't argue, but I didn't like it. My family didn't have much money, and it was this decadence that had sucked June in, offering her a glittering world so far from the one we'd always known.

Rolling off the bed, Roux darted to the wardrobe, pulled open the double doors, and rummaged through the clothes.

"Whoever picked this stuff has seriously sexy taste." She brandished what looked like a corset in my face.

Donors weren't allowed to bring anything with them; instead we had to give our measurements and shoe sizes on the application form so clothes could be provided, but our preferred styles were never considered. All that mattered was what the vampires wanted, and they didn't do casual—hardly surprising considering many of them had come from the era of corsets and crinolines.

"So many pretties," Roux crooned, pulling out an ivory lace dress.

New clothes were a luxury June and I had never had—we'd relied on castoffs from friends and neighbors, and despite myself, I was drawn to the wardrobe. I touched the sleeve of a soft leather jacket that probably cost a fortune. If only we got to take the clothes with us when we left—selling them off would bring in more money than I'd ever get from babysitting or dog walking.

June had come here primarily for the vampires, but she'd also hoped that the money she saved as a donor would help set her up for university, whereas I knew I could never go. Even if money wasn't an issue, what would I study? I didn't dream the way June did.

Roux rummaged through the wardrobe a little longer, then pounced back on her bed.

"So," she said, leaning her chin on her hands. "Have you got a special someone in mind to do the honors?" Baring her teeth, she mimed biting.

"No."

"Maybe you'll get Edmond."

"What makes you say that?"

"He swooped in to save you from the cameras when security could have handled it."

"Etienne helped too."

"True." Roux rolled onto her back and looked up at the ceiling. "Do you think he's *the* Edmond Dantès?"

I sat on my own bed, resisting the urge to run my hands over the soft satin and the feather-stuffed pillows. It was a bed, nothing more. With any luck I wouldn't even sleep in it for long. Once I knew that June was okay, I was out of here.

"What do you mean?" I said.

"You know, *The Count of Monte Cristo.*" Roux laughed at my blank expression. "The book by Alexandre Dumas, same guy who wrote *The Three Musketeers.* Any of this ringing a bell?"

"I've heard of the musketeers."

"It's about a guy called Edmond Dantès who gets wrongfully imprisoned, escapes, and plots revenge on the people who put him there. It's not a common name, and loads of vampires were around when the book was written, so was it actually based on true events, or did Edmond name himself after the character?"

"How do you know all this?"

"I'm not just a pretty face. Maybe if he bites you, you can ask him about the connection."

"He probably won't ask for me." I'd rather he didn't. The memory of his eyes was enough to do strange things to my heartbeat.

"I'm hoping that blond hottie will ask for me." Roux flopped back down on the bed.

"Who, Gideon?"

"No, the one with the ponytail—Ludovic."

Silence lingered, then Roux sat up again. "Do you think being bitten really feels as good as people say?"

"I don't know. They're sticking the equivalent of really big needles into our veins."

"Good thing I'm not scared of needles."

"Neither am I, but I'm nervous about someone biting me and drinking my blood."

Roux's face fell, and I felt a pang of guilt. It wasn't her fault I didn't like Belle Morte.

"People wouldn't keep signing up to be donors if it was painful," I reassured her.

"Do you think it's true that people can get addicted to bites?"

"Maybe, but it probably only happens in extreme circumstances." I was still trying to reassure her, but all I could think was how little people seemed to comprehend that vampires could be dangerous.

I didn't want to forget what they might actually be capable of.

As Roux chattered on about what life would be like here, I lay on my bed and thought of June.

CHAPTER TWO

Edmond

Edmond strode down the hallway of the north wing, Ludovic at his side. The donors had all settled in for the night; Belle Morte was still and quiet.

"Some of the new donors were, ah, interesting," Ludovic said. "Sometimes I forget that it's common for women to cut their hair so short these days."

"You're too old fashioned, my friend," Edmond said.

Ludovic gave him an amused look. "Didn't you recently dismiss the suggestion of installing CCTV because you don't understand how it works?"

"*Touché.*"

Edmond glanced at the chandeliers overhead. Even now, so long after electricity had become part of everyday life, he still marveled at it sometimes, still half expected to wake up with only a flame holding off the shadows. So much of the modern world was absolutely beyond him.

"The girl with the auburn hair—that's Irene Mayfield, isn't it?" Ludovic said.

"She said on her application that she prefers Renie."

"But that *is* her, yes?"

Edmond nodded.

"Is Ysanne sure she should have brought her here?"

"Ysanne knows what she's doing."

"Does she?"

Edmond hesitated. Ysanne wasn't just Lady of the House, she was his oldest friend. Their bond had been forged over hundreds of years, and June Mayfield was a secret that Ysanne had trusted him with. He should trust her in return. But he loved Ludovic like a brother, and they'd been through too much together for Edmond to simply fob him off.

"I'm not sure that keeping the truth from Renie is the best course of action," he admitted, "but it's the one Ysanne has chosen and we must respect that."

Something about Renie intrigued Edmond, and it wasn't just her beauty—although she *was* beautiful, all soft curves and tumbling autumn hair. Maybe it was how she'd acted when she'd climbed out of the limousine. Most donors relished posing for the cameras and answering questions, but Renie had done neither. He suspected she was here to find the truth, but did she really not care about the fame? If so, she was the first donor Edmond had met who'd felt that way.

Ludovic pushed back a strand of hair escaping from the ponytail at the nape of his neck. "Are you sure you can't tell me what's really going on? We all know Ysanne is keeping something from us, and it's to do with those Mayfield girls."

"You know I can't say anything."

"The truth will out."

"I'm sure it will."

Ysanne had told Edmond what was really going on because she knew she could trust him with her life, but he hadn't anticipated the weight of the secret. He hadn't anticipated how it would feel to lie to almost everyone in the house, especially Ludovic. They'd always been honest with each other. Now he'd have to lie to Renie too. It shouldn't matter—he didn't even know her—but he couldn't stop thinking about the vulnerable way she'd held herself when she was confronted by all those cameras.

Edmond shook his head.

It didn't matter how lovely or how intriguing she was. She was here for a reason, and when that was done, she would leave Belle Morte and he would never see her again. He'd spent a very long time building a wall around his heart, and no one was getting past that, including Renie Mayfield.

Renie

Satin sheets were part of the vampires' glamorous world but I couldn't sleep in them. I missed my own comfy duvet and the pillows I'd had since I was a kid, decorated with yellow flowers that had faded to grayish smudges. This new bed was too big and cold, the sheets too slick. Coupled with my black silk pajamas, I slid around like a greased seal. I should have picked one of the lacy nightgowns instead, but they'd seemed so over the top.

June would've loved them.

Would she be happy to see me or would she feel like I was muscling in on her dream? Even if she was cross, she'd get over it once she realized I wasn't staying, and probably laugh at me for getting so worried about her not writing letters anymore. Right?

Mum had said June was having too much fun here to check in with us at home, but I couldn't accept that.

Only eighteen months older than me, June had always treated me like a friend rather than a little sister, and the only thing that had ever come between us was her vampire obsession. She'd stopped confiding in me as much as she used to, and when her application to Belle Morte had been accepted, I'd told her she was making a mistake—ironically, the same thing that Mum had told me two weeks ago when *my* application was accepted.

But all the letters that June had sent had made it clear that she'd put aside any bad feelings, and it was hard to stay annoyed when she was so happy in her favorite vampire mansion.

I couldn't accept that she'd just stop.

Had something happened to her?

Or was I being paranoid?

I sat up. Roux was fast asleep, one foot dangling over the edge of the bed. The carpet almost swallowed my feet as I climbed out of bed and crept out of the room.

Belle Morte was in darkness, shadows dimming the edges of the walls and making the carpet look almost black. Paintings of historical figures seemed to look disapprovingly at me as I crept down the hallway. Had any of the vampires living at Belle Morte known these people in real life?

As I drew near the main staircase, a dark figure emerged from the north wing. I tensed. Maybe donors weren't supposed to wander the mansion this late.

The figure drew closer, and my breath caught in my throat as I recognized the ink-black hair and cut-glass cheekbones.

Edmond stared down at me. "What are you doing out here?"

"I couldn't sleep."

Suddenly I was very glad that I'd chosen pajamas over a nightgown— they hid the flush creeping up my neck.

In the darkness Edmond looked otherworldly, his face a contrasting artwork of shadows and ivory, his eyes diamond hard. He didn't exactly intimidate me, but I couldn't help feeling a twinge of discomfort, like I was facing a panther in the jungle, frozen in place as this beautiful, unpredictable predator considered whether it would eat me.

Irritation cut through the discomfort. Even watching vampires on TV had taught me they could be still in a way humans couldn't, avoiding facial tics or hints of expression that might betray anything going through their minds. Edmond could have been thinking everything or nothing at all.

"Am I not allowed out here or something?" I asked. "Because I don't recall anyone telling us that."

The slight lift of an eyebrow was the only reaction to my sharp tone. Maybe riling him up wasn't smart, but the way he stood and stared made my skin prickle. Vampires weren't human and they didn't act like humans. I didn't know how to react to them, and anger was the best defense.

"Most donors prefer to explore during the day," Edmond said. "Perhaps you were too excited to wait?"

"Too nervous, more likely."

"What do you have to be nervous about?"

The softness in his voice brought that flush back to my neck. There was a quality to it that was almost intimate, a purring lilt that made me think of whispers in the dark, murmured voices beneath twisted sheets.

"I'm going to see my sister tomorrow and I haven't seen her in a long time."

"Your sister?"

"June Mayfield. You must know her?"

Thinking of him sinking his fangs into my sister's skin was enough to banish the butterflies in my stomach.

Edmond stared in silence for so long it was like he'd turned to stone. I was considering prodding him in the eye, just to get a reaction, when he spoke again.

"Go back to bed, Renie."

His French lilt made my name sound soft and exotic, like it was something he could roll across his tongue. My skin heated.

"You didn't answer my question," I said.

He said nothing and his blank expression didn't change, but I could have sworn I felt the air shift around us, as if he was surprised that I didn't immediately obey his command.

His pale hand settled on my shoulder. "Go back to bed," he repeated.

There was little point digging in my heels. Edmond could lift me off my feet with one finger, and as a donor, I was replaceable. Hundreds of starry-eyed wannabes would kill to take my place in Belle Morte.

So I let Edmond steer me back to my room. My feet made whispering noises on the carpet but Edmond was as silent as a ghost—if it wasn't for the weight of his hand on my shoulder, I'd have thought I was alone. It was unnerving to know that someone was walking behind me and I couldn't hear him breathing.

When we reached my bedroom, I turned to Edmond—to say what, I don't know—but he was already gone. The imprint of his hand tingled through my skin.

CHAPTER THREE

Renie

I must have slept after that; the next thing I knew Roux was shaking me awake.

"Come on, sleepyhead. Are you going to snooze all day?" she sing-songed.

I sat up, scrubbing sleep from my eyes. The room took shape around me but its beauty left me cold.

"What time is it?" I mumbled.

Roux checked her new silver watch, courtesy of Belle Morte. "Quarter to ten."

"Seriously?" It felt like 5 a.m.

Roux shrugged. "It's the Belle Morte way—late nights and late mornings."

Apart from the watch, Roux wore only a fluffy red towel that matched our bedcovers. "The shower's awesome, but if you want to try it you need to hurry, or you'll miss breakfast," she said.

All donors ate meals together, so I wouldn't need to look for June—she'd be there at the breakfast table. That jolted me out of bed.

The bathroom was as fancy as the bedroom, with floor and walls of smooth cream tiles, a porcelain claw-foot tub standing close to a shower big enough for two, and a heated towel rack. Hanging on the farthest wall was a full-length mirror edged with wrought silver, and a toilet and basin stood in the opposite corner. Like the bedroom, the bathroom carried the faint fragrance of roses.

Roux was right; the shower *was* awesome, the heated spray pulsing out with enough force to feel like a massage on my whole body, but I was in only long enough to wash. I wasn't here to enjoy myself.

Wrapping myself in a towel, I went back into the bedroom. Roux was dressed now, in skintight jeans and a black lace T-shirt, with ankle boots that added another three inches to her height. She towered over me.

"Nice outfit," I remarked.

"I know." She twirled and blew me a kiss.

I rifled through the wardrobe, grabbing the first pair of trousers and the first shirt in my size. The trousers were soft, gray leather, the shirt delicate as tissue paper. I'd never owned anything so beautiful, and for the briefest moment I forgot they'd been provided by vampires.

My contract said I had to look presentable, so I slicked on mascara and lip gloss, ran a brush through my hair, then scrutinized my own reflection. Not bad.

"Ready?" Roux asked.

"Let's go and meet the other donors."

We made our way down the stairs to the first floor and turned right, heading for the dining hall. Just beyond the vestibule was a parlor, the corners softened with padded velvet seats and sofas, and one wall occupied by a door that opened into a small room.

Roux faltered, and I stopped with her.

Inside the room, a boy roughly our age sat in a wingback chair, his head tilted to one side. A vampire stood over him, her mouth clamped to his neck, her long hair mingling with his. The boy's eyes were closed, his mouth slack with bliss, but the vampire briefly lifted her head and looked at us, and her eyes shone red, the way all vampires' did when they were hungry.

Heat crawled along my cheeks. I'd never seen a vampire feed; it was like glimpsing something private.

"Don't worry, you get used to it," said a voice behind us, and we both turned. A girl stood there, a knowing smile playing around her lips. "I'm Melissa."

I knew the names of every donor in this House, same as I knew the names of every vampire, but Melissa's face was especially familiar to me. Two days before June had stopped writing, Belle Morte had hosted an art display, attended by everyone in the house as well as a select group of outside guests, and one of the photos from that night had been of June and Melissa, laughing together as they posed in front of a huge metal sculpture.

In the weeks following June's possible disappearance, I had spent hours studying that photo, looking for any clue that something was wrong.

"I'm Roux and this is Renie," Roux said, moving away from the open door so we didn't disturb either vampire or donor.

"Renie?" Melissa repeated, her expression wobbling.

"That's right," I said. "June's probably mentioned me?"

"June?" Roux said, frowning.

"My older sister. She's a donor here."

"I thought family members couldn't be donors at the same time."

That wasn't a rule I'd heard about, and my chest tightened with unease.

"But you do know June?" I pushed, watching Melissa's carefully schooled expression.

She looked away. "We should get to breakfast."

I needed to tread carefully here—Melissa knew something, and I didn't want to scare her away.

"How long have you been here?" I asked.

"Nearly seven months."

Roux whistled in admiration. Theoretically, donors could stay in the mansion for years if the vampires wanted them to, but they rarely stayed more than a few months. I guess there were too many other necks for the vampires to taste.

It wasn't hard to see why they wanted Melissa to stay. With an Afro like a dandelion puff haloing flawless deep-brown skin, big eyes, and feathery lashes, she was one of the most beautiful people I'd ever seen—she could have been mistaken for a vampire herself if she hadn't been blinking and breathing, her hands moving with the little gestures that are familiar to humans but lost on vampires.

"Is that really something you get used to?" I asked, glancing back at the room.

Melissa shrugged. "You don't have a choice. You're here to feed vampires, so you either get used to it or your stay here will really suck."

"No pun intended," Roux murmured.

"Amit's one of Catherine's favorites," Melissa said.

Although I knew that vampires had particular tastes, it hadn't occurred to me that they might develop attachments to specific donors. It should have made me feel better, reminded me that vampires didn't just see us as walking blood bags. It didn't.

Melissa lowered her voice to a conspiratorial whisper. "They'll be separated soon. Every donor is closely monitored to make sure they're not giving too much blood, and no vampire is supposed to favor a particular donor for too long."

Grudgingly, I had to admit the vampires seemed to be making sure their donors were happy and healthy, but why had Melissa reacted weirdly to June's name?

We walked into the dining hall. It was a large, rectangular room with the same parquet floor as the vestibule, and walls paneled with polished oak. The huge windows were sealed behind wooden shutters, carved all over with fruit and other food, and the only light came from a pair of chandeliers fashioned from beaten iron and little glass globes. A trestle table covered with a white cloth occupied the floor, and donors sat around it, talking, laughing, eating.

My eyes raced over them. There was no sign of June. There were still empty seats around the table; she probably hadn't come down yet, but my heartbeat sped up.

Stay calm.

I shoved down my fear and joined Roux where she was waiting for me at a smaller table piled high with food. Glass bowls filled with glistening berries stood alongside pots of organic yogurt and china racks of whole wheat toast. Platters of salmon studded with crisp lemon wedges jostled for position with a vat of creamy porridge. Glass jugs stood at each end of the table, one filled with orange juice, the other with a thick, pinkish smoothie.

My stomach ached; I couldn't remember the last time I'd eaten.

I filled a bowl with porridge and poured a glass of juice before following Roux to the trestle table. The other donors called out introductions, but the only ones I didn't already know were the ones I'd arrived with last night—Ranesh, Craig, and Tamara, apparently. I could barely absorb anything. I managed a wan smile for Jason, but everyone else's faces blurred together, and I hunched over my breakfast, hoping no one would talk to me.

Luckily, Roux talked enough for both of us, chattering about the lavish bedroom, the awesome shower, and the incredible clothes. I focused on the dining hall entryway, searching each new face as more donors trickled in, looking for the one I loved the most.

Roux nudged me. "Look at his neck," she whispered, subtly nodding at Amit, sitting farther down the table. I looked. Amit was talking to Tamara; he laughed, tossing his head back, and the collar of his blazer slipped to one side, exposing his neck.

Red puncture marks and tiny silvery scars pocked his skin, making him look like he'd been stabbed with dozens of needles. Fang marks.

Three girls around the table had long hair hiding their necks, and one boy wore a silk scarf, but I couldn't see marks on anyone else.

"I thought vampires didn't leave marks," I whispered.

Roux touched her throat. "I hope we won't end up looking like that."

Why some donors were marked and others weren't was a mystery I didn't have time for. Roux would have to find those answers herself.

I ate another spoonful of porridge, washing the milky oats down with cold, crisp orange juice. The food was delicious but I'd have enjoyed it more if I didn't know that it was all to improve the taste of our blood. We were just food being prepped for eating. My appetite withered and I put down my spoon.

"So which one's your sister?" Roux asked.

I looked around the table again, and an icy wave of fear washed over me.

June wasn't here.

Belle Morte never had more than thirty donors at a time, enough for the twenty vampires who lived here—the six of us who'd arrived yesterday were replacements for donors who'd come to the end of their contracts—and all thirty were at the table. I counted, then counted again, looking in vain for June's laughing eyes and hair a shade darker than mine.

But she *wasn't here.*

Something black and hollow stretched inside me. For weeks I'd told myself that June was too busy to write, that her letters had got lost in the post, that she'd breached some vampire rule and they weren't letting her write home as a consequence, that once I got here I'd see for myself that she was fine.

Now my worst fears were coming true.

One of the girls at this table had replaced my sister, but June had never left Belle Morte. So what the hell had happened to her?

CHAPTER FOUR

Renie

I gripped the edge of the table until my fingers ached. Panicking wouldn't help. There might still be a reasonable, rational explanation for June's absence—there *had* to be.

High heels clicking, a woman swept into the dining hall. Even if I hadn't recognized her beautiful, icy face, the sudden hush that fell across the room made it clear how important she was.

Ten years ago, a live news report covering the scene of a horrendous pileup on a highway had gone global after a woman calmly walked out in front of the cameras and tore the door off one of the crashed cars, freeing the young father and his baby who'd been trapped inside. Then she hauled another wreck out of the way to rescue an older couple from their car, and helped an injured motorcyclist out from under his bike by lifting the entire thing over her head like it weighed nothing. When she'd got everyone to safety, and the ambulances and fire engines had finally arrived, the woman had turned to the cameras and announced it was time the world knew the truth: she was a vampire.

Now that woman was standing in front of me.

Ysanne Moreau, the Lady of Belle Morte.

Dressed in an ivory blouse tucked into a camel-colored pencil skirt, she was probably only about my height, though her heels made her look taller. A diamond pendant nestled in the hollow of her throat, and her blond hair hung in a poker-straight sheet down her back, gleaming like it had been oiled. She surveyed us like a queen gracing the local peasants with her presence.

"Welcome to Belle Morte," she said.

Like Edmond and Isabeau, a subtle French lilt colored her voice.

"Isabeau has already informed you of the rules of my House, and I trust that everyone understands them. I do not take kindly to transgressors." Ysanne's smile was winter cold. "I am sure you will all be very happy for the duration of your stay."

Her pale eyes roved over us, settling on me. Her face gave nothing away—she was even better at the blank look than Edmond—but there was a piercing intensity to her gaze that pinned me to my chair and made me feel like she was turning me inside out.

Ysanne knew every single donor who arrived and left through the mansion doors—if anyone knew about June it would be her.

She said something about how lucky the new donors were to be admitted into this most prestigious of Vampire Houses, then she walked out of the room, her heels clicking loudly.

I didn't know how old Ysanne was—some vampires were surprisingly coy about their ages—but I was sure she was one of the oldest vampires in the world, and I wasted precious minutes planning how to approach her before realizing it didn't matter. My sister was *missing*—I didn't care how I got Ysanne's attention, only that I did.

Pushing back my chair, I jumped to my feet.

"Where are you going?" Roux asked.

"I have to do something."

"On your own?"

"Yes."

"Oh." Roux's eyes were big and wounded.

"Sorry," I mumbled.

She was probably wishing she'd been assigned a different roommate. Maybe once I'd learned the truth, I could explain it to her.

"I'll keep you company," Jason said, and her face brightened.

I left them to it.

Belle Morte was a big building, and for a woman in skyscraper heels, Ysanne moved fast. I didn't have a clue where she'd gone, and after rushing up and down unfamiliar hallways, I no longer had a clue where *I* was.

I stopped, trying to get my bearings. This hall was papered in forest green, the carpet a charcoal-gray color. More paintings lined the walls, and I turned away from their staring eyes.

"We're making a habit of running into each other."

Edmond's voice flowed over me like silk, making my stomach clench. I turned to see him standing behind me, beautiful as sin. Black trousers hugged his legs, and his white shirt was open at the neck, displaying a pale triangle of chest. Dark hair tumbled around his shoulders.

I licked my lips, telling myself the sudden dryness in my mouth was because I was nervous about being lost in a house full of vampires, and not because of Edmond.

"I'm looking for Ysanne," I said.

He arched an eyebrow.

"My sister isn't here and I want to know why. What have you vampires done with her?"

His face gave away nothing. Did vampires have to train themselves to maintain that statue-like blankness, or did it come naturally after living for so long?

"Do you know where Ysanne is or not?" His stillness was starting to irritate me.

"I'm afraid she's too busy to talk to donors."

"Yeah, I'm sure she's *very* busy posing for photo shoots, but this is important," I snapped.

"You should think carefully about what you say. Ysanne doesn't take impudence lightly."

"I'm shaking."

Edmond loomed over me, and the bravado died in my throat. Nervousness prickled along my skin. He wasn't human, and although vampires had been in the public eye for a decade, how much did we really know about them if they showed us only what they wanted us to see?

I didn't want Edmond knowing he made me nervous, but I couldn't help leaning back, away from the power of his presence. To my surprise, Edmond backed off, and the breath rushed back into my lungs.

"I will find my sister," I said quietly. "If seeing Ysanne is the only way to do it, I'll open every door in Belle Morte until I find her."

Edmond regarded me for a long moment, a hint of curiosity in his eyes. I felt like a performing animal that had just done something unexpected.

"Very well," he said at last. "I'll take you to her."

Edmond didn't speak as he led me to Ysanne's office. He didn't seem angry, but I couldn't shake my unease. What had he thought when I'd snapped at him? He was strong enough to break my neck with one hand, and many vampires had probably done that and worse during their lifetimes.

My treacherous little heart told me Edmond could use those elegant hands only for good things, but my head was louder and more insistent, and it told my heart not to be so stupid. I didn't know Edmond or what he was capable of, and I couldn't forget that, no matter how hot he was.

We stopped outside a door that was half-oak, half–smoked glass, and Edmond knocked.

"I'm busy." Ysanne's voice was sharp and cold, even through the door.

"Renie Mayfield wishes to speak to you," Edmond said.

A pause passed, during which I was sure that Ysanne was going to refuse me. Then she said, "Let her in."

The briefest flicker of surprise crossed Edmond's face, then he opened the door and ushered me in. I didn't expect him to follow me but he did.

Ysanne's office was more modern than I expected, a sharp juxtaposition to the classic glamour that dominated the rest of the mansion. The carpet was white, stark against dark wallpaper. Two chrome and leather chairs faced a black desk; behind that desk, Ysanne looked more like a high-flying businesswoman than an ancient vampire ruler. She regarded me as if I was an insect that had dared to crawl into her circle of existence.

"Renie's here to talk to you about her sister," Edmond said.

Ysanne's face didn't flicker. Her skin was marble, her eyes the color of frost.

"June Mayfield. She came here five months ago," I said. "But in November she stopped writing. I came here looking for her . . . but there's no sign of her. What's happened?"

Ysanne's eyes flicked to Edmond. "This is what you've interrupted me for?"

I bristled. This was my *sister* we were talking about.

"She believes something has happened to her sister," Edmond said.

Ysanne's face softened the barest fraction as she looked at him, and I wondered at the connection. Tabloids, magazines, and gossip sites avidly discussed which vampires might be sleeping with each other—it was hardly surprising if Ysanne and Edmond took the odd roll in the sheets.

They were both so elegant and beautiful—they'd make the world's sexiest couple. But I couldn't actually imagine either of them loosening up enough to tear off each other's clothes and leap into the sack.

Ysanne looked back to me, cold and impassive as ever. "June Mayfield isn't here."

"I'm aware of that. Where is she?"

"She was transferred to another House."

My heart started to thud. "I don't think so. Donors don't get transferred."

Ysanne smiled smoothly. "It's a new program."

"So new that no one's heard of it? And you never bothered to announce it to anyone? That's bullshit."

"Your feedback is noted."

"Okay, then I want to be transferred too. Which House is she in?" I demanded.

"That's not your business."

"The hell it isn't."

Ysanne's voice sharpened. "There will be no other transfers."

Blood pounded in my ears and my chest was so tight it was hard to breathe. "Tell me the truth."

"I already have."

I leaned forward, doing my best impression of a vampire's icy look of death. "You are *lying*."

Ysanne's stare put mine to shame. "Do I need to repeat myself?"

My hands shook, fear and rage a live current running through my body. How could she sit there and lie to my face?

"You may leave now." Ysanne flicked her hand.

"I'm not going anywhere until you tell me what's happened to June."

The vampire didn't move but I was suddenly aware of the anger rolling off her in almost tangible waves that brushed against my skin and made me tremble. Ysanne was ancient and powerful, not someone I wanted as an enemy. But I couldn't just accept her lie and walk away.

"Do I need to have you removed?" Her words were edged with frost.

Edmond touched my shoulder. A few minutes ago, I'd felt uncomfortable in his presence; now I wanted to lean into him. If Ysanne lost her temper and attacked me, Edmond might be the only thing standing between me and her. Equally, he might watch her rip out my throat.

Don't be ridiculous. Belle Morte wouldn't have achieved its status as England's most famous Vampire House if its vampires were in the habit of killing anyone who annoyed them.

But I didn't fight Edmond as he guided me out of the office. His hand was still on my shoulder; I could feel the strength in those fingers. If he clamped down, he could shatter my bones. I couldn't help June if I was nursing a broken shoulder. And I couldn't help her if I made Ysanne so angry that she terminated my contract and kicked me out of the house.

Tears pricked my eyes. Anger was a throbbing pulse inside me, adrenaline working itself into a hard knot that pressed against my chest.

"What the hell have you fanged bastards done to my sister?" I whispered.

Edmond's impassive mask cracked, compassion moving through his eyes. In some ways that was worse. I'd almost rather he look at me with a vampire's cold indifference than show a glimmer of human emotion.

"You're a donor, Renie. That's your role and you need to stick to it."

I had the sudden urge to jam both fingers into his stupidly compassionate eyes. That was the problem with these vampires. They'd been around so long that they'd forgotten how to *feel*.

"Fuck you," I snarled.

I stalked in the opposite direction as fast as I could without running, repressing my tears through sheer force of will. Whatever else happened, these monsters wouldn't see me cry.

CHAPTER FIVE

Edmond

There was a tangle of feelings in Edmond's chest as he watched Renie storm off.

It had been a long time since he'd stood in front of someone and really pitied them, but the anger and fear in Renie's eyes tugged at his heart. It shouldn't have been so hard to lie to someone he didn't know, yet somehow it was.

He was surprised too. Renie had come here for June, but Edmond had still half expected her to accept whatever Ysanne said, because that's what donors did. But Renie had fire in her. He couldn't remember the last time someone had spoken to Ysanne—or to him—like that, but in a way it was oddly refreshing, like a slap of cold air in a hot room.

He opened the office door without knocking.

"Perhaps it would be better to tell Renie the truth," he said.

Ysanne's lips tightened. "Now is not the time."

"It's not fair to her."

"This situation is more important than Irene Mayfield's feelings. I will decide when it's time for the truth."

Most other vampires couldn't have pushed Ysanne like this, but Edmond had known her longer than anyone. He could read her moods as easily as his own.

"It's a dangerous game you play, *vieille amie*," he murmured.

Ysanne leaned back in her chair, the rigid line of her shoulders softening. "I know, but the benefits to our kind could be momentous."

"*If* you succeed."

She smiled then, the same smile she'd given him many lifetimes ago when they'd huddled together against the bitterness of winter in rural France. "Have a little faith. I believe in this, and so should you."

Edmond nodded, but remembering the pain and rage in Renie's eyes, he couldn't ignore that sliver of doubt making him wonder if this time Ysanne was wrong.

Renie

I didn't know where I was going when I stormed away from Ysanne's office, but I wound up in the library.

It was smaller than the dining hall, and the thick burgundy carpet stole the noise of my footsteps. Crammed bookshelves lined the walls on either side, and here and there plush sofas were piled high with cushions. The chandeliers overhead were less ostentatious than the ones I'd seen everywhere else.

The library was my favorite room so far in the house—something about it felt more real than the glitz and glamour that saturated the rest of Belle Morte, and there was no one here, so I could be alone for a while.

The faint plinking of piano keys drifted in from the nearby music room.

June had wanted to learn to play an instrument, but we could never afford lessons. In her first letter, she'd gushed over the violins, guitars, pianos, and harps that Belle Morte's music room was equipped with—coming here had been a dream for her in ways that had nothing to do with vampires.

The rage in my chest became a steady ache, tingling up and down my arms. It made me want to run, shout, race back up to my bedroom and tear the clothes from their hangers, smash the mirrors, take a sledgehammer to the bathtub. I wanted to destroy the decadence that had sucked my sister in and spirited her away.

Instead, I paced, my feet scuffing up the carpet. Ysanne was lying—she *had* to be. Edmond . . . well, I couldn't decide if he was being genuine or if he knew more than he was saying. Was he blindly following Ysanne's orders? Regardless, I knew he wouldn't help me.

I was so lost in my own thoughts that I didn't hear the door open, didn't hear a thing until a voice softly penetrated the silence.

"Are you all right?"

For one stupid moment, I thought it was Edmond. But when I whipped around, Etienne stood in the doorway, a look of faint bewilderment on his handsome face. Maybe he didn't try as hard at playing the stoic vampire as Edmond and Ysanne, or maybe he was younger than them and simply hadn't developed that weird still look yet.

"I'm fine," I muttered.

I was glad he wasn't Edmond because I didn't have a clue what to say to *him* again, but at the same time I felt a quick flare of what could have been disappointment. I ground it under my boot heel.

I didn't care about Edmond.

I just wanted to be alone.

Etienne glided into the room, his body moving with the fluid grace particular to vampires. "You don't look fine."

"I'm just exploring."

He didn't move.

"Can I help you?" I said.

His mouth moved, like he was trying to shape words, but nothing came out. He looked at the floor, then back up at me, his gaze moving to my throat. "I was hoping I could feed."

That was the last thing I wanted right now, but contractually I couldn't refuse a vampire my blood. Thanks to my display in Ysanne's office, I was already on thin ice—if I refused Etienne, I could kiss Belle Morte good-bye before I knew the truth.

"Sure. Do we need to go to a feeding room or . . . ?" My voice trailed off as my eyes fastened on his mouth, where the tips of his fangs poked out. How could those things sink into my neck and not hurt me? I thought of Amit's scarred neck and pleasure-dazed face, and my stomach rippled uncomfortably.

"Here is good." Etienne moved his hand to the small of my back and guided me to the nearest sofa.

All the time I'd debated filling in an application and then waiting to hear if I'd been accepted, the weeks leading up to my arrival at Belle Morte, and the one night I'd already been here—I'd spent so much of it worrying how it would feel when a vampire bit me.

Now I was about to find out.

The sofa was marshmallow soft but it might have been filled with rocks for all the comfort it brought. My muscles were knotted tight as old cord, and nerves turned my throat to sand.

Etienne perched beside me but left several inches of space between us and I was grateful. "Would you prefer the neck or the wrist?" he asked.

I'd forgotten I had that choice. I gazed at my wrist, where bluish veins ran like tiny rivers beneath my skin. I didn't like the thought of Etienne sinking his teeth into those veins, but it was better than letting him suck on my neck.

"The wrist."

Taking my wrist between his thumb and forefinger, Etienne opened his mouth and I stared in fascinated disgust as his fangs grew even longer, pushing out of his gums.

"Relax, or it'll hurt," he advised. A red glow tinged his eyes.

I couldn't relax—a vampire was about to bite me.

Etienne bent over my arm and I waited to feel his breath tickle my skin, but of course it didn't. Vampires didn't breathe. His fangs sank into my wrist.

I bit my lip, fighting back a whimper of pain. *Ow, ow, ow.* I'd expected it to hurt, but this was white hot, lancing up and down my arm like fire.

Etienne began to drink, pulling my blood into his mouth with strong, even tugs. Tears gathered in my eyes and I blinked them away, biting my lip harder to fight the waves of pain. I'd thought that anticipating the worst would make it easier, but I'd been wrong, and for the foreseeable future, I'd have to do this whenever I was asked.

Nowadays, vampires had such a steady supply of blood that they needed to take only the equivalent of about five vials at a time, vastly less than if I was donating to a blood bank, but it still seemed like forever until Etienne drew back. Drops of my blood colored his lips, and I swallowed down my nausea. People actually *enjoyed* this?

Etienne's tongue flicked over the puncture marks in my skin. Vampires had healing properties in their saliva; the small cuts vanished.

"Are you all right?" he said, still holding my wrist.

I wanted to get away from him, away from all vampires.

"Can I go now?" I said.

Etienne nodded, pity softening his eyes, which had already returned to their normal color. He'd warned me it would hurt if I didn't relax, but now that I knew how much it hurt, how would I *ever* be able to relax in the future?

My throat burned with unshed tears as I stumbled out of the library.

I hated this house and the bastard vampires who lived here.

I hated Ysanne and her lies.

I found my way through the halls until I spotted a door with an exit sign above it, manned by Dexter Flynn in his black security guard uniform.

He nodded as I approached. I'd met him only yesterday, but it felt like much longer.

"Can I go outside?" I said. If Dexter said no, I might seriously lose it.

"Donors are free to wander the grounds, but only if they have an escort with them."

"An escort?" I just wanted to be alone.

"Either a vampire or a member of security has to escort donors at all times."

Was that for the donors' safety or to stop them in case they decided they'd had enough and made a break for freedom? Option two seemed unlikely, based on what I'd seen of the donors so far.

"I thought security always patrolled the grounds," I said.

"They do but Ysanne doesn't want guards on patrol to act as escorts."

"Fine. Who's coming with me?" My eyes slid to the wooden rack of black umbrellas sitting by the door. The older a vampire, the more resistance they had to the sun, but obviously some of the vampires in Belle Morte were young enough that they still needed to cover up when they went outside. No one knew exactly how long any vampire, new or old, could stay out in daylight for; they were very tight lipped about that little nugget of information.

"I can do it if you like," he offered.

"Doesn't the head of security have more important things to do?"

"Not right now." Dexter unclipped a small radio from his belt and muttered something into it. "Just arranging a replacement for the door," he said.

I noticed a sheathed knife hanging from the other side of his belt; what kind of security problems did he expect inside these lavish walls?

When another guard arrived to take his place, Dexter pushed open the door and I practically ran into the gardens.

The icy January air hit me like a slap—it was so warm in Belle Morte that I'd forgotten it was still winter outside. The ground was packed hard, the sun a weak smudge in a pale sky. My breath steamed on the air. The smart thing to do would be to go back inside and get a coat, but I couldn't face returning to the mansion. Not yet.

The pain from Etienne's bite had faded but I couldn't shake the memory of his mouth on my skin, his fangs coaxing the blood from my veins, the sweep of his tongue as he sealed the wounds. I felt dirty, and I hated that I'd have to do that again.

I stalked across frozen lawns and past sculpted hedges, trying to stamp out my rage and helplessness. The grounds of Belle Morte were barricaded from the outside by a tall stone wall—even out here I felt like I was in a cage, and with Dexter tailing me, I couldn't be as alone as I wanted. At least he kept a respectable distance so I could sort through the mess in my head.

Ysanne was lying. Vampires were sometimes transferred between Houses, but donors never were. Roux thought siblings couldn't be donors at the same time, but Ysanne had to know that I was June's sister. So why had she accepted my application? She would know I'd be looking for June. Or was she used to donors obeying her without question?

I glared up at the stone walls and shade-shielded windows of the mansion. Ysanne couldn't hide her secrets forever. I would find the truth if it killed me.

CHAPTER SIX

Renie

"What do you want to talk to me about?" Melissa asked, standing just outside the art room, where I'd asked her to meet me. My gaze slid past her to the boy standing at her side—Aiden.

"I was rather hoping to talk to you alone," I said to Melissa.

"If you can talk to me, you can talk to my boyfriend," Melissa said, taking Aiden's hand.

I'd forgotten that while vampires and humans weren't allowed to be together, there were no rules forbidding donors from dating each other. Donors who'd been in the same House together had even gone on to get married.

"Okay, fine," I said, and ushered them both inside the art room, closing the door behind us. With no TVs or computers to entertain us, donors relied on more artistic pursuits to pass the time. The music room was the favorite of those who could already play instruments and those who wanted to learn how. The small theater at the back of the house sometimes offered exclusive small showings of plays to guests, and the rest of the time it was open to donors if they wanted to stage their own productions for the entertainment of the House. There was always gardening work to be done, or reading in the library, and then there were the art rooms, where foldaway tables and easels filled the corners, and waist-high wooden shelving ran around the room, holding boxes of pencils, stacks of sketchbooks, and clay sculptures. A hanging display of glass shards caught the artificial light and scattered rainbows across the walls. Paintings hung above the shelves; one of them featured distinctive slashing brushstrokes and bold colors that I was pretty sure had been painted by a former donor who was now making waves in the art world.

"So what's this about?" Aiden asked, running his fingers through his close-cropped dark hair.

It was Melissa I really wanted to talk to. She'd been in that photo with June, before June stopped writing.

"How come no one's allowed in the west wing?" Maybe she'd lower her guard if I started with something non-June related.

Melissa leaned against the shelves. "I don't know. No one does."

"Has it always been off limits?"

Her forehead creased a little. "No, it used to be the spare wing for when vampires from other Houses came to stay."

"When did it become forbidden?"

Melissa's eyes slid away from me, suddenly very interested in the paintings above my head.

I waited, hoping the awkward silence would spur her to fill it.

"I guess . . . almost two months ago?" she said at last.

Her words hit me like a slap, and I struggled to keep my face neutral. "So about the same time that June disappeared."

"June hasn't disappeared. She was transferred."

"Even though that's never happened before, and there was no warning? I monitored all the major Vladdict social media pages for weeks before coming here, and none of them even mentioned it. Almost like nobody knows it happened. Why would Ysanne keep it a secret?"

"What do you want me to say?"

"The truth."

Melissa pushed off the shelves and wrapped her arms around herself. "Can't you leave this alone?"

"She's my sister, so, no."

"Take it easy," Aiden warned, glaring at me.

"All I know is several weeks ago Ysanne told us June had been transferred and we weren't supposed to talk about it," Melissa said.

I pounced on that, ignoring Aiden. "Why wouldn't you be allowed to talk about it?"

"I don't *know*."

"And none of this seems suspicious to you?"

She didn't answer.

"I'm just trying to find out what happened," I said, softening my voice.

"Well, we don't know anything, and neither does anyone else, so you're wasting your time if you question the other donors," Aiden said, putting his arm around Melissa. "They won't talk to you. The vampires won't either. No one will disobey Ysanne."

"She's not a fucking queen!" I snapped, my temper slipping out even as I tried to rein it in.

"In here she is," said Melissa. "I really liked June, but if Ysanne says she got transferred then that's what happened."

"I don't accept that."

"That's your problem," Melissa said, but she still had trouble meeting my eyes.

Frustration made me grit my teeth. Surely she could see that things weren't adding up here?

"I am going to find the truth," I told her.

"Fine. Good luck with that," Aiden said. "Come on, Mel, we're leaving."

"I don't think you really believe Ysanne's telling you everything, though," I said, and Melissa paused just before reaching the door. "Did anything strange happen the night that June disappeared?"

This time Melissa didn't correct my phrasing.

"No," she said, her voice starting to waver. "She seemed happy, okay? Really happy."

"About what?"

A shrug.

"She'd never said anything to make you worry?"

"No. She was a normal donor, and then one day they sent her to another House, and I don't know why but it's not my place to ask questions. The vampires know what they're doing."

I couldn't help but snort.

"I need to go," Melissa said, and I didn't try to stop her, because what was the point? Even if Aiden wasn't here, glowering at me from beside his girlfriend, I couldn't force Melissa to talk. At least now I knew more than when I first arrived.

Maybe the other donors could give me more to work with.

Unfortunately, Aiden hadn't been lying when he said no one else would talk to me. I tracked down donor after donor, anyone who had been here at the same time as June, and asked them the same questions that I'd asked Melissa, but I was stonewalled every time.

Maybe some of them, like Melissa, weren't entirely convinced that Ysanne had told them the truth, but none of them were willing to defy her and risk their place at Belle Morte.

After a day of fruitless interrogation, I slumped against the wooden shelves in the art room and tried not to cry. Had June painted any of the pictures around me? Had her hands shaped any of the sculptures? What hobbies and skills might she have discovered once money wasn't an issue anymore?

And where did I go from here?

Leave the mansion and go to the police? With what evidence? I had nothing.

What about the media? They'd jump at a juicy story like this. Or could I contact the Vampire Council? Made up of the five vampire lords and ladies who ruled the Houses in the UK and the Republic of Ireland, they were supposed to monitor what went on in each house, make sure everyone played by the rules, and liaise with Councils in other countries, but how in the hell was a donor supposed to get in touch with them? It's not like archaic, technophobic vampires had phones or email, and I couldn't exactly visit them. Donors couldn't choose to leave a House. The vampires had complete power over us, and the only way out was if they terminated our contracts. Once a donor left, they couldn't ever come back.

I had to stay in Belle Morte. The answers were here; I just needed to find them.

Jason came into the room. "Hey, you," he said. His black T-shirt was cut in a deep V at the neck, showing hints of a nicely sculpted chest.

"Hey." I managed a smile. If I was staying, I had to act as normal as possible.

"I just saw Amit and he said you've been questioning donors all day. What's going on?"

"I don't want to talk about it."

Jason nibbled his lower lip. "Are you okay?"

No, but what was the point in telling him that? He was a new donor so he wouldn't know anything, and I was exhausted from trying to get answers all day.

"I'm fine," I said.

Jason leaned against the wall next to me, pushing both hands into his pockets. "You've had your first bite, right? Who'd you get?"

Clarity rushed back in a cold wave—the sharpness of Etienne's fangs sinking into me, the suction of his mouth on my skin.

"Etienne. How about you?"

"Phillip. I hoped Gideon would ask for me and I even wore this sexy number just in case"—he plucked the T-shirt—"but nada. Still, Phillip's hot too."

Weren't they all?

"Maybe Gideon will ask for you tomorrow," I said, and Jason's face brightened.

The hope in his eyes made me want to scream. Didn't he understand? Gideon was a *vampire*. He wasn't a normal guy who Jason should be crushing on.

"I think I know who'll ask for *you*," Jason said, giving me a saucy smile.

I thought of Edmond and immediately wanted to kick myself.

I didn't want him in my head. I didn't care about his beautiful face or his smoldering eyes or the French lilt that made my toes curl.

For all I knew, he was off screwing Ysanne somewhere right now. Or maybe they were finished and were having a good, postsex laugh about the fool I'd made of myself this morning.

"I hear Etienne's already looking for you." Jason gave me a little nudge. "I don't know what kind of blood you're rocking, girl, but a certain red-haired vampire wants more of it."

Tears threatened again, then I mentally squared my shoulders. Etienne wanted another taste? Fine. Bring it on. Yes, it hurt like hell and I hated doing it, but it wouldn't kill me. Still, I couldn't help rubbing the spot on my wrist where he'd bitten me. The skin was smooth and unmarked, no sign that anything had happened, but I knew exactly where his fangs had pierced, as if the bite had left behind some invisible trace that nothing would ever get rid of.

"You went for the wrist, huh?" Jason said. "Next time you should do the neck. It's so good." He actually closed his eyes and smiled, as if savoring the memory of Phillip's bite. "I'm still disappointed that Gideon doesn't fancy a nibble, but . . ." He gave a happy little shiver.

"Seriously? You enjoyed it?"

"You didn't?"

"*No.*"

Jason seemed at a loss for words.

I shrugged, trying to pretend it was no big deal. "I just don't see anything sexy about someone taking a bite out of me."

"But isn't that one of the reasons you came here?"

I'd always thought people came to Belle Morte for the glamour and the fame it generated, but I hadn't considered that some people just really wanted to be bitten.

It made sense, though. Sex between donors and vampires was an obvious no-no, but there was definitely something intimate about being bitten. And if it felt as good as some people claimed, it was no wonder there was no shortage of volunteers.

"You don't like it here, do you?" Jason said.

I said nothing. The last thing I needed was for gossip to spread about how I was the only donor who hated Belle Morte.

Jason took pity on me. "Never mind. It's none of my business." Looking at the door, he lowered his voice. "Look, honey, I don't know why you don't like being bitten, but you know you can't refuse, right?"

Miserably, I nodded.

"So if I happen to run into Etienne, I'll conveniently forget I've seen you."

"Really?"

I'd pegged Jason as a classic Vladdict, someone who'd go out of his way to curry favor with anything that had fangs. I didn't expect him to lie to a vampire to protect me.

Jason put his hand under my chin and lifted my head. "It'll be okay, pretty girl. Don't be sad," he said.

I felt a rush of warm gratitude. I could actually have made some friends here if I'd had any intention of staying.

"Go on, get out of here. I'll throw him off the scent," Jason said.

I hurried out of the room. Even with Jason's help, I couldn't hide from Etienne indefinitely, so my best hope was that he'd be too impatient to wait and would find someone else to snack on.

I passed three feeding rooms; the big white space known as the meditation room, where three donors sat on padded mats on the floor, breathing deeply; and into another hallway where I found a life-size statue standing between two doors. It was of a tall man, carved so realistically that his mane of curls looked like they'd move if there was a breeze inside the building.

I slumped down next to the statue, letting its legs hide me from view. My wrist twitched as if it knew what was coming, and I considered what Jason had said about letting Etienne feed from my neck instead. I touched the smooth skin over my pulse and imagined a vampire biting me there, the sharp sting of fangs as they sank deep, and my stomach twisted into a queasy knot.

Nope.

A shadow fell over me and I nearly leaped out of my skin. My head thunked against the wall.

Edmond stared down at me, his face as blankly lovely as ever. "We're making a habit of running into each other. What are you doing down there?"

I patted the statue's stone thigh. "Just hanging out with my friend."

Edmond's eyes flicked to the statue, softening with familiarity. "Louis the Fourteenth. They called him the Sun King."

"Great. Thanks for the history lesson."

I expected him to admonish me, but all he said was, "You seem very unhappy, Renie."

"You think?" I burst out, unable to bottle it up anymore. "My sister is *missing*, no one will tell me what happened to her, and I'll have to let Etienne feed from me again even though I really don't want to—"

I broke off, afraid that even admitting I didn't want to feed the vampires was a violation of my contract.

Edmond didn't get a chance to respond.

Etienne appeared at the other end of the hallway. I closed my eyes, my fingers tightening around my wrist.

"Renie, I—" he started.

"I'm afraid I've already chosen Renie as my donor for this evening," Edmond interrupted, and my eyes flew open again.

"I see." Etienne sounded disappointed, but donors had to feed whichever vampire asked for them first. "Perhaps tomorrow, then." He looked at me, his eyes shadowed with . . . something.

Edmond waited until Etienne was gone before extending a hand. I ignored it, bracing one hand on the statue as I hauled myself up. "Why did you do that?" I said.

He didn't reply, just offered me his arm. "Shall we?"

Understanding dawned. Edmond had intervened because he knew I didn't want Etienne to feed from me, but *he* still wanted to bite me. Suddenly his gesture didn't seem so sweet.

But I couldn't refuse him, and if I was being honest with myself, if anyone had to bite me I'd rather it be Edmond. Was that completely messed up? After everything I'd thought about the other donors, was I really so different?

I couldn't deny that Edmond had this effect on me, but he was still a vampire, and he still represented everything I hated about their world. Maybe some weird attraction for him was brewing, but I was determined to fight it.

The alternative was unthinkable.

Edmond led me away from the Sun King statue and into the nearest feeding room, where the walls were pastel blue and the only pieces of furniture were a chaise longue upholstered in gray velvet and a small grand piano.

Suddenly I felt self-conscious. This wasn't like it had been with Etienne.

Sensuality clung to Edmond like a cloak, and his shirt was still open, offering a tantalizing peek at his chest. His skin never looked pasty or chalky like some of those cheesy old vampire films; his was an ethereal, unearthly sort of paleness, like he was carved from moonlight. His eyebrows were two dark brushstrokes, framing his piercing eyes.

My pulse kicked up a notch, my heart fluttering in my chest. *He's a vampire,* I sternly reminded myself. Reacting so strongly to him wasn't just pathetic, it was hypocritical. How could I pity Jason for crushing on a vampire when I was doing the same thing?

I banished that thought. I did *not* have a crush on Edmond. He was handsome and mysterious and tempting in a forbidden way, and I was reacting the way any girl would in the presence of a ridiculously hot man. That's all.

Edmond moved closer, taking my hand and turning it so my wrist was exposed. Gently he traced my veins with a fingertip. Heat rolled along my skin, and it was all me—as a vampire, Edmond's skin was permanently cool to the touch.

The little space left between us was charged with electricity. My head told me to pull away from him, but I couldn't move. Edmond's eyes pinned me in place, his languid stare igniting my blood, and a crazy thought skipped through my mind—would it be so bad if Edmond *did* bite my neck?

I couldn't go that far.

"Not my neck," I whispered.

Edmond's gaze traveled up my body, slowly, before pausing on my throat. My pulse almost burst through my skin.

No one had ever made me feel like this. Being around Edmond made every relationship I'd had seem like a silly fling, but that made no sense when I didn't know the first thing about him. All the ivory skin and hard muscles didn't make him a good person, and they wouldn't make up for whatever flaws he might be hiding beneath that gorgeous facade.

"Would you prefer to sit or stand?" Edmond's voice was low, rubbing across my senses like velvet. A hint of red crept into his eyes.

"I'll sit." It was either sit of my own accord or collapse when my knees gave out. Which they were in serious danger of doing.

Edmond sat beside me on the chaise longue, still holding my wrist. He murmured something in French.

"Huh?" I said.

The ghost of a smile touched his lips, bringing a lovely human quality to his face. "Relax."

But even though this was Edmond, not Etienne, I couldn't shake the tension that gripped my muscles.

Edmond opened his mouth and his fangs lengthened, sharp and gleaming white. I couldn't look away from them. They were slightly curved, like the canines of a tiger, but smaller and whiter, and beautiful in a lethal way. Kind of like the vampires themselves.

I closed my eyes as Edmond lifted my wrist. Maybe it would hurt less if I didn't watch. His fangs pierced my skin and a jolt of pain shot up my arm.

Nope.

How did the other donors manage it? How could *any*one relax when someone was *biting* them?

Edmond finished drinking and I relaxed my death grip on the back of the chaise.

"Would you like me to heal them?" he asked.

I started to look at the wounds, then decided I didn't want to. I nodded.

Edmond swept his tongue over my wrist like Etienne had done. Unlike with Etienne, heat rushed through me in an electric wave and my hand tightened on the chaise again—this time for a different reason.

"I didn't realize it was a choice," I muttered, snatching my hand back and rubbing the spot that Edmond had bitten. His eyes tracked the movement but he didn't comment. "Why would anyone not want them healed?"

Edmond leaned back, relaxed as a cat. "Some people think they're attractive, a form of body art. Others wear them as badges of pride, showing off the services they have provided vampires."

"That's just nasty," I said, before I could consider that might be offensive to a vampire.

"You don't appear to like vampires much."

I bit my tongue.

He waved a hand, and even that was graceful. "Sometimes honesty is the best policy."

"You really believe that?" His statement seemed hypocritical, considering that almost everyone in the house was lying to me.

"I'm genuinely interested."

"Yeah, right. I say anything you don't like and you'll rat me out to Ysanne."

He frowned, and I realized he didn't understand my turn of phrase.

"You'll tell her everything I say," I clarified.

"Anything you tell me will be in strictest confidence."

"Why do you care what I have to say?"

He spread his hands, palms upward. "I'm intrigued."

Still, I hesitated.

"Renie, I'm not going to hurt you if you say something I don't like. We're not monsters."

The jury was still out on that one. My thoughts must have shown on my face, for Edmond went very still, the humanity I'd glimpsed settling back into the blank mask of the vampire.

"You believe we are monsters."

"No, I just . . ." Why was I denying it? Wasn't that exactly what I thought? "I don't think anyone should be treated like a celebrity without having earned it."

"And you don't think we've earned it?"

Was he serious? Most vampires did *nothing*, and were still showered with money and fame, whereas people like my mum, a single parent who worked her butt off trying to provide for her two daughters, struggled to scrape together a living.

"What have you done? What makes you special?" I said.

The corner of his mouth lifted in the smallest smile. "Besides the fact that we're immortal?"

"Okay, so you're special, but I don't think that entitles you to automatic superstar status. People still don't really know anything about you."

Edmond lifted a pale finger. "Ah, now that is not true. I must admit I'm not familiar with the internet, but I am aware that a lot of people share information about us in this manner. We're talked about all over the globe."

"That's not what I mean."

"Please explain."

"People see what you want them to see." I gestured to the room around us and my own outfit, which probably cost more than my entire wardrobe had when I was growing up. "You present this image of glamour and lavishness, and people lap it up, but we don't know who you *are*. Not really. We don't know what you're capable of, and we know barely anything about the lives you've lived. I know this whole mysterious thing is part of your image, but I don't understand how people can worship creatures they know so little about."

Edmond was silent for a long moment, and I was afraid I'd said the wrong thing. I had only his word that I wouldn't get in trouble for speaking my mind.

"You think we should spill all our secrets?" he said.

"I think you shouldn't expect people to trust you just because you say they should. You shouldn't expect the world to bow at your feet without being honest about who you really are."

"But are vampires wholly to blame for that? We didn't ask humans for special treatment. They offered it."

"You didn't exactly discourage it."

"Would you?" Edmond's eyes searched mine. "If someone offered you the world on a platter, would you honestly turn it down?"

I started to answer, then stopped, not wanting to admit the truth, even to myself.

"Perhaps we're not as bad you think," Edmond said.

My anger and distrust of vampires was what anchored me and kept me from being swept away in a sea of silk and fangs and glitter and blood. If I let go of that, I was afraid of losing myself.

"How come vampires don't turn people anymore?" I asked.

June had often pondered that, trading theories with other Vladdicts, but no one knew for sure. Was I asking so I could clear up that mystery when I finally found her, or was I just digging for any scrap of information?

"We have everything we need, thanks to the donor system, so there's little point overcrowding our community with new vampires."

His words rang hollow. I tried to lift an eyebrow to mimic him, but from the funny look he gave me, it probably looked like a facial spasm.

"That's it?" I said. "That's the only reason?"

"You were expecting more?"

"Vampires established the donor system, so if you made new vampires, you could just build new Houses. The US built two new Houses in the last three years. Russia built four. There are rumors that Scotland will establish its own House in a few years."

Edmond's gaze drifted away from me, studying the piano opposite. "You want the truth?" His voice was barely a whisper.

I found myself leaning forward. My hand rested on the back of the chaise, almost touching Edmond's arm. "Tell me."

"Vampires walk a fine line with humanity and we all know it. People treat us like celebrities now because they see only the glamorous, immortal, romantic side of us. We don't want to remind them that a monstrous streak runs through our nature."

He lifted his eyes to mine, and I caught a glimmer of something raw, as if his vampire facade had cracked, allowing the tiniest peek at the man he might once have been. "You've been honest with me, Renie, so I'll be honest with you. Many vampires have blood-soaked pasts. Our histories are steeped in death and shadows."

It was no more than I'd always suspected, but hearing it still sent a chill through me.

"Do you know how a person becomes a vampire?"

I shook my head.

"You have to die." His voice brushed against my skin, making me tremble. "A vampire has to drain you and then feed you their own blood."

The only thing worse than letting a vampire bite me would be biting *them* instead.

"There's no guarantee of surviving the turn. You rarely just wake up as a vampire, there's a . . . transition. Some people who go through it simply die. If we were to start killing people, even to fulfill their wish of becoming a vampire, the public would turn against us. It's too dangerous. Humans vastly outnumber us, and they don't fear us like they once did."

That time, I knew he was telling the truth. The honesty in his voice was naked and raw, and I was overcome with the urge to lay my hand on his. But I didn't.

"*La vérité fait mal*," Edmond murmured.

I didn't have a clue what he'd said, but there was a soothing quality to his voice. It was velvet and caramel, sliding over my skin.

"I will not pretend with you, Renie. I've lived a long time and I have done some terrible things. But I'm still a man. Vampires are not as different from humans as you seem to think. If you prick us, do we not bleed?"

"Only for a moment and then you heal."

Edmond smiled, a wide, genuine smile that stripped the coldness of the vampire from his features and left me breathless.

But he didn't make me forget about June.

My earlier failure to find the truth crawled over my skin like ice, breaking the spell.

"I should go," I said.

Edmond climbed to his feet and held out his hand to help me up. This time I took it. His skin was cool; my own palm felt hot and clammy in response. Could vampires sweat?

He escorted me back to my room without another word, then I stood at the door, watching until he turned a corner and was gone.

I was thoroughly confused. I'd never been part of the Vladdict culture, and it had annoyed me that so many people were. I came to Belle Morte expecting to hate vampires, and then Edmond was there with those eyes and that smile and that aura of danger and eroticism, and I simply didn't know what to make of him.

But I couldn't forget that he was lying to me too. Even if he didn't know what had happened to June, he knew there was more to this than Ysanne was saying, and if none of them would tell me the truth, then they'd left me no choice.

I'd have to sneak into the west wing.

CHAPTER SEVEN

Renie

When I went into the bedroom, the bathroom door was open, steam billowing out in rose-scented clouds.

"I'm in here," Roux called, as if it wasn't obvious.

I peeked around the bathroom door. Roux was in the tub, almost hidden beneath a mound of bubbles, flecks of white clinging like snowflakes to her hair.

"You can come in," she said.

I sat on the closed lid of the toilet, suddenly exhausted. I couldn't attempt to get into the west wing until everyone was in bed, which meant I had hours to kill. I wanted to talk about this with someone but it didn't seem fair to drag Roux into this mess.

"How did your first feeding go?" I asked, for the sake of saying anything.

"Pretty awesome." She waggled her eyebrows. "I got Benjamin. How about you?"

"Etienne."

I didn't mention Edmond; those moments I'd just shared with him felt strangely private.

Roux hung over the side of the tub, dripping water and bubbles across the floor. "You've got something on your mind. Spill."

"What do you think about the vampires?"

"I'd say hot, but that's not the answer you want, is it?" One of Roux's long legs emerged from the bubble mountain, her toes pointing toward the ceiling. "They're creatures of mystery. They've been around a long time, but we don't always get exact dates; we know some of them have lived colorful lives, but we don't always get details; and they may be capable of terrible things, but they curb their darker impulses to fit in with the world."

I gaped at her.

She tapped the side of her head, leaving a blob of bubble stuck in her hair. "Not just a pretty face, remember?"

I felt a quick spark of shame. Judging people for their choices was one of my worst qualities. I'd assumed so strongly everyone who admired vampires must be ignorant at best and downright stupid at worst that I couldn't always see what was right under my nose.

"So why do you like them so much?"

Roux considered my question, dipping her leg back into the water and using her fingernails to carve little patterns in the bubble mound. "Why do people love tigers and wolves and other dangerous animals? Sure, they can rip out your throat, but they're so beautiful that you can't stop looking. And think of the history they carry around in their heads, think of everything they've seen and done. How can you not be fascinated with people who've lived that long?"

I'd never thought of it like that. I'd been so busy condemning the negative aspects of their immortality that I hadn't considered any positives. At school, I'd zoned out during history lessons because poring over textbooks was dull, but hearing it from people who'd actually lived it was another story. Maybe vampires should be teaching rather than posing for magazine covers. Of course, school taking place during the day would be a problem.

But two vampires in the US had released books detailing their experiences as slaves before they were turned. In Japan, a vampire who'd once been a genuine samurai now worked as a historical consultant on films and TV shows. Survivors of the Spanish Inquisition, the Salem witch trials, and the French Revolution had given interviews on TV.

Ysanne herself had brought vampires out of the shadows by publicly demonstrating her superhuman strength and saving multiple lives. Why weren't more vampires doing things like that? Why did they stay shut up inside their mansions like immortal hermits?

"Why do you ask, anyway?" Roux said.

"Just curious. I thought I was the only one here who didn't blindly worship them."

I think Roux shrugged; the bubbles around her neck shifted. "I know there's more to them than meets the eye, but I also believe that the past is the past. The things they did then and the people they once were aren't necessarily who they are now. Without knowing more about them, I don't feel in a position to judge."

Gripping both sides of the tub, Roux hoisted herself to her feet, water and bubbles sliding down her body. She faced me, unashamedly naked.

"Do you have *any* inhibitions?" I asked.

She grinned wickedly, putting one hand on her hip and posing. "With a butt like mine, why shouldn't I flaunt it?"

I couldn't argue with that. Roux's lean build hadn't given her much in the chest department, but her legs and backside were exceptional.

Roux struck another runway pose, and twirled like she was showing off a new outfit. Water slopped over the edges of the tub.

A laugh bubbled out of my throat. It was the first time I'd laughed since my donor application had been accepted—possibly the first time since June had stopped writing. It felt good, like all the fear and doubt that was weighing me down had lifted. Then reality crashed back down and the laugh died in my throat.

I'd been here a whole day and I still didn't have a clue what had happened to June. I was disgusted with myself for laughing with Roux and thinking about Edmond, all in the place where my sister had disappeared.

Tonight, I was getting answers.

*

Of course, "tonight" in Belle Morte wasn't what it was in the rest of the world. Vampires were more active at night, usually rising late in the morning and going to bed early the next morning. After 2 a.m. was the best time to snoop—when both vampires and donors were asleep.

My phone was stranded back at home, and setting the alarm on our clock would wake Roux, so I chugged several glasses of water before bed, counting on that to wake me up nice and early.

Which it did.

Roux didn't stir as I slipped on a dressing gown—black satin, of course—and crept out of the room. The hallway was thick with shadow, and the eyes of the paintings glared from their gilded frames. Cast in darkness like this, Belle Morte looked like the sort of house that'd feature in a horror film, monsters and murderers lurking behind every door. Ignoring the chills creeping up my spine, I strode down the hall, my footfalls muffled by the carpet.

The layout of Belle Morte's second floor was simple: the north and east wings were on one side, the south and west on the other. Shortly before reaching the main staircase, the hall branched off on my left, and I followed it until I reached a corner that turned onto a shorter staircase, leading up to another darkened hallway.

The forbidden west wing.

I gazed up the steps, squinting into the near-solid shadows of the wing that was supposed to be off limits to everyone.

So why was someone up there?

Edmond

Edmond couldn't sleep. He lay in bed, staring up at the ceiling and trying to stop thinking about what had happened today. But it was no good.

He'd never intended to taste Renie. He should have walked away and left her with Etienne. Renie hadn't asked for help, but the pleading look in her eyes had, even if she didn't realize it. She'd looked so scared and helpless, crouched on the floor, pulling Edmond back to the days when he'd stalked the shadows of the French countryside, or glided through the backstreets of Paris in search of a meal. So many people who'd caught a glimpse of his fangs had worn that look. He didn't want to see it on Renie's face.

Now he couldn't get her out of his head.

Eventually he gave up trying to sleep. He pushed back the covers and got dressed before quietly heading down to the place where he felt most at peace—the library. There, he slumped onto the nearest sofa, resting his head on the arm as he tried to quiet his buzzing brain.

When he'd told Etienne that he'd chosen Renie, he hadn't considered actually biting her, but he was sure that Etienne would know if he didn't. As far as Etienne and almost every other vampire in Belle Morte was concerned, Renie was just another donor, and no one needed to know that when Edmond looked at her he felt a spark of something he hadn't felt in a very long time, something he'd sworn he would never allow himself to feel again.

When they'd talked earlier, she'd slipped past his defenses. She'd made him smile. He couldn't allow that. He couldn't get close to Renie, even if he did feel some kind of pull toward her.

Edmond had lived for centuries, and he'd felt that pull before, but it had never ended well. For more than two hundred years he had avoided relationships because it wasn't worth giving your heart to someone only for it to be tossed back, beaten and raw. There were so many cracks in Edmond's heart, the scars of so many old wounds, and no one could fill those—especially not Renie.

When he'd bitten her, he'd told himself it was simply to prevent Etienne from doing the same thing, but at the first taste of her blood, all he could think was that he'd found heaven. When was the last time anything had tasted that good? Even the memory of it made his fangs lengthen, straining against his gums.

It would be harder to keep his distance now. Every time he saw her, he'd remember the rich sweetness of her blood filling his mouth.

He lay on the sofa until his thoughts finally exhausted themselves, his eyes grew heavy, and the need for sleep became more pressing than thoughts of Renie Mayfield, then he headed back to the staircase.

As of tomorrow, he would do whatever it took to avoid her and—

When he was almost at the top of the stairs, Edmond paused, listening.

Someone else was awake. No human could have heard the *shush* of bare feet moving on thick carpet, or the faint sound of a heart beating, but vampire hearing was far superior. A donor was nearby and their heart was fluttering like a frightened bird.

Edmond reached the second floor just in time to see a flash of auburn hair disappearing in the direction of the west wing. Renie? Despite himself, he smiled. She was determined, all right, and she wasn't backing down from this.

Then his smile vanished.

Renie genuinely didn't know what she getting into, and if someone didn't stop her, she was going to get hurt.

Silent as a ghost, Edmond followed the girl he knew he should stay away from.

Renie

I hugged the corner, peeking around at the stairs that led up to the west wing. The figure I'd glimpsed had disappeared into the depths of the hall, but I hadn't imagined it.

Maybe it was Ysanne herself—presumably the rules didn't apply to her.

Did I really want to come face to face with her again? *Nope.* She was one of the most powerful, dangerous vampires I was likely to meet, and I'd be happy to never see her again, but if June had disappeared at the same time that the west wing had become off limits, the two events had to be connected.

Was June up there?

Was *she* the figure I'd seen?

"Okay, Renie," I whispered. "You need to know what's going on, but you need to be careful."

"Why are you talking to yourself?"

Edmond's voice, materializing through the darkness, just about gave me a heart attack.

"What's *wrong* with you?" I clutched my chest. "Don't sneak up on people like that."

He regarded me with his usual calmness. In his black trousers and black shirt, he seemed part of the shadows themselves, his face an ivory sculpture shining in the dark. His hair spilled around his shoulders; I couldn't help wondering what it would feel like to run my fingers through it.

"Why are you talking to yourself?" he repeated.

"Why are you following me?"

"Because you're doing something you shouldn't."

"You said there weren't any rules about donors walking around at night."

There it was—the eyebrow arch. "You wouldn't be so defensive if you hadn't been caught doing something wrong."

True, but I wasn't about to admit it. Although when Edmond looked past me to the steps leading into the west wing, guilt was probably written all over my face.

"I don't know what you're talking about," I said.

Edmond glided closer. "Do you know that some vampires can tell when a human is lying to them?" He brushed my hair off my shoulder, exposing my throat.

I couldn't move.

"We can hear it in your heartbeat," Edmond murmured. His fingers trailed down my neck until they located my pulse. Guilt had already made it speed up, and now it was going into overdrive. Edmond was gentle but he left a trail of fire on my skin. I wanted his tongue to follow the path of his fingers, soothing those flames.

My legs trembled and my stomach turned to liquid. No one had ever affected me like this before, not even when I was doing far more intimate things. It was the sexuality that Edmond wore like a second skin. Everything he did made me tingle.

His gaze drifted down to my chest, and I was *very* glad that I was wearing pajamas. If I'd donned one of those nightgowns then not only would Edmond be getting an eyeful from his vantage point, but I'd be doing the dramatically heaving bosom thing.

"Guilt isn't the only thing we can discern," he murmured, and his voice was a caress.

I wanted to arch my body against his, turn my head to nuzzle against his arm. God, what was *happening* to me? I'd heard of physical chemistry but this was off the charts. My body wasn't just giving off sparks, it was about to combust. It was the closeness of his hard, muscled body, the way he loomed over me, his eyes blazing through the dark.

"Your heartbeat's getting faster," Edmond said, his eyes fixed on the spot where it beat beneath my rib cage. "But not with guilt this time. Do you know what else causes a heart to beat like that?"

I couldn't even shake my head. This wasn't supposed to be happening. But I couldn't seem to break away from the hypnotic spell of the beautiful vampire in front of me.

"Titillation," Edmond whispered. He moved even closer, and a hint of red crept into his eyes. "Desire."

He had to get away from me.

He had to get away right now or I would kiss him, and that absolutely couldn't happen.

I kicked him in the shin.

Edmond jerked back, his face astonished. It was the first time he'd been anything less than graceful, and for a moment he was a man rather than a vampire.

"What is up there?" I snapped, stabbing a finger at the west wing.

It occurred to me that everything Edmond had done might be diversionary, playing on my desire for him to distract me from my mission. He'd have to try a lot harder than that.

Edmond drew himself up, his face slipping back into the marble mask. "You're hardly the first donor to be curious about the west wing. But you're no more special than the others, and you won't be the one to crack Belle Morte's secrets."

The coldness in his voice stung as much as the harshness of his words, but I welcomed that. It cleared the butterflies from my head and reminded me who and what Edmond really was.

"I saw someone up there," I said.

His eyes flicked to the stairs but his face stayed impassive.

"What will you do if I go up there?" Maybe baiting him wasn't smart, but I was tired of stumbling around in the dark.

"I will pick you up and carry you back to your room."

"Try it, and your shin won't be the only thing I'll kick," I warned.

"These are the rules of Belle Morte. You signed the contract—you knew what you were getting into."

"I didn't sign up to be lied to. Why is everyone pretending that June was transferred? Do you all think I'm stupid or something?"

Gideon and Míriam appeared at the end of the hall. Míriam was as perfectly groomed as ever, and a few out-of-place strands of Gideon's hair were the only indication that he'd been sleeping—of course vampires didn't get puffy eyes and bed heads like us lowly mortals.

"What's going on?" Gideon asked.

"It's nothing," said Edmond. "I'm handling it."

Gideon's eyes slid past me to that dark hallway at the top of the short staircase, and the faintest flicker of uncertainty crossed his face. Did anyone apart from Ysanne actually know what was up there?

Edmond took my arm, pulling me down the hall and away from the other vampires.

"Ysanne does not take kindly to anyone flouting her authority, especially not donors. Understand?"

I glared at him.

"If you don't watch yourself, Ysanne will cast you out. Is that what you want?" Edmond said.

If she did, then my only hope of finding the truth would be gone. But if all I did was toe the line then I'd never get close to the answers. I bit back a scream of frustration. Everything I tried was met with a brick wall; I wanted to smash through it but I didn't know how.

I snatched my arm away from Edmond, and he let me.

"I can find my own way back to my room," I said, projecting as much ice into my voice as I could. Seething with anger, I stalked away.

Edmond

The cold bitterness of Renie's hurt and anger lingered on the air, and Edmond felt a stab of frustration. Lying to her like this was cruel, but he had no choice. She was getting too close to things that she wasn't ready to understand. Maybe she never would be.

Regret weighed like an anchor around his neck as he watched Renie leave. It was better this way. If she hated him, she wouldn't be such a temptation.

In the darkness of the hall, Renie's fiery beauty was brighter than ever, punching straight through the shields he'd spent the last two centuries building. Edmond had loved before, and it had ended bloody, almost every time—he wouldn't do it again. There was no place for someone like Renie in his life.

But it was hard to resist her when she had so much life, when she drew him in with all that spirit and passion. He still couldn't believe she'd actually *kicked* him.

When he was sure that Renie was gone, Edmond returned to the foot of the stairs that led up to the west wing. Gideon had gone but Míriam still lingered, her face troubled.

"Do you know what's going on?" she asked.

"You know I can't say anything," Edmond told her.

She moved closer. "Not even to me?"

Edmond wasn't the only Belle Morte vampire who carried lifetimes of painful memories and emotional baggage that couldn't be easily jettisoned, but avoiding love didn't mean avoiding physical needs. He and Míriam sometimes turned to each other to fulfill those needs, both of them aware that it would never be anything but sex.

He shook his head.

"I'm going back to bed. If you feel like joining me . . ." Míriam's voice trailed off suggestively.

"Not tonight."

She patted his shoulder as she left, which was about as affectionate as things ever got between them.

Another few moments passed before Isabeau finally emerged from the shadows of the west wing and headed down the stairs.

"What was all that?" she asked.

"Renie was nighttime exploring."

Isabeau shook her head, chestnut curls bouncing. "Ysanne should never have brought her here. None of this should be happening," she said.

"No," Edmond agreed.

In all the years of the donor system, none of them had ever faced a situation like this, and he couldn't shake that niggling feeling that Ysanne wasn't handling it in the best way.

Isabeau shook her head again. "I'm going to bed."

After she left, Edmond stayed, staring up at the west wing. Renie wouldn't give up until she knew the truth. Maybe it would be better for Ysanne to send her away, but Renie was the only chance they had, otherwise this had all been in vain.

"This," Edmond whispered, "is a mess."

Renie

Seething, I stalked back to the south wing.

Bastard Edmond, bastard vampires, *bastard* Belle Morte.

Beneath the anger I couldn't forget the way I'd felt when he'd leaned into me. For a crazy moment, I'd thought he would kiss me, and the worst part was I wouldn't have pushed him away.

If only I could go back in time to intercept June's application before she could submit it, to do whatever it took to stop her from becoming a blood bag for a bunch of vampires.

But she wouldn't have listened.

I squeezed my eyes shut, blinking back useless tears. Short of imprisoning her, I'd never have stopped June from coming here, and if she'd left thinking I hated her, maybe she wouldn't have written at all. Then I might never have known that something was wrong.

I tiptoed into my room, trying not to wake Roux, but she sat up as I was climbing into bed.

"What are you doing?" she said, sleepily.

"A dream woke me up, so I went for a little walk."

"A nightmare?"

When I was a kid and I had bad dreams, I'd always climb into June's bed and tell her about them. Sometimes she was grumpy that I'd woken her up, but she always got over it when she realized I needed someone to talk to. If I could talk about the dreams, they couldn't scare me anymore. My heart twisted.

"No."

"Ohhhh." Roux's expression turned mischievous. "A *sexy* dream."

"*No.*"

Roux patted her bed. "Details, now."

"There's nothing to tell," I protested weakly.

"It was about Edmond, wasn't it?"

"Don't be ridiculous. Why would I dream about him?" Even I could hear how hollow my words were.

"Hmm, let's see. He's smoking hot? He's got a body that Michelangelo would have begged to sculpt?"

"I don't care how hot he is. He's a vampire."

"So?"

I made a frustrated gesture with my hands. "So he's not *human*." Maybe if I repeated it enough, I could keep convincing myself of that.

"Do you really believe that?"

"Let's see." I mimicked her by counting off the ways on my fingers. "Vampires live forever. They can heal from wounds that would kill a human. They need blood to survive. Sunlight kills them if they're out in it long enough. I'd say they're pretty far from human."

Roux drew her knees up to her chest. "They can do stuff that regular people can't, but they're not another species."

I wasn't entirely convinced of that.

"And they were all human once, don't forget."

"*Once*," I stressed. But that was a long time ago, and I wasn't certain any of them remembered what it was like.

"If you hate vampires so much, why did you come here?" Roux's voice was unusually serious.

"I don't hate them."

"That doesn't answer my question."

A pause crawled by.

Roux's eyes bored into me, patient and nonjudgmental. She'd gone out of her way to try to be my friend, even when I didn't give her much worth befriending—she deserved the truth.

So I told her.

After my explanation, Roux frowned. "But if June's not here, then where is she?"

"I asked Ysanne and she said she'd transferred June to another House."

"You *asked* Ysanne?" The disbelief in Roux's voice made it seem like I'd waltzed up and interrogated the queen.

"Less vampire worship, please. Ysanne lied to me. Something's happened to my sister."

"How do you know she didn't stop writing because she was too caught up enjoying life here? Are you sure she hasn't been released from her contract?"

"No matter how much fun she was having, she wouldn't ignore me. She wouldn't ignore our mum, and if she'd been released from her contract, she would have come home. If she really has been transferred, like Ysanne keeps saying, then why does no one outside Belle Morte know about it? Why won't Ysanne tell me which House June's now in? Why are none of the donors allowed to talk about it? Why wouldn't the gossip magazines and websites be talking about it?"

"Yeah, I don't have an answer for that."

"Exactly. Ysanne's full of shit."

"Do you have any leads on what's really going on?"

Gratitude rushed through me. I rattled off what I knew about the west wing, and what had happened just now.

Roux looped her arm through mine. "Okay, think about this for a minute. You can't be suggesting that Ysanne keeps everyone out of the west wing because she's hiding June up there. The entire wing? To hide one teenage girl? Whatever's going on up there could be some spooky vampire shit, but I can't believe it's anything to do with June."

"You think the timing is just coincidence?"

"Maybe." Roux toyed with the edges of her covers. "How about we put our heads together and do some sleuthing over the next couple of days?"

"We?"

"Sure, you and me. We'll be like the Scooby gang, minus the boys and the dog. And the van." She grinned. "Velma and Daphne, that's us."

"But why do you want to help me?"

Roux rolled her eyes. "Duh. We're friends."

The last thing I'd come here to do was make friends, but it had happened without me even realizing it. Maybe that was a good thing. I didn't know how long I'd be stuck here, and a friend would help me weather the storm.

CHAPTER EIGHT

Renie

Roux wasn't my only unexpected friend. After finally returning to bed, I squeezed in a few hours of uneasy sleep before Jason bounded into our room, swatting both of us over the head with a cushion.

"Wake up, my lovelies," he said.

Roux threw her pillow at him; he caught it and waltzed around the room. It was hard to be sure since his dance partner was a pillow, but it looked like the boy had some moves.

"What are you doing here?" I asked.

I could have done with more sleep, but it was hard to be annoyed with Jason when he was beaming at me like a kid at Christmas.

"It's Friday," he said.

"So?"

Jason stared at me. "It's the Walls for All charity ball tonight. Did you forget or something?"

"The what now?"

"Of course." Roux scrambled out of bed and did a little dance, spinning so vigorously that her left boob almost escaped her nightgown.

I was still lost.

"Haven't you checked your calendar?" Jason said.

"What calendar?"

Jason went to my nightstand, opened the little drawer, and pulled out a small paper calendar. Some of the days were marked with neat, slanted handwriting. "These are all the planned events for the next three months. I can't believe you didn't look at it."

"What's happening tonight?" I said.

"The House is hosting a ball to raise money for that homeless charity Walls for All."

"Right." I forced a smile. If I wanted to stay in Belle Morte then I had to play the part of a proper donor, and a donor would be excited about an upcoming ball. They were a regular occurrence at Belle Morte—usually exclusive events, with tickets highly coveted since they were available to fewer than a hundred people, and almost always filmed live for the entertainment of Vladdicts worldwide.

For donors, it was our chance to put on beautiful gowns and elegant tuxedos and mingle with the vampires in a way we couldn't normally, as well as rub shoulders with well-known socialites, actors, musicians, and millionaires—I had to pretend to care about that.

"Okay, so we should sort our outfits now. We don't want to get all stressed trying to choose something later," Jason declared, sitting on Roux's bed and hugging her pillow.

"We've got hours until the ball," I pointed out.

"But I want to look my best. Maybe then Gideon will notice me."

Roux joined him on the bed. "You really have a thing for him, huh?"

"What can I say? I'm a sucker for hot blond Englishmen."

"Yeah, but it's not like there's a shortage of hot guys here. Even the other donors are hot. We're rolling in hotness!"

"It's not just about that. It's chemistry. Believe me, I've noticed this house is full of gorgeous guys, but there's something about Gideon. Don't ask me to explain it. There are other guys just as gorgeous as him, but he's the one I'm attracted to." He closed his eyes and smiled dreamily. "So, so attracted to."

That I could understand. When I was around Edmond it was easy to forget that there were other men in the world or that he wasn't the only incredibly good-looking one.

Roux bounded off the bed and headed for our wardrobe, where she rifled through the clothes. Alongside the daytime outfits and lacy nightwear there was a glittering assortment of formal dresses.

"This is a definite contender for me," she said, plucking out a plum velvet gown with lace panels at each side. "Renie, something in green would really set off your hair."

A lump rose in my throat. June would have loved this. When we were kids playing dress-up we used to pull the sheets off our beds and wrap them around ourselves, and make evening gloves out of old socks.

No wonder people signed up for this. Days spent luxuriating in bubble baths, drinking at the private bar, playing expensive instruments or pursuing projects, all the while dressed in designer-label clothing, and the only price was donating blood. Even that was seen as a good thing, considering how beautiful vampires were and how good it was supposed to feel.

Why *wouldn't* anyone want to sign up?

"So far the only pictures the world has of us are the snaps they took when we were getting out of the limo. We can all do better than that. So tonight we're going to look our most spectacular," Roux said. "Now get off your lovely butts and help me."

To my surprise, I ended up having fun. We tried on half a dozen dresses each, posing and prancing for Jason's approval, and when we had finally settled on our outfits, we went to his bedroom to help him select a tuxedo.

We completely missed breakfast. I'd thought that someone would come to fetch us when we didn't show up, but apparently we had the freedom to skip meals if we wanted to, and no vampires came looking for a morning nibble. They must have been busy with ball preparations too.

"Anyone fancy a drink?" Roux said, rubbing her hands together.

"It's not even midday," I said.

"So? That's the Belle Morte lifestyle. And what's the point of having a free bar if we never visit it?"

Jason and I exchanged looks.

"I'm up for it if you are," he said.

I shrugged. June was still the most important thing on my mind, but I couldn't get into the west wing during the day, none of the donors were talking, and it was pointless to think about interrogating the vampires themselves, so I might as well pass the time with my new friends rather than sitting around fretting.

"No getting wrecked, though. I plan on looking jaw-droppingly sexy tonight, which I can't do if I'm drunk," Jason said.

"Just one, I promise," Roux said.

I smirked at them. "Maybe two."

The more time I spent inside Belle Morte, the more I understood the appeal of it—heading down to the bar for cocktails at eleven thirty in the morning was how I imagined rock stars lived.

The bar was one of the smaller rooms, with a parquet floor to match the vestibule and dining hall, and slate-gray wallpaper decorated with twisting black vines and flowers that turned the space into a monochromatic jungle. High breakfast stools ringed the black marble bar, and behind that was a series of glass shelves filled with every kind of alcohol I'd heard of, and quite a few I hadn't. Glass boxes held glittering cubes of ice and fresh slices of fruit—they must be regularly topped up by the staff. A hardcover book of cocktail recipes sat beside the boxes.

The bar wasn't staffed, which surprised me. Letting the donors serve themselves seemed like playing with fire, but maybe that was the point. We were expected to follow Belle Morte's rules, which included not abusing privileges like the free bar.

Roux positioned herself behind the bar. "What can I get you?"

Jason scanned the shelves. "Something healthy, apparently."

Roux flicked through the cocktail book. "Gingered pear and brandy cocktail? No, thank you. Ooh, but pink grapefruit and lychee sounds good. Or maybe champagne pomegranate."

"I'll go with tried and tested. Cosmo, please," Jason said.

"Good choice. And you?" Roux's gaze switched to me.

"I'll have a mojito."

"Excellent."

Roux mixed the drinks, then slid them across the bar top on coasters made from squares of slate.

My stomach reminded me that I hadn't eaten yet, so I took only small sips. Tipsiness ruining the ball didn't worry me; flouting more of Ysanne's rules did.

"I guess bar snacks are out of the question," I said.

Roux promptly fetched the box of fruit and set it down in front of us.

"I think that's for the cocktails," Jason said.

"It can be refilled." She took a long sip of her drink and appreciatively smacked her lips. "I make a damn fine cocktail, don't I?"

Jason and I murmured our agreement.

"We haven't discussed hair and makeup yet," Jason said.

Roux pointed to her pixie crop. "I'm a bit limited on choice."

"Nonsense," Jason declared. He ran his fingers through Roux's hair, swept the front to one side, then changed his mind and ruffled the whole lot so it stuck up like an angry hedgehog.

"Renie's the one you can have more hair fun with," Roux said.

I'd always considered my hair my best feature—long and thick with a natural wave, it was a gorgeous autumnal color, auburn mixed with copper, and it looked even better under sunlight. Jason's eyes lit up as he lifted a section and examined it.

"You've got lovely natural bounce, but maybe we can turn these waves to curls. You've definitely got the bone structure for it."

"You sound like a pro," I teased.

"I studied hairdressing at college."

"Is that what you want to do for a career?" Roux said.

"It's a bit clichéd, I know—gay guy working in a hair salon—but styling hair is like creating art, and I love making people happy."

"You're welcome to create art with my hair. Saves me messing it up," I said.

"Same here. The whole reason I cut mine off was so I wouldn't have to bother with it," Roux said.

"I'm more than happy to oblige," Jason said. "Just don't ask me to do your makeup too."

"Leave that to me," said Roux.

Sitting at the bar, with two people who were becoming important to me, I felt a spark of something suspiciously like happiness, followed by a sharp pang of guilt.

I felt like I should be tearing this whole mansion down to find June. But I couldn't. I had to bide my time. I had to be careful.

When we were on our second round, Amit and Melissa drifted in. Amit wore a dreamy smile, his throat marred by a fresh bite mark.

"Uh-oh, I recognize that look," said Jason, chuckling. "Someone's in a bite daze."

Amit made a soft noise of appreciation. "Phillip."

"Oh, yeah, I had him yesterday."

Roux lifted her champagne flute. "Pull up a stool and join us."

They did, but Amit's movements were slow, like he was wading through something we couldn't see. The side effect of a good bite?

Roux poured them both cosmos, and Amit sipped his, the dreamy, half-lidded look never leaving his eyes.

Up close, his bite looked even worse. The holes themselves were neat enough, two more puncture marks among the many healing holes and scars scattered across his throat, but I still couldn't believe that someone actually *chose* that.

But anyone who saw Amit's throat would know he'd been a donor. Even after the interviews and offers for reality TV shows dried up, there were still enough Vladdicts who'd jump at the chance to take pictures with a former donor. Amit would always entertain a certain sort of status among them.

He caught me staring and ran a hand over the bite, almost lovingly. I couldn't help wincing.

"Doesn't that hurt?"

"Are you kidding? I've never felt so good."

"It's like sex," Melissa added, toasting us with her glass.

For the next hour, we sat and drank and chatted. Amit changed from cosmopolitan to martini to champagne before nearly falling off his stool.

"Whoops," he hiccupped. "I don't think you're supposed to drink straight after being bitten."

There was a new daze in his eyes, one that had nothing to do with postbite pleasure and everything to do with too much drink. He climbed off the stool, wobbling on his feet.

Jason offered Amit his arm and he took it, clinging to Jason like a limpet. "I'll take him back to his room so he can sleep this off before tonight."

"I'll give you a hand," Melissa said. She got up and slung one of Amit's arms around her shoulders, helping Jason steer him to the door.

Jason paused, looked back, and wagged a finger at us. "But don't forget, we're all getting ready together. I'm doing your hair, and you're going to help me look gorgeous."

"You're already gorgeous," Roux said.

He blew her a kiss as he and Melissa escorted Amit from the room.

Roux drained the last of her cocktail and set the glass down harder than necessary. "Well, I'm officially tipsy. So much for only having one or two." She hopped off her stool. "Hmm, maybe more than just tipsy."

"Fresh air—that'll sober us up," I declared. The room spun a little as I climbed off my stool.

"Excellent idea. Lead the way."

Roux linked her arm with mine as we exited the bar, which didn't help either of us walk in a straight line. But I liked it. This whole time I'd felt like I was alone in this, and now I wasn't. Now I had Roux, and she wouldn't let me forget it.

I led the way to the back door that opened onto the grounds. As before, Dexter Flynn stood on guard, his hands clasped in front of him.

"Don't you get bored standing here day after day?" Roux asked as we wobbled up to him.

"I don't watch the door every day."

"Okay, but when you do, doesn't it get boring?"

He lifted broad shoulders in a shrug. "It's a job and it pays well."

"Fair enough." Roux unlinked her arm from mine, and put one hand on her hip. "Are you going to let us out or do we need to say pretty please with a cherry on top?"

A smile ghosted across Dexter's lips. "You can say that if you like."

"We need an escort, don't we?" I said.

"No need. Isabeau and a few others are already outside."

Dexter pushed the door open and pale sunlight spilled into the hall. The cold air washed over us but we were both too buzzed to feel it.

"Why, thank you, kind sir," Roux cooed.

"Don't trip," he called after us.

"If we do, you'll have to pick us up," Roux called back.

We made our way onto the sprawling lawn, the heels of our boots thudding against the winter-hardened ground. The frigid air scoured my lungs—I really needed to remember a coat when I went outside.

Isabeau, helped by a pair of donors, was trimming the grass around the edges of a regimented flower bed while Míriam walked arm in arm with Catherine, quietly talking.

As we passed them I made a conscious effort to walk in a straight line so no one would know I'd been drinking. Unfortunately, I was so busy *trying* to walk in a straight line that I didn't look where I was going, and I almost lost my footing and fell into a flower bed.

Roux cackled with laughter.

We moved away from the vampires and into the shadow of the wall that circled the grounds.

"Right," Roux said, when we were out of earshot. "I'm guessing that if you wanted to tell Jason about June you'd have done it already."

I sighed, and my breath made a white shape on the air. "It's not that I don't want to. But I'm worried that I've ruined your experience here by dragging you into this, and I don't want to do the same to him."

"I wonder if there are any clues in June's old room. Do you know who her roommate was?"

"No."

"Okay, that's something we need to find out."

"What are you expecting to find?"

"Probably nothing, but it's worth a look. I got to know a few of the older donors yesterday, so I reckon I can find out who June used to live with, and then we can work out a time to search the room when no one's there. I'm not sure what else to do, to be honest."

"No, that's good. I hadn't thought of any of that."

Roux squeaked suddenly. "Edmond at three o'clock."

My heart stuttered.

The winter sun highlighted the ivory quality of his skin and made his hair shine like polished onyx.

Isabeau climbed to her feet as Edmond approached her, and they exchanged a few words that I couldn't hear. Edmond's eyes flicked in my direction. I didn't think they were talking about me because Isabeau didn't seem to have noticed me, but his stare was diamond sharp and just as bright, pinning me in place.

It wasn't until he strode back into the house that the magnetic pull felt broken. I blinked, and Roux squealed loud enough to make me wince.

"What the hell was *that*?"

"What? Nothing."

"Are you kidding? He couldn't take his eyes off you."

"I can't ever tell what's going through his head, and after last night, I was expecting him to cold-shoulder me."

"I think he likes you," Roux said, grinning.

"He probably just liked how I tasted."

Roux grabbed my arm. "Wait, when did he bite you? You never told me that."

"Must have slipped my mind."

"Tell me *everything*," she commanded.

Roux didn't manage to find out who had been June's roommate. Everyone was too focused on the upcoming ball to be in any mood for odd questions. She assured me we'd try again tomorrow—maybe people would be a little more open to suggestion when they were all hungover.

I took the time to scribble a quick letter to Mum, but I didn't mention June—what was I supposed to say? Until I knew what was going on, I couldn't make Mum worry. Besides, I guessed that if I mentioned my suspicions, whoever was in charge of inspecting letters wouldn't let this one leave the mansion. So I kept it short and sweet, and told her I was having a good time, and that I was looking forward to the ball tonight.

Now evening had come and it was time to get ready.

In our absence, the laundry basket had been emptied and the beds fitted with clean sheets. I knew that human staff worked here, collecting dirty clothes, changing bedding, and topping up anything in the bathrooms that was running low, as well as doing general cleaning throughout the mansion and preparing and clearing meals, but I hadn't yet glimpsed anyone besides security. If they were supposed to stay out of sight, they were doing a good job.

I sat on my bed and stared at the dress hanging on the wardrobe door.

All I could think of was June's prom night nearly three years ago. We'd found a dress in a second-hand shop, a long black gown covered in tiny imitation crystals, and it was slightly too big but Mum managed to do something clever with safety pins until it fit June like a glove. She'd worn her hair twisted up on top of her head and borrowed makeup from a friend at school, and my eyes had blurred with tears when she came downstairs so Mum could take photos. She'd looked so grown up, so beautiful, and despite how close we were, I'd felt like a kid next to her. My own prom had seemed forever away. And then suddenly that had come, too, and I hadn't been able to find a bargain dress so I'd ended up wearing the same one as June.

Now I was about to put on a gown by some fancy designer who I'd never even heard of, and it was too surreal.

Jason burst into the room, his arms full of tuxedos, a panicked expression on his face. "I had it all planned out but now I've changed my mind," he cried.

"Why?" Roux said.

"I just saw Amit, and he looks amazing. I have to look better than that."

"Okay, okay, calm down." Roux took Jason's outfits and laid them out on the bed. "Your favorite ladies are here to help with any clothing crisis."

"I was going to wear the silver-trimmed one, but it won't make me stand out enough, so I thought maybe this one." He picked up a red velvet tux. "But it's a hell of a statement, and I'm not sure I can carry it off."

"Put it on," Roux urged.

Unabashed, Jason stripped down to his boxers, then pulled on the velvet tuxedo and posed for us. It was a good fit, and the dramatic red complemented his blond coloring, but I could see what he meant—something about it wasn't quite right.

Roux circled him, tapping her finger against her chin. "Okay, you can pull it off, but if I'm honest it looks a bit try hard. You want to look effortless."

She flipped through the pile of tuxedos until she found what she was looking for. "Jason, baby, this one has your name all over it."

She handed it to him and he obediently put it on.

Roux wolf whistled. "Now *that's* what I'm talking about."

The tuxedo she'd picked out was midnight blue with black detailing; it perfectly hugged the muscles of Jason's body and brought out the paler blue of his eyes, dramatic without being showy, eye catching without being over the top.

Jason studied himself in the mirror. "Renie, what do you think?"

I answered truthfully. "I think you look hot."

He beamed. "This one it is, then. I'm guessing neither of you has had a last-minute panic?"

"Are you kidding?" Roux plucked her dress from the wardrobe, gazing at it with the pride and admiration a parent might give their newborn. "The only reason I'm not wearing this beauty now is because I want to sort my hair and face first."

"Let's get started on that, then."

Jason sat Roux at the dressing table and got to work with combs and mousse and hairspray, his hands flying over her head. He was right—it *was* like creating art.

"Wow," she said when he had finished, tilting her head to admire the result. He'd swept her hair to one side so the longest strands brushed the corner of her left eye, and had given it volume, fluffing it into subtle spikes. "How do you feel about doing my hair every day?"

Jason grinned and beckoned to me. "Your turn, darling."

My hair took longer than Roux's, hardly surprising since I had a lot more of it. Jason curled it, which seemed to take an eternity, but at least he didn't singe my ears with the curling iron. I closed my eyes and let him do his work, while in the background Roux busied herself with makeup.

By the time I opened my eyes again, Jason had gathered my curls into a huge, loose bun at the nape of my neck, tendrils springing free to cascade over my shoulders. It looked like a flurry of autumn leaves.

"It's beautiful," I said.

Jason looked thoroughly pleased with himself. "I know."

Roux took over my makeup, turning my eyes smoky and mysterious. The only thing left was to get changed.

Roux squeaked with excitement as she slipped her dress on. The layers of dark chiffon were sheer enough to offer tantalizing glimpses of her lithe body but not enough to appear indecent, and tiny flowers of red and white were scattered down the front of the dress, following the deep V of the neckline. She looked incredible and she knew it.

She took my dress from the hanger and handed it to me. "Almost showtime."

My dress was a sleeveless column of gold, red, and amber sequins. It should have clashed with my hair but instead it brought out the color and made it look more vivid, like I'd had highlights put in.

I faced myself in the mirror. The dress clung to my curves, throwing off a thousand sparkles every time the light hit it.

I looked like autumn.

I looked like I'd been dipped in treasure.

I looked like I was on fire.

Jason and Roux joined me, happily admiring their own reflections. "Those vampires won't know what hit them," Roux said.

*

The human guests arrived first, sashaying through the front door in their finest and posing in front of the staircase. The ball itself was being livestreamed, but a select group of photographers and reporters were gathered in the vestibule to snap photos of everyone's outfits and squeeze in some questions before the guests moved through the parlor and dining hall and into the ballroom.

Then came the vampires, emerging from the north wing and sweeping down the stairs like glittering butterflies.

Finally, it was our turn.

I wanted to walk down with my friends, but Belle Morte protocol dictated that we went one at a time, so I forced myself to smile as I descended the stairs. My mum would probably see these photos, and I wanted her to think I was having a good time. Even if she noticed that June wasn't in any of these pictures, that could be explained by saying that June was ill and couldn't attend.

In the parlor, I waited for Roux and Jason. There'd better be booze served at this thing because I really needed a drink.

We entered the ballroom together.

In here, the floor was made of creamy slabs of marble that formed a pattern of concentric circles that got steadily smaller until they reached a circular piece in the center of the room. The walls were richly gilded stucco sweeping up to a frescoed ceiling that was interrupted by two chandeliers that looked like they were about to collapse under the weight of their crystal embellishments. There were no windows. Human staff in black and white uniforms moved silently through the crowd, offering crystal flutes of champagne to the humans, and at one end of the room an orchestra played, filling the room with a flurry of violins. Several people had already split into pairs to dance.

Panicked, I clutched Roux's arm. "I can't dance."

I doubted it was optional. Events like these showed off the glamour of the vampire lifestyle, and happy donors were a part of that. Sullen wallflowers were not.

Roux scrunched up her forehead. "I can, but not the kind that's appropriate here."

Jason snagged three champagne flutes from a passing waitress and handed one to each of us. "Cheers," he said.

We clinked glasses and I took a long gulp from mine. The bubbles rushed down my throat, making my eyes water.

"Take it easy," Jason advised. "We've got all night to do this."

Melissa came over, champagne in hand, eyes bright with excitement. I looked around for Aiden, but he was on the opposite side of the room, talking animatedly with Craig and Ranesh—two of the donors who'd arrived the night I did. Events like these were the pinnacle of life inside Belle Morte, when each ordinary person became more than they'd ever been, when the cocoons split and the butterflies emerged.

In the middle of the room, I spotted two of the older donors dancing together—Hudson in a classic black tuxedo, and Mei in an embroidered cheongsam—while Tamara danced with a guest just behind them.

Roux nudged me. "Do you think the rumors about Benjamin and Alexandra are true?" she said, using her champagne to gesture to the vampires in question, dancing nearby and gazing deeply into each other's eyes. For almost a year gossip sites had speculated that something was going on between the pair, but neither vampire had ever confirmed anything. Maybe tonight was the night they would.

"I don't think friends look at each other like that," I replied.

Closer to the orchestra, Etienne was deep in conversation with Phoebe—a vampire I was seeing for the first time in the flesh—but when he caught my eye, he excused himself and looked as though he was about to head my way. He didn't get far before he was intercepted by Deepika, another vampire I'd only seen in photos. Deepika held out her hand, presumably asking him to dance, and he smiled and nodded, but as she pulled him onto the dance floor, his eyes met mine again. His expression was hard to read.

Catherine danced in front of us, one hand on Amit's shoulder, the other curling around the back of his neck. Any other time, the closest a donor could get to a vampire was feeding them, but on nights like these they could pretend they were equals. Catherine spun Amit so his back was to her chest, then she eased his head to one side and bit him. Amit stiffened, his mouth opening in a soundless moan of pleasure. He wasn't the only one—Abigail, who'd been among the last group of donors before I arrived, was pressed up against Stephen while he drank from her neck, while Hugh fed from Michelle.

"Holy shit," Roux muttered. "I forgot that fangs come out at these things."

"What happened to feeding being private?" I said.

The bite didn't last long—Catherine only took a taste.

"Things are different at balls. We get champagne, they get blood, but we've already fed them today so they only take little tastes. They get to drink from the guests too," Melissa told us.

She pointed. At the edge of the dance floor two vampires were talking with two human guests. Phillip, his black hair slicked back from his forehead, was smiling down at a woman in her thirties who I thought had once been part of some girl group. Eagerly, she tilted her head, exposing her neck. Close by stood Fadime, her rich purple gown matching her hijab, gesturing with her hands as she talked to an older man I didn't recognize. As we watched, she leaned in and delicately sank her fangs into his throat.

"It gives guests the chance to experience a vampire's bite without having to become full-time donors," said Melissa. "I think some of these people are more interested in that than in the actual charity."

"Can anyone be bitten?" I asked.

"See that guy over there? The one with a velvet ribbon tied around his wrist?"

"Yeah."

"Those ribbons mean the guest doesn't want to be bitten."

"We still get the choice of wrist or neck, right?" I said, glancing back at Fadime, who'd already stopped drinking.

"Yes, but Ysanne does prefer vampires to drink from the neck during special events. It looks sexier."

Screw that.

Melissa held out her hand to Jason. "Dance with me?"

"Sure." He let her lead him into the throng of swirling skirts and tuxedos. Unlike me, his feet moved with practiced skill; he was easily at home on the dance floor.

"He's good," Roux commented. She set her flute on the nearest tray. "Fancy a little boogie?"

"I wasn't kidding when I said I couldn't dance."

"As long as we don't give anyone a lap dance, I think we're free to do what we want. Someone will tell us if we're being inappropriate."

I chugged the rest of my champagne before venturing onto the dance floor—I wouldn't get through this without liquid courage.

Roux spun me in a circle, and I almost knocked over two human guests, both of whom shot me icy glares. Trying not to laugh, Roux reeled me back in.

"Wow, you really *can't* dance."

"Told you."

Jason and Melissa waltzed by, moving like professionals, but Jason wasn't looking at Melissa; instead, he peered over her head, scanning the crowd. He was looking for Gideon, I realized, my stomach twisting with empathy.

But Gideon, dancing nearby with Isabeau, didn't even look Jason's way.

"Don't forget to smile," Melissa told him. "Donors are expected to look happy."

Jason managed a grin, and stopped gazing at Gideon.

For a while we successfully mingled with the crowd. Roux danced and I swayed my hips without moving my feet—less chance of knocking into anyone that way—and so far no one had tried to chomp on my neck.

Then Edmond appeared.

CHAPTER NINE

Renie

The crowd seemed to part before Edmond, a path opening in the spinning layers of sequins and tulle. He wore black trousers and a black damask waistcoat over a white shirt with a lace cravat; completing the outfit was a tailored jacket woven all over with a silver fleur-de-lis pattern. It was a look too dramatic to be carried off by just anyone, but on Edmond it was perfect.

He looked good enough to eat, and I momentarily forgot everything bad I'd ever thought about him.

Then reality rushed back, bleak and ugly despite the beauty of my surroundings. No matter how sexy Edmond was or how nicely he dressed, I couldn't afford to trust him. My sister was still *missing*.

Edmond's eyes were fixed on my face as he approached; he didn't seem to notice that he was cutting into my dance with Roux. And she, the little traitor, just stood by and let it happen.

Edmond tilted my palm up, tracing a fingertip over the line of my veins. "May I?" he asked.

I kept a smile for the cameras as I said, "Do I have a choice?"

His expression didn't change, as beautifully blank as ever, but the pressure of his fingers decreased. "Would you prefer not to?"

If I said no, he'd let me go and melt back into the crowd, find some other donor to snack on. But I wouldn't get through the whole night without being bitten.

"If you're going to do it, just do it."

Edmond hesitated, scanning my face, but my perky camera smile didn't slip. He bit down on my wrist, and I stiffened like Amit had when Catherine bit him, but mine was pain rather than pleasure. Edmond only took a sip, then he licked the punctures closed.

"I don't want to hurt you," he said.

"Right—can't have those cameras seeing the donor system as anything less than happy and shiny."

"I don't care about the cameras." He glanced around to make sure no one was listening, but they were all too busy having fun. "I won't do this if it hurts you."

I didn't know what to say. Every time I thought I had Edmond figured out, he did something that stripped away my determination and left me raw and confused. It would be easier for us both if he just treated me like any other donor.

"If I can't drink from you, will you at least allow me a dance?" he said.

Behind him, Roux frantically mouthed, *Yes, yes, yes.*

I should have said no, but a wave of heat swept over me when I gazed into his eyes. When I opened my mouth, all that came out was, "I can't dance."

"Don't worry," Edmond said, his voice a velvet caress, smoothing away lingering doubt. "I can."

With one hand still holding mine and the other finding position on my shoulder blade, Edmond led me into a series of steps. I trod on his feet three times in quick succession and winced.

"I warned you."

Edmond just smiled. "Watch what I'm doing. Forward with the left foot, to the side with the right, then bring both feet together. Then step back with the right, side to the left, and back together again."

I tried to mimic him, and promptly trod on his foot again.

"Don't think about it so much," he advised. "Just let the rhythm take over, and don't worry about treading on my feet."

I copied his moves, and by the sixth or seventh go, I could keep pace without trampling him. And it felt good. I was at a ball and I was dancing.

With a vampire.

My smile, which had become genuine rather than a farce for the cameras, dimmed. It had happened again. Every time I had a moment of happiness, it was immediately extinguished by the reality of my situation. When I was with Edmond, things seemed slightly less bad, but he was part of the problem.

"Have you ever been to anything like this?" Edmond asked.

"Only my prom, and it wasn't quite in the same league."

"Why not?"

"I couldn't exactly afford a designer dress or anything better to drink than a few bottles of cheap beer."

"Did you enjoy it anyway?"

"It was okay."

The music was getting faster, and as I struggled to keep up, I almost knocked over a nearby couple that I vaguely recognized as presenters of one of the vampire gossip shows that June loved so much.

My throat knotted.

She was missing and I was dancing with the vampire who might know what had really happened.

Edmond's hand glided along my back, his fingertips soft and cool on my bare skin.

I shuddered. "Don't do that."

"You don't want me touching you?"

My mouth was desert dry and my heart was going wild; he must be able to hear it. I did want him touching me. I never wanted him to stop. But this *had* to stop. I couldn't keep falling into his voice and his eyes when I should be running as fast as I could in the opposite direction.

I snatched my hand away from him. "I don't want anything to do with you."

Edmond's face hardened into its usual mask. "As you wish."

He strode off, leaving me in the middle of the dance floor. I glanced around but no one seemed to have noticed. Time to get out of here before anyone else asked me to dance.

I was making my way through the crowd when a hand grabbed mine, and instinctively I tried to pull away until I realized it was Jason.

"You had a deer in the headlights look going on. I thought you could use rescuing," he said.

"My hero."

We danced in silence for a few minutes, my brief lesson with Edmond keeping me from trampling Jason's feet—at least for now.

A gap appeared in the sea of twirling partners and I spotted Ysanne prowling the edge of the dance floor, a queen surveying her subjects. She looked magnificent in a strapless gown of black velvet, slashed on one side so frothing layers of plum taffeta spilled out. Her lipstick was the color of blood.

Apparently, no one was bold enough to ask her to dance. I didn't blame them. Power rolled off the vampire lady, and though she wore a smile, her eyes were like ice.

"Things with Edmond looked a bit tense," Jason noted.

"I'm just not comfortable with this whole thing."

"I can tell."

Another few minutes of silence passed. The orchestra had segued into a slower piece, and couples danced around us, bodies melded together. I wondered if Edmond was dancing with anyone, then firmly told myself I didn't care if he was.

"I'm starting to think you didn't come here for the lifestyle," Jason said. "Do you want to talk about it?"

"Not right now."

"You sure?"

"I'll let you know when I'm ready to talk about it."

In my periphery, Roux was pressed tight against a male vampire who I thought was Benjamin, though it was hard to tell when his face was buried in her neck. Her lips were parted in a blissful sigh.

"See? It feels amazing once you learn to relax," Jason said.

"That won't happen any time soon."

"I hope for your sake that's not true."

I didn't answer, my gaze caught by a flash of silver fleur-de-lis. Míriam was wrapped around Edmond like a cat—unlike me, she danced gracefully, matching Edmond's steps and moving her entire body with slinky sensuality.

Jealousy sparked in my heart.

"Word of advice?" Jason said, following my gaze. "Don't fall for him. Even if vampires were allowed relationships with humans, it would end badly. They live forever. We don't."

"I'm not attracted to Edmond," I lied.

"Sure you're not."

"Says the guy who can't stop mooning over Gideon."

"I'm not *mooning* over him," Jason protested.

"Uh-huh. Who're you trying to convince—me or you?"

Jason didn't answer.

I was starting to feel claustrophobic. Despite the ballroom's size, it was packed with people and they were all too close to me, arms and legs jostling, the swish of skirts and clack of heels ringing in my ears louder than the orchestra. Every camera flash seemed blinding, dozens of miniature supernovas.

It would be different if June was with me. She couldn't dance, either, so we'd both have bumped and trampled and laughed our way across the floor, discussing the hottest guys here, and I might actually have had some fun.

Despite myself, I sneaked another look at Edmond.

Holding tight to his hand, Míriam was leading him off the dance floor and toward the entryway that led out of the ballroom.

I shouldn't care.

But I did.

If June had been here, she'd have declared him a bastard who wasn't good enough for me, and who was completely missing out by choosing someone else, and the memory of her voice was so loud in my ears that I actually looked over my shoulder, sure I'd see her there.

Of course she wasn't, and suddenly I couldn't do this anymore. I couldn't dance and smile and pretend that everything was okay when it wasn't.

"I need some air," I gasped, pulling out of Jason's arms and hurrying to the edge of the dance floor.

Security was tighter than ever during social events, stopping guests from leaving the ballroom unless they wanted to be escorted to a first-floor bathroom. Like almost everyone else on the planet, I was familiar with the case of Annabel Montrose, a young socialite whose parents bought her a ticket to a Belle Morte ball at a charity raffle two years ago, only for her to be kicked out after less than an hour when she was caught snooping around the rest of the mansion. Clips of her meltdown were still regularly circulated among social media sites.

But those rules didn't apply to donors, and no one stopped me as I slipped out of the ballroom.

Edmond

Edmond leaned against the wall by the music room, his hands tangled in Míriam's hair as she unbuttoned his waistcoat and pulled open his shirt. Her tongue was soft on his skin as she ran it over his chest, but his heart wasn't in it. Míriam looked beautiful tonight, wrapped in black satin, her eyes huge and seductive, but thoughts of a certain auburn-haired donor had got their claws into his head.

He couldn't shake the image of how Renie had looked tonight, that glorious hair swept up but for the few loose curls that kissed her bare shoulders, the glittering dress that clung to the soft curves of her body.

Irritated, he tried to push her from his mind. He had a stunning vampire woman ready to take him to bed, and all he could think of was Renie and how he wished she was here instead of Míriam.

"Stop," he whispered, gently pushing Míriam away.

Sleeping with her might take his mind off things, but he'd still be thinking of Renie, still imagining her lips on his, her tongue on his skin, her legs wound around his hips. There'd never been anything between him and Míriam but casual sex, but it still seemed grossly unfair to sleep with her when he was thinking about another woman.

Míriam gazed at him, her eyes shining red against her brown skin. "What's wrong?"

He shook his head, unable to explain.

Míriam sighed, and pressed one palm against his chest. "It's a good thing I'm not easily offended. You know where to find me if you change your mind."

Edmond watched her head back to the ball.

Renie wasn't the first donor who had tempted him, but in the past it had never been more than a fleeting attraction. Anytime he wondered if maybe, just maybe, he could risk his heart again, he remembered the women who'd held it before.

He remembered what had happened to them.

Edmond closed his eyes and leaned his head against the wall. People wanted immortality, seeing it as some wonderful, magical thing that would make them forever happy.

They didn't understand what a burden it could be. Immortality meant *living forever*, with every bad memory and ugly mistake, every betrayal and emotional wound. But people had to experience it to understand it.

He scrubbed his hands over his face, erasing any trace of Míriam's kiss. She would act as if nothing had happened if he went back to the ball, but he didn't want to go back. Renie was there.

Remembering the smooth warmth of her shoulder blade beneath his palm as they danced made his gums ache as his fangs emerged. The tiny taste he'd had of her blood wasn't enough to fill the hollow place inside him that raged for more. Vampires were predators; they always craved blood, but Edmond couldn't remember the last time he had craved someone like this.

He *wanted* her. That wasn't supposed to happen. He was supposed to remain impartial, keeping Renie from the truth as long as Ysanne wished it, but her fierceness and vulnerability had got under his skin somehow.

Edmond made his way to the library, where he knew he could be quiet and alone. But when he pushed open the door and slipped inside, he realized that someone was already there.

Renie.

Renie

Edmond stood there, frozen in the doorway. He obviously hadn't known I was here—the surprise on his face was genuine—but that didn't make me any happier to see him.

I'd come to the library for a break, looking for a little pocket of Belle Morte that was away from charity balls and fangs and cameras— away from Edmond. Yet he'd still managed to find me, even though he hadn't been looking.

"What are you doing here?" I said.

Edmond didn't seem to realize or care that his waistcoat and shirt were hanging open, baring the smooth, pale skin pulled taut over the muscles of his chest and stomach.

"Even vampires need to get away from crowds once in a while," Edmond said.

I looked pointedly at his bare chest. "Yes, I'm sure that's why you left the ball. Where's Míriam?"

Edmond's hands moved to his buttons, quickly doing them up. I'd have been disappointed at the loss of such a delicious view if it had been anyone other than Edmond. He sat next to me on the sofa and I pulled my feet up, using them as a spike-heeled barrier between us.

"Why did you leave?" he asked.

"I don't know, Edmond, maybe it had something to do with my sister. You know, the one you're lying about."

He averted his eyes.

"Why can't you just tell me?" I asked.

Nothing.

"Fine. Have it your way. I'll find the truth with or without you."

A tense silence settled between us but neither of us made any attempt to move.

"Do you like reading?" Edmond asked at last.

I shrugged. "Sure."

He reached over the back of the sofa, trailing his fingers over the leather-bound spines that lined the shelves behind him.

"Reading was a luxury I had to discover later in life. When I was human I couldn't read a word."

"Why not?" I asked, curious despite myself. I'd never describe myself as a bookworm, but I couldn't imagine not actually being able to read.

There was a bitter edge to Edmond's smile. "Reading wasn't a necessary skill for the peasants of France. It was hard enough just staying alive."

I couldn't picture Edmond as a peasant, not when he sat next to me dressed in clothes that cost a fortune, in the mansion he called home. Not when he thrived on decadence.

Edmond pulled a book from the shelf, his fingers tracing the embossed cover with something like reverence. "I discovered books once I became a vampire, and I've been in love with them ever since."

The honesty in his admission surprised me. One reason I'd always been convinced that vampires were different than humans was because of the lifestyle they led. Like so many celebrities before them, they'd lost touch with reality. I'd thought they couldn't possibly remember being human, not when they were so busy throwing balls, enjoying worldwide fame, and draping themselves in silks and diamonds.

But Edmond looked at the book in his hands like it was something new and magical. Most people took books for granted, but to Edmond they were still a luxury.

"Is that why you named yourself after a literary character?" I asked.

Edmond looked up, surprised. "*Quoi?* You don't believe that my name is real?"

"It just seems coincidental that you have the exact same name as a character from a famous book. I mean, Edmond Dantès? It's not exactly a common name."

"Did you ever consider that the character was named after me?"

"Was he? Did you really escape from prison?"

Again that faint, bitter smile. "I have escaped death sentences before, but I was never imprisoned in the Château d'If."

I assumed that was the prison in the book. Maybe I should read it.

"So how was the character named after you?"

"I met Alexandre Dumas back in the 1800s, and we spent an evening discussing ideas for the novel he was writing. I didn't realize that he'd used my name for his hero until I stumbled upon a copy of the book some years later. I never saw Dumas again, but *The Count of Monte Cristo* remains one of my favorite books."

Much as I was fascinated to get a glimpse of the real Edmond behind the vampire mask, one particular thing he'd said was going round and round in my head.

He'd met Dumas in the 1800s.

The *1800s*?

It was easy to know that vampires had lived for a long time when it was just some abstract thing, but I'd fantasized about kissing Edmond. Now his not being human didn't seem as much of an issue as his age.

"I'm sorry, but—how old *are* you?"

He regarded me for a long moment, his face frustratingly unreadable. "Do you really want to know?"

"Yes."

"*Si tu insistes*," he murmured. "I was born in rural France in 1648."

My chest felt like it had been slugged with a baseball bat. I'd panicked at the mention of the 1800s, and Edmond had been born more than one hundred and fifty years before *that*.

How could I ever hope to understand him? If all vampires were so old, it was no surprise that they sometimes treated humans as inferior. We were toddlers to them.

"I have to go," I said, standing up so fast I almost tripped over the hem of my own dress.

Edmond's expression darkened.

Despite my lingering resentment with him, I felt like a complete shit. Edmond didn't strike me as someone who talked about himself often, but he'd just tried opening up to me and I was repaying him by running away

But I couldn't stop myself.

I hurried out of the library and didn't look back.

*

Edmond

He didn't blame her for running. There were plenty of vampires older than him, but sometimes he himself struggled to come to terms with how long he'd lived and how much he'd seen, and he was the one who'd lived it.

But even as he didn't blame her, something hard and cold wriggled through his chest; it wasn't quite hurt and it wasn't quite shame, but something in between. He'd told her something personal about himself, and she'd fled. Still, it wasn't the first time he'd tried to open up and had it thrown back in his face.

Renie wasn't Charlotte; he had to remind himself of that.

But it didn't matter. There could never be anything between him and Renie, no matter how he felt.

And once she found out the truth about the west wing, she would hate them all.

CHAPTER TEN

Renie

Edmond was nearly *four hundred years* older than me. That echoed through my mind as I raced from the library.

I was a child compared to him. Worse, I was . . . an *embryo*. I was the twinkle in my great-great-great grandfather's eye, still generations from actual conception.

Deep inside me, so deep I struggled to admit it, there'd been the odd moment when I'd forgotten Edmond was a centuries-old vampire and had tried to think of him as just a man I could maybe become involved with.

I stopped walking, bracing my hand on the wall. There was a funny, tight feeling in my chest, a scream or a sob lodged there and making me feel like I'd swallowed a rock.

"You should be ashamed of yourself, Irene Mayfield," I told myself. "You came here to find June, not to make goo-goo eyes over some . . . *corpse*."

The word was ugly and savage in my mouth, but it was still true. For all his beauty, Edmond was a dead body that, by means beyond anything humans could comprehend, was still walking around, needing fresh human blood to survive. He had died hundreds and hundreds of years ago.

His heart would never beat again.

His skin would never feel warm.

He wasn't human.

If June was here now, she'd be telling me to go after the sexy vampire with everything I had. But she wasn't.

Had she ever mentioned Edmond? I could *see* her, sitting on the floor of our room, flipping through the glossy vampire magazines that a friend had given her because she couldn't afford to buy them herself, chattering away to me about all the vampires, but I hadn't listened because my disapproval of Vladdicts had seemed more important than her excitement. Now I couldn't believe I'd been so selfish.

Suddenly, I wanted to rip off my designer dress, to send the sequins scattering like sand across the carpet. I needed air more than ever, and there was only one way to get it.

Dexter wasn't on guard at the back door this evening; a young, sandy-haired guy stood in his spot. His gaze drifted over me as I approached, and he started to smile, but got a glare in response.

"I need to go outside," I said.

"Sorry, ma'am, but no donor can go out unescorted."

I ground my teeth in frustration. "The entire garden is surrounded by a massive wall. What the hell do you think will happen if I go out without someone to hold my hand?"

I didn't want a fucking escort. I wanted to be alone so I could try to sort through the tangled mess inside my head.

"I'm sorry, ma'am, but those are the rules." His voice was as bland and inflectionless as a vampire's—whoever trained security had done a good job with this one.

I was on the verge of physically fighting my way out when an arm slipped through mine and a cool voice said, "I'll escort the lady."

Etienne smiled down at me with probably the warmest smile I'd seen on a vampire. It was so human an expression that I faltered rather than snatching my arm away.

The guard shrugged and pushed open the door, standing aside so we could pass.

I thought about telling Etienne to go stuff himself, but then I wouldn't be allowed outside. I really did need the air, even though it wasn't the same with someone accompanying me, and none of this was Etienne's fault. In the end, I was too tired and too confused to argue, and I let him lead me into the garden.

Under the silver moonlight the wall looked solid black, as if it had been carved from a block of shadows. The winter-bare trees clutched at the night sky, their branches darker silhouettes against a star-sprinkled backdrop.

A frost had set in and our feet crunched on the grass. My breath came out in thick white plumes; within seconds, my teeth were chattering. Etienne gently draped his tuxedo jacket over my bare shoulders.

"Thanks," I muttered. Then I stiffened. "Please don't bite me," I said before I could think better of it.

"What makes you think I'm going to bite you?"

I fiddled with the lapels of his jacket. "You were looking for me yesterday, so I thought . . ."

Etienne said nothing and I peeked at him from under my lashes. He stared straight ahead, his profile so still he might have been carved from ice.

"I didn't want to bite you. I just needed to get you alone."

"Why?"

Etienne's jaw tightened, like he was holding something back.

I waited.

"I needed to get you alone so we could talk about June," he said. "I want to help you find out what happened to her."

"Are you serious?"

"Yes."

Tears burned my eyes and I swiped them away. Etienne put his arms around me, and my initial response was to push him away, but it felt so good to be held that I sagged against him for a moment, before easing out of his hug so I could wipe away another tear.

"June wasn't transferred, was she?" I said.

"I don't think so, no."

"Is she in the west wing?"

Etienne hesitated. "Ysanne doesn't trust me the way she does people like Edmond and Isabeau, and though I've lived in this house for a long time, I don't understand everything that goes on inside its walls. But . . . I don't believe that she is up there."

"Why?"

Another long pause.

"There's something I need to show you," he said.

Etienne led me farther into the grounds, around the sharp edge of the mansion and then over to the wall until we reached a great oak tree, its branches like gnarled fingers clutching at the sky. Etienne stopped.

"June must've disappeared sometime during her last night here. I saw her just after dinner, when she was heading up to her room with some friends. But the next morning she was gone, and all Ysanne would say was that she'd been transferred to another House and we weren't supposed to discuss it."

"So why are you? Won't you get in trouble?"

"If I'm caught, yes. But something is going on in Belle Morte, and I cannot pretend otherwise. The west wing was declared off limits the day after June's disappearance, and then there was this." He pointed.

The breath wound itself into a thick knot in my lungs. On the left side of the tree, right at the base of its trunk, was a large heap of disturbed earth.

"What . . . what is that?"

A bitter gust of wind whistled through the gardens and the branches of the oak tree knocked together, making a noise like bones rattling.

I watched Etienne's mouth shape an answer and braced myself for the terrible truth.

"I don't know," he said.

The breath rushed out of me in a gasp and furious tears burned my eyes, but I blinked them away. Crying wouldn't get me anywhere.

"It appeared three days after June disappeared. I asked Ysanne about it, but she told me it was none of my business. I asked Isabeau, since she spends a lot of time out here, and she said the same thing," Etienne said.

I wanted to move closer to the tree, but at the same time I couldn't bear to. "Tell me that's not what it looks like," I whispered, my voice raw. "Please tell me that's not a grave."

"I don't *know*."

I looked at him, and there was real fear on his face. I'd never seen a vampire afraid before.

"I don't know," he said again, quiet and frustrated. "I come out here to look at it sometimes, and the earth is always freshly disturbed, like someone is digging it up, over and over again."

My mind desperately raced, trying to fit together the pieces. "But if it's freshly disturbed then it can't be a grave, right?"

"I can't think of any reason why someone would need to dig up a grave," Etienne admitted, "but the fact remains that this wasn't here before June disappeared, and now it is. Maybe I'm wrong about this. Maybe the timing is purely coincidental."

"It can't be, not with the west wing too."

Etienne dipped his head in agreement.

The wind blew again, rippling Etienne's shirt against his body, but vampires didn't seem to feel the cold. Dimly, I was aware of goose bumps prickling over my skin, but I could barely feel anything other than a burning, building rage.

"There's one way to know what's going on," I said, and marched toward the tree.

Etienne grabbed my hand and pulled me back, looking left and right to see if anyone else was out here. Security always patrolled the grounds in case crazed fans or antivampire zealots tried to scale the wall—it had happened before—but if they were out here now, I couldn't see or hear them.

"What are you doing?" he hissed.

"I'm going to dig up whatever's buried there."

Etienne stared at me as if I'd gone completely mad. Maybe I had. A current of horrible energy was racing through me, making me feel shaky and slightly disconnected from myself, and so full of rage that I thought I could tear down Belle Morte with my bare hands.

That wasn't June's grave.

It *couldn't* be.

But what if it was?

I tried to pull away from Etienne but he had vampire strength on his side.

"Renie, just stop. Think," he said.

"You said you wanted to know what's happened to her," I snapped.

"I do, but we can't charge in with no thought for consequences. Ysanne will—" He broke off, his face grim.

"You're afraid of her, aren't you?"

"I'd be a fool not to be."

Finally he let me go, and I stumbled a couple of paces away from him, trying to suck in enough air to calm the storm inside.

"Renie, haven't you noticed that several donors have left Belle Morte since June disappeared, and none of them have said a word about this on the outside? Ysanne's influence is not just limited to this House." Etienne took both my hands in his. "I'm not saying we can't ever dig this up, but we can't do it now. Ysanne will notice if we don't return to the ball soon, and she won't be happy about it. We can't risk that."

He was right, even though I hated it. Ysanne probably knew that I'd questioned the other donors, and Edmond had almost certainly told her I'd been snooping by the west wing, so I was already on seriously thin ice. If she threw me out of the house there was no way back in.

I wanted to scream and cry and smash something. I wanted to get down on my hands and knees and tear up the truth, however bleak and ugly and devastating it might be, because at least then I'd *know*. If the worst had happened, at least I'd be able to say good-bye. My jaw hardened. And I'd make sure that June got justice.

Ysanne wouldn't get away with this.

"We need to go back to the ball and act as if nothing's going on, and I know that's incredibly hard, but there's no choice," Etienne told me. "We will find the truth, Renie, I promise you, but we can't do it tonight."

I gave a single nod. "Thank you."

He held my hand as we walked back to the mansion, but there was nothing romantic in it. We'd both been alone in wanting the truth, and now we had each other, and we needed that comfort. He let go before we went inside, though—even that contact was forbidden between vampires and donors.

We walked into the ballroom, and my treacherous eyes immediately fastened on Edmond, who was standing to one side, watching everyone dance. He glanced at me and his face hardened. Looking down, I guessed why—Etienne's jacket was still draped around my shoulders and Etienne himself was by my side.

Lifting my chin, I looked Edmond square in the eyes. I didn't feel for Etienne what I felt for Edmond, but Etienne had been honest with me. He was going to help me.

"Would you like to dance?" Etienne said.

"Why not?"

A mean part of me took satisfaction in the fact that Etienne led me onto the dance floor right where Edmond would be able to see us.

Sometimes Edmond acted like he had feelings for me and sometimes it seemed like he was trying to open up to me, but he was watching me go to pieces trying to get to the bottom of this mystery, and he'd done nothing to help. If watching me dance with Etienne hurt him in any way, it wasn't a fraction of how much he'd hurt me.

Etienne wasn't as smooth a dancer as Edmond, but he was good enough to guide me through the steps so I didn't make a complete fool of myself and I only trod on his feet twice.

My stomach was a greasy ball of nausea, but I managed to smile and act like a normal donor, as if fear for my sister wasn't a constant, pressing weight at the back of my mind.

I couldn't say how much I appreciated Roux's offer to help me solve this, but she didn't have the influence that Etienne did. He was a vampire of Belle Morte, and he would help me find the truth. For the first time since I'd arrived at the mansion, things didn't seem completely hopeless.

Etienne lifted my hand to his mouth, his gaze fixed hungrily on the veins forming delicate blue lines beneath my skin. He didn't ask permission, but the question was in his eyes, and I nodded.

Just relax, I told myself.

But I couldn't. When Etienne bit me, pain lanced up my arm and I stiffened.

Despite myself, I looked at Edmond again. He stared back, his face stormy. He'd stopped drinking the second he realized he was hurting me. Etienne hadn't, but maybe he didn't know I was in pain. Even if he did, he was the only one who hadn't lied to me about June and that meant more to me than Edmond's little gesture.

I looked away again.

The rest of the ball passed in a blur. I danced with Etienne some more and then Jason cut in, handing me a glass of champagne. I danced for a while with him before finding Roux in the crowd and sticking with her for the rest of the night.

No one watching us would have any idea that I was fantasizing about throttling Ysanne with her own dress and burning the mansion down around her.

When the ball finally came to an end, Roux and I made our way back to our room, Roux tottering slightly in her skyscraper heels.

As soon as the door closed behind us, she kicked off the shoes and peeled off the dress, leaving it in a puddle on the floor. In her underwear, she sat at the dressing table and started removing her makeup. A tattoo adorned her left shoulder, a snaking pattern of thorny vines and roses; I hadn't noticed it before.

"So where did you and Etienne sneak off to?" she asked, shooting me a sly glance.

"I needed some air and he came to see if I was okay."

"And then made the gentlemanly gesture of giving you his jacket." Roux fluttered her eyelashes. "Who said chivalry was dead? Although . . ." She spun in her seat, almost spilling onto the floor, and fixed me with a speculative look. "What about Edmond?"

"I don't want to talk about him," I said flatly.

My traitorous hormones still did a happy dance when I thought about him, and I didn't want them to. Edmond had *lied* to me. Okay, maybe he'd never expressly said he didn't know anything about June, but he'd never tried to help. He'd let me flounder away in the dark, and he'd watched while Ysanne had lied right to my face. That was just as bad as if he'd lied himself.

"So nothing happened with Etienne? No juicy details to share?" Roux asked, turning back to the mirror.

Etienne didn't know that I'd already confided in Roux. He didn't know that Roux was already planning on helping me, and maybe I should have checked with him before telling her about tonight, but Roux was willing to risk her once in a lifetime experience at Belle Morte to help me find the truth.

I couldn't lie to her now.

"He wanted to talk about June."

Roux spun back to me. She hadn't finished cleaning off her makeup, and the smeared mascara made her look like a startled panda. "What? He admitted that?"

I told her what had happened in the garden.

Roux's face went pale. "I don't know what to say."

Sitting on my bed, I pulled my knees up to my chest. The sequins on my dress prickled my chin. "I have to dig up that grave."

"But . . . it can't be a grave."

"Why not? What do we really know about vampires anyway—"

"No, I mean, if a Belle Morte vampire got carried away and killed a donor, wouldn't they have gone to more effort to hide the body? And why would the west wing still be off limits?"

"I don't know," I said, frustrated. "That's why I have to dig it up. I have to know what it is."

"Are you sure about this?"

"Yes."

"But, Renie . . ." Roux sat beside me and slipped her arm around my shoulders. "Let's say it *is* a grave. You realize that you might be digging up your sister's remains? And they *will* be remains by now. Are you really up to that?"

Images of bones and withered flesh crowded my head, and my stomach twisted. But what else was I supposed to do? Ysanne would never willingly tell me the truth.

"I don't have a choice," I said, and Roux nodded, like she'd known that's what I was going to say.

"Okay, then. We'll sneak out tomorrow before everyone's awake and see what we can dig up."

"What? No, I'm not asking you to do that."

"You didn't. I offered."

"Roux, you can't."

"Hey." Roux pointed a finger at me. "I said I'd help you and I'm not backing out of that."

Tears scratched the backs of my eyes.

Roux had come here for the donor lifestyle, and she was jeopardizing all that for me. Whatever she could offer, I was grateful for it—grateful for *her*.

There weren't many people in the world who'd help their friend dig up a dead body.

CHAPTER ELEVEN

Renie

Despite her good intentions, Roux was dead to the world when I woke up at the crack of dawn the next day.

I'd slept badly, my brain conjuring images of June rising from her grave, her eyes blood red, gore dribbling between her cracked lips, her hands scrabbling at me, trying to pull me into the ground, and when I begged her to stop, she wept tears of blood, pleading for me to save her.

I felt sick when I woke up, but that steely core of determination still pulsed inside me. Today was the day.

When I shook Roux, she groaned and swatted me. "Go 'way," she mumbled, burrowing into the covers.

Maybe I should leave her. This was my problem, not hers, and she didn't deserve whatever crap we'd find ourselves in when Ysanne realized we'd dug up that grave.

Then Roux pushed back the covers, blinking owlishly up at me. She'd slept soundly, barely shifting position all night, so her hair had more or less kept its style. Her face was pale without the makeup, making her ruby nose stud look even brighter.

"We're still doing this, aren't we?"

"Only if you want to," I said.

She squeezed my hand. "I won't let you down."

This time we both remembered to wrap up warmly in sweaters, coats, and boots.

"First problem," said Roux, as we crept out of our bedroom. "We don't have any shovels."

"That's not the first problem."

"What is?"

"Trying to dig up a grave with security following us around."

"Right, the escort thing. How can we get past that?"

"I was hoping you could be a distraction."

"Why me?" she said.

"Because I can't flirt to save my life."

"I really don't think flirting will do the trick, especially not for the amount of time it will take you to dig up a *grave*."

"You got a better idea?"

"Maybe we should wait for Etienne."

Fresh tears brimmed, and I pressed the heels of my hands to my eyes. "I *can't*. I need to know, Roux."

Last night, Etienne had reminded me that we needed to be careful, and that was still true, but after my nightmares, after my fears had had hours to twist and grow and spread, I couldn't spend another day pretending that nothing was wrong.

It was early enough that most people in Belle Morte were still asleep, which gave us a small window of time in which we only had to worry about security. If we waited, then we'd lose that window.

"And he's so afraid of Ysanne. What if he changes his mind about helping us?" I said.

Roux visibly braced herself. "Let's get on with it, then."

The guard on the back door looked surprised to see us. I didn't know him, but I was glad it wasn't Dexter Flynn, who I suspected wouldn't have fallen for Roux's charms.

"It's a little early to be up, isn't it?" he said.

Roux dazzled him with her best grin. "We don't need much beauty sleep."

"I can see that," he said, returning her grin.

"Listen." Roux sidled up to him. "We're a little fuzzy headed after last night, so we could really use some fresh air. I know we need an escort, but you can come with us, right?"

His face brightened. He was only in his twenties, not much older than us, and he spent his days surrounded by beautiful women, both human and vampire. But the vampires were off limits, and the humans usually only had eyes for the vampires. Was there even a rule about security and donors hooking up? If there was, this guy didn't seem too bothered by it.

"Sure, I can escort you. Just let me call someone to take over here."

A few minutes later, Roux and I were venturing into the gardens, the guard following us like an eager puppy. Despite our warm clothes, the freezing January air was a shock, tendrils of ice lashing our skin and curling around our bodies like cold fingers.

The grass was white with frost, and ice crystals dazzled the branches of the trees. The sun was a pale blob in a paler sky, wispy clouds trailing across it like a veil. My stomach sank. It would have been hard enough digging without any tools on a good day; how was I supposed to do it on a day like this? But waiting for the weather to improve could take weeks.

Roux stopped and caught the guard's arm, describing last night's ball in vivid detail, and how wonderful it had been except for the lack of real men. She was laying it on a bit thick, giggling and touching his biceps, but he seemed to lap it up. Most importantly, he wasn't looking at me.

I sloped away from them and headed to the oak tree. It seemed to glare at me, the knots and whorls in the wood like angry eyes, and its roots looked higher, more exposed, a web of thick fingers clinging to its secrets.

Tools or not, I was getting to the bottom of this.

Or so I thought.

All the good intentions and determination in the world didn't change the fact that the ground was frozen solid. I tried to dig my fingers in but the churned earth was as hard and cold as marble. I changed tack, sitting down and using my heels to scuff up chunks of earth. Nothing. I changed back to my hands, desperately trying to scrabble through the ground, but my nails splintered and broke, and the pads of my fingers rubbed raw.

Tears gathered in my eyes as a hot, sick feeling stung the back of my throat. All night I'd tossed and turned, terrified of what I would find, and now I wouldn't find anything because my stupid hands couldn't get through the stupid hard ground.

"Hey, what do you think you're doing?"

The guard stood behind me, his eyes wide with shock. Roux hovered behind him, wringing her hands, but I couldn't blame her— she'd said it wouldn't work.

"You need to stop that," the guard said.

I ignored him, resuming my attack on the grave. Blood welled up where I'd ripped a nail, and hard edges of stone and frozen soil dug into the sore patch, but I didn't stop.

"Hey!" The guard grabbed my arm but I flung him off. He hesitated, indecision flickering across his face. Stopping angry girls from digging up possible graves probably wasn't covered in Vampire Security 101.

He didn't touch me again, but I heard the *snick* as he unclipped the radio from his belt. He'd probably call for assistance, and then Dexter Flynn and a team would show up to drag me away from the grave. And then Ysanne would throw me out of the house, and I'd never know what the fuck had happened to June.

Despair and frustration made me beat my fists against the frozen ground, a half scream, half sob catching in my throat.

Then came a smooth, French-accented voice that I really didn't want to hear. "Let me handle this."

I didn't look at Edmond as he crouched beside me, couldn't bear to see his face.

"What are you doing?" he asked, his voice surprisingly gentle.

"I know June wasn't transferred," I snarled. "You bastards can lie all you want, but I *know*, and whatever the fuck you've done to her, I'm going to find out."

My breath was ragged, tearing at my lungs, and my chest ached with the pressure of built-up emotion.

Edmond put his hand on mine, but I snatched it away. "Don't touch me!"

"Renie," he said, as frustratingly calm as ever. "Do you really believe that if we had killed your sister, we would be careless enough to bury her in a shallow grave on our own grounds?"

Roux had said the same, but was Edmond telling the truth, or was that another ruse to throw me off the scent?

"You can keep digging if you don't believe me," Edmond said.

If there was a trick here, I couldn't see it, and now I had no choice but to continue. Once Edmond told Ysanne what I was doing, I wouldn't get a second chance. I scrabbled again at the frozen earth, but it would take me all day to dig more than a few inches. Roux kneeled and helped me.

"*Merde*." Edmond's shadow shifted as he guided my hands out of the way. "Let me."

Even without a shovel, his vampire strength meant he could plow through the ground with relative ease. If it had been any other situation, I'd have enjoyed watching Edmond getting his hands dirty, but dread was a black wave building higher and higher in my chest.

I didn't know what I was more afraid of—that Edmond was telling the truth and June wasn't here, or that he was showing me her body so I'd stop looking.

"Wait, what's that?" Roux pointed.

My heart turned over. Among the dark lumps of earth, whitish shapes were emerging.

Bones.

Roux gasped and clutched my arm, but I was already peering closer. "Those are too small to be human. What *are* they?"

Edmond didn't answer, just kept digging.

More shapes appeared through the earth; feathers and reddish clumps of fur, empty eye sockets, and open mouths, limbs stiffened in death. Finally Edmond sat back, letting us see the grave's contents in their grisly entirety.

The bodies of several foxes were entwined with the feathered corpses of a number of birds, and many more remains too desiccated to identify.

No June.

"What the hell is this?" I said.

Edmond didn't meet my eyes, gazing down into the animal graveyard. "I told you that you wouldn't find what you were looking for."

"Stop with the cryptic *bullshit*. You can pretend you don't know anything, but you're full of shit, and nothing will keep me from finding out what *happened* to her."

I was on my feet and running before he could respond. If June wasn't buried outside, then there was only one place she would be. The west wing.

The mansion was toasty warm inside, and I ripped off my coat, flinging it to the floor as I flew down the corridor.

Rounding a corner, I ran into Jason. He reeled back, grabbing my upper arms to steady us both. "Whoa, honey, where's the fire?"

I batted away his hands and ran down the hall without looking back. Jason called after me but his words were white noise. The truth was just beyond my fingertips.

I was almost there, the staircase leading to the forbidden wing bobbing ahead, when arms as strong as iron caught me around the waist, pulling me against a hard chest.

"Let me go," I spat, writhing in Edmond's arms.

If I'd been thinking clearly I'd have realized that this wasn't helping, but all I could think about were my terrible dreams about June and the hollow fear that had been eating away at me since she stopped writing.

I stamped on Edmond's foot but he didn't react.

"You won't get away with this," I cried, desperate tears burning my eyes. "I don't care how old vampires are or how much better than everyone they think they are—you can't *treat* people like this."

Roux and Jason appeared in my periphery, both wearing identical expressions of shock. Roux shifted from foot to foot like she was itching to rush in and save me, but didn't know how.

"What is the meaning of this?" Ysanne's voice cracked like a whip.

"I know you're lying about June," I yelled.

Ysanne's frost-colored eyes flicked to Edmond. "I repeat, what is the meaning of this?" She bit off each word, her voice filled with ice.

I stopped struggling; it was pointless. Trying to break out of Edmond's arms was like trying to smash through solid steel.

"I don't know why you're lying, but you are," I said, trying to calm myself down. "I thought you'd buried her by that oak tree, but it's just a bunch of dead animals there, which means the truth is somewhere inside your fucking mansion!"

"And how do you know there are dead animals buried by the tree?"

I hadn't thought it possible for Ysanne's voice to get any colder, but that one question proved me wrong. The temperature seemed to plummet, and words died in my throat.

But Ysanne didn't need words. She looked at Edmond, and I couldn't see his face, but the answer to Ysanne's question must have been written in his expression.

A snarl contorted Ysanne's face, turning that icy beauty into an animal mask. Quick as a blink, she lunged. Edmond shoved me out of the way; I hit the floor as Ysanne seized Edmond's throat and slammed him against the wall. His feet dangled several inches from the carpet.

Ysanne's face was terrible in her rage, her fangs gleaming and extended. Edmond was a vampire, he didn't need to breathe, but that didn't mean Ysanne couldn't rip out his throat.

This was the first time I'd glimpsed the true strength behind the cool composure and the tailored clothing, the first time I'd seen the beast straining to break free from the human facade.

Clarity and fear formed a sharp blade cutting through the haze of noise that had filled my head since I'd seen what was really in that grave.

I scrambled to my feet. "Don't hurt him."

Ysanne didn't give any sign that she'd heard me, and though she didn't move, something about the tense way she held herself made me think she was trying to control her savage side. She could so easily kill Edmond, and he just took it, dangling at her mercy, like he trusted her implicitly.

"*Please.*" I tugged Ysanne's sleeve, and she swatted me away.

Her strength was incredible—she knocked me off my feet. The side of my face hit the wall and I landed in a crumpled heap on the carpet.

The lights dimmed at the edges of my consciousness, and I remembered nothing more.

Edmond

It had been a long time since Edmond Dantès had truly been afraid, so when he saw Ysanne shove Renie, when Renie hit her head and fell to the floor, the explosion of fear behind his ribs startled him. He'd been cocooned in the safety of Belle Morte for so long that fear almost felt alien. Or maybe not alien, as he'd known enough of it to last him several lifetimes, but like something long dormant that was only just stirring back to life.

He couldn't tear his eyes away from Renie's pale, huddled form. Roux and Jason were frozen in place, Roux's mouth hanging open. He hoped for their sakes that they had sense enough to stay back.

He couldn't remember the last time that Ysanne had lost her temper, but he hadn't forgotten how dangerous she could be when she did. She'd already lived for years as a vampire when he was just a human boy, and the predator inside her was deeply ingrained in her psyche. She was a hunting tiger, beautiful and unpredictable, and when she lashed out, she did so with teeth and claws. When she lashed out, people got hurt.

But Edmond didn't care about the danger he might be in. His only thought was Renie.

"*Imbécile*," Ysanne growled, the usual smoothness of her voice giving way to harsh edges. "How dare you let her get this close. I'm not ready. And to go behind my back? What were you *thinking*?"

Her hand clenched even tighter around his throat—hard enough that she could have snapped his neck if he'd been human. Edmond didn't resist her; it would only make things worse.

"Explain yourself." Ysanne shook him.

Edmond pointed to her hand around his throat, the hand that was crushing his voice box. Ysanne let him go, and he landed neatly, with vampire grace.

"Renie believes June is dead. It's cruel to keep hiding the truth from her."

Ysanne swung to Jason and Roux. "If you know what's good for you, you will get yourselves and that girl out of my sight."

They scurried to obey, and Edmond fought the urge to help. He wanted to gather Renie into his arms, carry her back to her room, check her over to make sure that Ysanne hadn't caused any permanent damage. But disregarding Ysanne again would have serious consequences. Edmond hadn't survived as long as he had by not knowing which battles to pick.

When the humans had gone, Ysanne turned her attention back to Edmond.

"Why this betrayal, *vieil ami*?" Her eyes still burned red with anger, but there was sorrow in her voice.

Guilt swept through him, swift and sharp. He and Ysanne had known each other for hundreds of years, and they had supported each other through some terrible times. Over the ages, no matter where they ended up, they always found each other again, and they were always there when the other needed them the most.

As Lady of Belle Morte, Ysanne couldn't show Edmond overt favoritism, but he knew how much she trusted him. It had never occurred to her that he would go against her.

"Forgive me," he said, "but Renie needs to know. She should not have been brought here if you weren't ready. The longer you keep her in the dark, the worse things will become; it's better to tell her the truth and deal with the consequences."

"She will know nothing that I do not wish her to know."

"She came too close to the truth of her own accord."

Ysanne's face hardened, the predator shifting beneath her skin. "Of her own accord? You *showed* her."

"Only because she was already digging there. She was convinced that her sister's body was buried beneath that tree, and it was better to crush that notion than let it continue."

"Why would she dig there in the first place?"

"I don't know."

Ysanne stared at him for a long moment. The predator faded, the great beast curling back up to sleep, and she stretched a hand to his face, tracing his jaw.

"Tell me, Edmond," she said, and though her expression was relaxed, he caught the ice still threading her words. "Why do you care so much about this donor? Why has this *petite fille* got under your skin?"

Pointing out that, at eighteen, Renie wasn't a little girl, would be rising to the bait that Ysanne was dangling in front of him. Edmond knew better than that.

"This isn't about Renie. It's about what's best for everyone. She will cause further disruption in her search for the truth, and if she does that, people may start asking questions. You know everyone is already curious; do you wish to add fuel to that fire?"

Ysanne was silent, listening.

"Don't forget—you're the one who wanted to keep this a secret, and you cannot do that if Renie continues like this. Nor can you cast her out of the house at this point. I may not understand this internet phenomenon, but in the wrong hands it can become a weapon. It's bad enough that Renie is asking questions inside Belle Morte; imagine what would happen if she put those questions to the world."

"I need more time to get the situation under control."

"That, I think, is a mistake."

Ysanne smiled, that rare smile she kept hidden from the world, choosing instead to project the image of the icy vampire lady.

"*Mon garçon d'hiver,*" she murmured, stroking his face again.

There was affection in the gesture, though not the romantic sort. That kind of love had blossomed between them in the past, but it was a deeper, older bond they now shared, one that had begun with a frightened orphan boy, a hungry wounded vampire, and a lonely house in the winter-locked French wilderness.

"You must have faith," Ysanne continued. "I will admit, I did not anticipate this persistence from the girl, but she will know the truth soon enough. But it is not safe for her."

That, more than anything else, caused Edmond to nod. As much as it pained him to continue the lies, he couldn't see Renie hurt. He would do as Ysanne said. He would try to guide Renie through the storm until Ysanne turned on the light and allowed her to see.

And then a different kind of storm would hit her.

CHAPTER TWELVE

Renie

Consciousness trickled back in throbbing shards, blasting pain through my head. I opened my eyes, and immediately shut them again as light from the chandelier pierced my brain.

"Owww," I groaned.

The mattress shifted beside me, and Roux's voice filtered through the pain. "Open your eyes and tell me how many fingers I'm holding up."

I cracked open an eye. "Three."

"Good girl. Now tell me your name."

"What?" I squinted up at her as she hovered over me, her head blocking the chandelier.

"This is basic first aid for anyone who's been knocked unconscious by a seriously pissed-off vampire," she said, worry sharpening her voice. "Tell me your name."

"Irene Mayfield."

"How old are you?"

"Eighteen. Are you going to ask my weight and dress size next?"

A relieved smile broke across Roux's face. "Sorry, but I had to make sure she didn't scramble your brains."

Sliding her arm under my back, she helped me sit up. My jaw and cheek pulsed with pain.

"How long was I out?" I asked.

"Just a few minutes. Ysanne told us to get you out of her sight, so Jason and I brought you back here. You're lucky she didn't break your jaw."

"None of this would have happened if she'd just come clean with me."

"If June has been killed by one of Ysanne's vampires, she'll never admit it."

"But why did she even let me come to Belle Morte? Why not just reject my application?"

Roux chewed her lip, eyes troubled. "Yeah, that really doesn't make sense."

"Where's Jason?" I asked, noticing that he wasn't here.

"He wasn't allowed to stay."

Alarm shot through me. "They haven't hurt him, have they?"

"No, but Ysanne said you had to be locked in, and she wouldn't let Jason stay with us."

I jumped off the bed and tried the doors anyway. Locked, as Roux had said.

"Damn it," I whispered, resting my head against the wood.

I had been so close to the truth and now I'd probably never get another chance. Ysanne would throw me out and Belle Morte's doors would be closed to me forever. I'd spend the rest of my life never knowing what had happened to my sister.

"I guess Ysanne's off deciding my punishment," I said.

"Probably."

"Will they do anything to you?"

Roux looked sheepish, picking at my bedcovers. "I didn't tell them that I'd helped you. I'm sorry, but I was so scared after what Ysanne did—"

"I'm glad you didn't tell her. This is my fight, not yours."

"Screw that. I said I'd help, didn't I?"

"But you didn't say you'd land yourself in the shit as well. Look, Roux, I can't tell you how much I appreciate your help, but you didn't come for this, and you can't lose your place here because of me."

"It's not that simple now. Even if I stop helping you, even if Ysanne kicks you out and I never see you again, I can't pretend that everything's okay. I can't enjoy the vampire culture if I know something shady is going on."

"But if you're locked in here, too, surely Ysanne suspects you helped me?"

I could cope with whatever punishment Ysanne dreamed up, but I couldn't bear the thought of Roux suffering too.

"No. Ysanne sent Dexter to lock us in and I was supposed to leave with Jason, but I asked Dexter to let me stay. I didn't want you to wake up alone."

Rejoining her on the bed, I hugged her. "What did I do to deserve a friend like you?"

"Just lucky, I guess."

Roux told me that Ysanne had made her leave before she could hear anything useful, but that Edmond had mentioned me believing June was dead and how it was cruel to keep the truth from me.

"I don't want to give you false hope, but the impression I got is that June's not dead," she said. "I don't get it, though; if she's alive, why all the secrecy?"

"The answers have to be in the west wing."

Before we could discuss it further, we heard a soft *click*.

We both stared at the door, and Roux narrowed her eyes. "Was that . . . ?"

"Someone just unlocked the door."

We waited for someone to come in and tell us what was going on, but no one did, and the silence stretched out, thick as tar. Climbing off the bed, I approached the door. The handle turned smoothly in my hand, and the door swung quietly open.

"Is anyone there?" Roux asked.

I peeked out into the hallway, half expecting to see Edmond, but it was empty, just the paintings on the walls staring back at me with their unfathomable eyes.

"I think someone wants the Scooby gang to find the truth," I said.

Roux scrambled off the bed and joined me, peering over my shoulder at the deserted hallway. "Okay, Velma, what's the plan?"

"Why am I Velma? You're the smart one."

"Yeah, but Daphne's taller."

I couldn't argue with that. "I'm going to the west wing."

Roux put her hand on my shoulder, stopping me from charging out of the room. "Renie, sweetie, that's insane. You just tried that and look what happened."

"I know, but that's why I have to do it now. This is my last chance. And someone obviously wants me to finish what I started or they wouldn't have unlocked the door."

"But you don't know who unlocked it. It could be a trap."

"What would be the point? Ysanne has the whole house in a death grip, and I'm right where she wants me to be—out of the way. She doesn't need to set a trap for me. If she wants me out of the house, she can cancel my contract."

"I'm still worried about this."

"Me too, but what else can I do? I'm running out of time."

Roux's sigh ruffled my hair. "Then I'm coming with you."

The west wing had never seemed so far away.

We crept through the hallways of the south wing, pressing ourselves against walls and ducking behind statues and furniture, or into empty rooms, every time we heard someone coming. My nerves were stretched to a breaking point, frayed like old rope, and my stomach was a hard ball of tension.

We'd almost reached our destination when Etienne suddenly

turned a corner up ahead. I tried to duck out of sight but it was too late; he'd already seen us. His eyes widened as they took in my bruised face, his expression turning dark and angry.

"Who hit you?"

"Ysanne, but I'm pretty sure it was an accident."

"An accident," he repeated skeptically.

"Look, I don't have time to talk about it now."

Though it was unlikely there would *be* another time.

Etienne narrowed his eyes, looking from me to Roux. "Why did she hit you? What's going on?"

Roux and I exchanged looks, then Roux shrugged. "We're finding the truth."

Understanding dawned on his face. "You went back to the tree, didn't you? Without me."

"I thought you'd be too afraid of Ysanne to help," I said.

Etienne made a soft sound of frustration and gestured at my face. "Maybe now you understand why I'm afraid."

"So I'm guessing you're not the one who unlocked our bedroom door just now," Roux said.

"What? Why were you locked in?"

"Etienne, *please*, I promise I'll explain everything when I can, but I have only one chance to get into the west wing and I have to take it now," I said.

"The west wing?"

Damn it. I hadn't meant to let that slip.

Etienne studied me for a long moment, eyes churning. "Do you understand the risk you're taking?"

I touched my bruised cheek. "Oh yes."

Etienne closed his eyes, and if he'd been human, he'd probably have been taking deep breaths. "Right. We'd better get on with it then."

"We? You're not coming."

"Of course I am."

"It's too dangerous. The worst Ysanne can do is terminate my contract, but you *live* here. If you go against her, she'll never let you forget it."

Vampires weren't supposed to physically punish donors—although Ysanne had, arguably, just broken that rule—but nothing said they couldn't punish other vampires.

"I'm asking you as a friend to sit this one out. If I don't find what I'm looking for, if something goes wrong, if I get kicked out, I need to know there's at least one person still looking for the truth," I said.

How he would contact me if I was no longer at Belle Morte, I didn't know, but we'd cross that bridge when we came to it.

Etienne looked troubled. "Let me go instead of you," he said.

I shook my head. "It's essential that Ysanne doesn't know you're involved."

"I'm really not happy about this," Etienne said.

"Neither am I, but we've already wasted too much time discussing it. Please trust me."

Reluctantly, he nodded.

Leaving Etienne behind, Roux and I continued to the west wing.

"What do you think Ysanne will do if she finds out he's helping us?" Roux said.

"Something bad."

"She wouldn't kill him, though, right?"

"I think we can't begin to understand what Ysanne is capable of. I can't ask him to take that risk."

I didn't want Roux to take the risk, either, but she was human, same as me, and the worst we'd face was a terminated contract. Still, I had to say, "It might be better if you turn back now."

Roux snorted. "The hell I will. We're in this together." She pointed at me. "And don't try any of the stuff that you just said to Etienne. You can ask me, as a friend, to back off all you want, but I'm telling you, as a friend, that I'm not going anywhere."

We were almost there when Roux suddenly yanked me back.

Look, she mouthed.

Isabeau was coming up the main staircase, a blanket-wrapped bundle tucked under one arm. She turned right, heading into the west wing.

"I thought no one was allowed up there," Roux whispered.

"I bet she's the one I saw last time."

"But what's she doing?"

I couldn't answer that.

Whatever it was seemed to take forever. Every second that passed, I was convinced someone would discover that we'd escaped our room, and then we'd be locked in again, only this time with a guard at the door.

"Hurry up," I whispered, anxiety jittering through my limbs.

Roux squeezed my shoulder, the sound of her breathing a comforting presence behind me.

Finally Isabeau reappeared, hurrying down the hall as if she couldn't wait to be away from the west wing. The blanket-wrapped bundle was stained with fresh blood.

Roux's hand tightened on my shoulder, but neither of us dared speak with Isabeau so close. Vampires had incredibly good hearing. Even after she disappeared back down the stairs, we waited another few moments to make sure the coast was well and truly clear before darting into the west wing.

Even during the day, the hall and the short staircase it led to was shrouded in darkness; the lights were turned off, the chandeliers nothing but sculptures of wrought metal and dark bulbs. We paused when we reached those stairs, gazing up at another hallway, stretching away into shadows.

"You sure about this?" Roux asked.

"Not at all." I started up the stairs.

We paused at the top. The hall was decorated the same as the rest

of Belle Morte—flocked wallpaper and paintings of historical figures on the walls. The paintings looked even more ominous in the
darkness, as if they were ghosts trapped between the carved wooden
frames, left to gather dust in this gloomy piece of mansion. The air
smelled stale and musty, but there was also a trace of something pun-
gent, something I couldn't put my finger on.

Roux shivered. "This place is creepy."

Even her whisper sounded too loud. There was something oppres-
sive about the atmosphere, as if it hadn't been disturbed in a while,
even though Isabeau had only just been here.

I ran my fingers over a picture frame as we passed, picking up
dust. Clearly no one was cleaning up here.

Roux grabbed my arm, her face pale. "Did you hear that?"

As soon as she said it, I heard it—the *clunk* of rattling metal echoing faintly down the hallway. The hairs rose on the back of my neck,
a chill wriggling down my spine.

"What *is* that?" Roux hissed.

"I don't know."

I waited for her to say she'd had enough and wanted to go back,
but she didn't. Her hand slipped into mine, squeezing so tight it hurt.
I squeezed back.

Maybe I was completely wrong about this. Maybe this had nothing to do with June at all, and Ysanne really had a good reason to
keep everyone out of here. But I couldn't turn back now.

Doors lined the walls on either side of us, presumably leading to
the bedrooms that visiting vampires had once stayed in, but the noise
was coming from the end of the hall, where a heavy wooden door was
barred from the outside. Metal rattled again, louder this time.

I felt like I'd been dipped in ice. When I reached for the thick
iron bar that locked the door from the outside, my hand shook.
Roux's breathing hitched but she still helped lift the iron bar from
its brackets.

We laid it on the floor in front of us, inadvertently marking some sort of boundary line. It still wasn't too late to turn back, but once we stepped over that metal line it would be.

I stepped over the line.

Roux tried to follow me but I stopped her. "Stay here."

"But you don't know what's in there."

"Exactly."

If this was dangerous then I didn't want Roux in the middle of it, but telling her that wouldn't put her off. I'd need another excuse.

"I need you to stand guard. I don't know what I'm going to find in there, but we can't risk Isabeau coming back halfway through."

Roux looked doubtfully down the hallway. "I don't think she's coming back."

"I can't take that risk. Just stay here. If anyone comes, let me know."

Taking a deep breath, I pushed open the door and stepped into the room.

The door swung shut behind me with a dull thud. It sounded like a tomb closing, and goose bumps erupted on my arms. I hugged myself, peering into the depths of the room. With shades covering the windows and no artificial lights to chase away the shadows, it was almost impossible to see. A rank, metallic stench hung in the air, and my stomach twisted.

A blocky shape occupied the middle of the room but I couldn't work out what it was. Something shifted; a figure standing in front of the shape, and metal clinked again—chains, I realized.

A thick knot rose into my throat, making it hard to breathe. "Oh my god," I whispered, as my eyes adjusted. Dark though it was in this room, I would know that figure anywhere.

I'd finally found my sister.

CHAPTER THIRTEEN

Renie

When I'd pictured finding June, it hadn't been like this, not dressed in rags and chained to some sort of giant rack in a black room that reeked of death.

"June?" My voice choked.

She made a muffled noise—when I stepped closer, I realized she'd been gagged.

Fury turned everything inside me to fire.

My sweet sister had come here because she worshipped vampires, because she thought they were the most fascinating things to ever happen to the world, and this was what they'd done to her?

I rushed over, pulled the gag from her mouth, and cradled her face in my hands. "Oh my god, I've been so worried about you—"

A growl trickled out of June's throat, and I looked into her eyes.

Into her blood-red eyes.

Time seemed to stop as I struggled to comprehend what was happening, then June lunged, snarling and gnashing her fangs. They were already fully extended, long and lethal, tapering to dagger-sharp points.

"No," I whispered, tears blurring my eyes as I staggered back.

Thinking that June had been murdered was the kind of hell I wouldn't wish on anyone, but this—this was worse. My sister was a vampire, but not just any vampire. She was like a wild animal, her face chalk white and caked in blood, old gore crusted around her mouth. Her fangs sliced up her lips and fresh blood spilled down her chin, joining the rusty stains on her ragged clothing.

Many times I'd thought that vampires were monsters, but at least they'd always looked human. June truly was a monster: savage, blood clotted, frantically straining against her chains.

"June, it's me, you have to know me." The tears spilled over, hot and stinging.

She threw herself forward, the chains rubbing raw, bloody patches on her wrists. I finally understood why Ysanne wouldn't allow anyone into the west wing. But was Ysanne herself responsible for this? Or was she covering for one of her friends?

One of the chains restraining June's wrists came loose. The splintered ruins of her nails slashed through the air. Whatever the hell had happened here, I wouldn't get answers if my sister-turned-vampire broke free and butchered me.

I ran for the door.

A loud clang echoed through the room as the second chain unraveled from the wooden frame, and the thing that had been my sister was free. In the split second before she was upon me, I managed to register that she wasn't June anymore, and if I didn't defend myself she would tear me to shreds.

A mirror hung on the wall to my left; I snatched it from its hook and smashed it across June's head. Shards of glass scattered across the floor, dimly gleaming.

June barely slowed down.

She leaped between me and the door.

"Renie?" Roux's voice on the other side.

"Don't come in!" I screamed. "Do *not* fucking come in."

June advanced. I backed off until I hit the wooden frame in the middle of the room. I darted around it, using it as a shield.

"Renie, please, what's going on?" Roux sobbed through the door.

"Just stay outside. *Please.*"

I feinted to the left, then to the right, and June followed my movements like a wild animal, chains trailing from her bloody wrists.

Seizing my chance, I ran for the door.

June tackled me before I reached it, her fangs snapping a hairsbreadth from my cheek.

I slammed my elbow into her face, then dug my fingernails into the carpet to drag myself away. Pain splintered through nails I'd broken and fingertips I'd rubbed raw when I'd dug up what I thought was June's grave.

June snarled, ropes of saliva spattering me. I forgot that this had once been my sister and that I'd been willing to give up everything to find her, and saw a savage monster who would kill me if I didn't get the hell out of here. I fought her with everything I had, throwing clumsy punches and kicking any part of her I could.

I managed to wrestle her off me, but she clung to my ankle, tearing off one of my boots. I drew back my other foot and kicked her in the face. June reeled, rolling over and coming back up in a crouch. She snapped her teeth, and her own blood spilled down her chin as she sliced her lips to ribbons.

I was too scared to cry.

The door was just behind me. As I clambered to my feet, a shard of glass from the broken mirror sank into my heel, straight through the sock and into flesh. Blood welled up.

June froze, her nostrils flaring. Her eyes went even redder, and her ruined lips curled away from those huge fangs.

The nightmares I'd had of her last night were nothing compared to the terrifying reality.

June's terrible eyes fastened on the blood soaking through my sock. She gathered herself up and flew through the air like a huge, hunting cat.

Edmond intercepted her midleap, one powerful arm slamming into her chest and throwing her to the floor. June made a noise that was both inhuman and unlike anything that any animal could make.

A hand pulled me out of the way, and I looked up into Isabeau's tense face. Her other arm was thrust out behind her, holding Roux back.

Edmond hauled June to her feet. She clawed at his arms with her ragged nails and blood welled up, ruby red against the paleness of his skin. Seeing his blood was startling; it made him seem more human.

My foot was still bleeding and June could smell it. Her head swung in my direction, her red eyes bulging. With a shriek, she tried to charge, but Edmond looped an arm around her throat, dragging her back. Muscles bulged under his skin.

He could have tightened his grip and snapped her neck, but he was trying to restrain her without hurting her. Was that on Ysanne's orders, or was it for my sake?

Then Ysanne herself swept in, and the look on her face was so cold I half expected frost to blast the walls. Her cream shift dress and stiletto heels made her look like a starlet on the red carpet, not someone with Superman strength.

But she marched across to June, snatched her from Edmond with one hand and dragged her across the carpet. June snarled and writhed, but Ysanne was an unstoppable force. She dragged June back to the wooden frame and wrapped the dangling chains around my sister's arms, securing them so tightly that her flesh bulged out on either side, skin scraping away beneath the metal links.

Then she turned to us and the icy fury on her face reminded me that June wasn't the only dangerous thing in this room. She wasn't even the *most* dangerous.

"You." She stabbed a pale finger at me. "My office. Now."

"Perhaps she could have a moment to clean up." Edmond indicated my bloody foot, and Ysanne's nostrils flared.

"Very well," she said curtly. "But if you test my generosity, I shall have security drag you to my office." The look she gave Edmond was steel and ice combined. "Both of you."

"And this one?" Isabeau still had a hand on Roux's chest, holding her at bay. Roux was smart enough not to fight back.

Ysanne gave Roux a dismissive look, as if she was worth only a moment of the lady's time. "Get her out of my sight."

Isabeau guided Roux away before she could protest, and Ysanne followed Isabeau, her high heels stabbing the carpet with every step.

June's struggles had quieted, perhaps because she recognized the superior predator in the room, but when Ysanne left, she started to thrash again. I hadn't even noticed Ysanne replace June's gag, but she must have done so. June's slashed lips soaked the gag red, and my stomach heaved.

My worst nightmares couldn't have prepared me for this. Even if I'd considered that she'd become a vampire—and why the *hell* hadn't that occurred to me?—I'd have imagined her as one of the beautiful, elegant, cryptic creatures that graced the hallways and ballrooms of Belle Morte, not this ravening, blood-crazed . . . *thing*.

I turned away as if that could undo the terrible image that had been gouged into the backs of my eyes, but my sister's face would haunt me for the rest of my life.

The pain in my foot sparked to life, breaking through the adrenaline that had held it back this long. I tried to take a step, balancing on my toes, and gritted my teeth against the pain. I didn't dare pull out the shard of glass, not with June in the room.

Edmond strode over to me, put one arm around my shoulders, and bent as if he was going to lift me, but I smacked his hands away.

"Renie, I'm trying to help."

"Don't touch me. You knew about this, didn't you?"

Edmond was silent, his gaze traveling back to the ruin of my sister sagging in her chains, still making muffled growling noises behind her bloody gag.

"All this time you knew exactly what happened to her and exactly where she was. Was it funny watching me run around like an idiot, trying to find the truth?"

"Of course not." His voice was whisper soft.

"Then why did you do it?" The question burst out of me in a ragged cry.

Despite all my suspicions, I'd thought that the moments we'd shared were real, but he'd kept this terrible secret from me the whole time.

Edmond closed his eyes, looking achingly human. "Do you wish for explanations now, or would you rather I help you clean up your foot first? Ysanne was not making idle threats when she said she'd have security drag us to her office."

"Fine." I limped to the door, biting my tongue as every step sent sparks of pain shooting up my leg.

"This is ridiculous—you can't walk properly."

"I don't want you to carry me."

Maybe it was childish to turn down his offer of help, but I was afraid that if he cradled me in his arms, the rage I felt toward him would melt away, and I'd never want him to let me go.

"I won't." Edmond slipped a strong arm around my waist, holding me up. "Lean on me. It'll be easier on your foot."

I wanted to refuse that, too, but it wasn't a good idea to piss Ysanne off any more than I already had. So I let Edmond support my weight as I hobbled from the room. It would have been quicker and easier to let him carry me, but my heart hurt too much to let him do it.

There wasn't time to go to my bedroom so Edmond guided me to an empty room farther down the hall.

As soon as I could, I pulled away from him.

"It was someone in this house, wasn't it? One of you bastards turned my sister into a *vampire*. You fed me all that crap about why vampires don't turn people anymore, and all the time *you knew* she'd been turned."

"Yes," Edmond said.

"Who did it? *Who?*"

Edmond indicated the bed. "Please sit down. Ysanne will explain everything in a minute."

"Fuck you."

But I sat anyway, because the glass in my foot really hurt and I was suddenly too exhausted and emotionally wrung out to stand.

Edmond crouched in front of me, then gently lifted my foot and peeled away the bloody sock. The faintest hint of red touched his eyes as he watched each drop fall to the floor.

"Are you going to help me or just enjoy the view?" My voice was acid.

He looked up at me, pressing his lips together—I suspected to conceal his growing fangs. "This will hurt."

"I know, I know. Just get on with it." I tilted my head back so I didn't have to watch, and curled my hands in the covers.

Balancing my foot with one hand, Edmond pulled out the shard of glass. Despite my best efforts, a squeak of pain got past the tightly clamped barrier of my lips.

"Sorry," Edmond said.

"Is there a first-aid kit or something around here?"

"It's not as bad as it looks," Edmond said, studying my heel with equal parts clinical detachment and vampire hunger. "I can take care of it, if you'll let me."

I was too tired to protest. "Whatever."

Edmond ran his tongue over my heel. The pain subsided, and Edmond licked my foot again, his tongue sealing the cut as neatly as he'd sealed the puncture marks in my wrist.

Then he took my hands and pressed my fingertips to his tongue, healing them where I'd torn them up trying to dig through the ground.

I wanted to hug my knees to my chest, but blood still smeared my foot. "June's not a normal vampire, is she?"

"She's a rabid."

"What the hell is that?"

"Do you remember that I told you not all humans who are turned into vampires survive the transition? On rare occasions, some who *do* survive become . . . something else. The blood hunger consumes them, turning them into beasts."

I remembered the rage I'd seen on Ysanne's face right before she knocked me unconscious, the shadow of a predator shifting under her skin. What would happen if all trace of humanity was gone and only that predator remained?

June was what happened.

"Rabids are rare, but they are lethal. They are completely driven by their need for blood, and they are never satisfied. They exist only to kill. This is another reason why we don't make new vampires anymore, because it always carries the risk of the human becoming a rabid rather than a vampire. We cannot afford that."

I filled in the rest of the pieces. "Which is why Ysanne locked June away in the west wing."

"She was trying to keep the rest of the house safe."

"Why didn't she just tell me that?"

"That's for Ysanne to explain."

He fetched me clean socks from a dresser in the corner. One of my boots was still in that room with June, but I'd go barefoot the rest of my life before going back for it. Kicking off the other boot, I replaced my socks with the clean pair.

I ignored the hand Edmond held out to me, and after an awkward moment he withdrew it.

"I'm sorry you had to find out this way. Ysanne would have told you the truth sooner or later, but it shouldn't have been like this."

"*You* shouldn't have lied to me."

"I suppose it won't make you feel better to know that I never wished to."

"No, it won't."

For once Edmond's face wasn't impassive, but I didn't have a name for his expression.

"You know what the worst part is? You seem to think finding out my sister is a rabid is somehow better than finding out she was dead. But Edmond, this is *worse*." I looked up at him, unable to stop tears trickling down my cheeks. "My sister is suffering and I don't have a clue how to help her. She's a monster."

"I will admit the situation was handled all wrong—"

"But you won't say that to Ysanne, will you?"

He fell silent.

Of course he wouldn't. He would do whatever she said, like a good little puppy.

"Are you ready to go?" Edmond asked.

I wished I had enough guts to tell him where to stick it, but Ysanne didn't bluff. I'd rather go to her office of my own accord than have Dexter or any of his people drag me there.

"Let's go," I said, climbing off the bed and striding out of the room.

Ysanne was sitting behind her desk when we arrived, as cool and composed as ever, not a single strand of blond hair out of place. I could hardly believe she was the same woman who'd knocked me out, who'd lifted Edmond as if he weighed nothing, who'd handled June like a toy.

A shiver rolled down my back.

"Sit," Ysanne said, indicating the chairs in front of her desk.

I did so.

"I shall be frank with you, Renie," Ysanne said, and that alone surprised me. I'd half expected her to try feeding me more bullshit. "Your sister was happy here for the better part of her stay. She was a model donor."

"And then?"

Ysanne sighed and clasped her hands together on the desktop. "And then she was murdered."

The final word hit me like a slap. I'd been so focused on the horror of what I'd found, that it hadn't sunk in that in order to become a vampire June had had to die first.

June had *died*.

Anger almost choked me. "You've known about this the whole time, and you lied to my face. Who did it? Who the *fuck* did this to my sister?"

Ysanne glanced at Edmond. "I must confess that I do not know."

A disbelieving laugh escaped my throat, and Ysanne's eyes narrowed.

"You don't know," I repeated.

"That is what I said."

"Oh, that's fantastic. You're supposed to know everything that goes on in your House, but my sister was *killed* here and you don't know who did it."

Edmond made a warning noise, but I ignored him. Ysanne seemed unruffled by my outburst.

"Whoever turned June didn't anticipate her becoming rabid. It is lucky that I found her and secured her in the west wing before she had a chance to hurt anyone."

The June I knew wouldn't hurt a fly, but the thing lolling in chains upstairs wasn't my sister. She was dead and a monster wore her skin.

"I will find who is responsible for this, and when I do, they will be justly punished," Ysanne continued.

I couldn't imagine any punishment that would ever be enough.

"When someone turns rabid, we're supposed to kill them. Rabids are incredibly dangerous and will kill anyone they come across— both human and vampire. When your sister awoke from death, she became a threat to everyone in this house and many more people outside it. Any other vampire would have killed her the second they found her, but I thought I saw flickers of sanity in her. That's why I brought you here. Maybe it was foolish and naive"—two words that I never thought I'd hear Ysanne apply to herself—"but I hoped that you might be able to bring June back from the brink. Do you see? If you could get through the bloodlust, reach any part of June that might be left, then there's hope for all rabids." Ysanne gazed down at her clasped hands. "Becoming rabid is not just something that can happen to a person when they are freshly turned. It can happen to any vampire, at any time. Some vampires in the house have lost friends to it in the past, but with June I saw a chance to save future rabids."

I slumped in my seat. "Why didn't you just tell me that?"

"June's condition deteriorated shortly before you arrived. The sparks of sanity I had glimpsed were lost to the bloodlust. Until I could be sure that she was under control, it was not safe to let you near her."

I laughed again, a harsh, bitter sound. How fucking ironic. Ysanne had put me through hell and it had all been in some misguided attempt to *protect* me.

"I have some idea how you feel about vampires, but I can assure you, I hold myself responsible for my donors. When they sign them-selves over to me, they are putting their lives in my hands." Ysanne's eyes bored into me. "I let your sister down, and then I locked her up in a vain hope that she could retain enough of herself for you to reach her."

"Right, and it had nothing to do with you covering up that you'd let a donor get turned into a rabid. I bet that would be a black mark against your name if the Council ever found out. Not to mention the media."

Tension crackled through the room, and Ysanne's hands tight-ened. At my side, Edmond tensed.

"Perhaps that does have something to do with it, but it was not my only reason." For the briefest moment, Ysanne actually looked tired, a glimmer of humanity slipping through her icy exterior. "I feel responsible for what happened to June. She was supposed to be safe here."

I wanted to throw that back in her face, but the raw honesty in her voice stopped me. I believed her, whether I wanted to or not.

"I made a decision, Renie, and perhaps it was a risky one, but I cannot change it now. If June had escaped Belle Morte, she would have left a wake of death everywhere she went. You cannot fathom the level of butchery a rabid is capable of until you have witnessed it for yourself. They are a threat to everyone, but if we could reverse what has happened to them, then no vampire would have to fear turning rabid. Tragedies like June could be avoided. But I cannot reach her. She spoke of you often; if there's anyone she might respond to, I believe it is you."

I didn't know what to say.

"This affects everyone. If we can reverse the process then vampires who become rabid won't need to be killed, and humans won't ever be in danger from them. If you can get through to June, if you can help her recover her lost mind, then you will have your sister back."

"But she'd still be a vampire, right?" I said bitterly.

"That is correct. There is no reversal for the turn, and only death can release a vampire from this life. But isn't it better to have June as a vampire than a body rotting in the ground?"

I hated that she was right.

"I will continue my own investigations until I know who is responsible. The culprit will not escape justice—you have my word on that," Ysanne said.

That I believed. Ysanne wouldn't find June's killer to avenge her; she'd do it because someone had seriously broken one of her rules and she wouldn't allow them to get away with it.

"Why don't you send the other donors home if June's so dangerous?" I said.

"Because then the Council would know that something was wrong."

I smiled thinly. "That's right. In here you're the law, but outside Belle Morte, you're just one more voice on the Council."

"The only voice who wishes to save your sister rather than destroy her," Ysanne tartly reminded me.

Fair point.

"What if I hadn't applied to become a donor? What would you have done?"

"I would have found another way to bring you here. The important question now is whether or not you will help us," Ysanne said.

I stared at her impassive face and cool eyes, and looked at Edmond, standing silently by.

"It's the only way to save my sister. I don't have a choice."

"I am not forcing you to do anything. But if you don't help her, then no one else will be able to."

"Nothing like a little emotional blackmail to get what you want," I muttered.

She smiled, baring her fangs. "One thing you must learn about me, Renie, is that I am very used to getting what I want."

I just bet you are.

"I'll do whatever it takes," I said.

I didn't expect Ysanne to smile and I wasn't disappointed. A terse nod was all I got before her gaze switched back to Edmond, the light in them turning chillier.

"You showed Renie things that I had not given you permission to. Under the rules of this House, flouting your lady is a punishable offense."

Clearly this wasn't news to Edmond, and I wondered how much he'd actually risked for me. Some of the rage I felt toward him eased.

"However, as far as I am concerned, your actions do not constitute a public infraction so I am prepared to let the matter slide. But, mon garçon d'hiver, I will not be so lenient next time. I would appreciate it if you didn't put me in that position." Ysanne's words dripped icicles, and I fought the urge to shiver.

Edmond merely nodded.

I wondered again about their history. Was Ysanne genuinely holding off a punishment for the reasons she'd stated, or did it have anything to do with what they meant to each other—either now or in the past? Either way, I suspected that Etienne wouldn't have got the free pass that Edmond had. I'd done the right thing in not letting him come with us.

"Now," said Ysanne. "I personally secured June in the west wing because of the terrible threat she could pose to this house. It was no accident that she broke free today or that someone unlocked your bedroom door. Someone deliberately loosened June's restraints, but was that the same person who turned her, or does someone else stand to gain from all this?"

"I suppose the only silver lining is that it happened when Isabeau and I were there to prevent anyone from getting hurt," Edmond said.

"How did you know we were there, anyway?" I asked.

"I went to your room to see how you were doing and discovered you had gone. I knew at once where you were, and I went after you. Isabeau intercepted me on the way."

"It is extremely fortuitous that you were there," Ysanne said. "But I am more interested in *why* someone did this."

She and Edmond both looked at me, and I felt like I was standing under a spotlight.

"What?" I said, slow to catch on.

Ysanne fixed me with a look that was cold, but not without sympathy. "Renie, I believe someone may have been trying to kill you."

CHAPTER FOURTEEN

Renie

I fought the hysterical urge to giggle. This wasn't seriously happening, was it?

But I didn't laugh. Instead I buried my head in my hands and concentrated on taking deep, even breaths. Edmond shifted beside me, and through the gaps in my fingers I saw his hand twitch like he was fighting the impulse to comfort me.

"Why would anyone want to kill Renie?" A low note of anger threaded through Edmond's words.

"If I knew that, I'd know who is responsible, but I honestly cannot fathom why anyone would care about her," Ysanne said.

I rolled my eyes.

"Perhaps," she continued, "someone found out what I was planning on doing with June and Renie, and they don't like it. Perhaps they released June so I couldn't help her." Ysanne delicately frowned, a tiny wrinkling of her brow. "Or perhaps there's a bigger picture here that I cannot yet see. I do not like that."

I couldn't help myself. "Yeah, it must really suck having people keeping secrets from you."

Ysanne shot me an icy look.

"Maybe someone just disagrees with how you're treating June," I said.

"Would you care to explain what June's living conditions have to do with someone wanting you dead?"

Yeah, I didn't have an answer for that. Not that it stopped me from shooting back, "She deserves more than chains and rags."

Maybe June was a monster, but she was still suffering. And if what Ysanne said was true, then my sister might not be completely lost to me. Some part of June might still exist in that blood-crazed madness.

"I have made her as comfortable as I can without compromising anyone's safety, and she is fed twice a day. I think under the circumstances she has been very lucky." Ysanne spoke in clipped, cold tones.

"Fed how? I thought donors weren't allowed—oh." Realization struck me. "The animal graveyard."

The bundle that Roux and I had seen Isabeau carrying up to the west wing had been whatever animal they were giving June to eat. After she was done, they buried the bodies in the grounds. Even if other vampires and donors wanted to know what was going on, they wouldn't defy Ysanne by asking, and because it all happened inside Belle Morte's walls, the outside world knew nothing of it.

I should be glad that Ysanne wasn't letting June starve, but when I pictured my sister ripping into the throat of some poor fox or stray cat, nausea curdled my stomach.

Ysanne fixed me with a penetrating stare. "Why were you digging by that tree, anyway? Why did you think you would find anything there?"

Etienne flashed into my head, but I'd never betray him. "It looked like a grave and that made me suspicious. Why did you bury the remains in the grounds? Why not get rid of them with any food waste from the kitchen?" I said.

"My staff are completely unaware of anything that has been going on, and I would prefer to keep it that way. This is vampire business, and we deal with things in our own way," Ysanne replied, and her eyes shone with pale fire. "I may not have all the pieces yet, but I will get to the bottom of this."

"I want to help find June's killer," I said.

"That's my job, not yours. You are here to focus on helping June get better."

"Fine. When do I start that?"

"Certainly not today. You need time to digest everything, and June needs time to calm down."

"So I'm just supposed to wait until you say she's ready?"

"I think that's for the best."

I disagreed, but what was the point in arguing with her? Ysanne always thought she knew better than everyone else, though as far as I was concerned, she'd displayed some seriously shitty judgment regarding the whole situation.

The vampire flicked a hand at me. "You may go now."

Her casual dismissal rankled, but I wouldn't fight to stay in her company. I left the office and Edmond followed me.

"Come with me," he said, and I was too tired to protest.

He took me back to the feeding room where he'd first bitten me, and stood by while I sat on the chaise longue.

I hunched over my knees. "I'm guessing I can't tell anyone about this?"

"You guessed correctly. We cannot risk word reaching the Council."

"Would they really kill June?"

I thought back to what I knew about the other Houses. There were three more in England—Nox, run by Jemima Sutton; Lamia, run by Charles Abbott, and Midnight, run by Henry Baldwin—and one in Ireland: Fiaigh, run by Caoimhe Ó Duinnín. Fiaigh and Midnight were both bigger than Belle Morte, but did that mean their respective lord and lady had more say in the Council?

"I believe so. The Council put the Houses together, established the donor system, and laid down the rules by which all vampires now live. Any vampire in any House must answer to their lord or lady if they break those rules, but if any of the lords or ladies themselves break the rules, they must answer to the Council."

That meant I couldn't breathe a word of this to Etienne. He was the only one who'd been honest from the start, and I hated the thought of lying to him, but what if I told him the truth and he took it to the Council? It was too risky.

Edmond sank onto the chaise alongside me, graceful and languid as a cat. "When vampires agreed to reveal themselves to the world, we swore that the making of new vampires could only be done in absolute emergencies, and it had to be proposed to and agreed upon by the entire Council."

"I thought making new vampires was a no go in any situation."

"There are exceptions to every rule, but we don't broadcast that one; otherwise every donor who came here would imagine that they could be that exception."

I guessed that made sense.

"Ysanne herself did not turn June, so she is not accountable for that crime, but she failed to notify the Council, and she has flouted an important rule by allowing June to live."

"But Ysanne's trying to prevent vampires from becoming rabid in the future, or to bring back any who already have. Isn't that a good thing?"

"Regardless of her intentions, by harboring June she is breaking one of the rules that she herself helped set in place. The Council will not look kindly on that if they find out."

I hadn't considered that Ysanne might be putting herself at risk for June's sake. Not that she was doing it for June's sake, but she could have killed my sister on the spot and she hadn't. She had jeopardized her own standing to give June another chance at life and to give me a chance of getting my sister back. Maybe she was doing it for the good of vampires rather than humans, but I still stood to gain from her decision.

I sighed. "I still don't get why she didn't tell me the truth."

"Because June had deteriorated so drastically. When you arrived at Belle Morte, she was wild, beyond any kind of reasoning."

"She still is," I said, thinking of the crazed gleam in June's eyes when she attacked me.

"Ysanne feared that if you saw June as she is now, then you would only see her as a monster. You'd refuse to try to help."

I'd have said Ysanne was cynical, except her fears weren't far from the truth. When I'd seen what June had become, I hadn't hesitated to smash a mirror over her head. If someone had told me before seeing her that I could try to help her, I'm not sure I'd have believed them. I still wasn't sure. How could I get through that mad bloodlust?

"Ysanne had no intention of permanently deceiving you. But if she had told you from the start that your sister was a rabid, consumed with the urge to destroy everyone in this house, what would you have done?"

I sighed again, a hefty gust of air. "I would have insisted on seeing the truth for myself."

"Which Ysanne would not have allowed for the reasons I already mentioned. If she told you that June was a rabid but refused to let you see her, then she was opening herself up to blackmail. You could have forced her to tell you the truth or else risk you telling everyone else in the house and trying to make sure that word reached the Council."

As much as I liked the thought of having power over Ysanne . . . "Does she really think I'd have blackmailed her?"

"Can you blame her for not taking that risk? If she imagines the worst outcomes, it's because she's had hundreds of years to witness the worst of human nature."

I wrapped my hands around my feet and rubbed my thumbs along the new socks.

Perhaps now was a good time to discuss the possibility that someone in this house wanted me dead, but as soon as I reached for the words, they turned to hard knots in my throat. I couldn't talk about that yet—talking about it would make it seem oh-too-real, and I couldn't deal with that on top of everything else.

"Can I ask you something?" I said instead. I needed to think about something other than June, to give my battered brain a chance to process what it had learned.

"I have been nothing but honest with you today."

"What did Ysanne call you in her office?"

He cocked an eyebrow, unsure what I was referring to.

"She called you something in French."

"Mon garçon d'hiver."

"What does that mean?"

Edmond smiled, wistful around the edges. "You would translate it as *my winter boy.*"

"And that means what exactly?"

"It's what she used to call me when I was human."

I swiveled to face him. "Ysanne knew you when you were human?"

I don't know why that came as such a surprise—the donor system was only a few years old, so it was reasonable to assume that vampires could have befriended or even had relationships with humans before they stepped into the spotlight.

Edmond nodded, a faraway look in his eyes. "I was eighteen and living rough in Gascony when I first met Ysanne. Two years earlier, a wave of the Black Death had swept through my village, killing my entire family and the girl I planned to marry. I was left with nothing. For two years I struggled to survive in the wild, avoiding civilization in case of another plague attack. Then, one bitter winter's night, I met my first vampire."

"Ysanne."

"She was already immortal, and wealthy enough to travel with a convoy of guards. But times were desperate for French peasants, and even Ysanne's guards couldn't deter the gang of thieves that struck one night. Ysanne was wounded, her guards butchered, but even though she killed her attackers, she couldn't drink from them."

"Why not?"

"They were plague-ridden. Drinking diseased blood won't kill us, but it can make us sick. Ysanne found me hiding nearby, smelled that my blood was clean, and paid me to let her drink."

"You were the first donor," I realized, amazed.

"I suppose I was." Edmond looked a bit surprised, like he hadn't considered that until just now. "When she understood I was starving and wouldn't survive another winter, Ysanne took pity on me and brought me to one of her countryside properties. We lived together throughout a hard winter, just the two of us." He smiled, remembering. "We became friends. She drank my blood, and in return she hunted food for me and protected me from the thieves who sniffed at our door."

I tried to picture Edmond as a starving boy my own age, huddled in a house with Ysanne while ice and snow raged outside. My hand crept to my wrist, stroking the place where I'd been bitten. Since the first time, I'd privately raged at vampires for not understanding how much it could hurt, but I was wrong—they *could* understand because some of them had lived it themselves. Edmond had once been as I was now. It made me look at him in a whole other light.

"Does she deliberately speak to you in French, or does she even know she's doing it?"

"A bit of both—for me and her. I didn't learn a word of English until I emigrated here the first time, but I resumed my native tongue once I returned to France."

"But you were born French, so how come you speak mostly English now? Even your accent is faded."

"I suppose it rather has. But that is hardly surprising considering I permanently settled in England more than two hundred years ago."

That explained why he lived here rather than in one of the French Houses like De Sang or Dans l'Ombre.

"Why did you leave France?"

"Because I very nearly lost my head to the guillotine," said Edmond. His French lilt seemed stronger on that last word, a shadow flickering through his eyes. "After I escaped the blade, Ysanne and I fled Paris and traveled across Europe until 1802, when I returned to France and Ysanne chose to settle in Italy. But the Napoleonic empire wasn't to my taste. I wanted a quiet life, and Britain stood outside French control, so I returned here. I still traveled from time to time, but England had become my home."

"I've always wanted to travel," I said. "But I've never even left the country. We couldn't afford family holidays growing up, and I think that's why my mum encouraged June to come here, so she could get a taste of a life that she'd otherwise never get."

And June had, just not in the way Mum had ever intended. I blinked back fresh tears.

"Even if I save her, June won't be able to do anything like go on holiday again, will she?"

"Not in the way she could when she was human, but the older she gets, the more resistant she'll be to the sun."

"But she'll never be able to spend the day sunbathing on the beach, will she?"

"No," Edmond admitted.

"I used to google pictures of holiday destinations and imagine going there with June one day, even though I knew we could never afford it. It seems so stupid now."

"I don't think so," said Edmond gently.

"Yes, it does. No matter what I do, June will never have her old life back. Everything she dreamed of, everything she was working for—it's just gone."

"What was she working for?"

"June was a dreamer. She wanted to be a pop star, even though her singing voice sounded like a dying cat. She wanted to learn an instrument so she could be in a band, but we couldn't afford it. She wanted to be a model, an actress, a TV presenter—she just wanted to be *seen*. Before coming here, she'd been working in a bar, trying to scrape together a university fund, and the money she made as a donor would really have helped."

"What about you? What do you dream of?" Edmond said.

"Besides traveling? Nothing."

"What did you do before coming to Belle Morte? Were you working?"

"My dad left when I was a baby, and my mum worked herself to the bone to provide for us, but we've never had luxuries, and even though June's a dreamer, I've always had to be more practical. I have no special skills or vocational aspirations, and we need money, so I have to take jobs where I can. The last few months I've been working as a babysitter for various neighbors' kids."

"Do you enjoy it?"

"Honestly? I kind of hate it. I'm really not the maternal type," I admitted.

Edmond smiled a little. "You didn't have to leave anyone behind when you came here?"

"As in a boyfriend?"

"Yes."

I shook my head. "No, there hasn't been anyone for a while."

Was it my imagination, or did Edmond look pleased about that?

"So you and Míriam . . . you're not . . ."

"No."

"Have you and Ysanne ever been more than friends?" I asked.

I wasn't entirely sure I wanted an answer to that, but the more we talked, the calmer I felt.

"Yes, but not when I was human. I woke up one morning in that house we were living in, and she was gone. Thirteen years passed before I saw her again."

"What happened?"

"After several years alone, I headed to Paris, but the roads were plagued with thieves and Ysanne wasn't around to protect me anymore. By the time I reached the city, I was injured and half dead from exhaustion."

Gazing up at him, so beautiful and composed, his black hair tumbling across one shoulder, I couldn't imagine him like that, staggering the streets of a Paris unrecognizable from the city it was today.

"A few minutes after I arrived, I saw a band of thugs following a young man into an alley. With the last of my strength, I tried to warn him, but he didn't need my help. He was a vampire, and he ripped out his attackers' throats."

That was the side of vampires I'd always feared, the wild predator behind the civilized veneer. They controlled themselves now to fit in with modern society, but there had been times when they hadn't.

Then again, those men had been thieves at best, murderers at worst, so maybe I shouldn't judge anyone who fought back.

"The vampire's name was François, a French nobleman," Edmond continued. "Intrigued by the young peasant who'd tried to help him, he offered me a new life as a vampire. I accepted. I became François's companion and for several years I was happier than I had been since Ysanne."

I could sense a big "but" coming on.

"But François became careless and violent. Now I recognize those were early signs of turning rabid, but back then I didn't know, and he'd saved me from a wretched life, so I turned a blind eye. Other Parisians didn't." Edmond's eyes darkened. "In 1680, a mob descended on our home and slaughtered François. I managed to escape and hide on the streets, and when I needed to feed, I chose what I thought was an easy target—an unescorted young woman, who turned out to be Ysanne. With Paris on the alert for our kind, we fled the city. We traveled

France as friends for three years before eventually becoming lovers."

The sharp sting of jealousy took me by surprise. *Don't be so stupid,* I scolded myself. Of course Edmond had exes—he was nearly four hundred years old.

"How long were you together after that?"

"Ten years. In 1685 we moved to England and lived there before returning to France, where we established ourselves as wealthy nobility and lived a life of luxury. But the relationship eventually fizzled out and we parted ways amicably."

"But you stayed friends?"

"Actually, I didn't see her again until 1721, and then we reunited as friends only to go our separate ways shortly after. It would be decades until our next reunion, in the shadow of the French Revolution, and the next time we parted, it was the last I saw of her until the twenty-first century, when she tracked me down and shared her plans to reveal vampires to the world. We were lovers during only one of our periods together, but we have been friends for all that time, even during the long years when we did not see each other. I've always known she'll be there for me, and vice versa."

I quietly absorbed that, unsure if I felt better knowing that Ysanne and Edmond had once been a couple, or worse because I now knew they had, even though it had been over for a very, *very* long time. But if I didn't want to know, I shouldn't have asked. I did so only because I was trying to distract myself, but the moment Edmond stopped talking, June crept back into my mind, and my heart felt like someone had punched it.

"I guess that's why she trusted you with the truth of what happened to June," I said.

"Ysanne, Isabeau, and I are the only ones who know," he said.

"Except for the person who turned her." The words were bitter in my mouth. "Does Ysanne really not know who it is?"

Edmond shook his head. "Even I'm not privy to her investigation into whoever did this, but if she knew who the culprit was, she would have taken action against them already."

"But does she have any suspects? Do *you*?"

Another shake of his head.

"I guess that means you don't know who might want me dead either." I sighed.

Red flashed through Edmond's eyes. "No, but if they try again, they'll have me to deal with."

I looked at his arms, where June had clawed his skin. The cuts were almost gone already, and at the time he didn't seem to have noticed them.

"Tell me one more thing, Edmond, and I want the truth. Is there really a chance of saving June?"

Edmond looked me straight in the eyes. "I'm sorry, but I just don't know."

CHAPTER FIFTEEN

Renie

Roux was waiting when I finally made it back to my room, her face taut and pale with anxiety, and after she nearly hugged me to death, I told her everything. Edmond had warned me not to, but Roux already knew too much, and she couldn't go to the Council the way Etienne might be able to. The only thing I held back was that someone might be trying to kill me. Maybe that was foolish, but dealing with the reality of June's fate was hard enough; trying to comprehend anything else was just too terrifying.

I also said nothing about Edmond's past. He'd shared those secrets with me, and I wouldn't repay him by treating them like gossip.

A wave of exhaustion crashed over me. How could it have been only this morning that I'd planned to dig up what I thought was June's grave? It felt like days had passed.

I only meant to take a nap, but once my head hit the pillow, I sank into black oblivion.

June stalked my nightmares, a savage creature of claws and teeth and glowing red eyes chasing me through the shadows of my mind until I jerked awake in a tangle of sheets. My eyes felt gritty, like they'd been rolled in sand.

"Holy crap," I murmured when I checked the time. It was nearly 11 a.m.—the following day. I'd slept for . . . actually, I didn't know how long since I didn't know what time it had been when I went to sleep. So much for a nap.

Sluggishly, I climbed out of bed. Despite all the sleep, I still felt like I'd been awake for a week. My face ached where I'd hit the wall, and bruises colored my elbows where June had knocked me to the ground. Roux's bed was empty; she'd probably gone for breakfast. If I hurried, I'd make it downstairs before all the food was gone.

I showered and dressed quickly, dabbed concealer over my jaw, and then studied myself in the mirror. I couldn't completely hide the bruises, but if anyone asked, I'd make up some crap about falling down drunk.

There was a hard look in my eyes that I didn't recognize—horror tempered by steely determination. The world that my sister admired so much had chewed her up and spit her out, stripping her of everything that made her human and leaving a nightmare in its place.

But there was a chance I could do something about that.

"I promise that I will not give up on you. I will find a way to help you," I said, staring at my reflection as if it was June I was talking to.

Renie Mayfield didn't break her promises.

I almost walked into Etienne as I left my room; only his hands on my shoulders stopped the collision.

"What are you doing here?" I said.

"I came to see *you*." He glanced over my shoulder, then back over his own, checking that the coast was clear. "Renie, what *happened* in the west wing?"

I felt a pang of guilt. I'd had a hell of a lot on my mind, but I still should have found time to fill him in.

Only I couldn't.

He gave me a sad smile. "Ysanne won't let you tell anyone, will she?"

"I'm sorry," I said.

He was the only person who'd told me the truth when I'd got here, and now I couldn't do the same for him.

"It's not your fault," he muttered. "Just tell me one thing. Do you know what happened to June?"

"Everything's going to be okay," I said, and hoped with every fiber in my body that that was true.

"Will you tell me the truth when you can?"

"You'll be the first to know, I promise."

Movement caught my eye, and my heart stuttered. A couple of rooms down, a door had cracked open without us realizing, and Melissa stood there, watching us with hard eyes. What had she heard?

"I need to go," I told Etienne, and he nodded.

I didn't look at Melissa as I hurried past.

I snatched a quick breakfast in the dining hall and then made my way to Ysanne's office. Isabeau was just leaving as I arrived.

"How are you feeling?" she asked.

I shrugged.

"I know this is a lot to take in, but have faith in Ysanne."

I made a face and Isabeau frowned.

"You don't believe me?" she said

"Like you said, it's a lot to take in."

"Ysanne is a good leader, and she's doing what she thinks is best for her people. You must understand that."

"I'm not questioning her leadership."

"Not with your words, but your eyes tell a different story."

I looked away.

"Don't forget how long Ysanne has lived. She's made decisions that you cannot begin to fathom, and whatever else you might feel about her, you should at least respect her."

A soft glow lit Isabeau's face—did Ysanne have an admirer?

I went into the office. Edmond was already there, arms folded across his chest, eyebrows drawn over dark eyes that lightened only fractionally when I came in.

"This is a bad idea," he said.

"What is?" I asked.

"You starting to work with June so soon."

"You don't know I'm here for that."

The look he gave me was the closest to *oh please* that I think a vampire could get.

"Renie, you're nothing if not determined. Now that you know why you're here, you're not going to sit around waiting to be told that June is ready."

Maybe he knew me better than I thought. I wasn't sure whether to be happy about that or not.

"You're damn right I'm not."

"Even though you know that June is in no condition to be worked with," Edmond said.

I looked at Ysanne, sitting behind her desk, but she was studying Edmond, her face unreadable.

"Shouldn't this be my choice?" I pointed out.

"The whole point of keeping the truth from Renie was because June's too dangerous to be around at the moment," Edmond said to Ysanne. "Renie wasn't supposed to become involved until we knew June was under control." His face was as expressionless as hers, but there was a definite note of frustration in his voice.

He had a point there. I stared at Ysanne, silently willing her to look at me.

"Look, I know you're just trying to keep me safe," I said, "but this should be *my choice*. It's my life, and she's my sister."

Was my sister. Now I could barely fathom what she was.

Ysanne placed both hands palm down on the polished desktop, gazing at them as if the answers were written upon her pale skin.

"You're right, Edmond, but Renie knows everything now."

She pinned me with a shrewd look, like she was trying to see what I was made of, and I stared back, silently telling her that I might be just a donor to her, but I had a core of steel and I wasn't backing down from this.

"She has already demonstrated how tenacious she is, and it's foolish to assume she will sit idly by until I allow her to get involved," Ysanne said.

Tenacious or not, Ysanne *could* stop me seeing June if she really wanted to. She could have me locked up—if I got my way today, it was only because *she* wanted it.

"I still don't think this is a good idea," Edmond insisted.

The faintest hint of a smile touched Ysanne's lips, and I was reminded of what Edmond had told me yesterday. He'd kissed those lips. He'd seen the ice queen passionate and undone—assuming Ysanne was *capable* of passion.

"You have made your feelings very clear," Ysanne said. "However, June has shown no signs of improvement during the days that Renie has been here. There's little point asking her to wait for something that might never happen."

"So you want to throw her to the wolves?"

Ysanne's eyes flashed with warning, and Edmond fell silent. I felt like a deer, frozen between a pair of tigers.

"Don't I get a say in this?" I said.

Ysanne gave me that look again, the one where I felt like she was trying to decide my worth.

"Speak your mind."

"I agree with you." *Never thought I'd say that.* "If June isn't going to improve, then we're wasting time not working with her now, and we could throw away our only chance to save her."

"Ultimately the decision lies with me," Ysanne said, smoothing the front of her blouse though there wasn't a single crease. Her clothes were probably too *scared* to crease. "I think we have wasted enough time."

"And what of the danger to Renie?" Edmond asked.

Ysanne shrugged, the motion even more graceful than when Edmond did it. "As she said, it is her choice."

Only because she was allowing it to be, of course.

"Besides, we shall make sure that she has sufficient backup." Ysanne pointed at Edmond. "You, of course. And me."

That surprised me so much I almost fell off my chair. I'd expected Ysanne to send grunts to do her dirty work while she stayed here and looked authoritative.

"I should like one extra pair of hands with us to make sure no one runs the risk of getting hurt." Ysanne glanced at me, and the ice in her eyes seemed to soften. "I don't want June getting hurt either."

"It's a bit late for that," I muttered, and Ysanne's lips thinned.

I should have kept my mouth shut since Ysanne genuinely appeared to be trying, but did she think that the odd small gesture would make up for what had happened?

Even if this whole thing worked—and that was a *big* if—June would still be a vampire. Her life would never be the same. She would live forever and I would eventually die. My heart ached.

"I trust Ludovic de Vauban with my life. He will not breathe a word of this to anyone," Edmond said.

Ysanne didn't question him, just nodded.

I wondered why Ysanne hadn't let Isabeau join us—she already knew everything, so why introduce another vampire to the situation when Isabeau was available to help? But I knew Ysanne wouldn't answer if I asked.

Bundling up the fear and negativity weighing me down, I stuffed it into a little corner deep inside. If I didn't go into this believing it would work, then I didn't stand a chance.

It *would* work. I couldn't process an alternative.

*

After so long speculating about the west wing, it felt strange to go there with Ludovic, Edmond, and Ysanne, and not have to worry about anyone trying to stop me.

"I'm still not sure what I'm supposed to do," I said, hurrying to keep up with Ysanne. How could she walk so fast in those heels?

"In all honesty, neither am I," the vampire said without looking at me.

"Wonderful. You must have some idea; otherwise you wouldn't have planned all this."

"You have to try to reach any part of June that might still remember who she used to be."

"But how?"

Ysanne stopped, her posture as straight as a blade, disapproval radiating off her in chilly waves. "You know her, so you should know how to get through to her."

I glared at Ysanne's back. "No, I *knew* her. Thanks to one of your vampires, I don't anymore."

Edmond stepped in before Ysanne could turn and blast me with her Arctic death glare. "Consider treating this as if June has lost her memory," he said.

It was hardly a solid plan, but it was better than Ysanne's non-answers.

"Have we finished discussing this?" said Ysanne. If she hadn't been a vampire I think she'd have been tapping her foot.

The hallway leading to June's prison seemed much shorter without the trepidation of what I'd find weighing me down. Now I knew exactly what was there, and it terrified me.

It wasn't too late to back out. Ysanne could force me into the room with June but she couldn't force me to do anything else. But I'd do whatever it took to help June.

Pushing open the door, I stepped back into the room to face what my sister had become.

*

Knowing what I'd find didn't make it any easier, especially not when Ysanne turned on the lights, throwing the room into stark relief. June was standing, still chained to the huge wooden rack, her arms rubbed raw and her gag crusted with blood.

She shifted when she saw me, a growl trickling out of her throat.

I froze, my heart climbing into my mouth, beating wildly against my teeth. How in hell could I make this creature remember who she'd once been?

The three vampires standing behind me were statue silent, but the weight of their eyes on my back was like a trio of lasers. I inched forward, trying to put space between me and them while not getting too close to June.

My mouth was as dry as if I'd gargled sand, and I struggled to get a single word out. "Hi . . . June . . ." I coughed, tried again. "It's me, Renie."

Nothing—just another hungry growl and the rattle of chains as she tested them.

I took an involuntary step backward. On the way up here, Ysanne had assured me that she had checked and rechecked the chains so they wouldn't come loose again, but all I could see was them tearing away from that wooden frame and June launching herself at me.

"I know this must be really hard for you, but you have to remember who you are. You *have* to remember me," I said.

June thrashed, swinging her head from side to side. The hideous rattle of the chains set my teeth on edge. Her eyes glowed like hellfire, redder than the blood crusting her chin.

I glanced over my shoulder at where the vampires stood, watching me with their blank eyes and inexpressive faces. "You know, you're not helping just standing there watching. Talk about pressure."

"What did you expect us to do?" Ysanne enquired.

"I don't know, maybe stand outside the door. Just give me some space."

She shook her head, and I wondered how she managed it without a single strand of hair moving. "It's too dangerous."

"I thought you said she was properly restrained."

"She was sabotaged once, and I will not let it happen again," Ysanne snapped.

"Fine, but do you all have to be here? I feel like I'm on display."

I knew they were here to make sure that I didn't get hurt, but the whole point was for me to use the bond I'd shared with June in life to reach her now. I couldn't do that with so many people watching.

"Do you have a better idea?" Ysanne's face was as emotionless as marble, but her voice was dagger sharp and her eyes were like ice. I was definitely pissing her off.

"Yeah. You and Ludovic wait outside, and Edmond stays with me."

Edmond lifted an eyebrow, his gaze flicking between Ysanne and me. Her eyes were narrowed but she hadn't outright refused, so I plowed on.

"Edmond can handle June if anything goes wrong, and even if he can't, she won't get past the door if you're there."

She still didn't look convinced.

"Just let me try," I pleaded. "I can't remind my sister who she is with people I don't even like watching me."

Edmond's lips pressed together, but I couldn't tell if he was holding back a laugh or something else. It took my mind a moment to catch up with my mouth, and I bit my tongue. I'd just told Ysanne that I didn't like her. She couldn't stop me thinking it, but telling her right to her face was a whole other story.

And from the look she gave me—like I was a cockroach—she knew it too.

"It will be all right, vieille amie," Edmond murmured. "I'll be with her the whole time."

Ysanne's mouth narrowed to a thin line. "Very well. But if you suspect anything is wrong—even for a second—you must call me."

"Of course."

I waited until she and Ludovic were gone before speaking again. Their vampire hearing meant they could probably hear every word, but not having the pressure of their eyes on me made a world of difference.

"What did you just call her?" I asked Edmond, stalling for time so I didn't have to face my monstrous sister again.

"Old friend."

At least it wasn't a term of endearment.

June's chains rattled behind me, reminding me that I was trying to put off what I'd really come here for, but I couldn't bring myself to look at her. Edmond glided toward me and placed both hands on my shoulders, gently steering me around until I faced June.

"If you're not ready for this, we can come back another day," he said gently.

June swayed, her head lolling on her shoulders, quiet moans trickling from her throat. Seeing her like this brought a swift stab of pain to my heart. When she wasn't trying to kill me, it was clear how much she was suffering.

Tears brimmed in my eyes, and Edmond's hands tightened on my shoulders.

"Let it out if you need to," he said.

"I can't go to pieces now."

"You can, *mon ange*. If you fall apart, I will help put you back together."

For one searing, terrifying moment, all I wanted to do was close my eyes, melt against his chest, and pull his arms around me. I tried telling myself I was still mad at him for keeping this from me, but it was impossible to think straight when his presence surrounded me, smooth and delicious. The gentle weight of his hands on my shoulders made my skin tingle, even through my clothes.

"No," I whispered, then, breaking away: "*No.*"

Edmond let his hands slowly drop to his side, watching me with his usual inscrutability. Maybe I wouldn't feel so conflicted around this man if I could just guess what he was *thinking*.

Turning my back on him again, I faced June, wrapping my arms around my stomach. I had to forget that she was rabid and try to remember her as she had been. If *I* couldn't do that, how could I expect *her* to?

"You must be surprised to see me here." I gestured at the room around us. "I mean, Belle Morte? Not exactly my favorite place in the world. I know, I know, you think it's greater than Disneyland and Cadbury World combined, so you must have had a blast here—all the lovely clothes and fancy balls and delicious dinners. I bet it was everything you'd ever dreamed of."

She stared back at me, champing at her gag. Her hair was tangled in matted clumps around her neck and ears. Her skin was chalky rather than vampire pale, and her cheeks were sunken, almost concave. Whatever Isabeau had been feeding her wasn't enough. But Ysanne had said that rabids were never satisfied. If that was the case, then no matter what Isabeau did, June would always be starving.

I felt sick when I thought of the expensive, nutritious food that donors ate three times a day. That was what June had signed up for. Not this.

"I bet you never thought in a million years I'd set foot in here." I started to laugh but it turned into a sob.

June's red eyes were fastened on my face. Her feet shuffled, zombie-like, on the carpet, but her arms hung limply in their chains.

She wasn't trying to kill me, which was a huge improvement on our last encounter.

"I never thought in a million years I'd be here, either, but I am. I came for you, June. You need to know that. No matter what these vampires have done to you, you're still my sister, and I'm not giving up on you. I'm going to save you."

I took another step forward, gazing at the face that, despite everything, I knew so well. She was still my June, the girl I had shared my whole life with. She would be that girl again, vampire or not.

June's feet had stopped moving, her whole body vampire still. I thought I was getting through.

I was wrong.

"Renie—"

The rest of Edmond's warning cry was drowned out by June's snarl as she lunged at me. The chains held fast, snapping her body back into place, but I was already stumbling backward, tripping over my own feet.

I ran straight into Edmond's chest and then his arms were around me, one hand stroking my hair. He murmured to me in French, his voice low and soothing and comforting, though I didn't understand a word.

The door opened, and Ludovic said, "Is everything all right in here?"

"Minor setback." Edmond's voice sounded deeper when I had my ear pressed to his chest.

The door clicked shut again.

"Are you all right?" Edmond asked, gently tipping my head back with one hand.

I gazed up at him, into those eyes that were usually hard and bright as diamonds, but that softened when he looked at me.

The rattle of June's chains made me jump, and the moment where I'd almost fallen under Edmond's spell turned into me almost cracking my head on his chin.

"I'm so stupid. I really thought I could do it," I whispered, turning and gazing at the bloody patches on June's arms where the chains had scoured away her skin.

"Don't be so hard on yourself. No one expected you to have a breakthrough on the first day."

"It's just . . . I hate seeing her like this."

"I understand."

"No, you *don't*." I whirled on him, suddenly furious, and June shifted behind me, perhaps excited by the rush of anger filling the room. "How the hell could you understand? She's not *your* sister. She's suffering and I can't help her, and you don't have a clue what that's like."

Edmond stared down at me, his expression brittle. "I lost my entire family. I have lost almost everyone I ever loved, seen more friends go to their graves than any human could see in a lifetime. I have seen things you can't imagine, lived through things that your worst nightmares could not conjure up. Do not tell me I don't know what it's like."

The anger in his voice fractured and grief welled up, flashing across his face like a shadow.

Hot shame flowed over my skin, making my eyes prickle. It was a good thing I'd broken the only mirror in this room yesterday, because I couldn't stand to see my own reflection. Grief and loss weren't mine to monopolize.

"I'm sorry," I said quietly, and the anger in Edmond's eyes dimmed. "I'm being selfish, but I can only see what's happening to my sister, and it's tearing me up."

"I know." He beckoned to me, and, despite myself I went to him. "Try again," he murmured, laying his hands back on my shoulders.

I tried.

I reminded June of our clashes over her vampire obsession and Vladdict friends, managing to find humor in the memory of those arguments, and it was hard but Edmond was a constant source of comfort, reminding me I wasn't alone. Even though he was a vampire and he belonged to the House that had let this happen to June, even though he'd deceived me, I couldn't hate him.

But after a while, it became clear that my words were having no effect. June started to get more and more agitated, savagely chewing her gag and trying to break free of her chains; on her bare feet I glimpsed shiny spots beaded with blood where her struggles had given her carpet burn. As a vampire, they should have healed almost immediately, but the constant movement meant the wounds were always reopening.

I couldn't stand it any longer. Despair crushed my heart in a vice-like grip, the walls of this horrible room rushing in on me until I could hardly breathe.

"I have to get out of here," I said.

I ran for the door without giving Edmond a chance to respond, and pushed past Ysanne and Ludovic, fleeing down the hallway to the stairs.

The metallic rattle of June's chains followed me the whole way.

CHAPTER SIXTEEN

Edmond

Renie's hair streaked like a comet's tail as she fled, and Edmond stood and watched her go.

June's eyes latched onto him, her gag soaked with rusty-colored saliva. Vampires fed only from humans but rabids would take whatever they could get—if June got free, she'd go after him as surely as she would Renie.

Shaking his head, Edmond left the room.

Renie had told him it was crueler now that she knew the truth than when she'd thought June was dead, and he was starting to understand how right she was. By telling her there was a chance to save June they'd given her hope, which could be the cruelest thing of all. Renie would cling to that for as long as possible, and if this whole thing fell apart, it would destroy her. Maybe they shouldn't have given her that hope.

But that wasn't his decision to make.

"What happened?" Ysanne asked, as he shut the door behind him, sealing June in.

"It didn't work."

Her nostrils flared with delicate irritation.

"We cannot expect miracles straightaway," Edmond cautioned. "Renie still has a lot to come to terms with, and we must give her time to adjust."

"There's plenty of time for her to try again," Ludovic said, and Edmond nodded, both of them watching Ysanne for her reaction.

This was her crusade; the final decision was in her hands. But she wasn't foolish enough to think a single day would drive the rabid bloodlust from June's mind. This would be a long, grim fight, and Renie needed to be up to that challenge.

Edmond believed in her. From the moment Renie had arrived at Belle Morte, she'd made it clear that she would not be bullied or frightened off, and she had flat-out rejected the lies that Ysanne had tried to feed her. Edmond hadn't expected her fierceness or her determination, or the way she seemed so *alive*.

She was only a little fish in a big pond, but she was making some serious waves, and Edmond had noticed them. There was something special about Renie Mayfield. Anyone with that much life and grit and passion should not be underestimated.

But now all that passion had melted into grief, and seeing it in her eyes made something ache in the place where Edmond's heart once beat. He couldn't help her save June, but he could make sure that she wasn't alone in her endeavor.

If nothing else, he could be what she needed: a friend.

Renie

I had a feeling Edmond would come after me, and I was glad when he did. Angry energy surged through me, making my hands twitch and my feet want to run.

I really didn't want to unload even more crap on Roux, but I needed someone to talk to, so when Edmond strode up behind me, all I said was, "Follow me."

I took him to the library, glad it was as empty as ever, and made a beeline for the nearest sofa, but as soon as I sat down, I jumped up again, too churning with emotion to stay still.

Edmond took a seat. "Don't think of this as a failure," he said, his eyes tracking my short, angry bursts of movement. "Think of it as the beginning."

"I don't want to talk about that."

It was foolish to think I could have broken through the bloodlust so quickly, but I hadn't been able to stop hoping.

Now reality was crashing down like a sledgehammer. I would have to do this every day. I would have to go into a horrible room that reeked of death and see what June had become *every day*.

Edmond rested his arm on the back of the sofa, pale fingers dangling. "I can be silent if you wish."

"No, talk to me."

"About what?"

"*Anything*. I just have to keep my mind off June." Inspiration flashed to me. "Tell me about Ludovic."

Edmond didn't question my odd request, which was good because I didn't have a valid answer. Ludovic was a stranger to me, but he was Edmond's friend, someone he could talk to me about, and I needed to fill my head with anything other than the here and now.

"I met Ludovic in 1916 on the Western Front," Edmond said.

"You mean World War I?"

He nodded.

I gaped at the vampire who didn't look much older than me. "You fought in the Great War?"

"I can assure you, mon ange, there was nothing great about it."

For once I was speechless. I'd learned all about trench warfare in school, the false propaganda that had been used to entice young men to sign up, the brutal, bloody reality they'd discovered when they did. Meeting anyone who had seen and survived that was incredible under any circumstance, but the fact that Edmond still looked exactly as he would have then was jarring. It was almost impossible to imagine that he really had seen any of it—until you looked into his eyes. He could perfect the blank mask, but the closer I looked, the more I glimpsed the lingering shadows of past horrors.

"I couldn't feed on my fellow soldiers, so I was forced to drink from rats. There were always plenty of those and they were small enough that no one noticed me killing them."

I pictured their furry bodies, fat and bloated on the bodies of the dead, squeaking as they ran through the mud and slaughter, and my stomach twisted.

"Ludovic had lived in England since 1879, and when the war broke out he decided to fight for what had become his country. I was the first vampire he'd seen in a long time."

"You survived the war together."

Vampires could heal much faster than humans, but even they couldn't survive everything. They'd put their lives at risk when they signed up, the same as every other soldier who had huddled in those awful trenches.

Edmond was quiet for a moment, gazing into the distance. "Barely," he said at last.

I was still pacing, but less frantically now, my feet moving across the carpet rather than trying to stamp it into the ground.

"One night a bomb hit our little section of the trenches. Three men were blown apart in an instant, and another gravely wounded."

"Ludovic?"

Edmond lifted his eyes to mine, and the rawness I saw there was like he was reliving the whole nightmare. "Me."

I gazed at the impossibly beautiful man in front of me and tried yet again to picture him as anything less than perfection.

"What happened?"

"My injuries were too severe to heal on their own, and rat blood wasn't enough to help me. You may not understand this next part, but I won't hide it from you. I needed human blood to recover, more than any one person could give and survive. So Ludovic did what he felt he had to."

"He killed someone."

It shouldn't have come as a shock to me, not when I'd always preached about how little people knew of vampires and what many of them may have done in the past. But Ludovic always seemed so quiet, gentle even—for a vampire.

I could imagine him biting someone.

I couldn't imagine him killing anyone.

"Another soldier had been badly wounded that day." Edmond's voice was flat and steady, inflectionless. "Ludovic killed him and fed me his blood."

Finally I stopped pacing and sat beside Edmond on the sofa, careful not to get too close. "Would the guy have died anyway?"

It wouldn't be so bad if Ludovic had simply sped a dying man on his way, stealing his last hours so that Edmond might live.

"We'll never know. Maybe he would have survived and maybe he was at death's door; I wasn't exactly in any state to ask questions. Afterward, Ludovic refused to talk about it. When the war ended, he disappeared."

"Why? I thought you were friends."

"We were. But even vampires can be traumatized by the horrors of war. I'd already fought in two wars—the Spanish Succession and the Polish Succession—but Ludovic never had. He went to pieces after we finally emerged from those trenches, and I didn't see him again until the 1980s. By then we'd both had time to come to terms with what we'd seen and done, and we rekindled our friendship. We've been virtually inseparable ever since."

"What did you do after the war?" I'd wanted him to talk to me simply so I could focus on anything other than June, but now I was genuinely interested.

"I became something of a recluse. Most vampires have lived through one hell or another, and sometimes it's too much for us. Ludovic was the only real friend I'd had in a long time, and without him I was completely alone. I couldn't bring myself to fight in World War II, so I went to Ireland, looking for Caoimhe."

"The Lady of Fiaigh?" I said, thinking of the only Irish Vampire House.

"Yes. I first met her back in the 1800s, and I hadn't seen her in a long time, but that doesn't mean much when you're immortal. I went back to Ireland because I needed a friend and I didn't know where else to find one. But I didn't find her. In desperation, I went to Italy, vainly hoping to find Ysanne, but she remained as elusive as Caoimhe."

Since I was one of the few people I knew who didn't idolize vampires, I knew a little something about being lonely. But the worst loneliness I'd ever felt paled in comparison to Edmond's experience—hundreds of years old and without a friend in the world. I couldn't imagine traveling the world in a desperate search for a familiar face, or fathom the crushing disappointment that Edmond must have felt when he couldn't track down his old friends.

Edmond gave me a small smile, as if his words were of little consequence. "Eventually I returned to England and lived alone until finally reuniting with Ludovic."

It was little wonder that Edmond had flared up earlier when I'd accused him of not understanding my pain. Shame crept back into my cheeks, even though I'd already apologized.

But it wasn't just about that. How many times had I judged Edmond for being a vampire, thinking of him as somehow lesser because he wasn't human? He had fought during the war for this country, putting his life on the line to protect innocent people from the hungry wolves prowling at our shores. What the hell gave me the right to look down on him?

One thing I'd never thought about Belle Morte was that it would start exposing the cracks in my own character.

"You make me realize how much I don't know," I said.

"Some things you're better off not knowing."

Like the possibility of someone using my own sister to try to kill me.

I pulled my knees up and rested my chin on them. "I can't believe you fought in a world war. If only I'd known you when I was still in school; my history projects would have been brilliant."

"I could even have shown you a little piece of it."

"What do you mean?"

"When I was caught in that bomb blast, a piece of shrapnel hit my side. It's still there."

"You're kidding."

"Not at all."

I turned on the sofa, scooting forward so I was closer to him. "You're telling me that you've carried a piece of shrapnel inside you for over a hundred years?"

The smile he gave me was almost teasing, and a bolt of heat shot straight through my stomach. He was so damn delicious, and when he smiled at me like that, I forgot just about everything.

"You want proof?" Edmond started unbuttoning his shirt.

My mouth went dry as, little by little, the smooth expanse of his chest was revealed. His skin was flawless, the perfect ivory interrupted only by a faint shadow of dark hair that trailed below his belly button, disappearing into his trousers. I completely forgot that Edmond was trying to show me something, and stared like a gormless idiot at that gorgeous chest.

"Renie?" His voice was tinged with amusement.

"Huh? What?" I blurted out, tearing my eyes away from his body.

Edmond shifted position, angling his left side toward me. And there, marring that perfect skin, was a raised ridge about the length of a finger.

Before I could consider whether or not this was a good idea, I reached out and touched it. His skin was cool but not cold, soft and tempting as silk. The shrapnel was a hard lump, unyielding beneath my fingers.

"What is it?" I asked.

"I don't know. I was too busy bleeding to death to find out."

"How come you've never removed it?"

As a vampire, he could just cut it out and let the wound heal.

Edmond gazed down at the only flaw on his sculpted torso. "I didn't want to. Vampires cannot scar. We could be tortured almost to death, but when we heal, our bodies show no sign of what we've been through."

"You say that like it's a bad thing."

"When you live forever, it can be. Can you imagine what it is to never change the canvas of your skin? We can change our hair and our clothing, but our bodies stay the same. Scars are not always bad; sometimes they are memories." He touched the shrapnel beneath his skin. "I choose to keep this as a constant reminder of where I've been and what I've done."

Again, my fingertips traced what was probably a chunk of metal forever embedded in Edmond's side, and suddenly I *could* picture him injured in war, his broken, bloodied body fading away, those bright eyes turning dull.

What Ludovic had done was not necessarily the right thing—Edmond's life wasn't more valuable than another soldier's—but could I really say that I wouldn't have done the same in his position?

I was as prone to selfishness as anyone, probably just as capable of dark things to save the people I loved, so I couldn't judge Ludovic for the choice he'd made long ago in a nightmare where humans reduced each other to twisted lumps of meat.

I was suddenly aware that I was still touching Edmond, my fingers stroking up and down the shape of the shrapnel. Our bodies were almost touching, and I snatched my hand back as if his skin was red hot.

Edmond followed the movement, flowing toward me with almost inhuman grace. His hand cupped my cheek.

For the briefest moment I closed my eyes. He could do more with his fingertips on my cheek than any other guy had done in my whole life.

But—

"I can't," I whispered, pulling away.

This time he didn't follow, but remained still as I inched back, his eyes dark and unreadable.

"We can't do this," I said.

Edmond leaned back, lounging on the sofa as if we hadn't been an inch away from kissing.

"You're right," he said, and I felt a contrary flush of disappointment.

"But thank you," I said. "For everything."

I'd barely thought of June since we'd entered the library, and even now that she was filtering back into my exhausted brain, I didn't feel the same crushing panic and despair that I had when I'd rushed out of the west wing. Edmond had calmed me.

Edmond started buttoning up his shirt.

The door opened and Ludovic walked in, his face unreadable as he looked from Edmond to me, and back again.

"I should go," Edmond said, climbing to his feet.

"Will I see you tomorrow?"

Nothing could happen between us, but I still wanted him with me when I visited June.

He paused, his head turned in my direction though his eyes

focused on the bookshelves over my head. "Of course. I'll see you in the morning, Renie."

We both knew that this was how things had to be. So why did watching him walk away make something inside me feel like it was breaking?

Edmond

For a moment he'd almost lost control, and he couldn't decide if he was disgusted or amazed with himself. He should be disgusted that, after hundreds of years, he couldn't control himself around a pair of pretty eyes, but conversely he couldn't help being amazed that, in spite of everything, his bruised and battered heart still had the capacity to feel like this.

But he didn't want it to.

He had sworn never to love again.

Casual sex was one thing, but that was simply satisfying a physical need. That wasn't what he felt around Renie—at least not *only* what he felt around her. She made everything seem brighter and better, smoothing over the scars he carried inside him.

Leaning against the wall outside the library, he absentmindedly ran his fingers over the shrapnel, tracing where Renie's fingertips had been.

"It can never happen," Ludovic warned.

Edmond didn't insult his friend's intelligence by pretending he didn't know what Ludovic was talking about.

"Believe me, I'm cutting the strings."

Ludovic nodded, tipping his head back so it rested on the wall. "We both know how it ends."

Memories unspooled inside Edmond's head: Lucy, plague-ridden and tossed into a mass grave; the disgust and horror on Charlotte's face when she brought the mob to his door; Marguerite, dying in his arms; Elizabeth, growing old and happy without him.

Even if human-vampire relationships weren't forbidden, how could Renie ever feel comfortable knowing that she would age and die, and he wouldn't? Even if civilization turned to dust, leaving only the vampires standing in the ruins, Edmond would still look exactly as he did now. He would live forever, but human lifetimes ended all too quickly. He would have to watch her die.

Human and vampire relationships simply didn't have happy endings, and that wouldn't change because Renie had come into his life.

It couldn't work.

And of course he couldn't turn her.

People could only be turned in emergencies—falling for someone didn't count. Besides, Edmond had once tried to turn a woman he loved, and it had not ended well. He would never do it again.

Renie deserved a human man to give her everything she wanted. When she eventually left Belle Morte, she wouldn't look back. She would fall in love, get married, raise a family of her own, and live a happy mortal life, while Edmond would stay sealed away in the little haven that Belle Morte had created.

"The humans who long to be like us have no idea what they'd be letting themselves in for," he murmured.

"They see only the foolish fantasy, the dream of immortality. They cannot begin to fathom the reality of it," Ludovic agreed. "Mortals are not for us, old friend. They are too fragile, too delicate, too easily broken."

Words spoken from the heart; Ludovic knew the pain of loss as well as Edmond did.

"She will not break while I am here," Edmond said. "But she won't break me either."

He would harden his heart against the girl who didn't even

understand the effect she had on him. When the time finally came, she would be glad to leave him behind, glad when he was nothing but a memory.

And she would be only a memory to him, but it would be a shining one, a secret treasure that he would hold in the place where his heart once beat, and remember the tumble of her hair and the fierce flash of her eyes.

That was how he would remember her, even when she was dead and gone.

When they went to the west wing the next morning, Renie didn't mention the fact that they'd almost kissed yesterday, or act as if anything at all had changed.

But Edmond had to.

He had to be cool and distant with her, pushing her away, because it was time he accepted that he couldn't keep her.

They went into June's room and closed the door, leaving Ludovic to stand guard outside, this time accompanied by Isabeau.

"Why is Isabeau here now when Ysanne didn't want her joining us before?" Renie asked, her forehead wrinkling.

"I don't know," Edmond said, keeping his voice flat and remote, as though he was talking to a stranger.

Renie gave him a startled look, then June growled, and Renie focused on her sister.

For two hours she sat in front of June and talked, telling stories of their childhood and teenage years, the fights they'd had and how they'd made up afterward, and despite himself Edmond hung on every word, listening to the unfolding of this very ordinary life—the one thing he could never have.

But nothing she said had any effect.

When her throat ran dry and she couldn't talk anymore, she climbed to her feet and approached Edmond.

"I guess today's not the day."

"You don't seem upset," Edmond couldn't help saying, though he didn't look at her.

"I'm no longer under the delusion that I can do this overnight. It's going to take time and patience."

"Indeed."

Renie fidgeted with her sleeves. "Why are you being weird?"

"I'm not."

"Oh my god, is this about what happened yesterday?"

"Nothing happened yesterday."

"Okay, is this about what *didn't* happen yesterday?"

Frustration surged inside him. He had been alone for so long that he didn't know how to deal with this situation, and he was obviously handling it all wrong. Telling himself he had to push her away for both their sakes was a lot easier when she wasn't standing in front of him.

"What the fuck, Edmond?" she said.

"Don't you think it's better this way?"

Her jaw clenched. "I think you're being a dick. Just because we can't be together doesn't mean you have to be like this."

"It's for the best," he insisted, and maybe it was, but that didn't ease the sting of having Renie look at him like that.

"You sound like Ysanne. But it hurts much more coming from you."

"That's not what I wanted—"

"Then what *do* you want?" Her eyes flashed with anger and hurt.

Her. He wanted her more than he'd ever wanted anyone, but he couldn't have her, and he couldn't find the words to say that. But trying to keep her at arm's length wasn't working, and he didn't know how to say that either.

Renie made a soft, angry noise and pushed past him, walking out of the room.

Renie

Stupid vampire.

This thing between us felt deeper and more significant than mere chemistry, and even though we couldn't act on it, we could still be friends.

I hadn't grasped how much his friendship meant to me until he took it back.

Tears blurred my eyes, and I stopped in the middle of the hallway. This was ridiculous—crying over some guy I never had a chance with?

Edmond was right, even though I didn't want him to be. I wouldn't stay at Belle Morte once I'd saved June, so maybe cutting me off now would save us both an awkward good-bye later.

I couldn't imagine saying good-bye to Edmond.

I'd known him only a few days, but something about that gorgeous vampire had got under my skin. I wanted to hear more of his stories, learn more of his past. I wanted to kiss his pale lips and run my fingers through his dark-as-midnight hair.

I went to the library. It was as blissfully empty as ever, the books gazing down from their polished shelves; slowly, I walked the length of the room, concentrating on making each step measured and even.

I couldn't control the entire situation, but I could control how I felt about it and how I reacted to it. I *would* save June, no matter how long it took or how hard it was, and if Edmond wanted to push me away, then screw him. I didn't need him. It hurt now, but that wouldn't last forever. When I left the house, I'd never see him again. I'd move on, meet someone I could love and who could love me in return. Edmond could stay here in his fancy mansion, under Ysanne's ice-cold thumb, surrounded by an endless supply of pretty donor girls, until he no longer remembered my face.

My eyes stung. "Oh, for fuck's sake," I muttered, angrily swiping at them. "Get a backbone, Renie."

"Still talking to yourself, I see."

I almost jumped out of my skin as the smooth voice flowed over me like velvet. Edmond stood in front of the door, his dark eyes locked on me.

My mouth dried up, all thought fleeing my brain. When I was away from him, I forgot what a powerful effect he had on me, and it hit me like new every single time.

"Mon ange, what are you doing to me?" Edmond whispered.

He was across the room in three strides, not giving me a chance to answer, and then his mouth was on mine.

CHAPTER SEVENTEEN

Renie

My entire body turned to liquid. Nothing in the world could have prepared me for the feeling of Edmond's lips. I clung to his shoulders so my legs didn't give out, electricity shooting through every fiber of my body, and making my nerve endings sparkle.

No one had ever kissed me like this.

I didn't know it was *possible* to be kissed like this.

The flick of his tongue across mine, the growl in his throat as he pulled me harder against him—I was lost in a sea of sensation. I was drowning in Edmond.

My tongue brushed the hardness of fangs, and reality pierced the delightful fog I was floating in. I was kissing a vampire. But I couldn't stop.

By the time we came up for air, I was gasping, shuddering, burning with raw desire. Edmond's eyes glowed red, like two pools of melted rubies. It made his skin seem paler; his cheekbones sharper.

"What . . . why . . . ?" I felt drunk or drugged, my head stuffed with cotton, my lips tingling with the incredible imprint of Edmond's.

Edmond looked slightly sheepish, an expression that I'd never thought to see on his face. "Forgive me, mon ange. I could not help myself."

"Bite me," I whispered, wild recklessness stealing over me.

He stared back, uncomprehending.

I couldn't explain what was running through my head. I was balancing on a precipice, overcome with the urge to leap off the edge and plunge into the abyss to see what waited for me there. All I could think of were lips and teeth and glowing red eyes. I wanted more than Edmond's kisses.

"*Bite* me," I said again, shoving my hand in his face.

This whole moment felt like a dream, something wild and passionate and utterly disconnected from reality, like I could do anything and it wouldn't have consequences.

Edmond grasped my wrist. His fangs were fully extended, gleaming and razor sharp; for once I was fascinated by them. I wanted the pleasure that so many people said those teeth could give.

This time I would relax.

This time—

Edmond bit down and I squeaked in pain.

No, *no*, this wasn't fair. It wasn't still supposed to hurt. I wanted this, so why did my stupid body tense up like Edmond was challenging me to a fight to the death?

He promptly sealed the punctures and pulled back, the red light in his eyes dying, passion replaced by a somber look. Despite the incredible kiss we'd just shared, I still couldn't relax enough for him to bite me without it hurting like holy hell.

Weirdly, I felt like I should apologize for ruining the moment, but it wasn't my fault. The heart was willing, but the flesh was having none of it.

I gazed at him as he stood in front of me, his shirt wrinkled where I'd clutched it, my lips swollen from his kisses.

"What is this between us?" I said.

He took my hand, gliding his thumb across my knuckles. "I wish I knew."

"But you feel it, too, don't you?" There was no way he had kissed me like that without feeling the crackling electricity that we shared.

"*Oui.*" He brushed his lips across my hand. "I tell myself to stay away from you, but I cannot."

God, we were hopeless. Neither of us had the strength to stay away; there was some invisible cord between us, pulling us together even when we tried to fight it.

"What should we do about it?" I said.

"There's nothing we can do, mon ange. We both know the reality of this situation."

Knowing it didn't stop it hurting.

"I have to stay away from you," I said, taking back my hand.

That was the last thing I wanted but the more involved we got, the harder it would be to end it—we had to stop before either of us got in too deep. I ignored the voice in my head screaming that I was already in too deep and struggling to stay afloat.

"*Mon dieu*, you are right." Edmond half turned from me, passing a hand across his face. "I tell myself that I cannot have you, yet every time I turn around I am back in your arms."

"Tell me about it," I joked, trying to lighten the mood.

He didn't smile. "But I cannot be with you."

"I know, I know. Ysanne's rules."

"Were that the only reason." He cupped my cheek, his hand cooler than ever against my flushed skin.

It wasn't fair that he could see how much I wanted him, in my blushes, in my pounding heart, when I could only guess what went through his head unless he chose to share it with me.

"Renie, I am a vampire. Human lives are so short to us."

My chest ached, the threat of tears burning my eyes. How could a relationship between us work? We couldn't stay here at the mansion, so Edmond would have to forge a new life in the real world, where he'd be the target of crazed fans and violent antivampire movements.

Even if we managed to hide away from the rest of the world, I'd still grow older and older, while he would always look like this—perfect.

Eventually I would die.

Edmond wouldn't.

That wasn't fair for either of us.

The burning, overwhelming desire I felt for him wasn't enough to override reality.

"I don't want you to stop helping me with June," I said.

"If that is your wish, mon ange," he murmured. "But before I leave, I must do one thing."

He took my face with both hands and kissed me, slow, lingering, and tender. I closed my eyes, memorizing the taste of him.

This was the last kiss we could share.

For the next two days, I visited June every morning. Edmond was always with me, and even though we rarely spoke and never touched, I drew strength from his presence. But my determination was crumbling.

June wasn't getting any better.

Nothing I said made any difference.

"We have to try something else," I said to Edmond as we left the west wing on the afternoon of the second day.

"Do you have any suggestions?"

I led him to the first floor, and then into the nearest empty feeding room. A crushed velvet sofa sat against the far wall; I made a beeline for it.

"Right," I said, "I need to know more about vampires and rabids, because there's still so much that I really don't understand."

Edmond settled beside me, as languid and delicious as ever. "What would you like to know?"

"Where to even start?" I tried to organize the questions crashing around my brain. "Do you guys need to sleep?"

"What do you imagine we do in our bedrooms if not sleep?" Edmond sounded amused.

"I don't know. I just need a clearer picture of how vampires and rabids function."

"We can go longer than humans without sleep, but we do need it. From what we can tell, rabids need even less."

"Why?"

"We can't exactly ask them, but Ysanne's theory is that they simply can't sleep because they are so desperately driven by their need for blood."

"I can't imagine you sleeping," I said, without thinking.

Edmond just smiled.

"You said you lived off rats during the war. Is human blood better for you, or does it just taste better?"

"We cannot live off animal blood indefinitely. We need a lot more of it at a time than we would need to take from a human, but it doesn't sustain us the same way. Whether we like it or not, we always have to return to human blood. When Ysanne first discovered June, she didn't feed her at all, hoping that starvation might get through to her. But it quickly became clear that it only made her worse."

"Do rabids die the same way as regular vampires?"

"They do."

"And how's that?"

Ysanne wouldn't have trusted me with that information. Edmond did.

"Exposing us to sunlight for too long, burning, beheading, or stabbing us through the heart. We can also die from serious injuries if we don't get access to fresh blood. Like humans, we leave bodies behind, unless you leave us out in the sun where we'll eventually turn to ash."

"Wait, you die if you get stabbed through the heart?"

"Yes."

"But your heart doesn't beat."

"No."

"So how can being stabbed there kill you?"

Edmond spread his palms.

"Can you cry?" I asked.

"We can, but we find it much harder than humans do." He waited a beat before adding, "And our tears are red."

"Seriously?"

He nodded.

"But your saliva isn't." I'd have noticed if it was.

"That's correct."

I shifted on the sofa, trying to make sense of it all. "What about sweating? Can you do that?"

"I don't believe so. We're more resistant to extreme temperatures than humans are—we'd probably have to be in the Arctic before our fangs started chattering, and if we can sweat, I can't imagine how hot we'd have to be."

"You don't need to shower then."

"Technically not, but I believe the modern shower is one of humankind's greatest inventions."

I really, *really* didn't need to think about Edmond in the shower.

"June always said it was her privilege as the eldest to shower first, and then she'd take forever while I sat at the kitchen table, hugging my towel and worrying about missing the bus to school. More than once I gave up and had a sponge bath at the sink," I said.

It used to make me so angry, but now I'd give anything to hear her singing tunelessly in the bathroom again.

"Imagine having to splash around in an icy river because showers hadn't been invented yet," said Edmond wryly.

"You just said you don't feel the cold."

"I did when I was human."

"So your ability to feel cold just disappears when you become a vampire?"

"Apparently so."

"What else disappears? Can you still . . ." I made a vague gesture, and Edmond lifted an eyebrow.

"What are you asking?" he said, but I think he knew.

"Can you still have sex?"

"Why would you think we can't?"

"Your bodies don't function the same way as ours. For all I know, you guys don't have the blood flow necessary to get it up."

"I can assure you we do."

"Well, that's convenient."

Edmond's lips twitched. "I'm certainly grateful for it."

"I bet you are."

He laughed, and I couldn't help laughing too.

"But vampires don't need to use the toilet, right?"

"We don't."

"Ever?"

"No."

"That doesn't make sense. If you drink blood it should have to come out again."

Edmond shrugged.

"And you *can* bleed," I said, remembering the way June had clawed Edmond's arm. "You can even bleed to death. But you never drink much from a human at a time, so how can you have enough blood in your body to bleed to death?"

"I honestly don't know."

"If you could sweat, would it come out red?" I asked.

He tilted his head. "How would I know?"

"Right, stupid question."

Edmond's smile widened, like he knew what was on my mind. "Tears are our only bodily fluids that come out red, if that's what you're wondering."

"I wasn't," I muttered, but neither of us believed me.

A long pause.

"It just doesn't make sense, though," I burst out. "If your saliva is normal, then why are your tears red? How can you need to drink blood but not need to use the toilet? If you don't need your hearts to beat, then how can you die from stab wounds?"

"The same way we can be dead and not dead at the same time. Renie, not even vampires ourselves understand how and why we work. We are impossible things."

I absorbed that.

"Okay, so how different are rabids to vampires?"

"They need blood more than we do but they're never sated. They sleep very little but it doesn't seem to affect them. They can't speak."

I pounced on that. "Why is that?"

Another shrug.

"What happened with François? Did he forget how to speak one day?"

"If he'd become fully rabid, then yes, I believe he would have lost the power of speech, but he was killed before things got that far."

"How long did it take him to start going rabid?"

"He deteriorated over a matter of weeks."

"But June turned rabid as soon as she woke up as a vampire."

"Sometimes it happens. A person might turn rabid instantly, or it might happen years, decades, or even centuries down the line. We don't really understand how it happens, but it can happen to anyone at any time."

"Could it happen to you?" I asked, my stomach clenching.

Edmond looked down at his hands. "Theoretically, yes. But it is rare."

"Hasn't anyone really examined rabids before?"

"We've never had a chance. Until the donor system, vampires didn't have any kind of society. Humans have a nasty history of fearing what they don't understand, and killing what they fear. No vampire was ever able to linger too long in one place, or the people around us would start to notice that we never ate or aged, or that we could do things normal humans couldn't. Until Ysanne revealed us to the world, most vampires lived very lonely lives. If any of us discovered a rabid, it was our duty to kill them, both to protect everyone they'd butcher in their rampage and to prevent more people from learning about us."

"I'm guessing that's why vampires kept this secret even after the world knew about you."

"Ysanne thought it was for the best."

"Of course she did. Didn't she think that modern medicine might be able to help?"

"Haven't you ever wondered why we hide away in our houses like this?" Edmond asked, his dark stare pinning me in place. "For so many of us, it's the permanent home that we could never have as vampires, surrounded by our own kind, but it's also to protect us. Do you think you're the only person who wonders exactly how we function? Do you think there aren't people who'd jump at the chance to cut us up and examine us? Or that antivampire movements wouldn't slaughter us if they could? We stay in our houses because we're safe here, and to some extent that means maintaining distance from people. As far as Ysanne is concerned, rabids are a vampire business, and only vampires can deal with that."

In this instance, she was probably right, though. The world might not have been so quick to embrace vampires if they knew that rabids existed too.

In my head, I ran through everything I had learned, turning over each piece of information as if it would somehow help me with June.

"Vampires have preferences when it comes to who they bite, don't they? And younger blood tastes better than older?"

Edmond nodded.

"Does that mean blood tastes different when it comes from different people? Like, do blonds taste different than brunets? Do men taste different than women?"

"Yes. Your blood, for example, is the most exquisite thing I've ever tasted," Edmond said, that faded French lilt rubbing over me.

I swallowed hard and tried to focus. "Is it possible that feeding June my blood would make a difference?"

Edmond frowned, thinking it over. "I really don't know."

"But it is worth trying?"

"It's worth raising the suggestion with Ysanne," he said cautiously.

Jumping up from the sofa, I grabbed his hand. "Come on, then. Let's go talk to her."

CHAPTER EIGHTEEN

Renie

"Absolutely not," said Ysanne, reclining in the chair behind her desk.

I glared at her, trying to swallow the spark of anger in my chest. "Don't we even get to discuss it?"

"It's too dangerous. Nothing drives a rabid into a frenzy faster than fresh blood."

I'd seen that firsthand when I'd cut my foot in June's room, but that didn't mean this wasn't worth trying.

"What if she could recognize my blood somehow?" I asked.

"How? She's never tasted it," Ysanne pointed out.

I glanced at Edmond, sitting in the chair beside me, and he raised his eyebrows a little.

"Edmond's explained a lot about vampires and rabids to me," I said.

"Has he?" Ysanne shot Edmond a cool look.

"If no one really knows how or why vampires turn rabid, and there's no way of predicting who it will happen to, then you can't say for sure that this won't work. Has anyone ever tried it before?"

Ysanne took a long moment to reply, as if she was weighing up what to tell me. "I once heard of a human woman who tried to feed her blood to her rabid husband in the hopes that it would restore him. It didn't work. Instead it gave him the strength to break free of the room she had locked him in. He butchered her and their children."

Oh.

I resisted the urge to look at Edmond again. This was my fight.

"What if that rabid just needed more time? What if he needed his wife's blood more regularly for it to make a difference? You don't know what would have happened if he hadn't broken free," I pointed out.

Ysanne didn't look convinced but I pressed on anyway.

"If you're serious about trying to help June then you have to be willing to try everything."

"Very well," Ysanne conceded. "We shall try things your way."

"Thank you."

Surprise flickered across her face, quick as a blink.

"How are we going to do this? It's far too dangerous to allow June to bite Renie," Edmond said.

That I agreed with. "Can someone in the infirmary take my blood? We can feed it to June from an ordinary mug or something."

"Assuming that anyone is willing to risk injury getting that close to her," Ysanne said.

"I'll do it," Edmond said.

I wanted to take his hand, but of course I couldn't.

"Well, then," Ysanne said, her cool gaze settling on me. "I suppose you should make a trip to the infirmary."

"Are you sure you're okay with this?" I said to Edmond as we walked back up to the west wing, Ludovic and Isabeau following as usual.

In a plastic pouch, he carried half a pint of my blood, and I felt faintly sick whenever I looked at it. I'd never considered myself squeamish before, but that was *my* blood and the man I had feelings for was about to feed it to my sister.

"She won't hurt me," he said, but I couldn't help wondering if that blithe confidence was just to reassure me.

Ludovic and Isabeau said nothing.

They waited outside the door as we went in, and my nerves started to waver, faced again with the monster wearing my sister's skin.

I had to stay back as Edmond approached June. He checked her chains first, making sure they were secure, and then he removed her gag and opened the bag of blood.

June went wild.

Chains rattled as she thrashed against them, snarling and gnashing her teeth, her eyes blazing red. Edmond gripped her jaw with one hand, forcing her mouth open so he could tip my blood down her throat. I didn't want to watch this, but I wouldn't let myself look away.

Edmond poured half the bag into June's mouth, and let her go. She snapped at him, her fangs just missing his hand.

"What if this doesn't work?" I said.

"Then we try something else. We're not giving up."

I gazed up at him, more beautiful than anyone had a right to be. This wasn't his fight, but he treated it as if it was, refusing to let me face this alone. Something burned in my heart. I *wanted* him.

"Maybe I could read to her from her favorite books or play her favorite shows," I said, tearing my eyes away from him.

"Everything's worth trying, but let's wait and see if this works first."

It didn't work.

For another two days I visited June, watching Edmond as he fed her more of my bagged blood, but there was no sign of improvement, until reluctantly I had to admit that Ysanne was right.

It was time to try something else.

Since I didn't have a phone, I had to ask Ysanne about sourcing a laptop that I could use to play June's favorite shows. She assured me that Dexter would handle it, and a day later I was sitting cross-legged on the floor in June's room, queuing up old episodes of *Friends*.

If this didn't work, I'd play all her favorite music, and if that didn't work, I'd track down the books that Mum used to read us when we were kids. And if that didn't work I'd think of something else.

The flickering screen captured June's attention; she cocked her head, her gagged growls fading at the sound of canned laughter.

How many Saturdays had we spent on the sofa in our pajamas, watching reruns of our favorite episodes and quoting all the best lines? We'd never been able to agree on popcorn—I liked it sweet, June insisted on salty—so we'd quickly given up trying to share, and had each balanced a separate bowl on our laps.

June would never eat popcorn again. But if I could save her, then we could snuggle on that sofa again, watching our show.

Edmond laughed suddenly, and I looked up. Standing on my right side, where he could see both June and the laptop, he watched the screen with abject fascination.

"Haven't you ever seen this before?" I said.

"No." He didn't look away from the screen, his face bright and open, his lips parted in a smile that I don't think he was even aware of.

I'd thought of Edmond as beautiful, annoying, sexy, impossible, but this was the first time that I could only describe him as adorable.

My heart gave a sharp lurch.

How different would things have been if he was a normal human guy? I would have brought him home to meet Mum and June, and June would have been outraged that he'd never seen *Friends*. She'd probably have dragged him over to the sofa then and there and made him watch it, and later, after he'd gone, she'd have teased me about my poor taste in boyfriends.

For a fleeting moment that image was so real I could almost touch it.

Then June shifted, her chains clanking, and it was gone.

I sat for hours, playing episode after episode, quoting the lines we always used to, but for the first time they didn't make me laugh.

*

I'd almost forgotten that life in Belle Morte was continuing as normal for everyone else, other donors practicing music or creating art, all while I was trying to save my rabid sister. Then, the day after my *Friends* failure, Roux reminded me that the mansion was hosting another charity ball tonight. Unlike last time, we couldn't choose a gown from our wardrobes—this was a masquerade ball, which meant that a variety of outfits had been sent to our room.

"I really should have checked this thing." Sitting on my bed, I pulled the calendar of social events from the drawer in my nightstand and flipped through the pages. The days blurred into one inky smear.

"You've had more important things to worry about," Roux pointed out.

I tossed the calendar back in the drawer. "I wish I didn't have to go. I'm technically not even a donor."

Although I had fed a couple of vampires over the last few days, it was only so no one would become suspicious about my real purpose.

"Why not ask Ysanne if you can skip this one?" Roux said, tossing a layered satin dress onto her bed.

"She won't let me. The rest of the world needs to think that nothing's wrong, so I have to pretend to be a normal donor, like everyone else."

Roux stopped going through the dresses hanging from the wardrobe and sat beside me.

"Okay, I don't want to sound insensitive, but maybe this ball will do you good, help take your mind off things. You could use a break," she said.

It *would* be nice if my biggest decision of the day was what I'd wear to the ball, rather than what else I could try to get through to June because absolutely nothing was working.

"I feel like a shitty person for even thinking about having fun while June is suffering," I said.

"If June was here now, what would she tell you to do?"

I laughed and it came as out as a teary snuffle. "She'd tell me to put on the prettiest dress and dance with the sexiest vampire and have the time of my life."

"So what are you going to do?" said Roux gently.

I blinked away tears. "I'm going to try to have fun."

Roux hugged me. "You need it. Now let's choose our dresses."

"This is the one," she declared five minutes later, her face glowing.

It was one hell of a dress. The top was sheer, with flowers strategically woven across the chest, dropping down into a skirt of wine-colored silk. It came with a matching mask, adorned all over with tiny flowers.

"You're going to look hot," I said.

Roux beamed. "I know."

I sifted through the confections of satin and silk and velvet and tulle, glittering with crystals, boasting ribbons and fur, but I couldn't find one that leaped out and screamed *wear me*!

It wasn't until I'd dismissed the fifth dress that it dawned on me I was looking for one I thought Edmond would like. I wouldn't normally choose my clothes based on what my crush liked, but it wasn't that simple.

I wanted Edmond's eyes to flare with desire when he saw me. I wanted to see on his face that he felt for me what I felt for him. That was almost cruel, considering that we'd both agreed nothing could happen between us, but I was only human.

"Oh." The breath rushed out of me in a little gasp as I found what I was looking for.

It was made of peacock feathers, woven together to make a short, skintight dress that dropped into a glorious feathered train at the back, complete with a feathered mask. It was the most beautiful thing I'd ever seen.

"Wow." Roux came to stand behind me. "You're going to look amazing."

"You know what?" I linked my arm through hers, gazing at my dress. "I think so too."

Jason turned up to perform his magic on our hair, teasing Roux's pixie cut into tousled spikes, and building mine into a towering mass of curls.

Once my dress was on, I didn't recognize myself in the mirror. I didn't just look beautiful, I looked . . . otherworldly, like a faerie queen who'd stepped right out of myth and legend.

Next to me, Roux's wine-colored gown was a striking contrast to my feathered outfit.

When we looked like this, I could understand why the world was so fascinated with vampire culture. They were the gods and goddesses of old, fairy-tale kings and queens, creatures of beauty and eternity. They emphasized how ordinary humans were, how we lived and died in the blink of an eye, while vampires went on and on, watching civilizations rise and fall, seeing the whole turn of the world.

Jason looked wonderfully gothic in a satin tuxedo, his shirt complete with a foaming lace cravat, and a long velvet coat in place of a tuxedo jacket. His eyes twinkled behind a black mask tooled with onyx beads.

"My darlings, you look exquisite," he declared. "The belles of the ball." He winked and smoothed his cravat. "Besides me, of course." He extended an arm for each of us. "Shall we?"

We ran into Melissa outside our room. Her dress was metallic, a figure-hugging column of molten silver, and her mask looked like it had been shaped from delicately beaten metal, glittering against her deep-brown skin.

She smiled at us, but there was something empty about it, as if she was just going through the motions.

"You look amazing," Roux told her.

"Thanks." Melissa looked at me. "June would have loved this."

The statement was loaded somehow, and I wasn't sure why. I pretended to smooth down the feathers on my dress, trying not to meet her eyes.

That didn't deter Melissa. "Still, I'm sure she's having fun in another House, right?"

"Right," I mumbled.

"We should probably get going," Roux said, gesturing weakly down the hall.

"I'll walk with you," Melissa said.

I felt her eyes burning on me the whole way to the staircase.

The guests had already gone through to the ballroom, and the vampires were sweeping down into the vestibule to be photographed.

Nervousness formed a little ball in my stomach. I really hoped that I didn't trip in my heels, stand on my own train, or leave a trail of feathers behind me. I had a sudden, absurd image of the feathers peeling away from the dress, fluttering into the air until I was standing in front of the cameras wearing nothing but my heels and mask.

A laugh choked me. At least Edmond would definitely notice me.

I couldn't see him anywhere, and beneath the nervous knot in my stomach, something else spread over me, a sense of reckless abandon. It wasn't easy to tell who was who beneath their masks, and there was something wild and carefree about that.

Vladdicts across the globe would be watching and trying to guess who was behind each mask. Someone was probably taking bets. Someone else was probably turning it into a drinking game.

My heart clenched. June used to be glued to the TV screen when something like this was on, excitedly tweeting and texting her fellow Vladdicts.

None of her friends even knew she was dead.

It was my turn to walk down the stairs. I smiled and posed and looked pretty for the cameras, but my stomach was hollow. I needed this to take my mind off everything, but at the same time I felt like scum for putting on a dress and enjoying myself while June was rotting in the dark depths of the west wing.

Thousands of tiny bulbs were hung all over the ballroom, turning everything to a sea of shining light. As before, an orchestra occupied the farthest corner, and human staff milled about with silver trays of champagne, all of them uniformed and wearing masks. The orchestra and camera crew were the only bare faces in the room.

A vampire brushed past me and I thought I recognized Isabeau's curly hair, though it was hard to be sure when it was styled in a complicated updo. She was dressed in a white gown studded all over with pearls, her face covered with a pearl-studded mask, and a tiny pearl coronet sat in her hair.

Jason grabbed my arm. "Oh my god, have you *seen* Gideon tonight?"

I couldn't see which of the male vampires he was until Jason pointed him out. He did look rather delicious in a black velvet suit over a ruffled white shirt, a mask of black lace covering his eyes.

"Quick, dance with me," Jason hissed.

In my periphery, I saw a camera aimed at us, so I smiled and tried not to stab anyone's feet with my stilettos.

"Is he looking?" Jason asked, his eyes fixed on my face.

"I can't see over your shoulder."

Jason twirled me and I caught a brief glimpse of Gideon talking to a vampire wearing a mask shaped like a bat. He didn't look our way.

I tried to think of something more hopeful to say, but one look at Jason's disappointed expression told me there was no need; he'd already seen that Gideon wasn't paying us the slightest bit of attention.

"Weren't you the one who told me not to get attached?" I pointed out.

Jason winced, but that might have been because I'd just trodden on his foot.

"It's easy to give advice but not so easy to take it, you know?"

I certainly did. I couldn't even take my own advice.

"I know I'm being an idiot, pining over someone who barely looks at me, but I can't help it. The heart wants what the heart wants," Jason went on.

And when the heart decided it wanted something, it wasn't easy to deny it. That kicked in the chest feeling I got every time I remembered that Edmond could never be mine was proof enough of that.

Jason sighed, holding me against his chest so no one could see what a terrible dancer I was. I tried to recall what Edmond had taught me, but all I could remember of that night was the closeness of his body, the softness of his palm pressed against my shoulder blade, the dark glitter in his eyes when he'd gazed down at me.

"I tell myself I don't care about Gideon, but every time I see him it's like I melt into a puddle all over again. I know how stupid that is when there are so many hot human guys living here, but I can't help myself."

"Why are you so attracted to him?" I asked. Maybe if Jason could explain his infatuation with Gideon, I could understand mine with Edmond.

"I wish I knew. It's not like Edmond and Ludovic and Phillip and every other male vampire in this house aren't hotter than hell, but Gideon's the one I want. I don't think you can necessarily explain something like that."

We spun in a slow circle, and Jason pulled me even harder against him to keep me from stumbling into someone. In hindsight, maybe this dress wasn't the smartest choice. The train of feathers was heavier than it looked, and I had to keep sweeping it out of the way so it didn't trip me—or anyone else. Still, I looked damned good.

"Do you believe in love at first sight?" Jason asked.

The question caught me by surprise. "I don't think it's that simple."

It was hard to gauge Jason's reaction behind his mask.

It *couldn't* be that simple. Love was developed over time. It wasn't something that just *happened* when two people met. The dull ache in my chest wasn't because I had fallen in love with Edmond, it was because there was something between us that could be special if it ever had the chance to bloom, and I was feeling the pain of regret that we'd never know how special it might've been.

Jason stopped dancing. A small smile played around his lips.

"What?" I said.

He nodded over my shoulder. "I think someone wants to cut in."

Edmond's presence shivered over me, and I turned slowly to face him.

I'd meant to play it cool, to enjoy the look on his face as I dazzled him with my incredible, impractical dress, but my mouth was the one that dropped open.

Edmond was dressed in blue breeches trimmed with gold, and a golden brocade vest beneath a silk coat embroidered with a subtle pattern of interlocking leaves and flowers. His dark hair was tied at the nape of his neck, his face partially hidden beneath a midnight-blue mask. It was an extravagant style, and so old fashioned that I couldn't even guess what time period it was modeled on, but he looked more beautiful than I'd ever seen him.

My peacock dress didn't feel so wonderful now.

At least not until I looked at his face and saw the fire burning there—wonder and desire rolled into one, heating his gaze until my skin prickled.

"Dance with me," he said.

"We can't," I whispered.

He gestured at the sea of masked dancers. "Tonight we can be any-one we want."

That wild, reckless feeling crept back. Hidden behind my mask, I didn't have to be Renie Mayfield, the girl who couldn't be with the vampire she wanted. I could be the mysterious peacock who danced with the most gorgeous man here and didn't feel guilty for it.

"It'll only hurt twice as much when we have to stop dancing," I said.

He took my hand, his fingers soft against mine. "I can't imagine anything hurting more than not being able to dance with you when you look like this."

I looked into his eyes and was lost.

CHAPTER NINETEEN

Renie

Edmond's hand slid along my waist, pressing me against him, and I relished the hardness of his body against mine, the cool pressure of his palm on the small of my back, both of us finding the exact way to fit together.

The feathers of my dress *shushed* across the marble floor.

"You look incredible," Edmond murmured, devouring me with his eyes.

"Good enough to eat?" I teased.

He chuckled, though we both knew that I still couldn't relax when I was bitten.

The eerie notes of a single violin drifted across the room, spilling into a waltz, courtesy of a flute, until more violins chimed in to form a haunting melody that even I recognized.

"You know it?" Edmond asked, studying my face.

"It's the *Danse macabre*," I said. Roux would have been impressed that I knew that.

"The dance of death," Edmond whispered, spinning me in a dizzying circle before pulling me back in, clasping me to him so hard I gasped. "Do you know the story behind the music?"

I shook my head as the music became more energetic, brightly colored skirts forming spinning circles all around me as the other dancers picked up the pace.

"The legend says that Death appears every Halloween at midnight and calls the dead from their graves to dance for him. When the rooster crows at dawn, the dead must return to their graves until the following year."

There was something spookily appropriate about it, and not just that the dance of death was literally being danced by the dead. The masquerade ball gave people a chance to be someone else. It gave Edmond and me a chance to dance together and bask in the simmering sexual tension that we both felt.

But it was only for one night. Before dawn came, the ball would end, the masks would come off, and we would have to return to who we usually were.

A xylophone accompanied the flurry of violins, making me think of rattling bones. I gazed around the ballroom, picturing all this finery stripped away, and the flesh, too, until there was nothing left but a crowd of skeletons leaping around a dance floor.

Goose bumps broke out on my arms.

Edmond trailed his fingers down my face and my lips parted. We didn't dare kiss, but there was something strangely exciting about not giving in to what we really wanted.

He spun me again, this time bringing me in so my back was pressed against his chest. My heart thudded like crazy, but his hadn't beaten in centuries. That used to bother me about vampires, but with Edmond I barely noticed.

His lips grazed the side of my neck, too feather soft to be called a kiss, but enough to send shivers rolling through my body.

"*Je vous veux comme aucune autre,*" he whispered, one hand pressed flat against my stomach, the other stroking the veins in my neck, his fingers moving down to my bare shoulders and gliding along the jut of my collarbone.

My mouth was so dry I could barely speak. "What does that mean?"

"I want you like no other." His tongue brushed my earlobe and I swallowed.

It was a risky game we played, assuming that no one would recognize us behind our masks, but that was part of the thrill. We could flirt and tease in public, titillating the fans who would lap up every second of footage and feed the image of decadent sexuality that contributed to the vampires' overwhelming popularity. It would hurt so much in the morning, but the here and now was too delicious to resist.

Edmond's lips moved down to my pulse and he pressed a kiss against it, his tongue gliding over the spot. My pulse leaped and jumped in response, flapping like a trapped bird.

I swayed my hips against his, a suggestive flutter of movement, and he responded by nibbling the side of my neck. I felt the tiniest prick of his fangs, and the shadow of excitement stirred inside me.

He dipped me, bending me backward until I thought my head was about to touch the floor, and held me there, one hand easily supporting my weight while his eyes raked over me, blazing with desire. My breasts were about to spill out of my dress, and I didn't care. Edmond pulled me upright, his hand gliding lower than my back.

Behind his mask, his eyes shone ruby red.

Melissa spun into view in the arms of a male vampire I couldn't place thanks to his mask. She tilted her head to one side without being asked, and he sank his fangs into her throat. Through the crowd, I glimpsed Fadime hungrily feasting on Jason, and Etienne leaning over a girl with her back to me.

Suddenly I wanted Edmond to bite me.

The more I saw it happen, the more I understood how sensual it could be, the play of lips and tongue and teeth, the trust you had to place in someone.

I grabbed Edmond's hand. "Come with me."

I took him to the library, where the ghosts of our conversation still lingered, the fragile bonds we'd spun clinging to the silent air. The books didn't judge us or warn us that this relationship could never happen.

When the door had closed behind us and those books were our only witnesses, I removed Edmond's mask. His eyes burned red hot. "We cannot, mon ange."

"I know the rules, Edmond, but you're still allowed to drink from me." I tilted my head back, baring my throat. "So drink."

"*Non*. It hurts you."

"I don't care."

When I was behind my mask, clad in my gown of feathers, it felt like I could say or do anything. Any secret desires could be brought into the light, curiosities tested, new territory charted.

"Please, Edmond. I want this."

He turned my hand over to expose my wrist, but I snatched it back, hiding it behind my back. "Not there," I whispered.

I swallowed, and his eyes tracked the movement, focusing on my throat. If possible, his gaze turned even redder.

Edmond cupped my neck, sliding first his fingers and then his tongue along the sweet spot. The familiar tension crept into my muscles, but it was fleeting, a whisper of remembered fear that was swept away by a wave of certainty. For the first time I truly wanted this.

His lips parted, his fangs extending. How had it taken me so long to appreciate how beautiful they were? As he dipped over my throat, I closed my eyes.

A sharp sting throbbed through my neck as his fangs sank in, and frustration made me squeeze my eyes tighter closed. I'd thought this time I really was relaxed. I really had wanted it—

The pain faded away, exquisite pleasure sparkling in its place. "Oh my god," I whispered.

Edmond drank my blood, and each pull of his mouth sparked lights behind my eyelids, a molten core of pure pleasure throbbing inside me. *This* was what I'd been missing all this time? No wonder people became addicted to vampire bites.

I clutched Edmond's shoulders, my head hanging back. When my legs gave out, he caught me, never breaking his blissful hold on my neck. Soft gasps spilled from my lips in time to every pull of his mouth. If this was how it would feel every time, he could bite me every day. Twice a day. As many times a day as he could without me passing out from blood loss.

When his mouth left my throat, I whimpered in dismay. My legs still felt like jelly, but it didn't matter because Edmond had no intention of letting me go. His tongue swirled across the fang marks to seal them, and another jolt of pleasure sizzled through me.

"I don't want anyone else biting me ever again," I whispered when my voice came back.

Despite how incredible that had felt, I wouldn't be able to relax the same way for anyone else, and in a weird way, I was glad about that. What I'd just shared with Edmond was special; I didn't want to repeat it with anyone else.

Edmond gently kissed me, and I tasted a hint of my own blood on his tongue. Maybe that should have disgusted me, but I couldn't find anything disgusting about this moment.

"I could stay here forever," I whispered, gazing up at him.

The red in his eyes had dimmed, but they were still lit as though by fire. "Forever is a long time."

I wanted to kiss him again, to strip off his clothes and explore every part of him. But even I wasn't that reckless. I'd given him what I could, but this was a dream. When tonight ended, so did the dream. We couldn't cross a line that we couldn't come back from.

As we returned to the ball—Edmond's mask back in place—I refused to think about how little time we actually had. The ball wasn't over yet and I intended to enjoy every single second of it.

*

The next morning, I went to the west wing with Edmond, both of us acting like nothing had happened, and read to June from the Vladdict magazines that someone in security had procured for me. Once, June would have pored over these, devouring any scrap of vampire gossip and studying the glossy photos. Now I was reading her the gossip and holding up the magazines so she could see the pictures, while trying to ignore a growing sense of desperation— nothing was working and I didn't know what to do.

The next day we went back again, and I read to her from books that I thought she would like, and the day after that, I put on three Disney films in a row, hoping to trigger any memory of our childhood.

Nothing.

The brightest part of each day was the time I snatched with Edmond after my mornings with June, when we'd go to the library or one of the feeding rooms.

Sometimes he would bite me, but we were careful never to touch apart from that. He told me more stories about his past, and I filled him in on how the modern world had changed during the time he'd been at Belle Morte. Edmond was so unfamiliar with basic technology that had become part of everyday life for humans—computers, internet, phones. It was strange to explain it to someone who had seen and experienced so much, but I quite liked that I knew a lot of things that he didn't.

"You can't be serious," I said one day, as we sat on our usual sofa in the library. "You've only got used to electricity in the last twenty years or so?"

"I lived several lifetimes before it was even invented, and a lot of vampires thought it wouldn't last."

"But it's been around for more than a hundred years."

Out of everything he'd told me, this I really struggled with. Electricity was a basic part of the world, something that I'd never even known I was taking for granted until I met someone who remembered a world without it.

"Yes, and I've been around almost four times that long."

I shook my head in amazement. "There's so much I want to show you."

It was meant to be a flippant comment, but Edmond's face darkened. None of that technology existed inside Belle Morte, so the only way I could show him was when I left the mansion. But once that happened, I wouldn't be allowed back.

Since getting out of the limo that first night, I'd anticipated the day I would get to leave. Now part of me hoped that day didn't come too soon.

"Do you think the Houses will ever have computers?" I asked.

His eyes widened fractionally, which was as close to panicked as I'd ever seen him. "Are they really here to stay?"

"Computers are part of everyday life, Edmond. People use them for everything."

His face fell.

"Are the lords and ladies of the other Houses this antitech?"

Edmond laughed, and I wanted to wrap myself up in that sound. "Some of them are worse. Caoimhe would probably reject electricity in favor of candlelight if she could."

I didn't miss the familiarity in his voice when he mentioned her, and a cold finger of jealousy wormed through me. I'd always been very happy with what I saw in the mirror, but Caoimhe was gorgeous, even by vampire standards.

Had she and Edmond just been friends, or was there more to it? It shouldn't matter but I wanted to know.

"So . . . is Ysanne the only lady you've been with?" I winced as soon as I said it. "That was really obvious, wasn't it?"

He smiled wryly. "Yes. Do you really want to know?"

"You already told me that you and Ysanne used to do the nasty, so

I think I can handle hearing about your other girlfriends."

"Caoimhe and I were romantically involved back in the 1800s, after I met her while journeying around Ireland."

Well, I *had* asked. It wasn't Edmond's fault that the finger of jealousy suddenly swelled, turning to ice inside me.

Caoimhe was beautiful, immortal, and in charge of a Vampire House.

Ysanne was beautiful, immortal, and in charge of a Vampire House.

I was a human donor who couldn't even save her own sister.

"Talk about a lot to live up to," I muttered.

A slow smile spread across Edmond's face, that dazzling, honest one that he seemed to save only for me.

"Renie Mayfield, are you jealous?"

"No!" I answered too quickly.

He continued to smile.

"Okay, maybe a little, but can you blame me? They're both powerful and stunning and they're going to live forever."

"And my relationships with both those women began and ended a couple of hundred years before you were even born."

Ouch. Edmond had meant it to reassure me, but all it did was reawaken my previous concerns. Edmond was hundreds of years older than me. Even after he fed from me, I sometimes forgot he was a vampire, and his age frequently slipped my mind. Occasionally I'd remember and brush it off, and other times the reality of it hit me like a sledgehammer.

"How old are you?" I asked.

"I already told you—"

"I mean, how old were you when you died?"

It was a question that had niggled at me several times. Edmond couldn't help being immortal, but I'd never been sure if I wanted to know how much older he was in human years.

Edmond gazed at the floor for so long that I thought he wasn't going to answer. "I'd almost forgotten," he said at last. "I was twenty-two."

It seemed impossibly young when I knew how old he'd become after death. It was his eyes. They held the shadows of every love and loss he'd ever suffered, all the horrors he'd seen.

How much of a human life had he got to experience?

I leaned forward, clasping both my hands in my lap so I wasn't tempted to stroke his hair. "Tell me something else." It was a question that I hadn't thought about until now, but as soon as it was in my head I had to ask it.

"What was it like to die?"

Edmond was so still he might have turned to stone. His eyes bored into me, hard little pebbles in the perfect sculpt of his face. Had I crossed a line?

"It doesn't matter. Forget I asked," I babbled.

"No, it's all right." There was a curious quality to his voice, something slower and less velvety than normal—he sounded oddly human, and shockingly young. "I just haven't thought about that in a long time."

I couldn't imagine my own death not being something I thought of often, but then I'd never experienced it.

"It hurt," Edmond said at last, still in that soft voice. "You know how good it feels when a vampire bites you? When they bite to kill, it doesn't feel like that. They drain the blood right out of you, and that *hurts*."

I swallowed hard, touching my own neck. That had happened to June. She'd died in pain, miles away from her family.

"When you're a heartbeat away from death, the vampire feeds you their own blood." Edmond's voice dropped to a whisper, and he looked so vulnerable that I wanted to hug him. "Then you go through the turn. Sometimes it lasts days, locked in a bloodthirst you cannot imagine. Everything's dark, and you sink so far into it that you think you'll never come up, stuck somewhere between life and death."

He closed his eyes and his pain washed over me. I couldn't stop myself from taking his hand. These were clearly memories he hadn't visited in a long time, and I had the sudden fear that he was going to fall into them and not be able to find his way out. I held his hand so he wouldn't get lost.

"I'm sorry," I whispered.

Edmond shook his head, pulling himself out of the memory. "The moment you wake up, you know you're not human anymore. You try to remember who you were as a human, but the longer you live, the harder it is."

"That's why you never removed the shrapnel, isn't it? It reminds you of being human rather than this perfect vampire you've become."

If our conversation hadn't been so somber, he might have teased me about calling him perfect.

"When you're going to live forever, it's easy to forget that you can still be killed. I carry that shrapnel to remind myself that even though I'm a vampire, I should never stray too far from being human. And the scars from my human life remind me what it was like before I became a vampire."

"Scars?"

Edmond stood up and unbuttoned his shirt. It was only the second time I'd properly seen his chest, and for a moment all I could do was stare at the beauty of it. He looked like a marble sculpture under moonlight, each muscle clearly defined, every line perfect except for the small ridge of the shrapnel.

Then he turned around and I gasped. "Oh, Edmond."

The smooth skin of his back was marked by a series of scars—both faint, white suggestions of old wounds and thick, ragged lines of scar tissue.

Climbing to my feet, I gently laid my hand on the longest scar. Beneath my fingertips, Edmond tensed, as if he'd expected me to shy away. He was so physically beautiful in every other way that it seemed somehow wrong to see this kind of damage, like someone had graffitied a work of art.

"Were these the injuries you got on your way to Paris?"

"No, these are older." His mouth made a bitter shape. "Like I said, there were a lot of thieves on the road, and I had no one to fight at my side. The injuries I got on my way to Paris healed when François turned me. If it wasn't for him, I'd have died from them. That's the only time I was ever grateful to have been born a peasant."

"Why?"

"Because no one would miss me when I became a vampire. That's how many of us started life—as peasants, slaves, orphans, the bottom rungs of society. No one cared what happened to us or even noticed if we disappeared."

Maybe that was why wealth and fashion and luxury meant so much to so many vampires—because they'd come from such poor beginnings.

"François was a nobleman, right?"

Edmond shrugged his shirt back on, hiding the scars of his past. "Correct."

"It must have been a shock to you, going from peasant to prince practically overnight."

Edmond turned, his expression clouding over. "A shock, oui, and one that ended up leading me down a dark path."

I waited patiently for him to explain.

"During the 1700s, after Ysanne and I had parted ways, I found myself friendless and homeless. I'd lost so many people by then, I could find no purpose in anything, and I genuinely started to hate the life I had chosen. I even contemplated suicide."

I hated to think that he'd ever been that lonely, that unhappy.

"Increasingly disillusioned with life, I returned to Paris." He gave me a solemn, steady look. "As soon as I settled in the city, I started a greedy, selfish life as part of the French aristocracy, indulging myself with everything I wanted, forgetting my humble roots and ignoring that I was trampling over the peasants, even though I used to be one. I drank to excess, and I killed two innocent people."

I flinched at that part, even though Edmond was only confirming what I'd always suspected about vampires—that they had blood-soaked pasts, shadows of horrors that would cling to them no matter how far they ran.

"But I was never happy, and the unhappier I became, the more I indulged myself, desperate to fill the empty place inside me."

He fell silent, gazing around the library as if seeing the leather-bound books, plush sofas, and crystal-drop chandeliers for the first time.

"What changed?" I prompted.

"The French Revolution."

The words shivered through me, conjuring up images of bloodied guillotines, baskets filled with severed heads, crowds baying for the blood of the people who'd crushed them for so long.

"If I'd been paying attention, I would have seen the grounds of society shifting beneath my feet. But I was too selfish and too stupid, and then it was too late. A mob dragged me from my house and I let them because I felt that it was my time to die. I hated what I'd become. But when I was in the tumbrel, I was struck by the very human realization that I didn't want to die. I could do more with my life, but not if I became one more victim to that vengeful blade."

"How did you escape?"

"It was not hard for a vampire."

"Then you found Ysanne and fled Paris together," I said, recalling what he'd previously told me.

"So now you know that I have done terrible things," Edmond said, looking steadily into my eyes. "I'm not proud of it, but I cannot change it. And I cannot pretend I have not sometimes been the monster you once thought me."

His expression didn't change but there was a ragged edge to his voice as he dredged up those old memories. I stared back at him, my head whirling. It had been a while since I'd thought of vampires as monsters, and that was almost solely due to my bond with Edmond. Now he was the very person who'd reminded me that my worst suspicions about vampires actually were, in part, true.

Could I still look at him the same way?

I dropped my gaze to Edmond's hands, picturing them covered in blood. I could never condone what he had done, and I didn't think he would ever fully forgive himself. But hadn't he suffered enough already? It would be so easy to judge him, but I'd never been in his position. I would never know what immortality felt like, or what it could drive someone to.

I realized then that I'd always thought of vampires as another species. They looked like us and they talked like us, but they *weren't* us.

It had never really sunk in that every single vampire had once been a human being.

They'd all loved and lost, suffered and prevailed.

They carried a wealth of history inside them, and a lifetime of scars on their souls.

"There is no greater loneliness than immortality," Edmond murmured.

Another reason why Ysanne and the Council had created this system of Houses and donors—so vampires never had to be alone. They could live together in their extravagant shelters, safe among their own people.

"Have you ever regretted becoming a vampire?" I asked.

"Every time I buried someone I loved or looked for a friend and realized I had none."

"If you could go back in time to the night that François killed you, would you still choose this?"

"Without a doubt."

"Despite everything you've just told me?"

"You could not understand unless you lived the life that I did as a human. Peasants were crippled by hard labor, never far from starvation. Their children were more likely to die than live. They died in staggering numbers from cholera, smallpox, tuberculosis, influenza, malaria, typhoid, dysentery. If you lived like that and someone offered you a way out, wouldn't you take it? Even if you knew there would be dark times ahead?"

"When you put it like that, yeah, I probably would," I admitted. "I've always tried to be grateful for what I have because I know that my mum's worked so hard all her life to provide for me and June. But I can't pretend that I don't sometimes get jealous when I see people with more, or that I don't sometimes imagine a life in which we didn't have to scrimp and save. Sometimes I was even jealous of June for having dreams when I didn't have any. I felt like I should, but at the same time it was pointless because I didn't think I'd ever be able to pursue them."

I'd never told anyone that before. Edmond was baring his soul to me, showing me all the dark and ugly parts of his past, the things he kept hidden from the rest of the world. I'd judged vampires and criticized them, seeing only their faults, but I'd never once thought about what horrors might have driven them to vampirism in the first place.

Leaning forward, I placed a soft kiss on his lips.

Edmond wasn't just showing me the ugly parts of himself, he was inadvertently uncovering all of mine too.

CHAPTER TWENTY

Renie

I sat at the end of Roux's bed, staring down at my feet. Roux lounged across the pillows, her back against the headboard, one foot propped on her knee.

"So you're saying you may have been wrong about vampires all this time?" she said.

"I'm starting to understand there's a lot more to them than I thought."

"What's brought on this change of heart, hmmm? Edmond, by any chance?"

"What makes you say that?"

She rolled her eyes. "I'm not blind, Renie, I see the looks between you two. Every time you're near each other, little love hearts float over your heads."

Most of what Edmond had told me I would take to my grave. The secrets he had given me were gifts, little treasures that I valued and wouldn't cheapen by passing them on to someone else—not even the person I was starting to think of as my best friend.

But that didn't mean I couldn't tell her anything. "Edmond told me that many vampires come from pauper roots. I can't imagine what life must have been like for them back then, and how much some of them must have suffered before making the choice to become a vampire."

"You'd have to live it to understand," Roux agreed, echoing what Edmond had said.

"All my life I've thought I was pretty hard done by. June and I were the kids who relied on castoffs from friends and neighbors because we couldn't afford new clothes. We ate cheap food, and walked to school, and lived in a crappy little house that always smelled damp. But compared to how Edmond lived at my age? I was a fucking princess. I've got no idea what suffering is, but I've spent half my life judging vampires who *have* suffered."

God, when I put it like that, it was a miracle Edmond could stand to look at me.

"Don't be so hard on yourself, Renie. You can't blame yourself for feeling like you had a shitty deal in life just because you've found out that someone else has a shittier deal. Someone else *always* has a shittier deal."

She had a point. I couldn't change all the bad things I'd thought in the past, same as Edmond would always have the stain of blood on his hands. But self-pity didn't help me, and moping around in my bedroom whining about how my crappy life *hadn't* been all that crappy was just self-indulgent.

"Now," Roux said, narrowing her eyes, "are you going to tell me what's going on with you and Edmond? You were all over each other at the masquerade ball."

"You noticed that?"

"Yes, I have these wonderful things called eyes."

This was it—the moment when I either came clean and told her the truth or I bottled it up inside and kept Edmond a secret.

Roux had been there for me from the moment I arrived at Belle Morte. She'd joined my crusade without a thought for her own safety, and she'd sacrificed her once in a lifetime experience in a Vampire House for my sake. I hadn't known her long, but she'd already proven herself to be the best friend I'd ever had, and she deserved the truth.

So I told her.

A devilish smile spread across Roux's face. "Is this some sort of secret affair?"

"No."

But... wasn't it? Edmond made me feel things I'd never felt before. He made my heart race and my tongue turn dry, and his bite brought a pleasure that no other vampire's could. The moments we spent together were like tiny gifts, no less precious for their intangibility.

Roux cocked her head to one side and gave me a knowing look. "Really?"

"I don't know. He comes with me every day to see June, and we spend time together after that if we can."

"Doing what?"

"Talking."

Roux didn't deflate at the lack of juicy details, but she probably understood all the little things that built an attraction between two people. It wasn't just physical; it was all the secrets they shared, the smiles they exchanged, all the little parts of their souls they laid bare for the other person to see.

The importance of talking should never be underestimated.

"He tells me so much that he doesn't tell other people, Roux."

A little flash of jealousy passed through me as I considered that Ysanne and Caoimhe probably knew all this about him too. In fact, they knew more. Ysanne had had *years* to get to know him. She knew his stories, his smiles, the sound of his laughter, the shadow of his grief. She knew every inch of his pale, perfect body, had run her hands and lips over his skin, the lines and angles that shaped him. They'd shared things together that I never could, and in that moment I *hated* her.

"I've never felt this way about anyone," I confessed.

Roux's face softened. She didn't patronize me by telling me the same things that I'd been telling myself all this time: that we could never be together, that I was epically stupid for getting involved with him in any way, that there could never be a happy ending for us.

"Do you think he feels the same way?"

Helplessly I lifted my hands and let them drop. "Who knows? But it doesn't matter. It can't last so there's no point speculating about who feels what."

"Oh, yeah, the no-relationship rule." She paused. "Maybe he'll ask you to stay."

"Right, because Ysanne would allow that."

"Okay, let's talk hypothetically," Roux said, waving her hands as if batting Ysanne's decrees from existence. "If Edmond *did* ask you to stay, what would you do?"

The question hung in the air. It was the last thing I wanted to think about, but I'd be lying if I said it hadn't crossed my mind.

"No, I wouldn't stay," I said.

Roux looked disappointed.

"What would Edmond do once I got gray hair and wrinkles and my boobs sagged to my belly button?" I said.

"Love is about more than physical appearance."

"I agree with the sentiment, but I'd never want Edmond to be stuck looking after an old woman."

"He could always make you a vampire."

"Don't be ridiculous. The rules about not turning humans are in place for a reason."

"It happened to June," Roux pointed out.

"Yeah, and look how that worked out," I said bitterly.

For the briefest second I actually thought about what it would be like to be a vampire, to have the world know my name and hordes of fans obsessively following my movements online. I imagined living in Belle Morte, spending my days in decadent nothingness. Then I imagined drinking the blood of starry-eyed donors, and that stupid fantasy turned into a nightmare of blood and teeth.

"How long are you supposed to keep working with her?" Roux asked.

"As long as it takes."

Roux chewed her lip, her eyes troubled. "But isn't there any kind of time limit on this? I mean—what happens if nothing works?"

I went cold all over, because that was a possibility that I'd refused to consider. "I . . ."

"Ignore me, I don't know what I'm talking about," said Roux.

"But—"

Roux put a finger to my lips. "No buts. Forget I said anything. I have absolute faith in you. You are going to save June."

I felt a sudden wave of affection for this girl. "I'm glad I have you in my life," I said.

"Ditto. And no matter what happens, I'll always be your shoulder to cry on."

"Unless your contract gets terminated before mine."

"Then I'll wait for you on the outside."

"What if it takes a long time?"

"Then I'll wait a long time. Deal?"

"Deal."

I sat on the edge of my bed, digging my fingers into the satin covers. Roux was indulging in a long bath; she'd left the door open as usual, and clouds of rose-scented steam drifted into the bedroom.

There'd been a time when June was my go-to girl if I was having guy troubles. That was before she became obsessed with vampires, before my refusal to indulge her had driven a wedge between us, but if things hadn't come to this point and we were both still living at home, she'd have been there if I needed her. Regardless of our differences, we were sisters, and that would always count for something.

This was exactly the kind of situation she would have dropped everything for. But I couldn't talk to her about it because the vampires had turned her into a monster. And I couldn't stop thinking about what Roux had said. What if I *couldn't* save her? What the hell happened then?

Suddenly I needed to see her, even though she wasn't the June I loved and remembered anymore.

But I couldn't go to the west wing on my own. I couldn't ask Edmond—it was 2 a.m., and even the vampires were usually in bed by now. Even if I knew where his room was, donors weren't allowed in the north wing, and thanks to vampires and their infuriating superhearing, I couldn't sneak in.

What about Ysanne? Did she go to bed at the same time as every-one else, or was she too busy doing whatever it was the Lady of the House did?

I couldn't imagine Ysanne snuggled up in bed, her hair a mess and her tailored clothing replaced by pajamas, but if she wasn't asleep, there was one place she'd likely be—her office.

I poked my head around the bathroom door. Roux was almost hidden beneath a fluffy mound of bubbles, her eyes closed, her face the picture of utter bliss.

"Roux?"

She cracked open an eye. "You okay?"

"I need to go and see June."

Her other eye snapped open and she sat up, her shoulders emerg-ing from the bubbles. "Now?"

"Yeah." I couldn't explain why this suddenly felt so important. It was as if I was clinging to the memory of what June and I had once been and what we might be again, but if I waited too long, that thread might unravel and slip through my fingers.

"I'll come with you," Roux said.

I held out a hand in a *stop* gesture as she started climbing to her feet. She froze halfway up, patches of skin peeking through the sheath of bubbles.

"You can't go on your own."

"I'm going to ask Ysanne to come with me," I said.

"She's probably in bed like everyone else."

"I know, but it's worth checking."

Roux scrutinized me.

"I know you're not stupid enough to go and see June on your own," she said.

"Give me a little credit."

Roux sighed and sank back into the tub. "Okay, go see her, but if she's not there, you come straight back."

"Yes, Mum."

She flicked bubbles at me.

I left her to enjoy her bath and headed for Ysanne's office.

All too soon her door was in front of me, and my nerves were quaking again. It wasn't as bad when I had Edmond, or even Ludovic or Isabeau, acting as a buffer between me and Ysanne, but tonight I was alone. My face tingled with remembered pain. The bruises from where she'd knocked me into the wall were faint marks now, easily hidden beneath a light layer of makeup, but the memory was more deeply ingrained. I had to remember that there was a beast inside Ysanne, something ancient and volatile and dangerous.

Taking a deep breath, I knocked on the door.

Silence followed. My heart thumped in my ears and tension prickled my skin. I hated being afraid of Ysanne—hated that she could make me feel like this without doing or saying anything.

"*Entrez.*"

I went into the office.

Ysanne sat behind her desk, her hair perfectly sleek. Isabeau perched on the edge of the desk; she was avoiding my eyes.

"A little late for you to be up, isn't it?" Ysanne said.

I got right to the point. "I want to see June."

Was it my imagination or did Isabeau stiffen slightly?

"Of course you do. Why else would you be here?" Ysanne said.

It was a question that didn't need an answer, so I just stood in front of her desk, shifting awkwardly from foot to foot.

"Why is this so important now?" Ysanne asked.

"I just . . . I need to see her."

It seemed foolish now. I felt like a child in front of Ysanne, making petulant and unnecessary demands.

Isabeau slid off the desk. "I'll give you some privacy," she murmured, and left the office.

Ysanne regarded me steadily.

How could I explain the need to see my sister to a woman who had lived for centuries and had probably forgotten what it had ever been like to be human?

"Please," I said. "I can't go alone."

She leaned back in her chair, her eyes never leaving mine. "It's not like you to request permission for anything. Usually you go charging off with no regard for the rules of my House."

I resisted the urge to roll my eyes. "I would never confront a rabid on my own."

Her eyebrows twitched, and I wondered if that was her version of rolling *her* eyes.

"Please," I said again, trying to appeal to her better nature, if she had one. "I need to do this."

I expected her to refuse. It was late after all, and even Ysanne needed sleep, but she took me off guard when she said, "Very well."

It was strange being in this room with Ysanne rather than Edmond. She didn't stand with me as I approached June, but stood in front of the door like a beautiful bodyguard.

I sat on the floor, trying to see past the growling, blood-caked figure in front of me to the girl June had been.

"I don't really know why I'm here," I said. "Roux and I were talking, and it reminded me of all the times *we* used to talk. I used to be able to tell you anything and you never judged me, but I don't think I gave you the same consideration."

I scrubbed my hands over the floor, the carpet fibers tickling the pads of my fingers. "I should have been more supportive of you when you started following vampires."

That was what I hadn't realized until I'd come to Belle Morte—I hadn't wanted to face up to it. But I couldn't pretend anymore.

"I never understood why you liked them so much but I should have supported you anyway, the same way you'd have supported me. Do you remember what you said to me the day before you left for Belle Morte? We'd argued about it, and you asked me why I couldn't just be happy for you. I don't know why I couldn't."

June's feet shuffled along the carpet, her chains clinking. Her eyes shone red in the darkness.

"I miss you, June. Even when I pushed you away, I never wanted you to go far. And now you've gone somewhere I can't follow." A lump rose into my throat. "I want to bring you back."

Those red eyes locked on me, her mouth champing around her gag. Muted moans built in her throat.

"Do you remember your first kiss? You were thirteen. His name was Ryan Miller, and you met him at school. You talked about him every day, remember? Every morning you'd spend ages doing your hair, trying to decide what he would notice, and I told you that if you really wanted to get his attention, you should shave your head."

June had laughed and chucked her hairbrush at me. I'd teased her endlessly about her crush, but even though I'd never been sure what she saw in Ryan Miller, she'd liked him and I'd been happy for her. Why had I forgotten that when it came to vampires?

After three weeks of obsessing over Ryan she'd rushed over to me at the end of one school day, her eyes glittering with excitement, and squealed in my ear that he'd kissed her behind the stacks in the library.

I'd been so happy for her, and even a tiny bit jealous, since my first real crush had been unrequited.

"You said it would last forever, and it seemed like it at the time, didn't it? When you're thirteen and you think you're in love, it really seems like forever. You can't possibly imagine that it will fizzle out in just a few weeks."

June had cried when she and Ryan broke up, but only for the time it took me to rush out and buy a tub of cookie dough ice cream, and then she'd confessed that she was secretly relieved because she'd started crushing on a guy in her English class.

"You always treated me as your friend rather than your sister. We'd talk about the guys we liked, make plans to get them to notice us, and then chatter all night about how our relationships were going. Usually over brownies and ice cream."

June moaned, her fingers twisting into claws as she tested her chains. It was so hard to look at her and picture the sweet, beautiful girl she'd been before she'd come here, so I looked at the floor, dragging my fingers back and forth through the carpet.

"And we can't talk about this stuff anymore."

I wanted to tell her that I was falling hard and fast for someone I couldn't possibly have, and I didn't know what to do about it, but no way could I say that in front of Ysanne.

Unless I pretended I was talking about another donor. If I didn't mention names or say anything specific, then Ysanne would have no reason to question it.

"Meeting a guy was the last thing I expected when I came here but somehow it happened. I hate that I can't talk about it with you, June. I hate that I can't ask your advice."

June shook her head from side to side, her hair whipping across her face in matted ropes. The rank whiff of old blood and decay emanated from her body.

"I wish you could meet him," I said, trying to pretend that we were back in our bedroom at home, how it had been when we were kids—dirty clothes lying in heaps on the floor, posters on the walls, the smell of cheap cherry lip gloss lingering in the air.

We'd often complained about the tiny room, the way our beds were crammed too closely together, with zero chance of privacy, but looking back now I realized that some of my happiest memories were there.

"He's not like any guy I've ever met. For one thing, he's gorgeous." It wasn't that I hadn't gone out with good-looking guys before, but none of them held a candle to Edmond. "But that's not why I like him."

My mind flashed to the beautiful image of Edmond's bare chest, and a smile teased my lips. "Okay, that's not the only reason. He's so private, but with me he opens up. I can see the real"—I stopped myself from saying Edmond's name—"guy beneath the facade. I think he needs to talk to me, and I hate the thought that we won't get to leave Belle Morte together. If I leave before him, who will he have to talk to?"

June wasn't even looking at me, her head hanging, her feet shuffling over the carpet.

"Oh, June," I whispered, my eyes blurring with tears. "Don't you understand anything I'm saying? Isn't there any part of you that remembers me?"

Her only answer was a muffled growl.

I pressed my hands to my eyes, clenching my teeth with frustration. I was fighting and fighting and fighting, but I never gained an inch of ground, and I was beginning to lose faith.

And then Ysanne made it so much worse.

"I longed to believe that something could be done about this situation, but perhaps it has been nothing more than wishful thinking on my part. Perhaps there really is no bringing back a rabid." Her voice didn't change, despite the somber nature of her words.

I turned and found that she'd walked up behind me so silently I'd never heard her move. She stood over me, her arms folded across her silk blouse, her face a pale moon in the darkness.

"What happens if we can't save her?" I asked.

Emotionlessly, Ysanne looked down at me. "There is only one thing that can be done with a rabid."

Understanding crashed into me. If I couldn't save June, Ysanne was going to kill her.

CHAPTER TWENTY-ONE

Renie

I scrambled to my feet. "You can't do that."

Ysanne stared back at me, and I realized how stupid my words were. This was Ysanne's House—she could do whatever she wanted.

Technically, June was already dead, so who would bat an eye over Ysanne killing her again?

But June was still my sister. The hopelessness I'd felt a moment ago was drowned by a sudden wave of protectiveness. No, I hadn't made any progress yet, but I just needed more time.

"You can't kill her."

"I can if I deem her a threat to my House."

"She's already a threat," I snapped.

Maybe that wasn't the smartest thing to point out, but Ysanne had already risked Belle Morte by keeping a rabid here. She couldn't then use June's dangerousness as a reason for putting her down because things weren't going her way.

I tried to match Ysanne's icy look. "She is my *sister* and I won't let you hurt her."

"My dear girl, do you really think you could stop me?"

I couldn't, and deep down, in a part of me that felt sick at the very thought of it, I knew that Ysanne might actually be right. June *was* dangerous. If she got loose again, people could die.

But killing June wouldn't solve all our problems.

"Maybe instead of worrying about what June might or might not do, you should be trying to find out who killed her in the first place," I said.

Ysanne's expression hardened, and I resisted the urge to take a step back.

"That is precisely what I have been doing, as well you know—"

"But you haven't found her killer yet. You need more time, and so do I."

"You have been here for two weeks and you've made not an ounce of progress. How long until you run out of memories and pretty things to say?"

"She's my sister."

"I am aware of that," Ysanne snapped. "But the safety of my people comes first, and that will not change for you. I'll give you one more week, and if you have still failed to make any progress, then I will have to do my duty as lady of this house and destroy the threat."

Tears burned my eyes, but the hard lines of Ysanne's face didn't soften. She didn't care if I lost my sister. And the dark part of me actually understood that.

She was talking about the lives of everyone at Belle Morte compared to someone who was effectively dead already. She was making the decision that any good leader would, but I still hated her for it.

Suddenly I couldn't stand to be around her anymore.

I pushed past Ysanne and stalked down the hall, tears spilling down my cheeks.

Roux had gone to bed by the time I got back to our room, but how was I supposed to sleep after what Ysanne had just said?

I suppose I should always have known that this was a possibility, but I hadn't let myself consider it, focusing instead on my absolute determination to save June.

But what if I couldn't?

That grim reality was staring me in the face now; I had to acknowledge it. But I didn't know how.

Was I supposed to tell Ysanne that she was right, that I had failed, and then stand by and let her kill June?

After tossing and turning for a couple of hours, I climbed out of bed—I hadn't even bothered to get undressed—and crept out of our room.

The house was still and quiet as I made my way out of the south wing and downstairs, heading for the exit that would let me into the grounds, but I paused when my ears picked up the faint sounds of someone crying.

I thought it was coming from the feeding room on my left, but when I looked in, the room was empty. It must be next door then, in the first of the two art rooms.

Carefully, I opened the door. Melissa sat with her back to me, her shoulders shaking with muffled sobs, turning something over and over in her hands. Aiden sat beside her, rubbing her back.

"Melissa?" I said, taking a tentative step into the room.

She jumped, almost dropping whatever she was holding.

"What are you doing here?" Aiden asked, with an edge to his voice.

"I heard Melissa crying. Are you okay?"

"Like you care," Aiden muttered, still rubbing Melissa's back.

"What's that?" I asked, looking at the thing in Melissa's hands.

She held it up. "It was meant to be a clay bowl. June made it."

My stomach felt like I'd swallowed ice water, and I moved farther into the room, my eyes fixed on the bowl—if it could really be called that. It was a misshapen, lumpy little thing, the hardened clay still marked by the indents of fingerprints.

My hands trembled as I touched it, tracing the place where June's fingers had been.

"Sculpting wasn't exactly her strong suit," Melissa said, and I couldn't help laughing.

"In her defense, she'd never done it before."

"She knew she wasn't any good at it, but she really enjoyed it," Melissa said, stroking the edge of the bowl.

My throat constricted. There was a whole side of June that had blossomed inside these walls, and I'd never know those parts of her.

Melissa put the bowl on the nearest wooden shelf.

"What's going on?" she asked.

"What do you mean?"

"Don't play dumb," Aiden said. Melissa put her hand on his arm, and he fell quiet.

"First June is transferred," Melissa said, "but we're all supposed to keep it secret, then you arrive, even though only one member of a family is supposed to be a donor at a time. Then you start asking all these questions."

"I just wasn't sure—"

Aiden cut me off with a slash of his hand. "You don't join in with any of the activities here, and you've hardly made any friends. I've asked around the other donors, and most of the time no one even knows what you're doing with your days. A couple of people have told me they've seen you coming and going from Ysanne's office, and Amit insists he's seen you coming out of the west wing with Edmond, even though no one's supposed to be in there."

"A few days ago, you were talking to Etienne," Melissa said. "It looked pretty intense, and I heard June's name, so I'm going to assume that whatever's going on is all tied up with her."

"How are we doing so far?" Aiden snapped.

I said nothing.

"I thought it was weird that June left without a word, but I trusted Ysanne, and then you turn up and things start getting *really* weird," Melissa continued. "June was my friend, and I want to know what the hell is going on."

My heart ached for her, but I couldn't tell her, just as I hadn't been able to tell Etienne or Jason. The only reason I'd told Roux was because she already knew too much.

"Melissa," I started, then stopped. It hadn't been that long since I'd brought her in here to question her, and now our roles were reversed, and I *hated* it. "I'm sorry," I said.

Her expression flattened. "Is this because we didn't want to talk to you when you first got here?"

"No. I just . . . I can't."

I thought she was going to yell at me, but her shoulders slumped.

"Fine," she said, her voice quiet. "Let's go, Aiden."

He glared at me.

I watched them walk out of the room, feeling like a complete shit. But what was I supposed to do?

I was so lost in my own fears and frustrations that I forgot I couldn't go outside without an escort, and I skidded to a halt when I reached the exit, guarded as usual by a black-uniformed member of security.

Crap, crap, *crap*.

Ysanne's stupid rules closed in on me no matter where I was or what I wanted to do. It was like she was always right behind me, breathing down my neck.

"Can I get someone to take me outside?" I asked the woman on the door, and she gave me a slightly odd look, perhaps not used to donors wanting to go out before the sun was even up.

"There's no need. Edmond and Isabeau are already out there," she said.

I hesitated. Obviously I wanted to talk to Edmond about this, but I hadn't anticipated doing it now, and I definitely wasn't doing it in front of Isabeau, who'd probably defend anything that Ysanne said.

The security guard opened the door for me and waited. Cold air billowed in. "Do you still want to go out?" she said when I didn't move.

"Yeah," I mumbled, and walked into the grounds.

The air was bitter, and for a moment I couldn't breathe. I stopped dead, sucking in a gulp of air that was more like ice.

It was a clear night, the sky velvet blue, but the stars were fading, the world paling at the horizon where the sun would soon rise. A few birds hopped along the top of the wall that ringed the mansion; the rest of the grounds were silent and still, like a painting.

There was no sign of Edmond and Isabeau.

I took several breaths, trying to calm myself. Bleak as things looked, it wasn't over yet. Ysanne wanted me to succeed because of what it meant for vampires, so she wouldn't pull the plug on this immediately.

There was still time.

But what could I do in the one week that I had left? Ysanne was right—the last two weeks hadn't made any difference to June's condition, so what else could I try?

I turned in the direction of the oak tree before I even realized it, then stopped. Edmond and Isabeau sat on a stone bench in the shadow of the mansion wall; they stopped talking when they saw me. Isabeau's face was soft with sympathy, but I couldn't decipher Edmond's expression.

Isabeau murmured something, then rose to her feet and walked away. Edmond approached me. The predawn light made him look impossibly beautiful, shadows highlighting the razor sharpness of his cheekbones, the pitch blackness of his hair, the diamond brightness of his eyes.

"Are you all right, mon ange?"

"No," I whispered, my eyes burning.

I wanted him to hold me.

I didn't want to be touched.

I was so *tired*.

"I went to the west wing with Ysanne and . . ." I trailed off.

Edmond's face was solemn, his eyes filled with sadness. He looked at me like he knew my heart was breaking.

"You already know, don't you? Is that what you and Isabeau were talking about?" I moved away before he could answer, stalking over to the stone bench where they'd sat.

Adrenaline was building in my chest, making me shake.

Edmond glided up behind me, quiet as a whisper, and I turned to him.

Maybe he moved first or maybe I did; I couldn't be sure. All I knew was that we were in each other's arms, kissing with a passion that took my breath away. Edmond pushed me back against the mansion wall, pressing his body against mine. I felt wild, undone by pleasure; my hands locked around his neck, one leg sliding around his hips, pressing him harder against me. Fire sparked between our dancing tongues.

I'd never kissed like this; never felt that I couldn't get enough of a man. I shoved my hands under his shirt, my fingertips trailing the ridge of shrapnel before gliding up his stomach and chest. I placed my hand over the place where his heart used to beat. His skin was cool beneath my palm. I wanted to warm it with my hands, my tongue . . .

Edmond broke the kiss, grabbing my wrists and pinning them above my head. I was gasping for breath, my skin flushed, my heart thudding, but he was as quiet and pale as ever. Crazily, I wondered if vampires really could perform in bed, or if they'd spent so long being impassive statues that they couldn't remember what it felt like to let go.

But that couldn't be right. Edmond wasn't gasping for breath like I was, but his eyes blazed with desire. The hard bulge in his trousers pressed against me. My lips were swollen with the force of our kisses but I wanted more. I wanted to drink him down like wine, to tear off his clothes and explore every part of his body with every part of mine.

I wanted him so much it frightened me.

"Enough," Edmond whispered. His dark gaze roved over me, lingering on my chest, my lips. "We cannot do this, Renie."

I knew that just as well as he did, but I couldn't think straight. Pleasure was a thick fog filling my head, and all I could think about was how delicious Edmond tasted and how good he'd felt beneath my hands. All I could think about was getting another taste.

"You make me want to lose myself and that cannot happen," Edmond said.

He still stood so close that our breath would have mingled if he had any. But the overwhelming desire that had ripped through me had died down, and suddenly I wanted him away from me.

"Let me go," I whispered, and he did.

For a moment, neither of us moved.

"Ysanne told you what happened earlier," I said.

"She did," he said.

That awful shaky feeling swelled in my chest, and I struggled to form words.

"We can't let her do this."

"Renie—"

"What if we could get June out of here somehow? There must be somewhere we can hide her, somewhere she'd be safe—"

"Renie—"

"—there *has* to be, because we're not giving up on her—"

"*Renie.*"

I stopped, my throat raw and knotted.

Edmond took my hands, his cool fingers rubbing along my knuckles.

"Oh my god. You're on Ysanne's side, aren't you?" I whispered.

"This isn't about taking sides."

"But you do agree with her."

Edmond weighed his words. "I think we need to prepare ourselves for the worst."

"You told me you wouldn't give up on her."

"I know, but, Renie, nothing's working. June hasn't improved, and we may need to face the fact that she's not going to. We can't keep her hidden forever, and it's too dangerous to move her."

"So I'm just supposed to let her *die*?"

Edmond closed his eyes. "I would give anything to make this better for you, but I can't."

"I won't let Ysanne kill her," I snarled, snatching my hands away from him.

"Then what do you suggest?" His voice was gentle, and for some reason it only made me angrier. "At what point do you accept that we can't help her?"

"I'll never accept that, and I thought you had my back."

"I do, but June is dangerous, and she's suffering, and if you can't help her . . ." Edmond didn't finish the sentence.

He didn't need to.

Thick, hot humiliation curdled in my stomach, and my eyes burned with tears. June and I had once agreed that no matter how bad a guy hurt us, we would not cry in front of them, but I couldn't help myself.

I hadn't imagined that Edmond would agree with Ysanne, and that realization was like a knife sliding between my ribs. I glanced up at the sky. The stars had almost disappeared, just faint silver impressions upon a rapidly lightening sky.

"Fuck you, Edmond," I said. "*Fuck you.*"

I stormed past him, my arms wrapped around myself, both to protect myself from the cold and to quell the angry adrenaline shuddering through me.

Screw Ysanne.

Screw Belle Morte.

Screw Edmond.

No one was taking my sister away.

CHAPTER TWENTY-TWO

Edmond

Renie's words echoed through his mind, sharp and angry. He didn't blame her. He had given her hope and now he was taking it back, leaving her with nothing. But he had no choice.

He should never have got close to her; then he wouldn't have hurt her so badly. When Renie had first arrived he'd been determined to keep her at a distance, but she'd undone all his defenses, pulling him in with her passion and defiance. And yet that was exactly why he shouldn't have let things go this far. For all that passion, Renie was still so fragile, so breakable.

Humans could burn so brightly, but they were short lived and so easily snuffed out.

Faces flashed through his mind: Lucy, Charlotte, Marguerite, Elizabeth. Each of them he had loved. Each of them he had lost.

He'd sworn that he would never fall for anyone again. He would build a wall around his heart, harden it with ice, and never allow anyone with romantic intentions to pass beyond it. But somehow Renie had. She'd found the chinks in his armor and had slipped through to the vulnerable parts of him.

Something about that girl had started a fire inside him, and every time he tried to put it out, it blazed to life, hotter and fiercer than ever.

Edmond lifted a hand to his mouth, tracing his lips and remembering the sweetness of Renie's mouth. He knew he couldn't keep her, but he didn't know how to let her go.

Ysanne walked around the side of the mansion. A faint breeze passed through the garden, making her blond hair flutter. The way she dressed and the things she liked had changed, but she was still the same ethereally beautiful vampire who had saved an orphan boy a few hundred years ago.

"What happens if you do kill June?" he asked.

"I don't know," Ysanne admitted.

"Will you send Renie away? Or keep her here until we know who is behind this?"

"I haven't decided yet."

"Are you sure that someone *was* trying to kill her? It's been ten days, and there hasn't been another attempt."

"I suspect that's because she's been spending so much time with you. There are few vampires in this house who would attempt to take you in a fight."

"But why would anyone want Renie dead? This doesn't make sense."

"It's not your job to make sense of it. It's mine, and I will."

"Maybe you should allow Renie more time then."

Ysanne's gaze sharpened. "Tell me something, mon garçon d'hiver," she said.

He waited.

"There's nothing between you and the Mayfield girl, correct?" A steely note entered Ysanne's voice. "Because I cannot believe you would flout our rules like that."

In a world that treated vampires like gods, Edmond had become unused to feeling guilty. But since Renie had arrived at Belle Morte he'd been forced to reacquaint himself with those feelings—first, for keeping the truth about June from Renie, then for his subsequent treatment of Renie, and now for having to lie to his oldest friend.

"Of course not," he said, the words bitter in his mouth.

"Good, because you know why it cannot be," Ysanne said. "Humans look up to us and adore us, but in the end they always leave us."

A note of grief entered her voice, and Edmond knew she wouldn't show that vulnerability to many people.

He gazed around the garden, at the frost glittering on every blade of grass, ice forming lacy patterns on the naked branches of the trees. Vampires could barely feel the cold, and when he was with Renie it was hard to forget that the world wasn't sunshine and light.

"It was cold like this when we met," he said, changing the subject. "Colder."

It was so long ago, but Edmond could still remember the drifts of snow that choked the land, the knifelike wind that slashed through his rags to his starving body, that moment of horror and relief when he knew he wouldn't survive.

Then Ysanne had appeared, a blood-spattered angel in the snow.

He would never forget the winter they'd spent in that house, the vampire and the boy she'd taken pity on, huddled together in front of a fire while the wind howled outside.

"There's something I need to ask you," Edmond said.

He didn't know why he'd never asked before. Perhaps he'd been afraid of what she'd say.

"Why did you leave me?" he said.

She stiffened, her face smoothing into a hard mask.

Theirs had been a strange, symbiotic friendship—the boy feeding the vampire from his own veins, the vampire hunting food for the boy. They had talked to pass the frozen days and nights, they had played games, and they had forged a solid bond.

Yet one morning, when spring had broken through winter's brittle hold, Edmond had woken up to find that Ysanne had gone. There was no message, no warning, just the disappearance of the one friend he'd had in the world.

"Because I was afraid," Ysanne said.

It was the last thing he'd expected her to say. Ysanne didn't often admit to fear, not even to him.

"If you really must know, *mon cher*, I feared that our friendship was becoming something more."

That was hardly news to Edmond. He'd been a lonely, hungry, frightened boy, adrift in a world that didn't care if he lived or died. Ysanne was beautiful, immortal—almost magical in the way she had appeared to save him. It would have been strange if he *hadn't* started to fall for her. But he'd never suspected she'd felt the same. He had looked at her with a kind of hero worship, and in his young mind it wasn't possible that she could return his affections.

"I knew the way you looked at me, and in the last weeks of our time together, I realized that I was in danger of reciprocating," Ysanne said.

"Would that have been so bad?" They'd wound up in bed anyway, just several decades down the line.

"For me, yes. I feared that you would find your way into my heart, and I wasn't ready for that. My husband's death . . . it was still too raw." Ysanne took his hand. "But I do regret abandoning you. I thought of you often, and wondered what it would be like to find you again, and then fate brought you back to me."

"It never occurred to you to turn me?"

"No. All I saw was someone who had the potential to get into my heart, and at that time I couldn't allow it. I had to leave you because I was too afraid to keep you."

Edmond couldn't decide if she had exhibited the kind of strength that failed him when he was around Renie, or if it was cowardice that had driven her to slip out the door one day and leave him sleeping and alone.

Ysanne's eyes clouded over, a rare display of genuine emotion.

"Perhaps it was selfish, but if that is the case, I have more than paid the price for my selfishness since then."

Edmond took her other hand, clasping it between their bodies. "*Assez!* The losses you have suffered were tragedies but they were not atonement for past mistakes."

This was the side of Ysanne that she would never show the world, the parts that still ached with love and loss, with the vulnerable, human echoes.

"Forgive me for bringing it up," Edmond said. "I did not mean to open old wounds."

Ysanne placed her hands on both sides of his face and laid a cool, gentle kiss on his forehead. "No forgiveness is needed, my dear old friend."

Neither of them mentioned Renie again—Ysanne trusted that he had told her the truth, and he could not reveal how he was betraying that trust.

Even dear old friends had their secrets.

CHAPTER TWENTY-THREE

Renie

I didn't go back to my room. I wouldn't be able to sleep and it wasn't fair to wake Roux, so I went to my usual haven, the library, and tried to burn off some of the awful energy inside me by stalking up and down the room. The tears were gone, and there was only rage, clashing with fear until it felt like my chest was going to explode.

But after a while, the tears returned, and all that anger drained away, leaving me hollow and exhausted. I collapsed onto the nearest sofa, curling up in a ball. "I'm not giving up, June. I'm *not*," I whispered.

There was another way to help her, I just hadn't found it yet, but I would, I just needed to rest my eyes . . .

I jerked awake with a soft cry, and for a dizzy moment I couldn't remember where I was. The library came into focus around me, and I slumped back on the sofa, digging the heels of my hands into my eyes as everything flooded back.

I had no idea what time it was, but I needed a fucking drink.

The bar was empty.

I ignored the recipe books, threw some ice into a glass, and invented my own cocktail. It'd been a while since I'd eaten, so I knew I should pace myself, but I just didn't care.

My elbow caught the tongs I'd used for the ice; they fell to the floor with a loud clatter. "Shit," I muttered, bending to pick them up.

Jason poked his head around the door. "You okay? I heard a crash."

"I'm fine."

I sat on one of the high stools and sipped my homemade cocktail. A sharp crash of flavors hit my mouth, and I pulled a face. Maybe I should have stuck to the recipe book.

But maybe my own cocktail was strong enough to numb the ache in my chest.

"You're hitting the sauce early," Jason commented, coming up behind me.

"Nothing else worth doing."

"Uh-oh, this sounds bad." He claimed the stool next to me, swiveling so we were face to face. "What's up?"

"Nothing. Everything."

"Come on, honey, spill." He placed a hand on my knee and gave me a little shake.

"I can't."

"Hmm." Jason drummed his fingers on the marble bar top. "Secret stuff, huh? Maybe I should hit the booze as well."

I saluted him with my drink. "Yes, you should."

"You want to mix me up whatever it is you've got there?"

I hopped off the stool and walked around the bar. "It's new. I call it the Renie Special."

"Sounds sexy."

"Oh, it is."

I mixed up the drink as best I could remember and slid it across the bar. Jason took an experimental spin and blanched. "Jesus, what did you *put* in here?"

"Everything. It grows on you."

He took another sip, his lips puckering like he was sucking on a lemon.

Rejoining him on the other side of the bar, I clinked my glass with his. "Cheers."

"Are you going to tell me what's going on?"

I gazed down into the pinkish-orange depths of my drink.

"I'm not stupid, Renie," he said gently. "I know you're not just a normal donor. There's something going on with you, Edmond, Ysanne, and the west wing, and Roux's already told me she can't talk about it, and that's okay. But I am here if *you* want to talk about it. You know what they say—a problem shared is a problem halved."

"It would still be a bigger problem than I can handle," I muttered. "And I'm sorry, but I still can't talk about it."

We sat in companionable silence for a while, drinking, and when our glasses were empty I jumped up and refilled them. Already, pleasant warmth was spreading through my brain, the tension in my limbs melting away as the alcohol took over. Normally I didn't get drunk so fast, but I hadn't eaten and it was a *very* strong cocktail. Nonetheless, I didn't hold back as I mixed up two more.

"You're right, they do grow on you," Jason said.

We clinked glasses again, and I took a deep gulp, letting the alcohol wash through me and scour away all the anger and uncertainty.

"I'll give you my sob story instead. Gideon *still* hasn't asked to drink from me. Maybe I should just give up," Jason said.

"You did say not to get attached."

"I'm not getting attached; I just wanted to know what his bite felt like."

"Probably the same as every other vampire's."

"No, I think it would be better with Gideon, the same way sex is better if it's with someone you really, really like."

That made me think of the perfect expanse of Edmond's chest and the way my nerve endings flared when he kissed me, and I turned my head to hide the color creeping into my cheeks.

Giving blood to Edmond, kissing him—it surpassed anything I'd experienced, so sex with him would probably be better than any sex I'd ever had.

"Maybe it's better if you never find out," I said, and my words were as much for my benefit as Jason's. "If he'd fed from you and it had been amazing, then it would only be harder for you to not get attached. It's so easy to listen to your heart rather than your head, but these are vampires we're talking about. We're nothing more than a blip on their radar, easily replaced by the thousand other potential donors clamoring at the door."

Jason looked crestfallen but there was no point sugarcoating the truth. My heart felt like someone had stomped all over it; I didn't want Jason going through the same thing.

"We don't need them anyway," I said. "They can carry on hiding from the world in their stupid mansions, and we can both do better."

"Better than Gideon?" Jason sounded aghast.

"Better than any vampire."

I took a long gulp of my drink, as if that would bolster my belief in my own words. Jason scrutinized me.

"I'm no psychiatrist, but I'm guessing you're feeling down about a vampire."

Maybe it was because I was feeling tipsy, or maybe I was just sick of keeping it bottled up inside, but suddenly it spilled out.

"Edmond and I have kind of been having a secret relationship, but it has to end because he's a bastard and he's not on my side, and vampires can't be with humans, and I'm going to get old and die while he gets to look young and gorgeous forever."

Jason stared at me with wide eyes, and my stomach churned. I really shouldn't have said that.

"I knew you had eyes for Edmond—frankly, I don't blame you— but you two actually had a thing going on? Holy shit."

I grabbed his hand. "Please, you can't tell anyone. Except Roux, she already knows."

He rolled his eyes. "Of course I'm not going to tell anyone. What kind of gossip hound do you take me for?" He waited a beat before grinning mischievously. "Are you going to spill the juicy details or do I have to beg? Because I'll beg."

I laughed, nudging him with my foot. "It's really not that juicy."

"You guys didn't do the horizontal tango?"

"Not even close."

"Bummer. I've always wondered what sex with a vampire was like." His mischievous smile melted into something dreamy. "I bet it's amazing."

"Or maybe it's complete crap. Maybe *that's* why vampires and donors can't be together, because if a donor ever found out how bad vampires are in bed, their whole image would be shattered."

That was definitely the cocktail talking.

"Oh please. They've had hundreds of years to polish their moves. Do you really think Edmond's no good in bed?"

I started to lie, but the words refused to come. "I think he'd probably ruin me for every man on the planet. Which is why it's such a good thing that we never got that far."

"I bet Gideon's good in bed too."

"Here's to stupid vampires being excellent lovers that we will never experience for ourselves," I said, raising my glass.

"Hear, hear." Jason clacked his glass against mine so enthusiastically that he almost fell off his stool. "They probably know every position in the *Kama Sutra*, and then some."

"And they're probably all so flexible that half the moves can only be done with other vampires."

"They probably have BDSM dungeons in the north wing."

"Or sex swings in every bedroom."

We both snorted with laughter. It felt good to laugh, and the knot in my chest eased fractionally, even if it was only temporary.

Two donors—Ranesh and Abigail—wandered in, both bearing fresh bite marks and dreamy expressions. Jason waved to them, and Abigail waved back, but her hand was limp, flopping on her wrist.

"Is she okay?" I whispered.

Bite daze, he mouthed back. He shot another look at Abigail as she sidled behind the bar and examined the bottles on the glass shelves with the intense concentration of someone who was either drunk or drugged.

"She needs to be careful," Jason whispered. "She's looked like that every time she's been bitten lately. She's in danger of becoming an addict, and if that happens, her time here is over."

"What are you two whispering about?" Ranesh asked, sitting at the bar.

"Nothing," Jason said. Glancing back at me, he motioned with his eyes to the door.

I nodded. We drained our drinks and jumped off our stools, but before we left the room, I launched myself across the bar and snagged a bottle of tequila from the shelf.

"I don't think you're supposed to take the bottles out of the bar," Abigail said, slurring her words.

I pretended not to hear her.

We were barely out of the room when I unscrewed the bottle and took a swig. Tequila burned my throat, making me cough. Jason took the bottle and drank deeply.

"Oh man, we're going to get hammered," he said.

"Well on the way," I said.

"Crap," Jason suddenly hissed, and I spotted Gideon heading toward us.

I snatched the bottle of tequila and stuffed it under my jacket, crossing both arms across my chest.

Jason ran his fingers through his hair, and straightened his shirt, standing a little taller as Gideon drew near. But Gideon just looked at me oddly, not sparing a single glance for Jason. As soon as he was gone, Jason deflated like a sad balloon.

"Am I just invisible?" he said.

I glanced down. "I think I may have distracted him."

The way my arms were tightly folded over the bottle I held to my chest made it look like I was grabbing my own boobs.

Jason smiled when he looked down, but it was sad at the edges. The poor boy had it bad for Gideon.

"Goddammit," he muttered, looking after Gideon even though the vampire had already gone. "Why does he turn me on more than any guy I've ever met? I want to turn it off, but I can't."

"That's vampires for you. I wish I had something more positive to offer, but I'm fresh out of that."

"Right." Jason stuck his hand into my jacket and retrieved the tequila. "We both need cheering up, and I know just how to do it." Dramatically, he pointed the bottle down the hallway. "To your room."

Jason's idea of cheering us both up turned out to be an impromptu fashion show, which involved pulling every item of clothing from the wardrobe and seeing what he could fit into.

Between costume changes we both glugged tequila.

After I'd wriggled into a fur-trimmed velvet dress, Jason attempted to style my hair, but he was too drunk for his usual magic and gave up halfway through, leaving me with a very peculiar half-up, half-down do.

Now he'd stripped down to his boxers and was trying to squeeze into one of my gowns, dark-green lace with a sweetheart neckline. He wrestled with it, managing to get it over his hips but unable to pull it up around his chest, until finally there was a tearing noise and the dress slid halfway up his torso, brushing the edges of his nipples.

He scrutinized himself in the mirror. "What do you think? Too slutty?"

I laughed.

Gathering up his skirts, he walked to the far end of the room. "And now," he announced, "we have the latest creation by the world-famous Renie Mayfield, modeled by the ever-fabulous Jason Grant."

He strutted down an imaginary catwalk, pouting and tossing his head.

I laughed so hard tequila almost shot out of my nose. My ribs ached and it felt so good; I couldn't remember the last time I'd laughed like this.

Midway through Jason's catwalk triumph, Roux walked in.

Jason froze, one foot still lifted into the air. "Ladies and gentlemen, we seem to have encountered a slight interruption."

"Um . . . what are you guys doing?" Roux asked, eyeing the clothes scattered across the floor.

"Fashion show," I declared, proffering the tequila. "You want in?"

She frowned slightly, looking at me in my fur-trimmed dress and Jason in his ripped one, and her lips twitched. "Are you guys drunk?"

"Just a little," Jason said, holding his thumb and forefinger about an inch apart.

"Shh, don't tell anyone," I added, pressing a finger to my lips.

Roux closed the door. "Did you steal that tequila from the bar?"

"No," I said.

She narrowed her eyes.

"Maybe," I amended.

Jason chose that moment to perform a twirl, lace skirts billowing around him and showcasing the huge tear he'd made in the side of the dress.

Roux tutted. "Well, that's ruined now. What if Renie wanted to wear it tomorrow?"

I frowned blearily up at her. "Tomorrow?"

"You really don't check your events calendar, do you? Jemima Sutton, Lady of Nox, is visiting tomorrow with a small entourage, so we'll be having a little meet and greet with them."

I scoffed. "For people who've lived so long, you'd think they'd find more interesting things to do than dress up like dolls for endless parties. The whole vampire culture is ridiculous."

"You don't seem to mind wearing their culture," said Roux, her voice gentle but firm as she pointed at my dress and the clothes spread out around me in a sea of silk and suede, velvet and crystals. "And you don't seem to mind drinking their culture."

That shut me up.

"You'll have to forgive us. We're both brokenhearted," Jason explained. His eyes were tragically wide and he flung a hand to his brow in a theatrical semiswoon. Unfortunately, he tripped over his skirts and crashed into the side of Roux's bed.

Roux looked back at me. *Edmond?* she mouthed.

I nodded, unable to bring up June yet. I'd rather pretend that this was just about a guy who'd broken my heart, rather than addressing *why* he had.

Roux's expression softened. "I guess I can't let my friends have a party without me." She plucked the bottle from my hand and took a swig.

"You have to dress up if you want to join in. That's the vampire way," Jason said, looking up from his sprawled position on the floor. His skirts were up over his head, like a bridal veil.

"I can do that." Roux's outfit probably cost a fortune, like everything else in this place, but she slipped it off and tossed it in the corner like it was old rags. In her underwear, she crouched down and sifted through the clothes on the floor.

Jason picked himself up and applauded her.

We passed the morning in a blur of tequila and dresses, pretending we were celebrities walking down the red carpet, making up fictional interviews for each other, and acting out various celebrity scandals.

It was ridiculous, but it kept me from thinking about June, and that meant I never wanted it to end.

"You know what we're missing?" Jason slurred, gazing up at us from the floor. He'd fallen ten minutes ago and hadn't been able to get back up. I'd have helped him if I wasn't so wobbly myself.

"What?" Roux asked.

"Music. We've already done our catwalk and Oscars ceremony; now we need the after-party."

Roux, sitting on the floor next to me, looked down at her hands where they rested in her lap. "I guess . . . no, forget it."

"Forget what?"

"It's just . . . maybe I could sing for you both." Roux was never normally nervous, but now her hands twisted in her lap, her eyes not meeting ours.

"You're a singer?" Jason said.

She smiled weakly. "It's been a while."

Jason tried to pull himself into a sitting position, and fabric tore somewhere. There was no saving that poor dress now. He couldn't seem to maneuver his limbs into the right position, and eventually he gave up, accepting that lying on the floor in a sea of green lace was the best he could do.

Roux took a deep breath, still unable to meet our eyes.

I don't know what I expected, but the gorgeous, smoky quality of her voice as she launched into "The Sound of Silence" took me completely by surprise. Even though a couple of notes wavered at the beginning, where nerves had a death grip on her, she quickly gained confidence, that beautiful voice spilling easily from her lips.

Halfway through the song, she glanced up and offered a shy smile.

Jason pumped his fists when Roux finished. "Encore, encore!"

Roux hesitated only a second before starting to sing a slow, husky rendition of "True Colors."

By the time that was over, Jason had fallen asleep in the ruined heap of my dress, muffled snores trickling out of the rumpled layers of lace.

Roux smiled and shook her head. "Too much tequila."

I was starting to feel pretty queasy myself, alcohol writhing like a nest of snakes in my stomach. A little nap seemed more and more like a good idea.

"You told Jason the truth about Edmond, didn't you?" Roux said.

"How did you know?"

"Women's intuition."

"I probably shouldn't have dragged him into this," I muttered.

Not that I could change it now.

"We should wait for him, too, whenever we get out of here. I don't want to lose contact with either of you," Roux said.

I nodded.

There was a bitter irony in the fact that this House had taken away my sister, but had given me two friends that I'd never anticipated.

"I think I'm about to pass out, but I want you to know that I'm lucky to have you—both of you," I said. "And that's not the tequila talking."

"I know."

Roux added something about being glad she'd met me, but I was already sinking into a drunken, dreamless sleep.

CHAPTER TWENTY-FOUR

Renie

According to Roux, who had it on good authority from Melissa, Jemima was coming to discuss the possibility of a British version of *Vampire Dates*, an American show in which people competed to win a date with a vampire. It was a big hit in the US, and apparently there'd been a surge of donor applications since the first episode premiered two years ago, but I couldn't imagine any of the Belle Morte vampires participating. If it did become a reality, good luck to anyone who won a date with Ysanne.

The Nox vampires—Jemima and five others—arrived mid-afternoon the next day. I didn't understand why she needed an entourage to discuss a TV show with Ysanne, but maybe the Nox vampires had friends at Belle Morte.

Ysanne, flanked by Isabeau and Edmond, waited to greet her guests in the vestibule. Ludovic, Míriam, Etienne, Catherine, and Phillip formed a line behind her. The donors gathered on the stairs, and I got the impression we were supposed to be seen and not heard.

Jemima was smaller than Ysanne, a dainty slip of a woman who looked only about sixteen, with cascading blond hair and porcelain skin. She offered a hand for Ysanne to shake, and her wrist was as delicate as spun glass.

"Welcome to Belle Morte, old friend," Ysanne said. "We are honored by your presence."

Jemima smiled, and even that was dainty. "We are honored to be here."

"I am sure you're all thirsty, so please avail yourselves of my donors." Ysanne indicated us with a sweep of her hand. She might as well have been informing Jemima to enjoy the snack bar, which inside Belle Morte was really what we amounted to.

Nox was the second most prominent Vampire House in England, and though I didn't know the protocol for visiting vampires, Jemima probably got first pick of the menu.

She approached the staircase, her eyes sweeping us until they landed on me.

"I'll take that pretty young lady," she announced.

Amit shot me an envious look, and I resisted rolling my eyes. The other donors probably saw this as a huge honor.

"Irene, please escort Lady Jemima to one of our private rooms," Ysanne said.

I went down the steps to meet Jemima.

I led her to the feeding room with the piano in it, and she sank gracefully onto the chaise longue, looking at me with eyes that had seen more than I could comprehend. I wasn't sure how old she was, but if she ruled Nox, then she had to be one of the older vampires, maybe even on par with Ysanne.

It had surprised me to learn that Edmond had been only twenty-two when he died, but Jemima had either been amazingly well preserved in life, or she really had been a teenager when she died.

Somehow that made me vaguely uncomfortable.

Her old eyes seemed totally out of place in a face younger than mine.

I hovered by the chaise longue, and Jemima smiled gently. "This must be a bit odd for you."

"Odd?"

"You become used to the vampires that you live with, and then strangers come into your home and you don't know what to make of them."

Belle Morte wasn't my home, but there was little point saying that.

I sat down next to the vampire. It felt like the first time I'd been bitten all over again, nervousness and unease coiling tightly in my stomach.

Jemima's gaze drifted over my throat, a flash of hungry red heating her eyes.

"Um, I prefer the wrist," I said, holding up my hand. Only Edmond was allowed to bite my throat, but I supposed that was over now.

She nodded graciously and took my hand. "You're so tense. You must relax or it will hurt." Jemima actually sounded worried.

She bent over my wrist, her nostrils flaring as she caught the scent of blood pumping beneath my skin. Her lips parted, revealing dagger-sharp, fully elongated fangs.

As she bit down, I closed my eyes, the familiar pain rushing through me, and tried not to think about how different it had been with Edmond.

Jemima drank her fill, and sealed the wound with the daintiest sweep of her tongue. "Thank you."

Did I hear that right? No one had ever thanked me for my blood before.

Jemima seemed a gentler and more benevolent lady than Ysanne—if only June had requested to be a donor at Nox instead of Belle Morte.

"Are you looking forward to this evening?" Jemima asked.

Once her vampires had drunk from the Belle Morte donors, they would disappear with Ysanne to talk about whatever they needed to, until the party later on. Then I assumed they'd head home to their own house. Once, they might have stayed in the west wing, but they couldn't do that as long as June was there.

"Sure," I said.

A tiny line appeared between Jemima's eyebrows. "You don't sound convinced."

For a wild moment I thought about telling her everything. I didn't know what happened to Council members who broke the rules, but I rather liked the thought of Ysanne's title being stripped from her. If she wasn't in charge anymore, then she no longer had the authority to decide June's fate. Jemima seemed reasonable— maybe I could explain to her what we had been trying to do with June. Maybe she'd understand. The words climbed onto my tongue, but I bit them back. Jemima seemed reasonable, but I knew nothing about the rest of the Council and I couldn't gamble with June's life like that.

"I'm just tired," I lied. "I'll be okay by tonight."

Jemima seemed reassured, and I wished again that June had gone to Nox instead of Belle Morte. But wishes helped no one.

I climbed to my feet. "I should go."

"I'll see you tonight," Jemima said.

Edmond

Once the Nox vampires had gone to their separate feeding rooms with the donors they'd chosen, no one noticed Edmond slip away from the vestibule.

He supposed he should be glad that it was Jemima who'd chosen Renie, rather than one of the three male vampires she'd brought, but he didn't like the thought of anyone biting Renie except him.

He hadn't forgotten that first moment she finally relaxed, her soft body melting against him, her gasps as he drew her blood into his mouth. Perhaps it was selfish of him, but he wanted to be the only one who gave her that pleasure.

As he reached the hall that led to the west wing, soft footfalls sounded behind him, and he turned to see Ludovic following him.

"What are you doing?" Ludovic said.

"I don't know," Edmond replied honestly.

"Does Ysanne know about this?"

"There's nothing to know about." A pause. "But no, she doesn't."

"You're going to see the rabid, aren't you?"

Edmond stopped walking, looking firmly at his friend. "She still has a name."

Ludovic looked back just as firmly. "She's not June Mayfield anymore. There is nothing human left inside her, and there never will be."

Edmond wanted to protest, for Renie's sake, even though he'd destroyed things between them by admitting that he'd lost hope of saving June.

But he said nothing.

They walked to June's darkened room together and went inside, facing the pitiful creature that had been Renie's sister. The air was ripe with the smell of fresh blood running from June's wrists as she fought against her restraints.

"The kindest thing would be to put her out of her misery," Ludovic said.

"I know. But it'll destroy Renie."

"So will giving her continued false hope."

"I really wanted this to work, for all of us as much as for Renie. Imagine what would happen if we could save rabids."

"I would never have become a vampire," Ludovic mused.

His human life had ended violently, after being attacked by a rabid himself.

Edmond's mind drifted to François. When François had started becoming aggressive, killing rather than only taking as much blood as he needed, Edmond hadn't understood that François had been turning rabid.

And he'd been afraid.

François had been not quite a father, but perhaps a mentor. Or not quite that, either, but still, the man who had given Edmond a world far removed from his cold, brutal, and unforgiving human life. When his nature had started to change, Edmond hadn't known what to do about it.

Then an angry mob had taken care of the problem for him.

Edmond sighed as he raked his fingers through his hair. Memories built in his head, the pressure of the past weighing him down.

He hadn't understood what had happened to François until reuniting with Ysanne. She'd put the pieces together and taught him about the rabid threat.

She'd taught him that the only good rabid was a dead rabid, and now, hundreds of years later, she was ignoring her own advice.

June growled and rattled her chains, bringing Edmond back to the present. He watched June, her eyes glowing with blood-colored madness, her chained hands curling into claws, blood streaming down her wrists where the shackles rubbed through layers of skin.

Pity spiked inside him.

He took a step closer.

"I could end this," he murmured.

Ludovic looked sharply at him.

"I could kill June now, and it would all be over."

"Renie would never forgive you," Ludovic said. "And I don't think you want that. You care about her, don't you?"

"Yes," Edmond confessed. "I'm a fool, I know, but I can't help it."

Renie had so much life that it was almost enough to make Edmond's long-dead heart start beating again.

But it wasn't just that passion that drew him to her. It was her attitude—stubborn, defiant, and utterly, utterly determined. It was how she reacted to vampires. Most people treated Edmond's kind with awe and adoration, and though there were undeniable perks that came with being an immortal celebrity, there was also something tiresome about the world seeing only the vampire, never the man.

He was idolized, but he was lonely.

Renie didn't treat vampires like normal humans, but she didn't treat them like gods either. It made Edmond see her as a woman rather than a donor.

He hadn't looked at someone like that in all the years that Belle Morte had existed.

"It would be kinder, though," he said, taking another step toward June.

"Renie won't see it like that," Ludovic pointed out.

Charlotte flashed into Edmond's head.

By the time he'd met her, he'd been a vampire for less than fifty years. It had been several months since his relationship with Ysanne had fizzled out, and he'd been alone in the world. Then Charlotte had blazed into his life, a sweet peasant girl with freckled skin and dark curls, and Edmond had lost his heart to her so badly that he even admitted to her what he was. He'd thought she would understand.

He was wrong.

Charlotte had brought a mob to his door, who were as inflamed with self-righteous anger and religious zeal as she was. She'd stood at their head as they'd congregated outside his home, her beautiful eyes blazing with hatred, the lips he'd so often kissed now twisted with disgust.

"*Monstre!*" she'd spat at him, that one word like acid, burning a hole straight through his heart.

He had laid himself bare to that woman and she had turned him over to a mob that wanted him dead. The fact that he'd escaped physically unscathed didn't lessen the pain of Charlotte's betrayal.

It had been a long time since that night, but Edmond couldn't bear to see another woman he cared about turn on him with that kind of hatred in her eyes.

Through the ages, every time he'd fallen in love with a woman, it had ended badly—either because they'd died, left him, or betrayed him. Renie would be no different, but just because he couldn't have her didn't mean he could cope with her hating him.

Maybe in the end it wouldn't make any difference.

He was just a lonely old vampire with too many scars on his heart and too many dark spots on his soul. Renie deserved better.

Edmond turned away from June. "I can't do it."

"It's not your place. Ysanne set all this in motion, so if anyone's going to kill June, it should be her," Ludovic said.

"That's what she's planning to do. She's lost faith in this."

"When will she do it?"

"Soon."

"What happens then? June's death still has to be accounted for, and Ysanne's made things worse for herself. She'll have to tell the Council what really happened."

"She hasn't told me what she's planning," Edmond said.

Ludovic shook his head. "I always said the truth would out."

"But we had to try."

"I know." Ludovic squeezed Edmond's shoulder. "Best not to make things worse by getting involved with a donor."

Edmond had denied it to Ysanne because it was her job to enforce the rules of her House, but he didn't have to pretend with Ludovic.

"I know I can't keep her," he said. "But I want to."

"If Ysanne is going to kill June, then Renie's time here is almost over," Ludovic said.

Edmond gave a harsh laugh, and June stirred in her chains, growling softly.

"Believe me, I'm very aware of that."

They stood in silence and watched June for a little longer, then Ludovic squeezed Edmond's shoulder again. "We should go before someone misses us."

He opened the door, and Edmond paused before they left, looking back at June where she hung from the rack in the middle of the room. He'd barely known her during the time she'd lived here as a human, and he'd never bitten her, and now he felt a deep, aching sadness for this girl.

"I'm sorry," he said.

June growled.

Edmond shut the door.

CHAPTER TWENTY-FIVE

Renie

I was on autopilot for the hours leading up to that evening.

This was a small, informal event, no guests, no cameras, but donors were still expected to pretty up, so I changed into a knee-length cocktail dress, scattered all over with tiny crystals, and sat quietly while Jason styled my hair. Outwardly, no one would notice that anything was wrong, but inside, everything was twisted and tangled up.

Where did I go from here?

I tried telling myself to think positive thoughts, but failure after failure with June had reduced my optimism to tatters. It was like I was reaching the end of a long, hard road, and I knew I wouldn't like what waited for me at the end, but there was nowhere else to go.

What was I going to tell Mum?

When we were ready for the party, we went down to the dining hall. Apparently, the ballroom was reserved for more formal events. The huge trestle table that normally dominated the middle of the room had been pushed to the side, and drinks were laid out for the humans. There were no staff members besides security, and no orchestra, but someone had wheeled in a piano, and Fadime sat at it, her fingers flying over the keys, her gold-threaded hijab reflecting light from the chandeliered ceiling. Míriam was dancing with one of the Nox vampires, but I couldn't place his name, while Etienne talked to Catherine in the corner.

Aiden and Melissa danced together; she was laughing with him until I walked in, and then the laugh died on her lips.

At some point she'd have to know the truth. Everyone would.

What was Ysanne's plan for that?

Roux quickly spotted a Nox vampire she'd always wanted to meet, but I was hoping to avoid as much small talk as possible, so Roux and Jason went to introduce themselves while I made a beeline for the drinks.

I was almost there when a vampire I didn't recognize stepped in front of me. A prickle ran down my spine as he looked me up and down, like I was something he was considering buying, then without warning he grabbed me and pulled me close so he could bite me. I was so shocked I couldn't speak, so paralyzed with pain that I couldn't move.

Was this actually happening?

The vampire only took a nip from my blood—their equivalent of sipping champagne—before abruptly releasing me. I staggered, my hand flying to my throat.

"What the—" I didn't get to finish my sentence.

Ysanne, dressed in a figure-hugging red dress that made her look as though she'd been dipped in blood, swept over and grabbed my arm.

Not bothering to look at me, she addressed the vampire. "Adrian, I do hope you are enjoying yourself."

"Indeed," he replied. "Let it never be said that Lady Ysanne does not know how to take care of her guests."

Ysanne smiled graciously, but her grip on my arm didn't relax. Rather than risk glaring at her, I stared at the floor.

Only once Adrian had moved away, eyeing the other donors with the same cold hunger that he'd given me, did Ysanne release me. I snatched my arm back, rubbing the spot where her fingers had left indents.

"I hope I do not have to warn you to behave yourself," Ysanne said, her voice low enough that only I could hear, but laced with frost. "Jemima and her entourage are our guests, and they are to be treated with the utmost respect."

"They should ask before biting," I shot back.

"Donors cannot refuse blood to any vampire under this roof," Ysanne reminded me, emphasizing the word *donors*.

I could read between the lines. I hadn't come here to be a donor, but it was imperative that no one knew that—especially anyone from Nox. However nice she was, none of us could risk Jemima discovering something was wrong and reporting back to the rest of the Council.

So I kept my mouth shut and forced a smile, while on the inside I silently seethed. All of the visiting vampires seemed to want a bite, and all I could do was let them, crushing my true feelings deep down.

Jason made his way over to me. There were a couple of fang marks on his neck where the vampires who'd fed from him hadn't bothered to seal up the punctures, and little beads of blood still welled from the holes.

Jason gave a shaky smile. "I'll end up looking like Amit at this rate."

"Does it hurt?" I asked.

"No, but I don't like it."

I glanced around the room, seeing if anyone else was coming for a bite; my eyes locked with Gideon's, and then he was pushing his way through donors and vampires toward us.

"Great," Jason sighed. "I spend all that time trying to make myself look good in the vain hope that he'll notice me, and by the time he does, I look like an extra from *Friday the 13th*." He tried to mop up his bloody neck with his sleeve.

Isabeau intercepted Gideon before he could reach us, and he said something that made her purse her lips and look over at us.

"Oh, goody, and he's bringing his girlfriend," Jason muttered.

Remembering the way Isabeau's face had glowed when she talked about Ysanne, I wasn't sure Gideon was her type.

Gideon frowned as he reached us. "Our guests shouldn't be marking the donors like this."

He touched Jason's jaw, gently turning his head to one side so he could look at the bites on his neck. Jason seemed to have forgotten how to breathe.

"Would you like these marks gone?" Gideon asked, his hand still on Jason's face.

Jason nodded.

Gideon leaned in, his body almost touching Jason's, and gently ran his tongue across each of the bites, sealing them. Jason shuddered, melting against the vampire.

Was it my imagination, or did Gideon hold on to Jason slightly longer than was necessary?

Slightly breathless, Jason said, "Would you like to drink?" He turned his head a little more, offering up his throat to Gideon.

The vampire's gaze traveled along the veins arching beneath Jason's skin, then he shook his head. Jason's face fell.

"Do you have any bites that you wish to be sealed?" Isabeau asked me.

"I'm good, thanks."

She nodded, then looked at Jemima, who stood at the other end of the room. "Perhaps we should have a quick word with her."

Gideon didn't look back as he followed Isabeau over to Jemima, beautiful in floral chiffon, and the small blond vampire's face brightened when she saw him. She hugged him.

Jason looked half elated, half deflated, emotions clashing across his face. "Okay, what was that about?"

"I'm not sure."

Jason sighed, touching the place where Gideon's tongue had been. "I'm going to get a drink."

He'd only just walked off when a pair of strong hands settled on my hips and pulled me back a couple of paces. Adrian grinned down at me.

"I assume you don't object to dancing with me?" he said.

I refrained from telling him that the polite thing to do would have been to ask *before* pulling me away.

"How are you enjoying your stay at Belle Morte?" Adrian asked.

His hand drifted to the small of my back, pressing me against him more tightly than I was comfortable with. I tried to ease back, but he was too strong.

"It's wonderful." The lie came automatically to my lips.

"I'm glad to hear it. Donors are very precious to vampires." His hungry eyes moved down my throat and settled on my cleavage. I half expected him to lick his lips.

Yeah, we're precious to you, all right, I thought, darkly. *As precious as any other inanimate object you like the look of.*

Adrian's hands wandered from my waist to my butt. That was where I drew the line; grabbing his hand, I firmly returned it to my waist. Adrian's eyes hardened, red sparking in their depths.

"Have you been here long?" he asked.

"Just a couple of weeks."

Adrian's hand wandered back down to my butt, and I removed it again. He clasped me hard against him, grinding his pelvis into mine.

I slapped a hand against his chest. "My contract says I have to give you my blood, not my body, so get the fuck off me."

He grinned and it was nasty, showing off the tips of his fangs. "Don't play coy. You're just another starry-eyed Vladdict who wants to know what it's like to be with a real vampire."

"I'm really not," I said, ignoring the fact that I had spent more time than I would ever admit thinking about what sex with Edmond would be like.

That was completely different. I'd thought about sex with Edmond as a man I was desperately attracted to, rather than about sex with him as a vampire. He wasn't some novelty that people could try out just to see what he was like. I was weirdly offended on his behalf, even though I was the one being insulted.

"Let me go," I said, trying to twist out of Adrian's arms, but he held me firm.

"I think I'll take another taste," he said, leering at my neck.

I managed to bring my arm between us, shoving my wrist against his face, but he knocked it aside.

"Sorry, but I prefer the throat."

He bit me, and pain was a hot starburst in my neck. As my blood flowed into his mouth, his hands relaxed and I seized the opportunity to pull away. Adrian's fangs cut a shallow slice across my neck, and blood trickled down my skin and between my breasts.

Adrian's eyes blazed red as he licked my blood from his mouth.

Fear coiled and tightened inside me as I stared at the predator in front of me. He was everything I'd always feared about vampires— that behind the polished, civilized veneer they'd developed for the world, they were still the fanged predators that stalked the night.

Seizing my arm, Adrian pulled me forward. I wasn't strong enough to fight him off, and, regardless of Ysanne's warning, I opened my mouth to scream even as Adrian was swooping back over my neck.

He hadn't reckoned on Edmond, who cut through the crowd like a blade through silk, his eyes on fire.

"Get your hands off her," he growled.

He took my arm, drawing me out of Adrian's clutches, and his face hardened when he saw my bleeding neck.

"You should teach your donors some manners," Adrian said.

He made a sudden grab for me and Edmond moved like lightning, his fist plowing into Adrian's chin. Adrian flew backward, knocking into a knot of vampires and donors, and skidding across the floor.

The piano music continued for a couple more heartbeats before Fadime noticed the melee, and her hands faltered. Silence descended, but only briefly, and then it was punctuated by gasps and whispers. From the horror-struck faces around me, I realized that Edmond had just done something very wrong.

Ysanne swept over, her face like thunder. Jemima flanked her; she looked at Adrian as he wiped blood from his mouth, and then at Edmond, a question in her eyes.

Adrian climbed to his feet, suddenly contrite.

"Come with me," Ysanne said, her voice whisper soft and laden with menace.

She strode out of the dining hall, people parting for her like receding waves. Jemima followed in her wake, and Adrian and Edmond brought up the rear.

I tried to follow them, but a hand caught my arm and I looked up at Ludovic, grave faced and steely eyed.

"Don't," he warned. "You'll only make things worse."

"What's going on?"

"By hitting a guest, Edmond has publicly insulted Nox, and publicly insulted Jemima herself. That cannot go unpunished."

Fear crept over me. "What will they do to him?"

"I don't know."

Edmond

He'd crossed a line tonight, but he didn't regret it.

The moment he'd seen Adrian's hands on Renie, and the fear in her eyes, it had filled him with a protective rage that he hadn't felt in a long time.

Ysanne led the way to her office, and when all four vampires were inside, closed the door with a softness that belied the anger that Edmond could sense pouring off her.

"Would someone explain to me precisely what just happened?" she said.

"It's my fault. I'm afraid I got . . . carried away," Adrian said.

"He was sexually harassing one of our donors," Edmond snapped.

"I never meant any harm to the young lady."

"Treating her like a piece of meat *is* harming her."

Ysanne held up a hand and Edmond fell silent.

"I apologize profusely for Adrian's behavior," Jemima said, shooting him a glare that made him cringe. "There is no excuse for it. Ysanne, I am truly sorry for the insult to your donor, and I can assure you it won't happen again."

Ysanne nodded.

"However," Jemima said, giving Edmond a glance that was sympathy tinged with regret, "your vampire has insulted me most grievously by raising a hand against one of my own. If he believed that Adrian was behaving improperly, he should have informed you or me, rather than taking matters into his own hands."

Furiously, silently, Edmond seethed.

He was older than Jemima and he probably could have ruled Nox or one of the other UK Houses if he'd wanted to.

Now Ysanne had no choice but to punish him.

Adrian's insult to Renie was not considered as offensive because of what she was—human. Vampires might treasure their donors, but insults against them were not in the same league.

Ysanne looked steadily at Edmond. "I cannot deny the truth in your words, Jemima. Edmond may have acted in what he believed were the best interests of my donor, but his actions were inexcusable. He shall be silver whipped, if you feel that is an appropriate punishment."

Jemima slowly nodded. "Unpleasant but fair." She gestured to the door. "Come, Adrian. Perhaps we can salvage what's left of the night."

Ysanne waited until the door closed before speaking again. "I am sorry, my dear old friend, but you must have known this would have grave repercussions."

"I was aware of that, my lady."

Ysanne waved a hand, irritated. "*Pour l'amour du ciel!* I may be lady of this house but I am still your friend, and it is as a friend that I wish to speak to you."

Suddenly tired, Edmond looked straight at her. "What do you want me to say? That bastard was manhandling one of our donors. He ignored her request to feed from the wrist and forced himself on her neck. That is not how we treat our donors, nor is it how we should allow them to be treated."

Ysanne folded her arms, leaning one hip on the edge of her desk. "But this isn't about the disrespect toward a donor, is it? It's about the disrespect toward *her*."

The last word was heavy with disgust.

Edmond held his tongue. There was no point pretending he didn't know exactly who Ysanne was talking about.

"You are attracted to the girl, are you not?" Ysanne said.

"It's nothing. Humans burn so brightly and sometimes we cannot help being drawn to them."

"Yes, and they always burn us in the end."

"I know that as well as anyone."

"And yet you have not learned from your past mistakes."

She knew about the women who had flitted in and out of his life, leaving his heart in tatters. There was nothing that he had kept from her during the years they'd spent together, either as lovers or friends.

"You are wrong," Edmond said softly. "I have learned. I do all I can to keep my distance from her, but you cannot expect me to stand by and watch as another man uses his status as guest to abuse her."

"I expect you to handle it as one of my most trusted friends should, rather than a lovesick fool," Ysanne snapped. She closed her eyes, the cold lines of her face softening. "But at the same time, I cannot blame you. Love makes fools of us all in the end."

Edmond felt a sudden, strange ache in his chest, as if his long-dead heart had given a single beat.

Love?

He felt things for Renie that he hadn't felt in a long time, but he couldn't possibly be in love with her. Could he?

Ysanne took Edmond's hands. "You will be beaten tomorrow morning, before Jemima leaves."

Edmond nodded. From the moment he had charged across the ballroom to Renie's defense, he'd known he would suffer for his actions. But Renie was safe, and that was worth all the punishment in the world.

Ysanne was still watching him, her eyes lit with the compassion that she didn't often show other vampires. She kissed his head just once, the same way she'd done hundreds of years ago, on the last night they shared before she slipped away into spring's embrace and left him alone.

"Truly," she whispered. "I am sorry."

CHAPTER TWENTY-SIX

Renie

Ludovic hadn't left my side since Edmond and the others disappeared from the dining hall.

I wanted to linger at the entryway and wait for Edmond to come back, but Ludovic warned me that Edmond was in enough trouble; the best we could do was pretend everything was normal, like everyone else was doing.

Fadime had started playing again, something fast and lively, and Ludovic quickly started dancing with me, keeping us moving so that no one could ask what was going on. I hated that I had to dance and smile and pretend while not knowing what was happening to Edmond, but I wasn't stupid enough to ignore Ludovic's advice.

Jemima and Adrian came back into the room, melting seamlessly into the crowd.

A shiver rolled through me. Adrian looked so normal now, as smartly dressed and handsome as any vampire, but I'd never forget the way his eyes had gleamed red with hunger and violence, the bruising grip of his hands, and the way his fangs had stabbed into my neck.

Ludovic deftly repositioned himself so he was standing between me and Adrian, a wall of solid chest protecting me from the man who scared me.

He'd offered to seal the cuts on my neck, but I couldn't shake my fear of anyone going near my throat.

A hand touched my shoulder and I turned to see Jemima.

"I offer my sincerest apologies for the way Adrian behaved toward you. That is not how I run things in my House, and I can assure you he will receive due punishment once we return to Nox. In the meantime, I hope that you are all right," she said.

"I—I'm fine," I stuttered, because what else could I say?

Even I, with my sparse knowledge of vampire politics, suspected that throwing Jemima's apology back in her face probably wasn't smart.

"I'm glad to hear it," Jemima said, then someone caught her attention behind us. "Excuse me," she said and walked away.

Ludovic hadn't let go of my hand, and there was something comforting about that.

"I'm impressed. It's rare that a lord or lady apologizes to anyone, much less a donor," Ludovic said.

"I don't think Jemima's like the others."

Finally, Edmond came back into the dining hall and my whole body ached to run to him, but Ludovic held me back, a warning in his eyes. I wasn't sure if he knew about me and Edmond, but regardless, I couldn't broadcast my feelings to the whole room.

Edmond made his way toward us, ignoring the looks and whispers as people speculated what exactly had happened between him and Adrian. His gaze met Ludovic's and neither of them spoke, but their eyes seemed to say all they needed to, wordless understanding passing between them.

Edmond held out his hand to me, his solemn expression giving away nothing. "Will you do me the honor of a dance?"

As I took his hand, Roux disentangled herself from a nearby dance partner and scurried over to us.

"What happened? Are you okay?" she hissed.

"Can we talk later?" I said. I hated to turn her away, but finding out what was going on with Edmond was more important.

Roux nodded. She looked Ludovic up and down, assessing him. "You fancy a dance, gorgeous?"

Ludovic blinked, apparently lost for words.

Roux didn't need confirmation; she grabbed his hands and pulled him onto the dance floor.

One hand holding mine, the other gently resting on my waist, Edmond led us both into a simple box step, as he'd taught me before. The rhythm was all wrong for the music that was playing, but neither of us cared.

"You didn't have to do that," I said.

"Yes, I did, and I'd do it again in a heartbeat."

"But aren't you in trouble?"

He smiled and shook his head. "It doesn't matter, mon ange. It was worth it."

"You always call me that, but I don't know what it means."

He paused before answering, studying every detail of my face, his gaze lingering, bright with an emotion I couldn't name. When he spoke, his voice was a whisper, stroking along my skin like a caress.

"It means *my angel*."

Despite what had happened between us last time, I ached to kiss him, burning with the need to press myself against his cool, hard body. But all I could do was hold him.

This wasn't supposed to happen.

The last thing I had come here to do was fall for someone, but it had happened and I couldn't stop it. We were falling together, clinging to one another as the wind rushed around us.

What would happen when we hit the ground?

Edmond was immortal; maybe his heart could cope with the pain of loss better than mine could. Or maybe his was even more fragile because he had loved and lost more terribly than I ever could. Maybe when we hit the ground we'd both shatter together.

For now, I just wanted to keep falling.

*

Later, when Edmond had healed the cuts on my neck, and the party was over, Roux and Jason and I ended up back in my room, all huddled together in one bed. It wasn't quite big enough for three, but after tonight, I didn't want to be alone.

As we lay in bed, Jason wedged between us girls, I told my friends what had happened, but didn't dare speculate what would happen to Edmond.

His actions would have consequences. I just didn't know what they were.

I was abruptly awoken the following morning, when Melissa burst into our room. "Something's happening outside," she cried.

We all poked our heads out from under the covers at the same time: three sleep-scruffy bed heads and three pairs of bleary eyes.

"Oh wow," Melissa said. "I didn't know you guys were into that."

Roux raked her fingers through her hair, making it stand on end. "Into what?"

Jason flopped back on the pillow between us, burrowing beneath the covers. "She thinks we had a threesome," he mumbled.

My cheeks flamed red, and Roux cackled with laughter. "It's not what it looks like," she said.

"Seriously, though," Melissa said when none of us got up. "Jemima and Ysanne took Edmond into the gardens about ten minutes ago. I think all the vampires are out there now, but I just tried going out to see what's happening, and security wouldn't let me. Donors aren't allowed out of the house this morning."

My heart started to thud.

"Nothing like this has ever happened before." Melissa fixed me with a penetrating look. "Do you know what's going on?"

"Oh my god," I breathed. "They're punishing him for hitting Adrian yesterday."

I clambered over Jason and out of bed. I hadn't taken my hair down after the ball, and an uneasy night had turned it into a wild mass of twists and curls and hairspray, like I'd been dragged through a hedge backward.

There was no time to change; I stuffed my feet into the nearest pair of boots, threw a coat over the crystal-encrusted cocktail dress that I hadn't bothered to change out of, and ran for the door.

Amit was talking with a small group of other donors in the hallway; they all looked at me as I charged out of my room, and one of them started to ask me something, but I was too busy running.

I tore out of the south wing and down the staircase. My stomach felt like I'd swallowed something cold and heavy, and I couldn't get enough air into my lungs.

Dexter stood at the exit door, his face grim. He raised a hand as I skidded to a halt in front of him.

"No one's allowed out at the moment."

"Why?"

He gave me a look, part sad, part frustrated.

"Let me guess, you're not allowed to tell me," I said.

"I'm afraid not."

It wasn't his fault, but I wanted to scream at him, to throw him out of the way so I could get out into the gardens to stop whatever was happening.

"Please," I whispered, my voice breaking.

I'd been so angry at Edmond for agreeing with Ysanne that June might be beyond help, but the thought of him suffering was like shards of glass in my heart.

"I'm sorry," Dexter said, and he sounded like he meant it. "But you should go back to your room."

A hand touched my arm, and I jumped. Roux stood there; I hadn't noticed she'd followed me.

"Come on," she said.

In a daze I let her lead me back to our room. Jason was sitting on Roux's bed, hugging a pillow. Melissa was pacing the floor, and Aiden leaned against the wall. His eyes narrowed as I came in.

"Well?" Melissa said, as we came in.

"I have no idea," I said. The words tasted sour, like failure.

"But it's all to do with you, isn't it? Anytime something strange happens in this house, it's tied up with *you*." Aiden sounded frustrated rather than angry.

"I didn't ask for any of this," I said.

"But everything changed when you got here."

"That's not my *fault*," I snapped.

Roux stepped between us. "Time out, guys. Let's all just relax."

How could I relax when something awful might be happening to Edmond?

A horrible thought hit me and I staggered, clutching Roux's sleeve. "They wouldn't kill him, would they? They haven't taken him outside to . . . to . . ."

"No," said Roux at once, clasping my hands. "Don't even think that, Renie. That's not what's happening."

"You don't know that."

"We can take a pretty good guess," Jason said. "I don't know exactly why punching Adrian is such a big deal, but they're not going to kill Edmond over it. Vampire laws might be different from human laws, but their sense of justice can't be that badly skewed."

"Then why aren't we allowed outside?"

"Because vampires are cryptic bastards?"

"Or," said Roux calmly, "because they want to preserve their image and not frighten their donors."

"Maybe they shouldn't be doing anything that would frighten us," Melissa muttered, wrapping her arms around herself. Aiden hugged her.

I leaned against the foot of my bed, acutely aware of his eyes on me.

"I really don't know what's going on," I told her, sensing that he was about to ask.

"You know a lot more than you're saying," he snapped.

Roux looked at me and lifted her eyebrows, but I shook my head. We couldn't tell Melissa or Aiden.

Jason lifted a hand. "I don't fully know what's going on, either, but it would be nice to."

"Please, just don't," I said, pinching the bridge of my nose. "Not right now."

Jason looked disappointed, but he didn't push.

"What happened to you, Renie?" Melissa asked. "You came here because you were worried that June was in trouble, and now what? You're helping cover something up?" Her voice was pleading.

"It's not that simple."

God, I *hated* this. Melissa cared about June; she deserved to know the truth, but telling her could put June's life at risk. Logically, Melissa had no way of contacting the Council, but what would happen if she told the other donors? What would happen if she left Belle Morte and told the world? It was a gamble I just couldn't take.

"Why did Edmond punch Adrian?" Melissa said.

"Because he had his fucking hands in places they shouldn't have been."

"I've been in this house for months, and that's the first time I've seen Edmond do anything like that. Once again, it all comes back to you."

"He was just looking out for me."

"That's not actually his job, though. It's Ysanne's job to make sure that her donors are taken care of."

I sighed. "What do you want me to say?"

"I want you to be honest about what you know."

I pressed my lips together and said nothing.

The last thing I needed was this interrogation, but it was impossible to blame Melissa.

I needed to see Ysanne.

I *had* to know what she was doing to Edmond.

"Where are you going?" Melissa asked as I headed for the door.

Roux caught my eye. *Go,* she mouthed.

I took that to mean Roux would stop anyone from coming after me, even if she didn't know where I was going. What had I done to deserve a friend like her?

I slipped out of my room.

I had no idea if Ysanne was still outside with the other vampires, but she'd have to come in at some point, and when she did, she'd find me waiting at her office.

As I was going down the stairs, a security guard came through the front door, brushing white flakes from her shoulders. "It's snowing," she said, smiling up at me.

I tried to smile back, but my cheek muscles felt frozen. My throat was a hard knot.

The first time I remembered it truly snowing was when I was six. I'd seen snow before, but only ever a weak flurry that never settled, and then one morning, June and I woke up and knew something had changed. The light coming through the windows was different, and the usual noises outside were muffled, and when I'd opened the curtains, the whole world had been transformed while we slept.

We'd been so excited that we'd rushed straight out in our second-hand Disney pajamas, not even bothering with shoes. We hadn't registered how bitterly cold it was, how the snow was like teeth on the soles of our feet, until Mum yelled at us to come back.

Once we were bundled up in hats, coats, scarves, boots, and gloves, we'd spent the rest of the day playing in the snow. At the time it had felt like the greatest, most magical day in the world. It was all over too soon—by the time I opened the curtains the following morning, all that beautiful snow had melted—but it remained one of my happiest early memories.

None of my memories had been enough to bring June back.

Everything we'd shared—a lifetime of laughter and squabbles and jokes and misunderstandings and deep love—had been wiped clean the moment June woke up rabid.

How could I have let her down so badly?

A short distance from the office, I stopped. Ysanne and Isabeau stood in front of the smoked-glass door; Isabeau lifted Ysanne's hand and planted a lingering kiss on the other woman's knuckles, and Ysanne stroked Isabeau's face with a gentleness that I hadn't thought her capable of.

She said something and Isabeau nodded, releasing Ysanne's hand and walking away.

"What do you want, Renie?" Ysanne said, without looking at me.

"What happened to Edmond?"

Ysanne turned. Her face was as blank as ever but there was something strained in the shape of her mouth and the way she held herself. "For his insult to Lady Jemima and the House of Nox, Edmond paid penance in blood."

"What the hell does that mean?"

"It means that he was publicly whipped. It's over now, and it won't be brought up again, by either Belle Morte or Nox."

My head felt all foggy. "You *whipped* him?"

"No. Phillip did."

"Why?"

"He's a neutral party."

I gaped at the vampire in front of me. "How *could* you? Edmond is supposed to be your friend, and you let that happen to him? Do you even remember having a heart?"

Thunderclouds formed in Ysanne's eyes, and I bit off whatever else

I'd been about to say, suddenly very aware that I was alone with a vampire who had knocked me unconscious before.

But Ysanne's anger faded as quickly as it had come. "I do not expect you to understand."

"Good, because I don't."

"When we established these Houses and the donor system, we had to put certain rules in place to govern our kind. Our acceptance in the human world will exist only as long as each House remains civil and courteous to the others. We are known for being beautiful, graceful, and ancient, not for civil disputes and petty infighting. To maintain that balance, we must maintain a certain sense of propriety toward each other. Edmond violated that by striking an honored guest."

"Yeah, to save me from being groped by that sick fuck."

"There are ways to handle situations like that. Public violence is not one of them and Edmond knew that."

"And whipping someone isn't public violence?"

"That is a public punishment. It's not the same thing. If Edmond felt that Adrian was abusing our hospitality, he should have come to either Jemima or me, and we would have dealt with it. But he didn't. He lashed out, gravely insulting Jemima and her House, and that cannot go unchecked. Edmond *knew* this."

But he'd still done it in defense of me. Something twisted inside me and my eyes burned, but I couldn't cry. I was too angry to cry.

"Being a leader requires making difficult, sometimes unpleasant choices. There is a great deal of pressure on the lords and ladies of each House to make sure that everything runs smoothly, that our integration into the human world is not upset, and we cannot tolerate that kind of aggression."

"You were pretty aggressive when you knocked me out," I snapped.

Ysanne opened her office door. "In," she commanded.

I marched into the room. Ysanne took a seat behind her desk.

"Everything I do is for the good of my people. What do you think would happen if humans stopped loving us?" She didn't give me a chance to answer. "Public favor would turn against us. Donors might stop coming, the world would view us as dangerous, and then do you think we would be safe in our mansions, or would people come in angry mobs to drive us out, like they have before in our history? It is essential that I quell violence in my vampires."

I'd never fully realized just how much of the vampires' way of life depended upon the way humans reacted to them. They seemed so far above us and they acted as if they were so much better than us, so it seemed impossible to think we could topple their glittering empire.

But Ysanne obviously thought we could.

I was still livid, but even so, I recognized how candid Ysanne was being, talking to me as an equal rather than a donor, trusting me with this information. But I still couldn't accept it.

"What you did was wrong, no matter the reasons," I said.

"I should have known that you wouldn't be mature enough to understand this." Ysanne's voice was cool and steely, her eyes like blades digging into me.

I started to snap back, but Ysanne wasn't finished.

"I have lived lifetimes. I have caused suffering, and I myself have suffered more than you can possibly imagine."

Her frank admission startled me.

"I have seen the depths of human evil and human depravity, and I know what they are capable of inflicting on vampires they consider a threat. The decisions I make may be hard, and I may not want to make them, but they are necessary. I will not be lectured to by some silly little girl."

She stabbed a finger at me, and despite myself I fell back, remembering how much power she had in just her hand.

"I assure you that Edmond's punishment could have been worse.

I have allowed him to get away with infractions in the past, where another lord or lady would not. I'm not the monster you think I am, but I cannot allow Edmond to get away with so flagrantly breaking the rules that are in place to protect us all."

She looked me up and down, her gaze so cold that goose bumps broke out on my skin.

"Edmond knew what the consequences would be when he chose to defend your honor. As far as I am concerned, it was a mistake. Aside from the punishment itself, the humiliation is not something he will easily forget. It's not often that one of his standing falls so low, and all for a donor."

The way she said it, Edmond might as well have risked his reputation for a maggot.

"Rather than throwing a tantrum with me, you should be appreciating the sacrifice that Edmond made for you," Ysanne said.

I wanted to throw something at her head. The worst part was that some of what she was saying actually made sense. I didn't fully understand vampire politics, or how fragile their position in the human world was, and I couldn't fully grasp what would happen if the balance between humans and vampires was upset, because I would never be in that situation. But I did understand that humans could turn on vampires. Edmond had told me how an angry mob had descended on François and destroyed him, and much as I wanted to believe we'd come a long way since then, I wasn't naive enough to think that we weren't still capable of the same violent prejudice.

"You punished Edmond for breaking the rules, but you're doing the same thing," I said quietly.

"Excuse me?" Ysanne's voice was ice.

"You hid June. That's against the rules but you did it anyway because you believed it was for a greater good. Why do you get that leeway but Edmond doesn't?"

Ysanne's lips whitened.

She'd said she wasn't a monster, and part of me believed her. Part of me tried to understand how difficult it must be to balance her friendships with her duties as a leader. But it wasn't fair that Edmond was *whipped* for breaking the rules, while Ysanne blatantly got away with it.

Someone knocked on the door.

"Entrez," Ysanne snapped, not taking her eyes off me.

Ludovic walked in, and my heart gave a little leap. Ludovic and Edmond had been friends longer than I was alive; if Edmond was seriously injured then Ludovic would never have left him. Right?

"Edmond is settled in his room and he'll remain there until he's healed." Ludovic spoke in clipped tones, focusing on Ysanne's desk rather than the lady herself.

I expected her to challenge his cold attitude, but all Ysanne said was, "Thank you."

Ludovic nodded once and left the office, shutting the door a little harder than I thought he might normally do.

I hovered inside the office, unsure what to do. Ysanne and I would never agree on this issue.

"Is there anything else?" Ysanne asked, but she didn't bother to look at me.

"No," I mumbled.

She gestured to the door, and I left quietly.

CHAPTER TWENTY-SEVEN

Renie

Ludovic was waiting for me outside. I started to speak, but he put a finger to his lips, looking meaningfully at Ysanne's door.

We moved farther down the hall, away from the office and Ysanne's keen hearing.

"Is he okay?" I asked.

Ludovic's face was grim, his eyes as hard as marbles. "He's been better."

"I didn't mean for this to happen."

"It's not your fault. He's been asking for you, wanting to know how you are."

I laughed shakily. "He's the one who was just whipped, and he's asking if *I'm* okay?" I scrubbed my face with both hands, smoothing my palms up to the tangle of my hair.

Ludovic intently scrutinized me. "You care about him, don't you?" he said.

I hesitated. Ysanne wasn't stupid; she'd probably guessed that Edmond's actions yesterday were a knee-jerk reaction because he had feelings for me. It still felt risky to admit out loud that there was anything between us, but Ludovic wouldn't betray Edmond's secrets.

"Yes, I do. I know I shouldn't, but I can't help it." Fresh tears stung my eyes as I thought how much he must be suffering now.

Ludovic lowered his voice. "Do you want to see him?"

My head whipped up. "What? But I thought donors aren't allowed in the north wing."

"They're not. But Edmond wants to see you and you want to see him. I know it's breaking the rules, but I'm willing to take that risk."

"Even knowing what Ysanne will do if she catches you?"

Ludovic's face hardened. I wondered what he actually thought of Ysanne—what any of her people thought of her.

"I know why Edmond had to be punished, even though I'm not happy with it. I also know the one thing he wants right now is to see you. So yes, I am willing to risk Ysanne's ire if it will get my best friend that one thing."

I still wasn't sure, but it might be my last chance to see Edmond. If Ysanne had caught on to us, then she would probably ban us from seeing each other. While a day ago I might have welcomed that, now all I could think was that I couldn't *not* see Edmond, even if it was the last time.

"Take me to him," I said.

Fate must have been smiling on me for once, because we made it to the north wing without anyone spotting us. My heart was in my throat the whole time, thudding loudly. Ludovic stopped before an ornately carved wooden door and quietly turned the handle.

I hadn't registered that he'd be taking me to Edmond's bedroom until we were already inside.

The decor wasn't so different to my own room: the walls were flocked velvet, only these were dark blue rather than pale gold, and the curtains were black brocade. One wall displayed a pair of mounted swords. The carpet was deep enough to swallow my feet. The room was dominated by a four-poster bed, each post carved from thick oak and hanging with swaths of dark fabric.

Edmond lay on his front in bed, a black towel spread out beneath him, his back a mess of blood and gashed flesh.

He lifted his head with an obvious effort. "Renie?"

He looked so weak, so very human, and I flew across the room and climbed onto the bed beside him, choking back tears.

Ludovic quietly left the room.

"Why aren't you healing?" I asked, gazing in horror at the raw ruin of his back.

"The whip was silver tipped, and vampires are allergic to silver. It delays the healing process," Edmond explained, his voice strained. "I'll still heal, but it will take longer than if a normal whip had been used."

The cruelty of it wrenched at my heart.

Edmond couldn't prop himself up to look at me, so I lay down next to him, bringing our faces as close together as I dared. Pain had carved lines on his face and left bruise-dark circles under his eyes. He looked more human than I'd ever seen him, and warmth swelled inside me. This was how he would look if he wasn't immortal—still gorgeous, but without that impossible vampire perfection.

"Why did you do it? Ysanne said that if you'd told her what was happening, she would have stopped it," I whispered.

His hand slid across the covers, clasping mine. "I wasn't thinking clearly. I saw him put his hands on you, saw him bite you when you didn't want it, and all I could think about was getting him away from you. He's lucky I only punched him; I wanted to tear his head off."

"But look what's happened to you." I raised my eyes to the bloody slashes layered over the scars left over from his human life, but just as quickly looked away, unable to bear it.

He managed a taut smile. "It was worth it."

"Why would you do it for me when we know that this thing between us can't become anything?"

Edmond trailed a finger along my cheek. "It already *is* something. It's foolish to keep pretending that it's not."

He shifted, moving fractionally closer to me, but even that movement caused pain to twist his face. His other hand clutched a fistful of bedcovers. I'd never seen him in pain before.

"Is there anything I can do? Clean you up?" How I'd handle mopping the blood off his ravaged back, I wasn't sure, but I couldn't stand leaving him lying here like this.

"No. The silver will keep the wounds bleeding until they start to heal. There's no point cleaning anything until then."

I wasn't sure I agreed, but maybe cleaning the wounds would make them bleed more. Edmond was more familiar with pain and the extent of his healing abilities than I was, so I had to trust what he said.

"Can I feed you? That would speed up the healing process, right?"

"It would, but I can't. The wounds have to heal on their own; it's part of the punishment."

"I can't believe Ysanne did this to you."

"She had no choice."

"Yeah, yeah, she's already explained all that to me, but I still can't believe it."

"She explained it?" Edmond sounded surprised. "You realize that Ysanne is not in the habit of explaining her decisions to donors?"

"So why did she?" I said.

"The only reason I can think of is that she genuinely wanted you to understand."

"What, because she doesn't want me thinking she's a monster?" I was kidding, but Edmond frowned, mulling over my words.

"I know what you must think of her, but she does care about me."

"She's got a funny way of showing it."

"She has duties and rules to uphold, and she cannot make exceptions for my sake. If she is seen to have favorites, then another vampire might challenge her right to rule Belle Morte."

I hadn't considered that, and doubt crept into my mind. I could see only the injustice in front of me, rather than the fact that it might have been necessary for the stability of vampires worldwide.

But who could blame me for struggling to see the bigger picture when Edmond was bleeding and hurting next to me?

"I didn't realize that anyone could challenge her," I said.

"It's rare, but it does happen. Members of the Council are among the oldest and strongest of us all, but there are others who would like to lead. Power is a dangerous temptation, for vampires as well as humans."

"Has anyone ever challenged her?"

"Ysanne? Non. But challenges have been issued to other Houses. Henry of the House Midnight has been challenged twice, and Jemima has been challenged once."

I couldn't picture dainty little Jemima fighting off a potential usurper, but Ysanne herself didn't look like she could lift a man off his feet with one hand, and I'd seen her do just that to Edmond.

"Obviously unsuccessfully," I said.

He offered a half smile. "The lords and ladies rule the Houses for a reason, and none of them are willing to relinquish that position."

"I couldn't imagine Ysanne giving up anything without a serious fight," I said.

"She wouldn't. Belle Morte means more to her than anything, and woe betide anyone who tries to take it away."

I knew I shouldn't touch him but I couldn't keep myself from stroking a hand up his arm, my palm ghosting over the muscles beneath his skin. I wanted to explore every beautiful inch of him, to kiss him and never stop, to welcome him into my body and let him take me to a place where only bliss existed.

"Thank you," I whispered.

"For what?"

"For doing what you did. I hate that you're suffering, but thank you for rescuing me."

He gazed at me, his eyes shining like stars even though his face was still drawn tight with pain, and I pressed my palm to his face, gliding my thumb along his cheek.

This wasn't fair.

I'd had relationships before, even a couple that I considered serious, but this was beyond anything I'd ever felt.

Everything was brighter and better when Edmond was around.

Every time he smiled, everything inside me melted.

Every time I saw affection flicker in his eyes, I felt a pang that this couldn't work.

Every time he touched me, it was pure bliss.

It was grossly unfair that the one person I felt all this for was the one person I could never have.

I clasped his hand to my chest. My gaze drifted to his lips, wishing that I could kiss him. But I didn't dare. It was hard enough that I'd have to let go of his hand and climb off this bed, but I doubted I'd be strong enough to do that if the taste of him was still on my lips.

"I should go," I whispered.

I started to move, but he wouldn't let me go.

"Please don't," he said.

I'd never heard him sound so raw, so uncertain, and I knew then that I'd stay with him for as long as he asked me.

"We could get in trouble," I said, settling back on the bed, closer to him this time—or at least as close as I could get without disturbing his injuries.

"I don't care."

Still, I didn't kiss him, and he didn't kiss me. We both knew there was a line we couldn't cross. But we huddled together on the bed, our hands clasped tightly, and if this was the best we'd ever get, I was at least grateful for that.

*

When I cracked open an eye, I was completely disoriented. How long had I been asleep?

Careful not to disturb Edmond, I sat up. My crystal dress had left small indents in my skin where my arm had pressed into my side, and I couldn't imagine what a horror show my hair must be.

Edmond was still asleep. With his eyes closed and his fangs hidden, his face soft and relaxed, he could have passed for human. His hair fell across his forehead, a shadow against his pale skin.

My gaze moved to his back, checking his injuries. Blood had clotted on the slashes, the red crusting to black, but they weren't properly healed yet. I'd hoped they would be by the time I woke up.

What would it be like to wake up with him every morning?

What would it feel like to fall asleep with him every night, his strong arms pulling me into the curve of his body?

Why did I keep torturing myself with thoughts of things that I couldn't have?

Edmond opened his eyes. He started to stretch, then stopped, wincing. He smiled up at me. "I wasn't sure you would stay."

"I'd never sneak off and leave you."

"Are all your pajamas this fancy?" he said, pulling gently at the crystals on my dress.

Crumpled and creased, the dress was a little worse for wear, and my makeup was probably smeared across my face, but Edmond gazed at me as if I was the most beautiful thing he'd ever seen.

"This old thing? Please," I teased, trying to ignore the wrenching feeling in my chest. "My other pajamas make this look like rags."

Edmond chuckled. "Then I look forward to seeing them."

The laughter died in both our throats as his words fell into the space between us. Edmond couldn't possibly see what my pajamas really looked like because this—us being in a bed together for any reason— could never happen again. For just a moment, we'd both forgotten that, and now it came rushing back, stark and cold and miserable.

"Thank you for staying," Edmond whispered.

Bending over him, I planted a gentle kiss on his head. It was meant to be soft and chaste, but he grabbed my hips and pulled me down the bed, maneuvering his body over me. His lips met mine, electricity sparking between us.

I just had time to acknowledge this was a very bad idea before the deliciousness of Edmond's mouth chased all other thoughts from my mind. I clung to him, one hand gliding through his hair, the other sliding along his shoulders. Edmond braced himself on one arm, his free hand roaming over my hip, making its way up to my chest. I held my breath as his fingers lingered on the glittering bodice, a hairsbreadth from where I knew he really wanted to touch. He gazed down at me as if I was a precious jewel, one he was almost afraid to handle.

I took his hand, intending to move it farther up, but Edmond shifted position at the same time and hissed suddenly, squeezing his eyes shut.

"What's wrong?" I asked.

As soon as the words left my mouth, I could have smacked myself. What's wrong? His whip lashes were still raw and open. My other hand rested on the top of his shoulders; if I moved it down I'd find crusted blood and torn skin.

"I'm sorry," I whispered, though I wasn't sure what for.

Sorry because I hated that he was hurting and I couldn't take away the pain?

Sorry that we'd both let this go on when we knew it was a mistake?

Sorry that I was human and he was a vampire?

Edmond shook his head, silently telling me not to apologize, but he moved away from me, settling back in the indent he'd made in the covers.

"Perhaps it's a good thing I'm out of commission," he said, with a wry smile.

Heat filled my cheeks, my stomach doing a little shimmy. If Edmond wasn't injured, I was pretty sure that nothing would have stopped us. We'd have lost ourselves in each other, regardless of the consequences.

But much as I wanted it, I was glad we hadn't got that far. It was already hard enough knowing I'd have to walk away, but if I experienced everything he could give me, I was afraid I wouldn't be able to let him go. And I'd have to eventually, because Ysanne would make me. It was better to walk away than be dragged from Edmond's arms.

I noticed a book lying on the bedside table; a battered leather-bound thing that looked like it was about a hundred years old. I tilted my head to read the title etched in gold on the spine.

"'*The Count of Monte Cristo*,'" I murmured.

Edmond smiled up at me from the pillow. His face wasn't usually this expressive, and I wondered if it was because he was too tired and in too much pain to maintain the usual vampire facade, or if it was because we were in the privacy of his bedroom. He didn't have to pretend with anyone here; there was only me, and I didn't think there were any secrets left between us.

"Once I realized that Dumas had used my name for his hero, I bought a copy of the book. It hasn't left my side since," Edmond said.

I looked at the book with a new respect, trying to imagine clinging to a single object over so many years.

"I bet Dumas would have liked that," I said.

I couldn't think of anything else to say. I didn't want to go, but the reality of the situation was filtering back to me, and fear was gathering in the pit of my stomach.

In one week, Ysanne would kill June if I couldn't help her.

If Ysanne caught me in Edmond's bed—even if he was in no shape to *do* anything . . . I didn't want to imagine what she would do.

"I have to go," I whispered, curving my body around Edmond, and winding my fingers into his hair. It was as soft as I'd always thought, like silk.

"I don't want you to."

"I know, but I have to."

I bent to kiss him but stopped, recalling what had happened last time.

There was nothing else to do but slide off the bed in my beautiful dress. I looked down at Edmond, taking a mental snapshot of this moment so I could keep it through all the years when he'd no longer be with me. Maybe someone else would have taken my place by then, a gorgeous vampire girl who'd never grow old and die.

A spike of pain jabbed into my chest.

It was starting to feel like everything I'd ever wanted was lying in that bed, bloody and weak, but still so beautiful I could hardly believe it.

Edmond tensed and lifted his head. "Someone's coming," he whispered.

I didn't even have time to panic when there was a soft knock at the door. "Edmond? Are you awake?"

Etienne.

If it had been anyone else, I'd have hidden under the bed. But I was so goddamn sick of lying and sneaking around.

"I trust him," I whispered, and Edmond nodded, because he trusted me.

I went to the door.

Etienne was visibly taken aback when I opened it, rocking back on his heels slightly.

"Renie? What are you doing here?"

"I came to see how Edmond was doing," I said honestly.

Etienne looked past me, to where Edmond lay on the bed. "You're not allowed in the north wing."

I shrugged. I wasn't about to bring Ludovic into this, even if I did trust Etienne.

"I'm leaving now, anyway, but I'd really appreciate it if you didn't say anything to anyone," I said.

"Of course I'm not going to say anything." He sounded vaguely insulted.

"Will you make sure she gets back to the south wing without anyone seeing?" Edmond asked.

Etienne nodded.

"You don't have to—" I started to say, but Etienne held up a hand.

"Renie, I consider you a friend, and I don't want anything to happen to you. I'm doing this," he insisted.

My throat knotted as I looked back at Edmond and tried to say good-bye, but my mouth wouldn't form the words.

"What would Ysanne say? I didn't think vampires and donors were even allowed to be friends," I said, as we carefully made our way through the north wing, pausing every now and then while Etienne listened, making sure no one was coming.

"Technically, we've never been told that. The no-relationships rule has been hammered home, but Ysanne's never actually forbidden us from befriending donors. Besides, I don't really care what she thinks about it."

First Ludovic, now Etienne. Not that I was complaining, but did anyone respect Ysanne's rules?

Maybe they were all just pissed at her for what she'd done to Edmond.

"Who knew vampires could be this nice?" I said.

It was meant to be a joke, but Etienne's smile was a little on the sad side.

"People see only what they want to," he said.

I'd said something very similar to Edmond once, though it felt like years ago. Time really did seem to stand still in this place, the days melting into one another, an endless string of fashion and parties and good food and sharp teeth.

Despite myself, I was starting to wonder how I would adjust to the real world.

We made it out of the north wing without running into anyone, and Etienne stopped a few feet from my door in the south wing.

"Thank you," I said, giving his hand a little squeeze.

"Anytime."

I watched him walk away before going into my bedroom. Jason had gone, but Melissa was sitting on Roux's bed, her head downcast, while Aiden and Roux faced off in the middle of the room.

"I care because I love Melissa, and all this shit is upsetting her," Aiden snapped, bristling with anger.

Roux opened her mouth, then shut it when she saw me.

Aiden whipped around. "Where have you been?" he demanded.

"Nowhere."

He snorted. "Another lie. I don't understand—why can you tell Roux and not us?"

My eyes slid to Roux. She made a helpless gesture with her hands.

"Tell her what?" I said carefully.

"Whatever it is you won't tell us." Melissa spoke up. "Roux knows something. I don't know if this thing with Adrian and Edmond is connected to June, but everything started happening once you got here, and you only came for June. So I'm going to assume it's all linked somehow."

She waited, maybe expecting me to say something.

Thanks to what had just happened, Etienne had probably guessed there was something between Edmond and me, but I still hadn't told him about June, and I still couldn't tell Melissa or Aiden.

I shook my head.

Tears shone in Melissa's eyes.

Aiden clenched his fists. "Fine. We all know where the answers are, and if you won't give them to us, I'll get them myself."

Shoving past me, he stormed out of the room.

"Wait, what does he mean?" Roux's eyes widened and she caught Melissa as the other girl jumped off the bed. "He's not going to the west wing?"

Oh shit.

"Stay here," I told Roux, and went after Aiden.

He'd only had a few seconds' head start on me, but Aiden could *move.* I didn't dare call after him—the last thing we needed was an audience.

"God*dammit,*" I whispered.

Aiden's head bobbed ahead of me, then he veered off to the left, heading into the hall that led to the west wing.

I put on an extra spurt of speed, but Aiden was too fast. He was bolting up the short staircase into the darkened stretch of the wing while I was still rounding the corner.

Terror sliced into me. This wasn't just about June being discovered anymore—it was about Aiden running blindly into serious danger.

"Aiden, stop," I called, heedless of who might hear us.

Aiden paused at the top of the stairs, head cocked, but it wasn't me he was listening to. It was the faint rattle of chains coming from the end of the hall.

"Please," I begged, reaching the stairs, but he was past listening.

He ran down the hallway, toward the room where June was imprisoned.

Desperation fueled me, and I raced after him, faster than I'd thought I could run, but I still wouldn't have caught him if he hadn't faltered a little way before the door.

"What the hell is that noise?" he demanded as I grabbed his arm.

"You can't be up here," I panted. "Aiden, please, I'll explain every-thing, but—"

Chains rattled again, closer this time, and the words died in my throat.

That noise . . . it was way too close to the—

The door was suddenly torn from its hinges.

June stood in the doorway, her eyes glowing bright red, like hell-fire, her filthy hands twisted into claws. The ragged gag hung around her neck, and her fangs were out, poking into her lower lips like spear points.

My blood turned to ice.

There was no reasoning with this creature.

"Run!" I screamed.

June snarled like a wild animal, her chains rattling behind her as she gave chase. We could outrun her: she'd hesitated for a split second when she emerged from the room, perhaps adjusting to her sudden freedom, and the long chains still dangling from her limbs would slow her down.

I was moving so fast I almost overshot the staircase; I swung my whole body in that direction, trying to correct my course, and my feet slipped from under me.

I fell, and rolled down the stairs, each step battering my body. My head swam, the walls around me flickering in and out of focus. I was lying on the floor at the foot of the staircase, my limbs splayed; I tried to move but pain pulsed through my head and my vision darkened.

I couldn't pass out. June was . . .

A scream.

A thud.

Blackness swallowed me.

CHAPTER TWENTY-EIGHT

Renie

Awareness trickled back in, the world taking shape around me. My body *ached*, but I was alive, which was more than I'd expected.

Noise filtered into my consciousness, a wet, slurping sound. Fear crawled down my bruised spine.

Slowly, carefully, I turned my head to the side.

Aiden lay close by, his throat torn so deeply that his head was almost separated from his body. June crouched over him, her face buried in the wet ruin of Aiden's throat.

A tiny gasp escaped my mouth.

June looked up and growled, gore dripping from her fangs. Ice-cold terror sliced through me. Despite my throbbing skull and aching body, I scrambled to my feet and fled.

Snarling, June charged after me.

Mental screams rang through my head, the terror that I couldn't actually vocalize. Or maybe it was the memory of what must have been Aiden's last scream, imprinted on my brain.

Suddenly I realized that the screams weren't in my head, but were actually drifting through the walls of the mansion.

Veering wildly around a corner, I slammed into Ludovic's chest. His eyes were lit red, his blond hair escaping its usual ponytail, and in one hand he held an actual freakin' sword.

"June's free," I cried.

"The house is under attack," he told me.

A beat passed while we absorbed each other's revelations, and then June surged around the corner, snarling and gnashing her fangs.

Ludovic pushed me behind him. "Run."

"But—"

"*Now*."

Much as I hated to leave Ludovic with the monster that June had become, he was better equipped to handle it than I was. So I fled.

The sound of screaming grew louder as I tore out of the hallway that led to the west wing, my heart hammering in my chest.

Belle Morte was under attack?

What the fuck was going on?

I was almost at the south wing when I skidded to a halt, a different kind of terror forming a thick knot in my stomach. If Ludovic was here, then Edmond was alone and undefended in his room. And he was in no shape to fight off any attackers.

"Edmond," I whispered.

I had no idea how I could possibly defend him, but I ran back toward the north wing anyway, fueled by wild fury and desperation. I'd do whatever it took to keep him safe.

As I reached the main staircase, three vampires barreled into my path, fighting furiously—Miriam and two vampires I'd never seen before. One of them seized her by the throat and threw her to the floor, then stamped on her chest hard enough that I heard ribs splinter. The second vampire suddenly turned, his nostrils flaring as he spotted me. I cast about for a weapon, but there was nothing.

The strange vampire started to advance.

And then Edmond appeared like some beautiful avenging angel. He grabbed my would-be attacker, lifted him off his feet, and cracked the vampire's back across his knee. The vampire screamed and Edmond kicked him down the stairs. His body flopped in a horrible way as he rolled down the steps, but he was still alive when he reached the bottom, glaring up at us with hate-filled eyes.

His friend cowered, pressing himself against the wall. Edmond advanced on him but the vampire vaulted over the banister, landing neatly on the parquet floor below.

I was too stunned to move. It had all happened in the space of a few seconds, and my poor brain was struggling to keep up.

Edmond helped Míriam to her feet and leaned her gently against the wall, then turned to me.

"What are you doing here?" he said.

"I was coming to protect you." It sounded silly when I said it out loud, but Edmond's whole face softened. He caught me in his arms and kissed me.

My hand slid across his back and felt dampness seeping through his shirt. I frowned and pulled away from him, looking at my red-stained palm.

"Oh my god, you're still injured," I cried.

Now that I looked closer I could see the strain on his face, the tightness around his mouth and eyes, and the stiff way he held himself.

"It doesn't matter. The house is under attack."

"By who?"

He looked grim. "I don't know. We're trying to corral the attackers in the ballroom, so you need to get back to your room and stay there."

I tried to protest, but he took my arm, propelling me to the south wing. He was so much stronger than me that it was pointless to resist, and I was afraid that even trying would make his injuries worse.

"You can't stay out here. You'll get yourself killed," I cried.

"I am not abandoning my House. I can't."

"But it's dangerous."

Edmond just looked at me.

It wasn't like he was a stranger to pain and danger—the man had served in multiple wars—but I hadn't known him then. I only knew him now, and all I could feel was gut-wrenching terror that he wasn't strong enough to fight yet, and rushing off while his wounds were still so fresh could get him killed.

"I don't want you to go," I whispered. "Please stay with me."

Edmond stopped and cupped my cheek with his palm. "Renie," he said, his voice soft. "You cannot ask me to hide while my fellow vampires fight to defend Belle Morte. You know that's not who I am."

I did know that. Edmond wasn't a coward and he wouldn't abandon his friends when they needed them. That didn't ease the knot of terror in my chest.

"Then at least drink. It'll give you strength," I said, rolling up my sleeve.

He protested, but I shoved my wrist at his face. We couldn't risk him drinking from my neck; one of us needed to keep an eye out for more attackers.

"Thank you," Edmond said, giving my lips a quick kiss before biting down on my wrist. There was no pleasure this time, just the burning pain, but I was only vaguely aware of it through the drumbeat of adrenaline in my veins.

When he finished, he sealed the cuts with his tongue, and we continued to my bedroom. At my door, he kissed me once more, then pushed me inside.

Roux, white faced and shaking, grabbed my arm. "What's happening?" she whimpered. Melissa was huddled in the corner, her eyes wide.

"The house is under attack."

"By who?"

"I don't know."

Roux sank onto her bed, shoulders hunched like a wilting flower.

I hated to be the bearer of more bad news, but: "June's loose."

Roux gaped at me, her eyes swimming with tears.

It was better to tell her the truth than lie and pretend that my blood-crazed sister wasn't stalking the hallways of Belle Morte.

"What do you mean, she's loose? She's *here*?" Melissa said. "Wait, where's Aiden?"

The words stuck in my throat as I remembered the awful ruin of Aiden's throat. How was I supposed to tell Melissa that my sister had just murdered her boyfriend?

A crash sounded somewhere outside, and we all jumped. Roux grabbed my hand and pulled me over to the bed. Her hands were shaking, her teeth sinking into her lower lip so hard they left red marks.

I stared at the door, and the churning fear inside me settled, forming a cold ball of determination. Edmond was still out there. My blood had helped, but it wasn't enough to fully heal him, especially not when the wounds had been made with silver. He was still at a disadvantage, and I couldn't leave him like that. He had said to me he couldn't hide out while his fellow vampires fought and bled and died, and suddenly I truly understood that. Edmond had shut me in here for my own safety, but I couldn't hide in my bedroom while he put his own life at risk. That wasn't who I was either.

"I have to go after him," I said.

"Are you *crazy*?" Roux cried.

"Edmond's out there, and I can't leave him."

There wasn't much in the room that could be used as a weapon—except the solid brass Venus de Milo on my nightstand. I grabbed it.

Roux shoved her fingers through her hair, tears spilling down her face. "You can't go out there."

I started for the door but she grabbed my arm and held me back.

"Please stay," she whispered.

My earlier words to Edmond, repeated back at me—I didn't miss the irony.

"I have to go."

"No! You don't. You can't risk your life for some guy—"

"Roux, I love him."

I don't know which of us was more shocked by my words. Roux gaped at me and I was fairly sure my own mouth was hanging open. I really had just said that, hadn't I? But I couldn't . . . I mean . . .

But I did.

"I love him," I repeated. The enormity of it smashed into me, and I actually reeled. "Oh my god, I love him." I grabbed Roux's shoulders. "Velma would never abandon the man she loved, right?"

Roux sniffled, nodded. "And Daphne would never stop her."

I had no idea what good I could do, but I wouldn't hide in my room while Edmond was fighting for his life, and I didn't know what future we possibly had, but it didn't matter. All that mattered was Edmond, and I would not leave him to die.

I slipped out of my bedroom and went to find the vampire I loved.

It wasn't long before I stumbled upon a body—a man lying at the end of the hallway, his throat a bloody ruin. I couldn't tell if it was June's handiwork or the work of an enemy vampire. I edged around him, trying not to look at the wet crater in his neck or the grimace of agony stretched across his face. His black uniform told me he was one of Belle Morte's security team, though not one I recognized.

I was relieved that it wasn't Dexter, and then immediately felt guilty. This poor guy probably had a family too; not knowing him didn't make his death any less awful.

I paused and turned back to the body. Like all members of security, he had a sheathed knife clipped to his belt, which was a better weapon than the decorative statue I'd armed myself with. I bent over the body and inched my hand toward the knife, but stopped before I actually touched it. It was bad enough being so close to a dead body—I was trying to push the horror of that to the back of my mind until I could deal with it—but taking anything from him felt so much worse.

But I didn't have a choice. He didn't need the knife anymore—I did. I couldn't ignore the chance to defend myself out of some sense of propriety.

I slid the knife from the sheath. The blade was long and wide, razor sharp on both sides, and coated with silver. I had no clue how to properly wield it but maybe if I made enough stabby motions, I'd get lucky.

Edmond had said the Belle Morte vampires were trying to drive the intruders to the ballroom, so that's where I headed.

I reached the staircase. The vampire whose back Edmond had broken still lay at the foot of the stairs, his head now separate from his body. I hoped Míriam had done it.

I didn't know her, so the sudden wave of protectiveness that rushed through me caught me by surprise. Belle Morte might not be home to me, but it was home to these vampires—Edmond's friends—and it was home to the donors. It had been home to Aiden, and even June for a while.

Regardless of how *I* felt about Belle Morte, the vampires who lived here didn't deserve this.

Shouts and screams, coupled with the harsh clash of metal on metal, echoed from the direction of the ballroom. I crept down the stairs, knife in hand. The main door leading into the mansion hung open but I didn't dare try to close it, not when I didn't have a clue what was going on.

As I crept through the vestibule, I stumbled on two more bodies: one was a vampire I didn't know, the other was Abigail. They were practically torn apart, Abigail's arm attached to her body only by a ragged string of sinew, and the vampire ripped almost down the middle, the chasm in her chest wide and wet and red. Blood pooled on the parquet floor around them, and my stomach lurched.

The sounds of fighting grew louder as I ventured through the vestibule and into the dining hall, but my nerve didn't fail. It wasn't too late to turn back. I could run back to my room, hide with Roux and Melissa until this was all over, and no one would blame me for it. But I would blame myself.

I loved Edmond. It had taken me long enough to realize what that hot, heady feeling in my heart was, and now that I knew it, I couldn't ignore it.

Two figures lurched into the dining hall, grappling fiercely with each other. Isabeau's tumble of chestnut curls was immediately familiar; her hand was around the throat of a strange male vampire I didn't recognize, but he was so much bigger than her, and he was pushing her steadily back. Her fangs were out, lips pulled back in a snarl, but there was fear in her eyes.

Charging across the room, I plunged the silver-coated knife into the male vampire's back. The blade slid between his ribs and stuck there. He screamed, rearing back and releasing Isabeau. He swung around and swiped a clawed hand at me, but pain made his movements slow and clumsy, and I ducked.

But he wasn't down yet. He advanced, his eyes flashing red, fangs jutting over his lip. Isabeau pulled the knife from his ribs and plunged it into the back of his neck, wrenching the broad blade to the side and severing his spinal column. He collapsed to the floor, twitching horribly. Isabeau rolled him over, set the edge of the knife against his throat, and pushed down. I could never have cut through the thickness of a man's neck like that, but Isabeau was a vampire. With her strength, the blade sank through the vampire's neck and his severed head tilted away from his body.

Isabeau straightened up. Blood splashed her face and clothes, matching the color of her eyes. Flipping the knife over, Isabeau handed it back to me, hilt first. I took it, the blood that had spattered the hilt sticking to my palms.

"I think you just saved my life," Isabeau said, staring at me in amazement.

A shudder rolled over my body. I'd just stabbed someone. Yes, he'd have killed me and Isabeau, but that didn't change the horrible memory of sharpened metal sliding into flesh, scraping against bone. It didn't wash the blood off my hands.

"You shouldn't be here," Isabeau said. "Go back to your room and let us handle this."

I shook my head, gripping the knife more determinedly. No way was I turning back now.

"It's not safe, Renie."

"I don't care."

I expected her to persist, but Isabeau just shook her head. "It's your life, and you're free to throw it away if you wish."

She stepped over the vampire's body, heading for the ballroom. I scuttled behind her, bloody knife at the ready.

The ballroom looked like a war zone. The walls were a mural of red splashes, the marble floor so stained with blood and thicker things that it was starting to resemble the tapestry-patterned carpets elsewhere in the mansion.

Mutilated bodies lay here and there, limp and tangled. The vampires still standing tore at each other like wild animals, all fangs and fire and rage.

It seemed impossible that we'd danced in this room; that an orchestra had played beautiful music while a camera crew had broadcast the event to an eager audience.

What would that audience think if they could see the bloodbath the ballroom had become?

I spotted Edmond, and my heart gave a great leap. Blood was splashed on his face—I couldn't tell if it was his own or someone else's—and his dark hair stuck to it. Even with his eyes glowing red and his fangs fully extended, he was still beautiful, still my Edmond.

How had I only just realized that I was completely in love with him?

Isabeau threw herself into the fray but I hung back by the entryway. I'd found Edmond—now what?

If I ran into that crowd, I was going to get killed. The stupidity and futility of being here crashed into me like a speeding train. I'd come because I couldn't bear the thought of Edmond fighting alone, but how exactly had I thought I could change that? Fight alongside him? I'd last three seconds if I was lucky.

I wasn't a vampire. I was just a girl with a knife that I didn't know how to use.

An enemy vampire slammed into me and knocked me to the floor. I managed to keep hold of the knife, but when I tried to get up, my feet slid over the blood-slick floor. I slashed wildly with the knife, but stabbing that vampire before had been lucky, taking advantage of his distraction. This vampire just jumped out of the way, grinning nastily as he licked his fangs.

I slashed at him again but he grabbed my arm, his fingers impossibly strong. He squeezed my wrist until tears of pain sparked in my eyes—he was going to break it and I couldn't stop him.

A strange noise sounded behind him, like a baseball bat hitting a melon, and the vampire stiffened, his eyes rolling up in his head. His hand slipped from my arm and his legs folded beneath him. As he hit the floor, I saw blood pouring from a dent in the back of his head.

Roux stood over him, her chest heaving. The brass pole that used to hold our bedroom curtains was clutched in both hands; one end was wet with blood and strands of hair.

"Holy fuck. Is he dead?" Roux cried.

The vampire groaned then started to get up, and Roux screeched, bashing the curtain pole over his head again and again until his skull caved in, and bits of bone and brain sprayed across the floor.

Roux retched and clapped a hand to her mouth.

Another vampire charged toward us, and Roux cracked the pole against his ribs, but it barely slowed him down. I swiped with my knife, but he batted me aside like I was made of paper. I landed hard on my elbows and the vampire promptly kicked me in the stomach. Pain jolted through me, and bile burned the back of my throat.

Roux screamed and I scrambled to my feet, ready to fight for her to my last breath.

But someone got there first.

A whisper of metal cleaved the air, then the vampire's head rolled on the floor in front of me, tongue lolling between his fangs.

Ludovic stood in the ballroom entryway, sword in hand and fire in his eyes.

"My hero!" Roux exclaimed.

I climbed to my feet, pressing one hand to the burning pain in my stomach.

Ludovic shot me a dark look. "I told you to go back to your room, not bring your friend to a battlefield."

Before I could explain, a terrible roar slashed through the air. I knew what I'd see even before I turned.

June had shed her chains, freeing her arms to slash and tear and maim. She wasn't graceful like normal vampires but she was just as fast and strong, and as she carved a bloody path through the ballroom, I fully understood why rabids were feared.

Tears blurred my eyes.

A vampire sailed—literally sailed—over the heads of the fighting masses and hit the far wall with a sickening crunch.

Ysanne stood in the very center of the room, and I was willing to bet that she was the one who'd thrown him. Despite her modern clothes, she looked like a furious, bloody angel, chunks of gore clinging to her long hair, her eyes blazing like molten rubies. Jemima fought with her, the two ladies back to back as they fended off their attackers.

Isabeau was heading toward them when a female vampire reared up behind her and plunged a knife into Isabeau's shoulder. She shrieked.

With a roar, Ysanne lunged forward and ripped out the attacking vampire's throat. Flesh and bits of . . . *something* dangled between her fingers. Isabeau yanked the knife from her shoulder and grabbed the front of Ysanne's clothes, pulling her forward. Their lips met in a brief, passionate kiss.

June moved like lightning, flickering in and out of view. Blood splashed her like paint, both from the carnage around her and from the wounds that other vampires had managed to inflict. She rushed in our direction, and Ludovic leaped in front of us, expertly wielding his sword. One flick of the blade sliced a deep wound across June's stomach.

She screamed and reeled back, and for just a moment I thought I saw a glimmer of intelligence in her red eyes, something more than the beast.

Clutching her wound, June streaked past us, fleeing the ballroom.

"Renie, no!" Roux yelled, but I was already giving chase.

June tore through the house, leaving a trail of blood droplets that led me to the back exit. The door hung open, creaking in the wind, and snow billowed inside. There was no sign of security.

Someone had released her.

Again.

Had they been trying to kill me again, or was this all part of some bigger plan? It had to be connected to the strange vampires attacking the mansion, but what did they have to gain from it?

The answers would have to come later.

If June got over the wall around Belle's Morte's grounds, she'd be loose in Winchester—more than a hundred thousand people lived there.

I couldn't leave all those lives at risk, not even for June's sake.

Clutching my knife, I stepped out into the snow.

Edmond

Edmond stepped over the body of an enemy vampire. The beast inside him roared to life—hungry, demanding blood. His hands were covered with it, his shirt soaked through and sticking to his skin. Some of it was his, streaming freshly from the whip wounds on his back. Far more was from the vampires he'd fought in defense of Belle Morte.

The smell of gore hung thick and heavy on the air.

He'd glimpsed June once or twice, tearing through the fighting vampires with no regard for whom she was killing. She needed to be stopped. Even if it meant that Renie never forgave him, Edmond couldn't let June run wild to kill more people.

Then he heard something that made his blood run cold.

"Renie, no!"

Renie was here somehow.

Suddenly nothing else mattered but getting to her.

A vampire took a swing at him and Edmond knocked her to the ground, stamping on her throat and crushing her windpipe. He stamped down again, shattering her rib cage, immobilizing her without fully killing her. In the heat of battle, it was impossible to see how many enemy vampires had died, how many had escaped, and how many were still here, but Ysanne would need living hostages to pry information from. They had to know who was behind this and why.

Roux was pressed against the wall by the entryway; Ludovic stood in front of her, shielding her.

"You have to stop her. She's gone after June," Roux cried.

A wave of pain rushed over him, and Edmond braced a palm against the wall for support, stifling a groan.

"You shouldn't even be here in this condition," Ludovic snapped.

Edmond didn't waste his breath answering—every second that

passed could be life or death for Renie. Pushing off the wall, he ran from the ballroom.

All these long lonely years he had feared for himself, feared that if he gave his heart to anyone else, it would come back in pieces, like it always did. Now Renie was in danger of leaving him in the worst possible way. He could cope with never seeing her again as long as he knew she was safe and happy. He could not cope with losing her to a rabid.

He heard Ludovic curse and give chase, but he didn't slow down.

Realization was unfolding inside him, fragile and fluttering, but bright with possibility. He wasn't just drawn to Renie. He was in love with the stubborn, impossible girl.

And he'd die before he let anything happen to her.

Renie

Snow still drifted from the darkening sky, making it difficult to see clearly. Every time the wind whipped the flurries into swirling shapes, my heart almost punched out of my chest, terrified that June was creeping up on me.

As I passed the oak tree, the disturbed earth packed hard beneath a thick layer of snow, I came upon another body. The snow was already starting to bury him, and his face was white and stiff in death, but I still recognized him—the young guard Roux had flirted with on the morning we'd gone to dig up a grave.

I'd never found out his name.

The snow made everything in the garden seem unfamiliar, the lines and edges blunted and reshaped by a heavy white blanket. The gathering dusk cast a strange light, reflecting back off the snow.

The garden walls towered around me, and I tried to calculate how high they were. Fourteen feet? Sixteen? Even if a vampire couldn't jump that high, they could climb a tree and leap from the branches.

If June really wanted to get out of here, she would.

Unless someone stopped her.

"June," I called, wishing my voice didn't shake so much. "It's me."

Something moved in my periphery, and I spun around, my heart hammering, my blood-sticky palm tightening on the knife hilt.

A shape detached itself from the shadow cast by the wall.

"Etienne? What are you doing out here?" I cried.

He moved closer, snow settling on his red hair.

"It's not safe out here," I said. "I'm sorry, I should have told you, but June's rabid—"

"I know."

I stared at him, uncomprehending. "I don't . . . *how*?"

Etienne's eyes were full of sympathy but it was tempered with something hard and icy. "Because," he said, "I'm the one who turned her."

CHAPTER TWENTY-NINE

Renie

I couldn't absorb his words because this was *Etienne*, my friend . . . Movement flickered to my left, and I spun again. June emerged from the veil of falling snowflakes; a terrible, bloody figure. Snow settled on the tangle of her hair, mingling with the blood smeared across her face. She stalked toward me like something out of a nightmare, softly growling through her fangs.

"Oh my god," I whispered. "Did you try to kill me too?"

"I'm sorry," Etienne said.

"*Why?*" I cried, my throat raw.

He didn't answer.

"Tell me," I snarled. "You lied to me, you pretended to be my *friend*. You owe me the truth."

Etienne inclined his head. "It wasn't personal. I do like you, Renie, but you're in my way. I can't have you interfering with June."

She growled softly, as if she recognized her name, but why was she just standing there? Why wasn't she attacking?

"Why did you do this to her?" I said.

"I didn't know she was going to turn rabid."

"Answer the *fucking* question," I screamed.

Etienne's face hardened. "I did it because it was necessary. A revolution is coming and the vampire world is going to change. I'm sorry you have to die, Renie, I really am, but that's how it has to be." He looked past me to June and made some gesture that I didn't understand.

Growls trickled out of her throat, and she edged forward, but she was still so slow and controlled, and despite the terror churning me up inside, I found a glimmer of hope, too, because if she wasn't attacking then maybe she could still be saved.

"I know you don't remember me, but I love you, June. I always have and I always will, no matter what," I said.

She hesitated, head tilted, her red eyes studying me.

"Do you remember the first time it snowed like this? Do you remember how happy we were?" I said.

June didn't come any closer but she didn't run either. Half-wrapped in shadows, she shuffled her feet restlessly through the snow, eyes glued to my face.

She still hadn't attacked—she was actually *listening*. Tears melted the snow on my face, and I stretched out a hand.

"It's me, June. It's Renie."

June shuffled closer.

It was working.

Somehow I was getting through to her.

A knife flashed in June's hand, and I just had enough time to wonder why the hell a rabid was carrying a knife, before the white-hot punch of pain as it plunged into my chest.

Edmond

He knew he was too late before he'd made it outside. The smell of Renie's blood rushed into his nostrils, overwhelming him. There was a terrible feeling in his chest, like his heart had started beating again and was trying to pummel through his rib cage.

He found Renie lying in the snow a short distance beyond the huge oak that marked the place she'd once thought was June's grave. There was no sign of June herself, only Renie's small form lying in the snow.

Edmond's footsteps faltered before he reached her, and the sharp stab of pain in his unbeating heart made him double over. There was so much blood spilling out of Renie's chest and soaking into the snow, but even if he couldn't see the deep wound in her chest, he'd have known she was dying. Her heartbeat was too weak, struggling.

Collapsing to his knees, Edmond gathered her into his arms. Her eyelids flickered.

"Edmond?" she whispered, and the pain in her voice tore at him.

If he'd been faster, he could have protected her.

Instead, he was watching another woman he loved die, feeling another piece of his aching heart wither away.

"I'm sorry," he whispered, cradling her. "I should have been here."

She tried to smile, but blood bubbled on her lips.

"No!"

Edmond heard Roux's cry behind him, the soft thump as she fell to her knees. When he turned his head, Ludovic and Míriam stood with her.

"I couldn't save her," Edmond said.

Roux brokenly sobbed, her voice muffled by the ever-falling snow.

"Etienne . . ." Renie whispered. ". . . killed June . . ."

Míriam made a sharp noise of disbelief. "*Etienne?*"

"We need to tell Ysanne," said Ludovic.

"I'll do it. You stay here." With a flick of dark hair, Míriam rushed back inside.

Edmond could barely focus.

Renie was bleeding to death.

Even if they called an ambulance, they couldn't save her. He could hear it in her heartbeat. She had minutes left.

"It wasn't supposed to end this like," he whispered, pressing his face to her hair and trying to breathe in the smell of her. But all he could smell was blood.

Ludovic put a hand on his shoulder. "It doesn't have to."

Edmond couldn't process his friend's words. He'd known all along that Renie would leave him, but he'd never imagined it would be because he was too slow to save her.

Self-loathing filled him.

Ludovic tightened his grip. "Edmond, this doesn't have to be the end."

Edmond managed to tear his eyes away from Renie's pale face to look at his friend. "What are you talking about?"

Ludovic's mouth set in a grim line. "You could turn her."

The Council would never allow it.

Edmond gazed down at her, so small and fragile in his arms. Blood darkened her auburn hair, making it stick to her white face. The blood on her lips looked shockingly bright. He hadn't even had time to tell her how he felt.

Fuck the Council.

Edmond had a chance to save the woman he loved, and he wouldn't let that slip through his fingers for the sake of *rules*.

He felt something wet on his cheeks and thought it was snow, until Renie's eyes widened.

"You're crying," she whispered, her breath rattling.

Edmond touched his cheek then gazed at the redness on his fingers.

He hugged her against him, pressing his lips to her ear. "Let me turn you."

The fluttering of her heartbeat was getting fainter; soon she'd be gone.

"You're dying, Renie. The only way to save you is to turn you into a vampire, but I won't do it without your permission."

If she'd rather die than become a vampire, that was her choice—Edmond wouldn't force this life on anyone.

"Please, Renie. If you want me to save you, just say yes. Please say yes." More bloody tears spilled down his cheeks, dripping onto Renie's face.

Renie's lips parted, struggling to speak through lungs full of blood. "Yes," she whispered.

Edmond sank his fangs into her throat.

Renie

My eyes snapped open.

The pain in my chest was gone, that terrible feeling of slipping away replaced by a new kind of energy unlike anything I'd ever felt before. The world around me was dark but at the same time it seemed brighter and sharper than I'd ever seen it, and I could hear a steady *thump, thump* that sounded familiar, though I couldn't put my finger on what it was.

There was a strange taste in my mouth, something rich and metallic, but not in an unpleasant way. I ran my tongue over my lips, sucking the taste down, and brushed the points of small fangs.

Fangs.

I had fangs.

Recollection crashed back in a flurry of images—Etienne, June, the knife, Edmond's whispered plea.

I had said yes.

I was a vampire.

Suddenly, I knew what that thumping noise was—a heartbeat.

I pressed a hand to my own chest, but nothing would beat there again.

I had died and Edmond had brought me back. The taste in my mouth—that was his blood.

The heartbeat I could hear was Roux's; she knelt in the snow a couple of feet away, staring at me with wide, teary eyes. Ludovic stood next to her, his hand resting on her shoulder. His face was unreadable.

A hand cupped my cheek and I gazed up into Edmond's eyes. He looked even more gorgeous through my vampire vision, all the colors and angles of his face brought into clearer focus. The bloody tears he had wept for me left red trails down his cheeks.

"Renie," he whispered, and my name had never sounded so beautiful. His hand lingered on my cheek, then moved to touch my chin, lips, nose, reassuring himself that I hadn't gone.

I had so very nearly gone.

Blood soaked my clothes but there was no sign of the wound.

I sat up and agony spiked through me, as if I'd been stabbed all over again, but this pain was lower, pulsing and writhing in my stomach.

A moan trickled from my lips. I doubled over, clutching Edmond's shoulders as red-hot waves wracked me, turning my vision dark.

"What's happening to her?" Roux cried.

She tried to approach me but Ludovic held her back.

I was a vampire—I should have been stronger than ever, but instead I felt as fragile as bone china. I wrapped my arms around myself and moaned again.

"It's all right, mon ange. It's just the hunger pangs. They will pass," Edmond whispered.

He scooped me into his arms, straightening up and turning in the direction of Belle Morte. "I'm going to take care of you."

Ysanne, standing just before the doorway, stopped us before we made it back inside. Her hair was blood drenched, her face as chillingly white and blank as ice.

"Oh, my dear boy, what have you done?" she said.

Edmond faced her defiantly. "What I had to."

"Not everyone will see it like that."

"I'll deal with that when the time comes. But please, let me help Renie through the rest of the turn."

Ysanne looked at me, not a spark of emotion in her eyes. She gave Edmond a little nod, and he carried me inside.

"What happened?" I murmured.

The screams had all gone quiet.

"The fight's over," Edmond said. "I don't know if Etienne was behind that, too, and I don't know what it all means for the future of Belle Morte. Vampires and donors and staff have died, and Ysanne will be held accountable for keeping a rabid here and"—he broke off, his eyes darkening as he looked down at me—"and what's happened to you will need to be explained to the Council."

I sensed there was more to it than that, but the hunger pangs had sunk iron claws into my stomach and I couldn't think past the raging need. Everything was going dim, the world fading.

Edmond kissed my forehead. "Nothing else matters, mon ange. All questions can wait. For now, I just need to look after you."

There was nothing else I could say to that. I had no idea what adjusting to being a vampire was going to entail, or how long it would take. All my questions would have to wait.

A whole new life was about to start.

ACKNOWLEDGMENTS

Writing this book has been an absolute labor of love, so firstly I need to thank Bram Stoker, who made me fall in love with vampires in the first place.

To my family, who've always had faith in me and always believed that one day my books would be on the shelves.

To my cat, for only occasionally trampling the keyboard while I'm working.

To Liz, who always believed I'd make it, and who sadly is no longer here to see this book.

To Robyn and Deanna, for that first video chat that changed my life and for championing my story every step of the way since.

To Jen, my amazing editor, for endless patience when I prove, yet again, how bad I am with technology.

To all of the Wattpad Books team, for helping prepare my little story for the big wide world.

To my special Wattpad group, Kimbers, Jyfrit, L. B. Shimaira, Shaun, and Katherine. Thank you for the daily chats, the writing discussions, the support, and of course, the cocktails.

To all my incredible Wattpad readers. Thank you for the comments, the votes, the messages, and the absolute love shown for my world and my characters.

To all my new readers who are taking their first journey with me. Here's to many more in the future.

ABOUT THE AUTHOR

Bella Higgin fell in love with vampire fiction after reading an illustrated copy of *Dracula* as a kid, so it was inevitable that her debut novel would be about vampires. She currently lives in a small English town not far from the sea, where she writes full time. Her works on Wattpad have amassed more than twelve million reads. One day she hopes to have enough money to build a TARDIS in her garden.

Turn the page for a sneak peek of

REVELATIONS

Book two in the Belle Morte series

COMING WINTER 2023

CHAPTER ONE

Renie

I drifted into darkness, blind and deaf to anything but the constant, gnawing ache in my stomach. Every so often, a warm, sweet liquid slid down my throat, and the hunger pangs faded, but never for long. That terrible hunger always surged back, like fire.

Occasionally, there were snatches of awareness: the sensation of cool hands touching my face, the faint murmurs of a male voice. At the back of my fevered brain, I was aware that I knew that voice, *loved* that voice. But then the hunger roared back and everything was lost.

It could have been days, months, or even years before I finally cracked my eyes open. A corniced ceiling took shape above me, bright spots of light coalescing into a crystal chandelier.
Pieces of memory filtered back into my battered brain.

Belle Morte.

I was lying in a huge, four-poster bed, tangled in black satin covers, and the walls around me were indigo blue, much darker than the pale-gold bedroom I shared with Roux. Light from the chandelier winked off a pair of swords mounted on the wall.

I knew this room—this was *Edmond's* bedroom.

And standing by that bed was Edmond Dantès himself, the vampire that I'd fallen in love with. He looked like a dark angel, all coal-black hair and ivory skin, eyes glittering like diamonds, and my breath would have caught in my lungs at the sheer beauty of him . . . but I no longer needed to breathe.

I touched my throat, then pressed my palm to my chest. No heartbeat.

Memories rushed back, making me reel: June's escape from the west wing, the attack on Belle Morte, my final attempt to help her that had ended with her plunging a knife into my chest, and—

"Etienne," I gasped. My lungs felt rusty, and my lips were dry.

The vampire who had pretended to be my friend, who'd helped me find the truth about June, only to reveal that he was the one who'd killed her and turned her into a monster.

Edmond slid onto the bed next to me, as graceful and as fluid as a cat. "Hush, *mon ange*. Don't worry about that now," he soothed.

I recoiled from him instinctively, and Edmond went very still.

Emotion roared in my head, making it hard to think.

I was dead.

I had died out there in the snow.

All I'd wanted when I'd come to Belle Morte was to make sure that June was okay, and now I couldn't even comprehend what the future held. I'd never grow older than eighteen. I'd never have a career. It would be years before I built up enough UV resistance to spend any real time in the sun. All the things I'd taken for granted as a human were lost to me now.

The pain of all those lost *maybes* caught in my throat, making my eyes burn, but no tears fell.

My palm was still pressed to my chest, vainly waiting to feel the thump of a heart that would never beat again. Probing my teeth with my tongue, I flinched at the sharp points of fangs. When I'd first opened my eyes as a vampire, cradled in Edmond's arms on the snowy grounds of Belle Morte, I'd been aware of these changes but in an abstract sort of way.

Now the reality of this was hitting me like a hammer to the brain.

I was a vampire.

For the rest of my life, I'd have to rely on human blood to survive.

I'd become the very thing I'd once feared.

"What have you done to me?" I whispered.

A shadow of pain swept across Edmond's perfect face.

Nausea curdled inside me, and I clutched my stomach. The sweet liquid I remembered drinking when I was lost in the darkness, the only thing that had quelled the hunger pangs—that had been blood. I'd been drinking *human blood*.

"I'm a monster," I rasped.

Still Edmond didn't move, didn't speak, but the look in his eyes was devastated, like something inside him was breaking.

I'd given him permission to turn me—I knew that—but I didn't know how to cope with the monumental change that had come over my body and my life. I was scared and angry, and I had no idea what I was supposed to do with myself.

An aching wave of hunger rolled over me and I groaned. My fangs pricked my lower lip, and my gums throbbed.

Ignoring my harsh words, Edmond pulled me gently against his chest. "The hunger will pass. You're almost there," he murmured.

His voice was like velvet, wrapping me up in warmth and safety, and the room dimmed, blackness rushing up to welcome me back. My last thought was that, despite what I'd said to him, I was glad that Edmond was here, holding me.

*

Edmond

Sitting on the edge of the bed, watching Renie toss and turn in a restless sleep, Edmond wished there'd been another way to save her.

He'd once told her that if he could go back in time, even if he knew all the terrible times that awaited him as a vampire, he'd still choose this life. But he wouldn't have chosen it for *her*.

Etienne's treachery had given Edmond what he desperately wanted—Renie to stay with him. Now she would never grow old and die while he watched helplessly. They had a chance to actually be together.

But that meant nothing if Renie wasn't happy with the choice she'd made.

The door opened and Ysanne Moreau swept in, Ludovic following tentatively behind. The Lady of Belle Morte cast her eye over Renie's sleeping form, but her cool expression didn't change.

"How is she doing?" she asked.

"Better," Edmond replied, stroking the tangled mess of Renie's auburn hair, brighter than ever against her pale vampire skin.

Ysanne knew about his feelings for Renie now, but he'd lied to her about it, and he knew Ysanne wouldn't forget that. Their friendship had been forged through the ages, love and loss binding them together, and Edmond had hated to lie to the person who'd known him longer than anyone. But relationships between vampires and donors were strictly forbidden, and when Edmond realized that he couldn't fight his feelings for Renie, he'd had no choice but to lie to his oldest friend.

"Do you believe she's through the worst of it?" Ysanne asked. "Because the Council will be coming soon, and you can't be here when they arrive."

Edmond closed his eyes. Turning a human without permission from the Council—the collective rulers of the British and Irish vampire houses—was one of the most serious crimes a vampire could commit. Ysanne should have punished him immediately, but she'd stayed her hand so he could help Renie through the turn. It was not a reprieve that anyone else would have granted. But even Ysanne couldn't hold off his punishment forever, especially when she herself was in serious trouble with the Council.

Under her watch, June Mayfield had been killed and turned, but instead of waking up as a vampire, she had woken up rabid. Vampire law decreed that rabids were too dangerous to live, and Ysanne should have killed June the moment she'd found her. She hadn't. Instead she'd hidden June in the mansion's west wing, and then she'd brought Renie to Belle Morte under the guise of being a donor, hoping that Renie might be able to help June recover her sanity.

But Renie had failed. Rabids could not be saved, and by the time Ysanne realized that, it was too late—Etienne had already turned June loose on the house just as Belle Morte had come under attack from enemy forces.

The bodies of the people who'd died because of that had been removed, but the house still smelled of blood.

Edmond's illegal turning of Renie was just one of the many bleak shadows darkening Belle Morte.

"Edmond?" Ysanne prompted, and he realized he hadn't answered her question.

He gazed down at Renie again, curled up in his bed where she'd been for the last three days, her hair spread over his pillow like a shower of autumn leaves. He could tell Ysanne that he needed more time with her, but it would be a lie. Renie was through the worst of the turn—the next time she awoke, it would be as a true vampire. Edmond had helped her as much as he could, and he wouldn't disrespect the time Ysanne had given him by asking for more. He wouldn't lie to her again.

"Yes," he said, his heart feeling like a rock in his chest. He had no idea what punishment he had incurred by turning the girl he loved.

Ysanne's icy mask slipped for a fraction of a second. "*Vieil ami*, you know I have no choice."

Edmond climbed off the bed and approached her—the woman who'd first opened his eyes to the vampire world, and whom he'd loved as both a friend and a partner. "I would never blame you," he said. "The choice was mine, and I'd make it again, regardless of the consequences."

Ysanne kissed his cheek, a soft brush of her lips, and then the cool mask was back in place.

"It's time to go," she said.

Edmond looked back at Renie, memorizing every line of her face, every strand of her hair. He remembered the way her lips curved when she smiled at him, the way her eyes could flash with anger or glitter with laughter. He committed every part of her to memory because he didn't know when he'd see her again.

Ysanne left the room, and Edmond started to follow her but stopped when Ludovic put a hand on his shoulder.

"I'll take care of her," Ludovic said.

Edmond laid his hand on Ludovic's. "Thank you," he said.

Then, with one last look back at the girl who'd stolen his ancient heart, Edmond left to pay the price for saving her.

Renie

The next time I woke up, Edmond was gone. Ludovic and Isabeau stood close to the door, speaking in low voices. I was a vampire now, and I could hear every word they said. Too bad I didn't speak French.

They both looked over as I slowly sat up, and Ludovic approached me. His face was unreadable. "How do you feel?"

"I . . . okay." The crippling hunger pangs had faded to a dull ache in the pit of my stomach.

I climbed out of bed, expecting my legs to feel shaky, but they were strong. My whole body felt strong.

This was it then. I really was a vampire.

When I was first turned, I hadn't had time to process the enormity of it; I'd literally just died, after all. In my conscious moments during the turn, I'd registered only the worst parts. Now I was calmer, more able to think about the decision I'd made.

Yes, I was a vampire, and while I was technically no longer *alive*, I would still *live*. Possibly forever. I had never imagined something like this happening to me, and it would take some serious getting used to, but the knife that June had plunged into my chest had not ended everything.

June . . .

A sharp pain sliced through my heart, and I sucked in a breath that I didn't need anymore.

"What happened?" I asked.

"How much do you remember?" Isabeau asked, clasping her hands in front of her. Her thick hazelnut curls were pulled back into a low ponytail, and her expression was solemn.

"I remember Etienne being the bastard who murdered my sister," I said in a low, hard voice. "Where is he?"

Ludovic and Isabeau exchanged a look.

"We don't know," Isabeau said.

"What?"

Ludovic took over. "After June stabbed you, she and Etienne

disappeared. By the time Edmond and I reached the gardens, they'd gone. We have no idea where they went."

"Roux? Jason?" I said.

I hadn't come to Belle Morte to make friends, but my roommate, Roux Hayes, and Jason Grant, another donor who'd arrived at the same time as us, had quickly found their way under my skin and into my heart. They were the best friends I'd never expected to have.

"They're fine," Isabeau said, but there was something in her voice that made me pause.

"How long have I been here?" I asked.

"Three days."

"Where's Edmond?"

Another look passed between the older vampires, and Ludovic's face darkened.

"Renie, you must understand that Edmond did something very serious by turning you," Isabeau said gently.

My stomach turned to ice. Something was wrong.

"Where is he?" I repeated.

"He's been imprisoned for turning you without permission," Ludovic said.

His eyes were hard as he looked at me, and I wondered if he blamed me for what had happened. Edmond was his best friend, someone he'd survived the hells of war with, and Edmond wouldn't be locked up if I hadn't come to Belle Morte.

Then the ice in my stomach turned to fire.

No, Edmond wouldn't be locked up if *Etienne* hadn't murdered my sister.

"Did Ysanne lock him up?" I demanded.

I wanted Ludovic to say no, that it had been done by another member of the Council. Just days ago, Ysanne had had Edmond whipped with silver for defending me against another vampire; I couldn't bear to think that she'd punish him again.

"Yes, she did," Ludovic said.

I closed my eyes.

There were bigger things going on here than just Edmond and me—I knew that—but the thought of him suffering, *again*, for my sake, was almost more than I could bear.

Edmond no longer loved Ysanne romantically, but he still loved her as a friend. He still trusted and respected her. Did that count for nothing?

"Can I see him?" I said.

Isabeau shook her head. "I'm afraid not."

This wasn't fair. Edmond had only turned me to save my life—he'd had no choice. How could Ysanne punish him for that?

"I need to see Ysanne," I said.

Isabeau's expression was sympathetic but firm. "I don't think that's a good idea."

Rage suddenly blazed through me, faster than I could rein it in. "I don't *care* what you think. Maybe you blindly support everything Ysanne does because you're sleeping with her, or whatever you two are doing, but I'm not standing by while she does this to him. Not again."

Isabeau's eyes flared red, her lips pulling back from her fangs. "Watch what you say," she warned.

"What's Ysanne going to do—terminate my contract? I'm not a donor anymore."

As I spoke, I felt a strange swell of power—not physical power but something else. I was a *vampire* now, and Ysanne couldn't brush me off the way she had when I was human.

I stalked across the room and threw open the door so hard it left a dent in the fancy wallpaper.

Isabeau strode after me. The red had faded from her eyes, but her face was set in hard lines. "Don't be foolish, Renie."

Her hand touched my shoulder, and I shook her off. I spun to face her, my bare feet sinking into the thick carpet that lined Belle Morte's many hallways. Rage blistered me, so hot and fierce it felt like I would combust on the spot. My gums ached as my fangs emerged, sliding to their full length.

This wasn't just about Edmond. It was about my sweet sister dying in this house and coming back as a blood-crazed monster at the hands of a man that I had trusted. It was about that man escaping justice while Edmond was punished for *saving my life*.

Isabeau regarded me, her face infuriatingly blank. If I'd hoped that becoming a vampire meant I could better decipher what they might be thinking, I was wrong.

Ludovic stood a little behind her, his eyes fixed on me. When Edmond had leapt to my defense against Adrian, the vampire who'd groped me during a welcoming party for visitors from House Nox, Ludovic had made sure no one else had bothered me while Edmond and Adrian were removed from the ballroom. He'd shielded me from Adrian when he returned, and then a few hours later he'd broken Belle Morte's rules and smuggled me into the north wing, where the vampires slept and no donor was meant to go, so I could see Edmond after his beating. I wasn't sure how he felt about me at this point, but I hoped he understood that the rage I felt was on Edmond's behalf.

Pieces of memory clicked together in my head, and I remembered what I'd said to Edmond the last time I'd woken up. Some of my rage died down, replaced by scalding shame. I'd called myself a monster— and him, by extension. I'd blamed Edmond because, however horrible and unfair it was, in that moment I'd needed to blame *someone*. It had been a while since I'd truly thought of vampires as monsters, but when I'd felt the prick of my fangs and realized I'd been drinking human blood, my old fears had resurfaced and spilled cruelly from my mouth.

I had to see Edmond, and Ysanne was the only person who could give me that.

"I told Edmond I would take care of you," Ludovic said, still watching me.

"You can't stop me from going to Ysanne."

He could, but that didn't stop me saying it. And it didn't stop him from replying: "I know."

Turning my back on the two vampires, I walked off to find Ysanne. I had no idea what I'd do when I did, but I couldn't leave Edmond like this.

He'd saved me. Now I would save him.

Turn the page to read a preview of

Available now in print and ebook,
wherever books are sold.

CHAPTER ONE

Every day is the same mind-numbing routine. I wake up, venture from the tunnels, serve breakfast for the hunters, weed the gardens, make lunch, clean the tunnels, and then cook dinner. And finally, the most important step—go back into the tunnels and don't leave until sunrise. I thought that by the time I turned nineteen I would've been able to hunt like everybody else. That I'd already have ventured farther than the tree line that guards our village. I was wrong.

"Did you slice the carrots, Milena? Remember, Charles likes them extra thin."

The carrots on the chopping board lie in crooked chunks beside the blunt knife. "Yes, Cynthia."

Her gray hair pops up from behind the wooden countertop, her thick eyebrows pulled together as she eyes the hacked-up carrots in front of me. Darius, her thirteen-year-old son, lingers behind, pulling a face behind her back. In charge of food preparation, Cynthia has been bossing me around for half my life now, so her disapproving tone barely affects me.

"That's *not* thin." Her nose wrinkles. "You're turning twenty this week, child, yet you still don't know a slicer from a knife."

My best friend, Flo, who stands beside me, warns me to keep my mouth shut with a shake of her head, and I bite my tongue. The only time I ever talked back to Cynthia, I was put on cleaning duties for a month. Alone. I couldn't go more than a few hours without having to pick dirt from my fingernails.

"I'm sorry. I'll try again."

"Good." She brushes her hands on her apron. "All the vegetables need to be sliced and in the pot. You have an hour before the hunters return, two before the sun sets. Make sure dinner is prepared and ready in the tunnels."

"Yes, Cynthia," Flo and I chime. The matron turns on her heels, grabs Darius's hand, and drags him outside, the door swinging shut behind them.

Flo's shoulders slump, red hair spilling over them. "She's *such* a nightmare. I know the hunters are important, but I'm pretty sure how thin the carrots in the stew are is the last thing on their minds when they get back."

"Yeah." Still, I'm slicing the carrots as thinly as I can manage. "Who would've thought that I'm days away from turning twenty and still stuck on cooking and gardening?"

"You get to clean sometimes too."

"Oh, joy."

"Come on, Millie." Flo picks the bucket of potatoes up off the floor and dumps it on the wooden countertop. "It's not *that* bad."

"Easy for you to say. Charles let you hunt the moment you came of age."

"You turn twenty soon," she says without looking at me. "And then you'll get your wish."

"Everyone else only had to wait until they turned sixteen." Flo peels the potatoes, as there's nothing she can say to make me feel better. She knows it's true. My entire life, I've been prohibited from venturing into the forest. While everyone else had some freedom starting at sixteen, Charles kept me here, wanted me safe. "Come on," I say. "Let's weed the garden while we wait for the stew to boil."

Chucking the carrots and the rest of the potatoes into the simmering pot, Flo follows me out of the wooden shack we use as a kitchen. The sun glares down at us as we wander toward the vegetable patch behind it. The village we live in doesn't look like much. With one, sole building aboveground, the rest of the clearing consists of gardens and a thin stream before a large, clear area that separates us from the reaches of the forest. To a passerby, the building would be as inconspicuous as a run-down shack.

As Flo tugs at some weeds, I lean back on my heels and gaze across the clearing at the tree line. The sun bathes the tips of trees in gold as it begins its descent, dipping between the distant mountains. Figures of hunters form in the gaps between the trees. Charles is first to come into the open, a dead boar thrown over his shoulder and four hunters following behind. Like every other day, a crowd gathers around the entrance to the tunnels beside the kitchen shack, mostly children, welcoming the hunters back. Life seems normal, like a regular day of hunting. But it isn't. The hunters never return early.

I nudge Flo. "What?" she asks, still pulling weeds from the ground.

"The hunters. They're back early. They're *never* back early."

She shrugs. "I'm sure it's nothing."

Charles weaves through the villagers, eyes scanning the crowd.

"Charles." Cynthia greets him first. "You're back early."

He nods. His movements are stiff and intentional. Different. "I'd like everybody in the tunnels. Curfew starts early tonight."

Cynthia scurries away, ceaselessly obedient. Charles surveys the crowd, the limbs of the animal on his shoulder flopping left, and then right as he turns. A gentle breeze blows my dark hair across my face. "We should get the food." I tug on Flo's arm to pull her up. "Cynthia will be angry if we're not ready."

She drops her tools and together we hurry back to the kitchen. I peer over my shoulder as we fly through the center of the village. Charles is looking at me from across the clearing, green eyes sharp. A silent message passes between us—I know what he's trying to tell me. Night is coming, and so are they.

~

Dead—my mom, my dad, my whole family. Charles says there was a raid the day I was born. That the creatures broke into the tunnels and killed my parents. He raised me, and though he provided me with the necessities, there was never any warmth in his embrace.

"The stew is good," Charles says once we're secure in the tunnels. He sits at the head of the tunnel with a group of hunters. "Thank you, ladies."

"You're welcome, Charles." Flo smiles brightly.

Even though she's one of my only friends, the way she sucks up to Charles annoys me like nothing else. I move my piece across the checkerboard and kick Flo to let her know it's her turn. She nearly knocks her bowl off the table as she turns back.

"Milena," Charles calls. "Come here. I want to speak with you."

Pushing myself to my feet, I move toward him. "Yes?"

He nods to one of the hunters sitting beside him, who gets up and moves away. "Please sit." As I do, the other hunters at the table stare at me, but I ignore it. I do their cooking and cleaning, but I'm not allowed to hunt, and that makes me an outcast. "What'd you do today?" Charles asks.

"What?"

"I'm asking what you did today." He lifts his spoon to his mouth, stew catching in his gray beard. "I'm trying to have a conversation."

Charles never tries to converse with me. My childhood consisted of instructions and scolding; I can count the number of casual conversations we've had on one hand.

"Cooking and gardening with Flo, like every other day."

"You didn't do anything . . . unusual?"

"No. Why?"

"No reason." He stirs the spoon in the bowl. "You can go now."

"Charles, what brought the hunters back early?"

"We finished early."

"You never finish early." He ignores me, turning to say something to the woman next to him. "I'm turning twenty in two days, Charles. I finally get to hunt. Isn't it time you let me in on things? Isn't it time I get to learn a thing or two about the hunts?"

I've never been afraid of Charles, and although he's never been kind, he's never hurt me either. But as he stands and stares down at me, I feel so very small. "We finished early. The reasoning is none of your concern."

"Right. Sorry."

"Go. I'm sure Cynthia could do with some help cleaning up."

I step away as he ventures around the corner to the cleaning station. We're in the room designated for dining and recreation, separated from the stone walls blocking the entrance by a mere three steps. And despite the fact that there are fewer than two hundred of us living in the tunnels, the rooms always feel crowded.

"You okay?" Flo appears at my side and puts her hand on my arm. "I know he's harsh, but he cares about you. He doesn't want you to get hurt."

Memories of my childhood blur my mind: begging Charles to carry me through the tunnels, crying when he refused; scraping my knees against the ground and hanging my head in shame when he told me to grow up. If Charles won't allow me to hunt because he cares too much for me, he has a funny way of showing it.

"I'm going to have an early night," I say. "See you tomorrow."

Before she can respond, I take the two steps that lead to the narrow halls. Unlike the main rooms in the tunnels, the hallways aren't well maintained. Carved from compacted dirt, they're thin, winding passageways littered with dips in the ground and badly attached pipes that drip water. Their only purpose is to connect the various rooms. I take the familiar corner, ducking my head to avoid a low-hanging pipe protruding from the entranceway of my room.

When I was younger, I stayed with Charles in his quarters—the largest and most extravagant of the rooms. But when I turned ten, he left me in a box-sized room right at the end of the passageway, separate from the rest. He said it was time for me to mature, to grow up and start being more independent. I cried out for him every night for the first two weeks. But tonight, lying in my stone room void of anything save for a lumpy bed and set of drawers, I enjoy the loneliness. The blanket scratches against my skin as I pull it to my chin. I trace the crooked letters Flo and I scratched into the wooden bed frame when we were kids—an *F* and an *M*—with my finger. The distant howls coming from above provide a familiar comfort. They allow me time to sort through my racing thoughts.

My entire life I've waited for my twentieth birthday. I thought people would be more inclusive, would accept me as one of them—a hunter. But the closer the day gets, the more secretive Charles becomes, and the more ostracized I feel. And today was no exception.

Bang. I jolt up in bed. *Bang.* The screeching starts. It rebounds off the stone walls, rattling my brain. I put my hands over my ears and listen: deep, familiar growls echo through the tunnels— sounds that make my chest burn. But these growls aren't coming from above. Shouting fills the halls. Footsteps barrel past my quarters. I slide out from beneath my covers, throw a coat from the floor on, and pull the sheet covering the doorway open—then leap back in fright.

Charles stands in the doorway. "You're still here," he says, relieved.

"What's going on?"

"Don't leave this room."

"Charles—"

"Listen to me: do not leave this room until I come back for you!" His voice shakes me to the bone. I can do nothing but nod as he slips from the room, the sheet billowing as he exits. His footsteps get farther and farther away. Panic blazes through my body like wildfire. I stand frozen, staring at the door. Night has broken into the tunnels, and so have the creatures who own it.

~

The screaming ends before the night does and a piercing silence takes its place. I don't leave my room. I don't venture into the halls. I don't disobey Charles. I stay in my quarters, hugging my knees and waiting for the screaming and growling to start again. It never does.

When Charles finally appears in my doorway, I know, from the absence of howling, that the sun has risen. "You did as you were told, good." His shirt is torn across the chest, his head of gray hair mussed.

"Yes."

He clears his throat, the dark circles under his eyes more prominent than usual. "Cynthia called for you. They're preparing breakfast in the kitchen shack."

I grab his wrist before he can leave. Why is he acting like everything is normal? Nothing like last night has ever happened before. "Charles, what happened last night?"

"Everyone is safe and accounted for." He pries his hand from my grip. "The rest is none of your concern."

He spins and exits without another word, not addressing my curiosity. Whatever happened last night, however abnormal, I'll have to ask somebody else about it. I throw on a light-blue shirt and braid my black hair to the middle of my back before venturing into the cocoon of the morning sun. The village is quiet, the songs of birds wafting through the trees surrounding us. On a warm day like today, children are usually playing in the small stream that runs through the clearing, but everyone is still in the tunnels.

"Millie!" I turn as I reach the kitchen to see Flo rushing toward me, Darius's hand clasped in hers. She wraps her arms around me and squeezes. "You're okay! I couldn't find you anywhere last night."

"What *happened*?" I ask.

"Don't tell me you slept through it," Darius says, blue eyes wide.

"I heard screaming and growls. Charles made me stay in my room."

Darius opens his mouth. "They caught—"

"You're okay, that's all that matters," Flo says, shooting Darius a look.

"It was *terrifying*," he says. "The entrance wasn't sealed properly. Someone—something—broke in. It had red eyes and matted fur, and it was in the tunnels."

"A creature of the night . . . you saw one?"

"No. But Flo did," Darius says. I stare at Flo but her eyes are focused on the ground. "She said it almost killed her but the hunters got there just in time."

"They killed it?"

"No." He leans closer. "They *caught* it. It's down in the tunnels, chained up."

A creature of the night alive and in the tunnels. It broke in and we're still alive. *What's it like? Why didn't they kill it? Why didn't anybody tell me?*

"Hey!" Cynthia appears behind Flo, hands on her hips and a scowl on her face. "What do you think you're doing?"

"Mom!" Darius yells. "They have one in the tunnels. Flo said the hunters caught it and—"

"Stop spreading nonsense and complete your chores, Darius," Cynthia snaps, looking at Flo and me. "Get inside and get to work. The hunters need a meal before they leave."

We follow her timidly into the kitchen and stand to attention. A gust of wind rattles the pots hanging on the wall. There are three other girls present—Allison, and the twins, Katie and Alexis. The twins started in the kitchen with me and Flo less than a year ago, but this will be their final year before they're promoted to hunting. "Allison and Flo, Charles wants you on the hunt today," Cynthia says. "The rest of you: gardening, cleaning, and cooking."

"I'll clean the tunnels," I say.

"You're on breakfast."

"After breakfast, then. Instead of gardening. I need a change of scenery."

"Fine," she says, and the tension in my shoulders releases when she looks away. "Get to it."

Flo gives me a sheepish look before exiting with Allison to prepare for the hunt. Alexa hands me a pot full of water collected from the stream. I kneel down to the basket of supplies Cynthia brought from the tunnels, for once glad I'm not getting my chance to hunt today even though I'd like to go with Flo. Today, I have other plans. None of what Darius said makes sense. They should have killed the creature. Stopped it before it got to the entrance. But as the hunters leave soon, the tunnels will be unguarded, and I'm going to see a creature of the night.

© Grace Collins, 2021